From Anne & John.
August 1st, 1927

"Aquitania"

A WREATH OF CLOUD

A WREATH OF CLOUD

BEING THE THIRD PART
OF 'THE TALE OF GENJI'

By
LADY MURASAKI

TRANSLATED FROM THE JAPANESE BY
ARTHUR WALEY

BOSTON AND NEW YORK
HOUGHTON MIFFLIN COMPANY
The Riverside Press Cambridge
1927

PRINTED IN GREAT BRITAIN

TO
RAYMOND MORTIMER

PREFACE

THIS is the last volume but one of *The Tale of Genji* proper. Between volumes IV and V there is a gap of eight years, during which Genji has died. Volumes V and VI contain the sequel, 'the ten Uji chapters,' as they are called in Japan, which deal with the fortunes of Genji's supposed son Kaoru, and his grandson (the Akashi Princess's child) Niou. The name 'Genji' (member of the Minamoto clan) applies equally to his descendants, so that in Japanese the sequel too can be called *The Tale of Genji*. But in English it needs a new name, and I have called it *The Tale of Kaoru*. Thus *The Tale of Genji* itself will be complete in four volumes, and will be followed by a sequel in two volumes.

I wish here to thank Mr. R. C. Trevelyan and Miss Sybil Pye for the care with which they have read the proofs of the present volume. The fact that the heroine of the story and the writer of it are both called Murasaki is somewhat confusing. I will therefore here point out that the name 'Murasaki' was given to the authoress as a nickname, in allusion to the heroine of her book. Her real name is unknown to us. For the origin of the nickname, see below, p. 23.

CONTENTS

	PAGE
PREFACE	7
LIST OF MOST IMPORTANT PERSONS	11
SUMMARY OF VOLUMES I AND II	13
INTRODUCTION	15

CHAPTER		
I.	A WREATH OF CLOUD	35
II.	ASAGAO	68
III.	THE MAIDEN	91
IV.	TAMAKATSURA	147
V.	THE FIRST SONG OF THE YEAR	200
VI.	THE BUTTERFLIES	218
VII.	THE GLOW-WORM	240
VIII.	A BED OF CARNATIONS	264
IX.	THE FLARES	291
X.	THE TYPHOON	296

LIST OF MOST IMPORTANT PERSONS

(ALPHABETICAL)

AKASHI, LADY OF	Whom Genji courted during his exile.
AKASHI, PRINCESS FROM	Daughter of the above by Genji.
AKIKONOMU, EMPRESS	Daughter of Rokujō.
AOI	Genji's first wife.
ASAGAO, PRINCESS	Daughter of Prince Momozono Shikibukyō, courted by Genji since his boyhood, without success.
ATEKI	Daughter of Tamakatsura's old nurse.
BUGO NO SUKE	Brother of the above.
CHŪJŌ, LADY	Tō no Chūjō's eldest daughter (called Kōkiden in the original, but this renders her liable to confusion with Genji's step-mother).
EMPEROR, THE OLD	Genji's father.
FALLING FLOWERS, LADY FROM THE VILLAGE OF	Sister of one of the Old Emperor's Court-ladies under Genji's protection.
FUJITSUBO	Consort of the Old Emperor; loved by Genji.
GENJI	Son of the Old Emperor by a lady-in-waiting.
HIGEKURO	Brother of Suzaku's consort Lady Jōkyōden.
HYŌBUKYŌ, PRINCE	Murasaki's father.
KASHIWAGI	Eldest son of Tō no Chūjō.
KŌBAI	Brother of the above.
KŌKIDEN	Consort of the Old Emperor; Genji's wicked 'step-mother.'
KOREMITSU	Genji's retainer.
KOREMITSU'S DAUGHTER	Gosechi dancer, admired by Yūgiri.
KUMOI	Younger daughter of Tō no Chūjō.

Momozono, Prince . . .	Brother of the Old Emperor. Father of Asagao.
Murasaki	Second 'wife' of Genji (never, technically speaking, his *kita no kata* or formal wife).
Nyogo, Princess . . .	Younger sister of the Old Emperor.
Oborozuki	Consort of the ex-Emperor Suzaku. Loved by Genji.
Ōmi, Lady of.	Bastard of Tō no Chūjō, reclaimed by him in error while searching for Tamakatsura.
Ōmiya, Princess . . .	Mother of Aoi and Tō no Chūjō. Sister of the Old Emperor.
Rokujō	Widow of a brother of the Old Emperor.
Ryōzen, The Emperor .	Reputed son of the Old Emperor, but really son of Genji and Fujitsubo.
Sanjō	Yūgao's maid.
Shōni	Husband of Tamakatsura's nurse. Father of Ateki and Bugo no Suke.
Sochi, Prince	Genji's step-brother.
Suyetsumu	Fantastic lady with red nose, daughter of Prince Hitachi.
Suzaku, The Ex-Emperor .	Genji's step-brother; son of Kōkiden.
Tamakatsura	Child of Tō no Chūjō by Yūgao.
Tayū	Swashbuckler in Tsukushi.
Utsusemi	Wife of a provincial governor; loved by Genji.
Yoshikiyo	Faithful retainer of Genji; followed him into exile.
Yūgao	Loved first by Tō no Chūjō, then by Genji. Dies in a deserted mansion.
Yūgiri	Genji's son by Aoi.

SUMMARY OF VOLUMES I AND II

GENJI is an illegitimate son of the Emperor. At the age of twelve he is affianced to Lady Aoi, daughter of the Minister of the Left; but she is older than he is, and looks down upon him as a mere schoolboy. Genji falls in love with Rokujō, a widow eight years older than himself. She is passionately jealous of his wife, and relations with her become very difficult. Genji turns for consolation to Utsusemi, wife of a provincial governor: to Yūgao, a discarded mistress of his friend Tō no Chūjō: to the fantastic Suyetsumu, the 'lady with the red nose.' Utsusemi is carried off to the provinces by her husband; Yūgao dies, withered by the virulence of Rokujō's jealousy. Meanwhile Genji succeeds in establishing better relations with his wife, Aoi, only to lose her through the operation of the same baleful force that had destroyed Yūgao. Since his childhood he has passionately admired Fujitsubo, his father's second wife. He has a son by her, who is believed by the public to be the Emperor's child.

Genji's enemies, in particular Kōkiden, who had been his mother's rival, are striving to get rid of him. He simplifies matters for them by starting an intrigue with Oborozuki, a much younger sister of Kōkiden.

At the end of Vol. I Genji marries Lady Murasaki, a niece of Fujitsubo; some years before he had taken her into his house and adopted her.

In Vol. II, Rokujō leaves the capital and goes to live at Ise, where her daughter is Vestal Virgin. Genji is caught making love to Oborozuki, and knowing that his enemies now have him in their grasp he retires as a voluntary exile to Suma. Here a storm destroys his house, and the Old

Recluse of Akashi (a neighbouring bay) persuades him to move thither. Here he falls in love with the Recluse's daughter (the Lady of Akaski), by whom he has a child (called the Princess from Akashi). Genji, after three years of exile, is recalled, and wants to send for the Lady of Akashi to live with him in his palace. But she fears that her position there will be humiliating, and will not consent. Finally he instals her in a country house at Ōi, several miles from the capital. In this volume both Utsusemi (the governor's wife) and Rokujō re-appear at the capital. There is also a further encounter, of a diverting kind, between Genji and the lady with the red nose.

INTRODUCTION

Murasaki

MURASAKI SHIKIBU was born about 978 A.D. Her father, Tametoki, belonged to a minor branch of the powerful Fujiwara clan. After holding various appointments in the Capital he became governor first of Echizen (probably in 1004); then of a more northerly province, Echigo. In 1016 he retired and took his vows as a Buddhist priest.

Of her childhood Murasaki tells us the following anecdote[1]: 'When my brother Nobunori[2] (the one who is now in the Board of Rites) was a boy my father was very anxious to make a good Chinese scholar of him, and often came himself to hear Nobunori read his lessons. On these occasions I was always present, and so quick was I at picking up the language that I was soon able to prompt my brother whenever he got stuck. At this my father used to sigh and say to me: "If only you were a boy how proud and happy I should be." But it was not long before I repented of having thus distinguished myself; for person after person assured me that even boys generally become very unpopular if it is discovered that they are fond of their books. For a girl, of course, it would be even worse; and after this I was careful to conceal the fact that I could write a single Chinese character. This meant that I got very little practice; with the result that to this day I am shockingly clumsy with my brush.'

[1] *Diary*, Hakubunkwan text, p. 51.
[2] Died young, perhaps about 1012, while serving on his father's staff in Echigo.

Between 994 and 998 Murasaki married her kinsman Fujiwara no Nobutaka, a lieutenant in the Imperial Guard. By him she had two daughters, one of whom married the Lord Lieutenant of Tsukushi and is reputed (very doubtfully) to be the authoress of an uninteresting novel, the *Tale of Sagoromo*. Nobutaka died in 1001, and it was probably three years later that Murasaki's father was promised the governorship of Echizen. Owing to the machinations of an enemy the appointment was, at the last minute, almost given to some one else. Tametoki appealed to his kinsman the Prime Minister Fujiwara no Michinaga, and was eventually nominated for the post.

Murasaki was now about 26. To have taken her to Echizen would have ended all hope of a respectable second marriage. Instead Tametoki arranged that she should enter the service of Michinaga's daughter, the very serious minded Empress Akiko, then a girl of about sixteen. Part of Murasaki's time was henceforth spent at the Emperor's Palace. But, as was customary, Akiko frequently returned for considerable periods to her father's house. Of her young mistress Murasaki writes as follows [1]: 'The Empress, as is well known to those about her, is strongly opposed to anything savouring of flirtation; indeed, when there are men about, it is as well for any one who wants to keep on good terms with her not to show herself outside her own room.... I can well imagine that some of our senior ladies, with their air of almost ecclesiastical severity, must make a rather forbidding impression upon the world at large. In dress and matters of that kind we certainly cut a wretched figure, for it is well known that to show the slightest sign of caring for such things ranks with our Mistress as an unpardonable fault. But I can see no reason why, even in a society where young girls are expected to

[1] *Diary*, p. 51.

keep their heads and behave sensibly, appearances should be neglected to the point of comicality; and I cannot help thinking that her Majesty's outlook is far too narrow and uncompromising. But it is easy enough to see how this state of affairs arose. Her Majesty's mind was, at the time when she first came to Court, so entirely innocent and her own conduct so completely impeccable that, quite apart from the extreme reserve which is natural to her, she could never herself conceivably have occasion to make even the most trifling confession. Consequently, whenever she heard one of us admit to some slight shortcoming, whether of conduct or character, she henceforward regarded this person as a monster of iniquity.

'True, at that period certain incidents occurred which proved that some of her attendants were, to say the least of it, not very well suited to occupy so responsible a position. But she would never have discovered this had not the offenders been incautious enough actually to boast in her hearing about their trivial irregularities. Being young and inexperienced she had no notion that such things were of everyday occurrence, brooded incessantly upon the wickedness of those about her, and finally consorted only with persons so staid that they could be relied upon not to cause her a moment's anxiety.

'Thus she has gathered round her a number of very worthy young ladies. They have the merit of sharing all her opinions, but seem in some curious way like children who have never grown up.

'As the years go by her Majesty is beginning to acquire more experience of life, and no longer judges others by the same rigid standards as before; but meanwhile her Court has gained a reputation for extreme dullness, and is shunned by all who can manage to avoid it.

'Her Majesty does indeed still constantly warn us that

it is a great mistake to go too far, " for a single slip may bring very unpleasant consequences," and so on, in the old style ; but she now also begs us not to reject advances in such a way as to hurt people's feelings. Unfortunately, habits of long standing are not so easily changed ; moreover, now that the Empress's exceedingly stylish brothers bring so many of their young courtier-friends to amuse themselves at her house, we have in self-defence been obliged to become more virtuous than ever.'

There is a type of disappointed undergraduate, who believes that all his social and academic failures are due to his being, let us say, at Magdalene instead of at St. John's. Murasaki, in like manner, had persuaded herself that all would have been well if her father had placed her in the highly cultivated and easy-mannered entourage of the Emperor's aunt, Princess Senshi.[1] ' Princess Senshi and her ladies,' Murasaki writes, ' are always going off to see the sunset or the fading of the moon at dawn, or pursuing some truant nightingale amid the flowering trees. The Princess herself is a woman of marked character, who is determined to follow her own tastes, and would contrive to lead at Court a life as detached as her present existence at the Kamo Shrine. How different from this place, with its perpetual : " The Empress has been summoned into the Presence and commands you to attend her," or " Prepare to receive his Excellency the Prime Minister, who may arrive at any moment." Princess Senshi's apartments are not subject to the sudden alarms and incursions from which we suffer. There one could apply oneself in earnest to anything one cared for and was good at ; there, occupied perhaps in making something really beautiful, one would

[1] 963–1035. Vestal at Kamo during five successive reigns. One of the most important figures of her day ; known to history as the Great Vestal.

have no time for those indiscreet conversations which at our own Court are the cause of so much trouble. There I should be allowed to live buried in my own thoughts like a tree-stump in the earth; at the same time, they would not expect me to hide from every man with whom I was not already acquainted; and even if I addressed a few remarks to such a person, I should not be thought lost to all sense of shame. Indeed, I can imagine myself under such circumstances becoming, after a certain amount of practice, quite lively and amusing!'

While pining for the elegance and freedom of Princess Senshi's Court, Murasaki was employed by her earnest young mistress for a purpose that the world would have considered far more improper than the philandering of which Akiko so sternly disapproved. The Empress had a secret desire to learn Chinese. The study of this language was considered at the time far too rough and strenuous an occupation for women. There were no grammars or dictionaries, and each horny sentence had to be grappled and mastered like an untamed steer. That Akiko should wish to learn Chinese must have been as shocking to Michinaga as it would have been to Gladstone if one of his daughters had wanted to learn boxing. Murasaki had, as we have seen, picked up something of the language by overhearing her brother's lessons. She did everything in her power to conceal this knowledge, even pretending (as she tells us in the *Diary*) that she could not read the Chinese characters on her mistress's screen; but somehow or other it leaked out: 'Since the summer before last, very secretly, in odd moments when there happened to be no one about, I have been reading with her Majesty the two books of "Songs." [1] There has of course been no question of formal

[1] The third and fourth body of Po Chü-i's poetical works, including *Magic, The Old Man with the Broken Arm, The Prisoner, The Two Red Towers*, and *The Dragon of the Pool*, all of which are translated in my '170 Chinese Poems.'

lessons; her Majesty has merely picked up a little here and there, as she felt inclined. All the same, I have thought it best to say nothing about the matter to anybody. . . .'

We gather, however, that what in the long run made Akiko's Court distasteful to Murasaki was not the seriousness of the women so much as the coarseness and stupidity of the men. Michinaga, Akiko's father, was now forty-two. He had already been Prime Minister for some fourteen years, and had carried the fortunes of the Fujiwara family to their apogee. It is evident that he made love to Murasaki, though possibly in a more or less bantering way. In 1008 she writes: 'From my room beside the entrance to the gallery I can see into the garden. The dew still lies heavy and a faint mist rises from it. His Excellency [1] is walking in the garden. Now he has summoned one of his attendants and is giving directions to him about having the moat cleared. In front of the orange trees there is a bed of lady-flowers (*ominabeshi*) in full bloom. He plucks a spray and returning to the house hands it to me over the top of my screen. He looks very magnificent. I remember that I have not yet powdered my face and feel terribly embarrassed. "Come now," he cries, "be quick with your poem, or I shall lose my temper." This at any rate gives me a chance to retire from his scrutiny; I go over to the writing-box and produce the following: "If these beyond other flowers are fair, 'tis but because the dew hath picked them out and by its power made them sweeter than the rest." "That's right," he said, taking the poem. "It did not take you long in the end." And sending for his own ink-stone he wrote the answer: "Dew favours not; it is the flower's thoughts that flush its cheeks and make it fairer than the rest."'

The next reference to Michinaga's relations with Murasaki

[1] Michinaga.

is as follows: 'His Excellency the Prime Minister caught sight of *The Tale of Genji* in her Majesty's room, and after making the usual senseless jokes about it, he handed me the following poem, written on a strip of paper against which a spray of plum-blossom had been pressed: "How comes it that, sour as the plum-tree's fruit, you have contrived to blossom forth in tale so amorous?" To this I answered: "Who has told you that the fruit belies the flower? For the fruit you have not tasted, and the flower you know but by report." [1]

'One night when I was sleeping in a room which opens on to the corridor, I heard some one tapping. So frightened was I that for the whole of the rest of the night I lay dead still on my bed, scarcely daring to breathe. Next morning came the following poem from His Excellency: "More patient than the water-rail that taps upon the tree-root all night long, in vain I loitered on the threshold of your inhospitable room." To this I answered: "So great was your persistence that for a water-rail I did indeed mistake you; and lucky am I to have made this merciful mistake."' [2]

Again, in 1010: 'To-day his Excellency had an audience with the Emperor; when it was over they came out of the Audience Chamber together, and banqueted. As usual, his Excellency became very drunk and, fearing trouble, I tried to keep out of his way. But he noticed my absence and sent for me, crying out: "Here's your mistress's papa taking dinner with the Emperor; it is not every one who gets the chance of being present on an occasion like this. You ought to be uncommonly grateful. Instead of which your one idea seems to be how to escape at the earliest possible moment. I can't make you out at all!"

[1] 'You have neither read my book nor won my love.' Both poems contain a number of double-meanings which it would be tedious to unravel.
[2] *Kui-na* means 'water-rail' and 'regret not.'

He went on scolding me for some time, and then said: " Well, now you are here, you must make a poem. It is one of the days when the parent's [1] poem is always made by a substitute. You will do as well as anybody; so be quick about it. . . ." I was afraid at first that if I showed myself he would behave in such a way as to make me feel very uncomfortable. But it turned out that he was not so extraordinarily drunk after all; indeed, he was in a very charming mood and, in the light of the great lamp, looked particularly handsome.'

It has often been observed that whereas in her commonplace book (the *Makura no Sōshi*) Sei Shōnagon [2] scarcely so much as mentions the existence of the other ladies-in-waiting, Murasaki refers constantly to her companions, and to one of them at least she was evidently very strongly attached. Her great friend was Lady Saishō. ' On my way back from the Empress's rooms I peeped in at Saishō's door. I had forgotten that she had been on duty at night and would now be having her morning sleep. She had thrown over her couch various dresses with bright-coloured linings, and on top of them had spread a covering of beaten silk, lustrous and heavily scented with perfume. Her face was hidden under the clothes; but as she lay there, her head resting on a box-shaped writing-case, she looked so pretty that I could not help thinking of the little princesses in picture-books. I raised the clothes from her face and said to her: " You are like a girl in a story." She turned her head and said sharply: " You lunatic! Could you not see I was asleep? You are too inconsiderate. . . ." While she was saying this she half raised herself from her couch and looked up at me. Her face was flushed. I have never seen her so handsome. So it often is; even those

[1] The parent of the Empress.
[2] Lady-in-waiting to the Empress Sadako, Akiko's predecessor.

whom we at all times admire will, upon some occasion, suddenly seem to us ten times more lovely than ever before.'

Saishō is her constant companion and her fellow victim during the drunken festivities which they both detested. The following is from a description of an entertainment given on the fiftieth day after the birth of the Empress Akiko's first child : ' The old Minister of the Right, Lord Akimitsu, came staggering along and banged into the screen behind which we sat, making a hole in it. What really struck us was that he is getting far too old [1] for this kind of thing. But I am sure he did not at all know that this was the impression he was making. Next followed matching of fans, and noisy jokes, many of which were in very bad taste.

' Presently the General of the Right came and stood near the pillar on our left. He was looking at us and seemed to be examining our dresses, but with a very different expression from the rest. He cannot bear these drunken revels. If only there were more like him ! And I say this despite the fact that his conversation is often very indecent ; for he manages to give a lively and amusing turn to whatever he says. I noticed that when the great tankard came his way he did not drink out of it, but passed it on, merely saying the usual words of good omen. At this Lord Kintō [2] shouted : " The General is on his best behaviour. I expect little Murasaki is somewhere not far off ! " " You're none of you in the least like Genji," I thought to myself, " so what should Murasaki be doing here ? " . . . Then the Vice-Councillor began pulling about poor Lady Hyōbu, and the Prime Minister made comic noises which I found very disagreeable. It was still quite early, and knowing well what would be the latter stages of an entertainment which

[1] He was now 64.
[2] Fujiwara no Kintō (966-1041), famous poet ; cousin of Michinaga.

had begun in this way, I waited till things seemed to have come to a momentary pause and then plotted with Lady Saishō to slip away and hide. Presently however the Prime Minister's sons and other young Courtiers burst into the room; a fresh hubbub began, and when they heard that two ladies were in hiding they tracked us down and flung back the screen behind which we had ensconced ourselves. We were now prisoners. . . .'

The *Diary* contains a series of notes chiefly upon the appearance but also in a few cases upon the character of other ladies at Court. Her remarks on Lady Izumi Shikibu, one of the greatest poets whom Japan has produced, are of interest: 'Izumi Shikibu is an amusing letter-writer; but there is something not very satisfactory about her. She has a gift for dashing off informal compositions in a careless running-hand; but in poetry she needs either an interesting subject or some classic model to imitate. Indeed it does not seem to me that in herself she is really a poet at all.

'However, in the impromptus which she recites there is always something beautiful or striking. But I doubt if she is capable of saying anything interesting about other people's verses. She is not intelligent enough. It is odd; to hear her talk you would certainly think that she had a touch of the poet in her. Yet she does not seem to produce anything that one can call serious poetry. . . .'

Here, too, is the note on Sei Shōnagon,[1] author of the famous *Makura no Sōshi*: 'Sei Shōnagon's most marked characteristic is her extraordinary self-satisfaction. But examine the pretentious compositions in Chinese script which she scatters so liberally over the Court, and you will

---

[1] See p. 22. Shōnagon was about ten years senior to Murasaki. She was lady-in-waiting first to the Empress Sadako (died, 1000 A.D.); then to Sadako's sister Princess Shigesa (died, 1002 A.D.); finally to the Empress Akiko.

find them to be a mere patchwork of blunders. Her chief pleasure consists in shocking people; and as each new eccentricity becomes only too painfully familiar, she gets driven on to more and more outrageous methods of attracting notice. She was once a person of great taste and refinement; but now she can no longer restrain herself from indulging, even under the most inappropriate circumstances, in any outburst that the fancy of the moment suggests. She will soon have forfeited all claim to be regarded as a serious character, and what will become of her [1] when she is too old for her present duties I really cannot imagine.'

It was not likely that Murasaki, who passed such biting judgments on her companions, would herself escape criticism. In her diary she tells us the following anecdote: 'There is a certain lady here called Sayemon no Naishi who has evidently taken a great dislike to me, though I have only just become aware of it. It seems that behind my back she is always saying the most unpleasant things. One day when some one had been reading *The Tale of Genji* out loud to the Emperor, his Majesty said: "This lady has certainly been reading the Annals of Japan. She must be terribly learned." Upon the strength of this casual remark Naishi spread a report all over the Court that I prided myself on my enormous learning, and henceforth I was known as "Dame Annals" wherever I went.'

The most interesting parts of the *Diary* are those in which Murasaki describes her own feelings. The following passage refers to the winter of 1008 A.D. : 'I love to see the

---

[1] Murasaki suggests that Shōnagon will lose Akiko's confidence and be dismissed. There is indeed a tradition (*Kojidan*, vol. ii) that when some courtiers were out walking one day they passed a dilapidated hovel. One of them mentioned a rumour that Sei Shōnagon, a wit and beauty of the last reign, was now living in this place. Whereupon an incredibly lean hag shot her head out at the door, crying ' Won't you buy old bones, old rags and bones ? ' and immediately disappeared again.

snow here,[1] and was hoping from day to day that it would begin before Her Majesty went back to Court, when I was suddenly obliged to go home.[2] Two days after I arrived, the snow did indeed begin to fall. But here, where everything is so sordid, it gives me very little pleasure. As, seated once more at the familiar window, I watch it settling on the copses in front of the house, how vividly I recall those years [3] of misery and perplexity! Then I used to sit hour after hour at this same window, and each day was like the last, save that since yesterday some flower had opened or fallen, some fresh song-bird arrived or flown away. So I watched the springs and autumns in their procession, saw the skies change, the moon rise; saw those same branches white with frost or laden with snow. And all the while I was asking myself over and over again: "What has the future in store for me? How will this end?" However, sometimes I used to read, for in those days I got a certain amount of pleasure out of quite ordinary romances; I had one or two intimate friends with whom I used to correspond, and there were several other people, not much more than acquaintances, with whom I kept up a casual intercourse. So that, looking back on it now, it seems to me that, one way and another, I had a good many minor distractions.

'Even then I realized that my branch of the family was a very humble one; but the thought seldom troubled me, and I was in those days far indeed from the painful consciousness of inferiority which makes life at Court a continual torment to me.

'To-day I picked up a romance which I used to think quite entertaining, and found to my astonishment that it no longer amused me at all. And it is the same with my

---

[1] At the Prime Minister's.   [2] Her parents' house.
[3] After the death of her husband.

friends. I have a feeling that those with whom I used to be most intimate would now consider me worldly and flippant, and I have not even told them that I am here. Others, on whose discretion I completely relied, I now have reason to suspect of showing my letters to all and sundry. If they think that I write to them with that intention they cannot know very much of my character! It is surely natural under such circumstances that a correspondence should either cease altogether or become formal and infrequent. Moreover, I now come here so seldom that in many cases it seems hardly worth while to renew former friendships, and many of those who wanted to call I have put off with excuses. . . . The truth is I now find that I have not the slightest pleasure in the society of any but a few indispensable friends. They must be people who really interest me, with whom I can talk seriously on serious subjects, and with whom I am brought into contact without effort on my side in the natural course of everyday existence. I am afraid this sounds very exacting! But stay, there is Lady Dainagon. She and I used to sleep very close together every night at the Palace and talk for hours. I see her now as she used to look during those conversations, and very much wish that she were here. So I have a little human feeling, after all!'

A little later in the same winter Murasaki sees the Gosechi dancers [1] at the Palace, and wonders how they have reached their present pitch of forwardness and self-possession: ' Seeing several officers of the Sixth Rank coming towards them to take away their fans, the dancers threw the fans across to them in a manner which was adroit enough, but which somehow made it difficult to remember that they were women at all. If I were suddenly called upon to expose myself in that fashion I should completely lose my

[1] See below, p. 125.

head. But already I do a hundred things which a few years ago I should never have dreamed myself capable of doing. So strange indeed are the hidden processes which go on in the heart of man that I shall no doubt continue to part with one scruple after another till in the end what now appears to me as the most abandoned shamelessness will seem perfectly proper and natural. Thus I reflected upon the unreality of all our attitudes and opinions, and began sketching out to myself the probable course of my development. So extraordinary were the situations in which I pictured myself that I became quite confused, and saw very little of the show.'

The most direct discussion of her own character comes in a passage towards the end of the diary : ' That I am very vain, reserved, unsociable, wanting always to keep people at a distance—that I am wrapped up in the study of ancient stories, conceited, living all the time in a poetical world of my own and scarcely realizing the existence of other people, save occasionally to make spiteful and depreciatory comments upon them—such is the opinion of me that most strangers hold, and they are prepared to dislike me accordingly. But when they get to know me, they find to their extreme surprise that I am kind and gentle—in fact, quite a different person from the monster they had imagined ; as indeed many have afterwards confessed. Nevertheless, I know that I have been definitely set down at Court as an ill-natured censorious prig. Not that I mind very much, for I am used to it and see that it is due to things in my nature which I cannot possibly change. The Empress has often told me that, though I seemed always bent upon not giving myself away in the royal presence, yet she felt after a time as if she knew me more intimately than any of the rest.'

The *Diary* closes in 1010. After this we do not know one

solitary fact concerning Murasaki's life or death; save that in 1025 she was still in Akiko's service and in that year took part in the ceremonies connected with the birth of the future Emperor Go-Ryōzen.

The Composition of Genji

It is generally assumed that the book was written during the three or at the most four years which elapsed between the death of Murasaki's husband and her arrival at Court. Others suggest that it was begun then, and finished some time before the winter of 1008. This assumption is based on the three references to *The Tale of Genji* which occur in the *Diary*. But none of these allusions seem to me to imply that the *Tale* was already complete. From the first reference it is evident that the book was already so far advanced as to show that Murasaki was its heroine; the part of the *Tale* which was read to the Emperor[1] was obviously the first chapter, which ends with a formula derived directly from the early annals: 'Some say that it was the Korean fortune-teller who gave him the name of Genji the Shining One.' Such 'alternative explanations' are a feature of early annals in most countries and occur frequently in those of Japan. Lastly, Michinaga's joke about the discrepancy between the prudishness of Murasaki's conduct and the erotic character of her book implies no more than that half-a-dozen chapters were in existence. It may be thought odd that she should have shown it to any one before it was finished. But the alternative is to believe that it was completed in seven years, half of which were spent at Court under circumstances which could have given her very little leisure. It is much more probable, I think, that *The Tale of Genji*, having been begun in 1001,

[1] For the Emperor's remark, see above, p. 25.

was carried on slowly after Murasaki's arrival at Court, during her holidays and in spare time at the Palace, and not completed till, say, 1015 or even 1020. The middle and latter parts certainly give the impression of having been written by some one of comparatively mature age. In 1022 the book was undoubtedly complete, for the *Sarashina Diary* refers to the 'fifty-odd chapters of *The Tale of Genji.*' In 1031 Murasaki's name is absent from a list where one might expect to find it, and it is possible that she was then no longer alive.[1]

The Empress Akiko lived on till 1074, reaching an even riper age than Queen Victoria, whom in certain ways she so much resembled.

[1] Murasaki was outlived by her father, so that it is improbable that she reached any great age.

NOTES

ON GENJI'S HOUSEHOLD.

Polygamy in Japan as elsewhere was confined to the upper classes, who alone were able to support the expense of so costly an institution. The actual wife (*kita no kata*, ' north side ') of a man in Genji's position had to be of the same social class as the husband, a condition fulfilled by Aoi, but not by Murasaki, who was never strictly speaking a *kita no kata*, but merely a *tai no uye* (' lady of the wing '). It will be remembered that Murasaki's mother was not of noble birth. Falling Flowers, Akashi and the rest were theoretically on the same footing as Murasaki. The number of ladies in an establishment was limited not by law or religion, but by expense and above all (in a case such as that of Genji) by the difficulty of dealing with the emotional situation that arose from large households. Did polygamy create different emotional situations from those to which we are accustomed —if, for example, it were so much taken for granted that jealousy ceased to exist—a novel dealing with a polygamous society would make very little appeal to us. It is because in *Genji* the re-actions of the characters are precisely the same as ours would be under similar circumstances, that the book holds our attention.

Another point concerning Genji's household that perhaps requires comment is the apparent ability of persons to live years in the same house without ever having met. But such a thing happens frequently at English University Colleges, and we must envisage Genji's palace as more like a college than a house,—consisting, in fact, of separate courtyards and cloisters, joined by covered galleries. Hence it comes about that, in the story, Genji's various favourites tend to be isolated from one another in a way which is not always advantageous to the construction of the book. Later on the authoress realizes the danger of the tale falling into a series of disconnected episodes, in which the personality of Genji is the only common factor—and takes pains to bring her heroines into relation with one another.

On the Time-scheme in Genji.

A pamphleteer has recently shown how complete and elaborate is the time-scheme that underlies Emily Brontë's *Wuthering Heights*. It is obvious that *Genji* is based upon an equally precise scheme. Here is no 'Oriental vagueness'; indeed it is inconceivable that Murasaki had not prepared for herself some species of chronological chart, which she kept constantly by her when at work. If it has appeared to any reader that her sense of time is vague, the fault is entirely mine. In one case, indeed, I am conscious of having created this impression by translating inappropriately a phrase about the young Emperor Ryōzen, whereby I make him seem much older than the chronology warrants. But there is never a moment in the story at which the authoress has not got a precise idea about the age of every character in it.

A WREATH OF CLOUD

A WREATH OF CLOUD

CHAPTER I

A WREATH OF CLOUD

AS winter drew on, the Lady of Akashi in her house by the Ōi river became very dispirited. Formerly the prospect of a visit from Genji was sufficient to rouse her from her melancholy; but now he found her always in the same dejected posture morning, noon and night: 'How much longer is this to go on?' he cried impatiently. 'Do, I beg of you, make up your mind to come to my palace and use the quarters I have reserved for you.' But he could never persuade her that she would not be thus exposing herself to a hundred indignities and affronts. It was of course impossible to be quite sure how things would go, and if, after all his assurances, the move did not turn out well, her vague resentment against him would henceforth be transformed into a definite and justified grievance. 'Do you not feel,' he said, 'that it would be unfair to your child to keep it here with you much longer? Indeed, knowing as you do what plans [1] I have made for its future, you must surely see that you are behaving towards it with a lack of proper respect.... I have constantly discussed this matter with my wife and she has always shown great interest in the child's future. If it is

---

[1] Genji had promised in due course to marry the child to the Heir Apparent, son of the Emperor Ryōzen.

put for a while under her care, she will no doubt be willing to stand sponsor to it; so that it will be possible to carry out the Initiation ceremony and other rituals of induction[1] with full publicity.' So far from being convinced by his arguments, she saw herself now being inveigled into doing precisely what she had always suspected with horror that he would one day ask of her. 'Take the child away from me if you like,' she said at last, 'and give her to these grand people to bring up as though she were their own. But just when you think you have repaired the accident of her birth, some one will let out the secret, and where will you be then?' 'Yes, we must be careful about that,' answered Genji. 'But you need have no fear that the child will not be properly looked after. As you know, though we have been married for many years, Lady Murasaki has no children of her own, and this very much distresses her. She badly needs companionship, and when at one time there was some question of her adopting Lady Akikonomu, the former Vestal Virgin, she was obviously delighted at the prospect, though this lady was already a grown-up person. But when it comes to a child,—at an age, too, when such creatures have an irresistible charm—it is quite certain that she will welcome it with alacrity and henceforward devote all her time to its care. Of that there is no doubt at all . . .' and he proceeded to a general eulogy upon Murasaki's docility and charm. But while he was speaking the Lady of Akashi recalled the stories of Genji's adventurous past, and of numerous other attachments with which rumour credited him. It seemed on the one hand very unlikely that Lady Murasaki would not ultimately suffer the fate of her predecessors, and why should her child be entrusted to a favourite who might soon be forgotten or thrust aside? If on the other hand Murasaki

[1] Buddhist ceremonies corresponding to the Christian 'Confirmation.'

were indeed endowed with such pre-eminent qualities that she alone of all her rivals and predecessors was destined to enjoy permanent favour, then as long as mother and child remained in their present obscurity there was little danger that this magnificent lady would regard them as worth a moment's thought. But as soon as one or both should make an appearance in the Nijō palace, Murasaki's pride would be affronted and her jealousy aroused. . . . Her mother, however, was a woman who looked beyond the difficulties of the moment, and she now said with some severity : ' You are behaving very foolishly. It is natural enough that you should dislike parting with the child ; but you must make up your mind to do what will be best for it. I feel certain that His Highness is perfectly serious in his intentions concerning its future, and I advise you to entrust it to him at once. You need have no misgivings. After all, even Royal Princes are of very varying stock on the mother's side. I seem to remember that Prince Genji himself, who is reckoned the greatest gentleman in the land, could not be put forward as a successor to the Throne because his mother was so far inferior to the other ladies of the Court ; and indeed, judged from that point of view, he is a mere waiting-woman's son. If such disadvantages are not fatal even in the most exalted spheres, we lesser folk certainly need not trouble ourselves about them. . . .' The Lady of Akashi took the advice of several other persons who had a reputation for sagacity in such matters, and also consulted various soothsayers and astrologers. In every case the answer was the same : the child must go to the Capital. In face of such unanimity she began to waver. Genji, for his part, was still as anxious as ever that his plan should be carried out. But the subject was evidently so painful to her that he no longer attempted to broach it, and in the course of his next letter merely asked what were her wishes concerning the Initiation ceremony. She answered: 'I see now that, being what I am, I cannot keep the child with me without injuring its prospects. I am ready to part with it; but I still fear that amid such surroundings . . .' He was very sorry for her; but all the same he ordered his clerks to search the calendar for a suitable day, and began secretly to make preparations for the child's arrival.

To hand over her own child to another woman's keeping was indeed a bitter trial; but she kept on repeating to herself that, for its own sake, this sacrifice must sooner or later be made. The nurse whom Genji had originally sent to Akashi would of course go to take charge of it at the palace, and the prospect of losing this lady, to whom she had long confided all her sorrows, finding in her society the one solace of her monotonous and unhappy existence, added greatly to her present distress. 'Madam,' the nurse would say to her, 'I shall never forget your kindness to me ever since the day when, so unexpectedly, yet as I think not without the intervention of some kind fate, it fell to my lot to serve you. You may be sure that I shall all the while be longing to have you with me. But I shall never regard our separation as more than an expedient of the moment. In the end I am convinced that all will come right. Meanwhile, do not think that I look forward with any pleasant anticipations to a life that will take me so far from your side.' She wept; and thus day after day was spent in sad forebodings and preparations till the twelfth month was already come.

Storms of snow and hail now made the situation at Ōi more than ever depressing and uncomfortable. It appalled the Lady of Akashi to discover what manifold varieties of suffering one can be called upon to endure at one and the same time. She now spent every moment of the day in tending and caressing her little girl. One morning when the fast-falling snow was piling up high on every side she sat with the child in her arms, again and again going back in her mind over all the miseries of the past, and picturing to herself the yet more desolate days that were to come. It was long since she had gone into the front of the house. But this morning there was ice on the moat, and she went to the window to look. She was clad in many wraps of some soft, white, fluttering stuff, and as she stood gazing before her with hands clasped behind her head, those within the room thought that, prince's daughter though her rival was, she could scarce be more lovely in poise and gesture than their lady in her snowy dress. Raising her sleeve to catch the tears that had now begun to fall the Lady of Akashi turned to the nurse and said: 'If it were upon a day such as this,[1] I do not think that I could bear it. . . .' And she recited the poem: 'If country roads be deep in snow, and clouds return, tread thou the written path, and though thyself thou comest not, vouchsafe a sign.'[2] To comfort her the nurse answered through her tears: 'Though the snow-drifts of Yoshino were heaped across his path, doubt not that whither his heart is set, his footsteps shall tread out their way.' The snow was now falling a little less fast. Suddenly Genji appeared at the door. The moments during which she waited to receive him put her always into a state of painful agitation. To-day guessing as she did the purpose of his visit, his arrival threw her immediately into an agonizing conflict. Why had she consented? There was still time. If she refused to part with the child, would he snatch it from her? No, indeed; that was unthinkable. But stay! She had consented;

[1] That Genji fetched the child.
[2] There is a play on words: *fumi* = 'letter'; also 'treading.' *Ato* = 'the tracks of feet,' but also 'tracks of the pen,' σήματα.

and should she now change her mind, she would lose his confidence forever. At one moment she was ready to obey; a moment afterwards, she had decided to resist by every means in her power.

She sat by the window, holding the little girl in her arms. He thought the child very beautiful, and felt at once that her birth was one of the most important things that had happened in his life. Since last spring her hair had been allowed to grow [1] and it was now an inch or two long, falling in delicate waves about her ears like that of a little novice at a convent. Her skin too was of exquisite whiteness and purity, and she had the most delightful eyes. To part with such a creature, to send her away into strange hands, —he understood well enough what this must mean, and suddenly it seemed to him that it was impossible even to suggest such a sacrifice. The whole matter was re-opened, and a discussion followed which lasted the better part of the day. 'Whether it is worth while depends on you,' she said at last. 'It is in your power to make amends to the child for the disadvantages of its birth. And if I thought that you meant to do so . . .' she was worn out by the long discussion, and now burst into tears. It was terrible to witness such distress. But the child, heedless of what was going on about it, was lustily demanding 'a ride in the nice carriage.' The mother picked it up and carried it in her own arms to the end of the drive. When she had set it down, it caught at her sleeve and in the prettiest, baby voice imaginable begged her to 'come for a ride too.' There framed themselves in the lady's heart the lines: 'Were all my prayers in vain, or shall I live to see the two-leaved pine from which to-day I part spread mighty shadows on the earth?'; but she could scarce speak the words, and seeing her now weeping wildly Genji

---

[1] Babies' heads were shaved, save for two tufts.

strove to comfort her with the verse : ' Like the little pine-tree that at Takekuma from the big one grows, grafted to my deep roots long shall this stripling thrive secure.' ' Wait patiently,' he added. She strove hard to persuade herself that he was right, that all was for the best. But now the carriages were moving away. . . .

With the child rode the nurse and also a gentlewoman of good family called Shōshō, holding on their knees the Sword, the Heavenly Children [1] and other emblems of royalty. In the next carriage followed a band of youths and little girls whom he had brought to form the child's escort on the homeward way. All the time they were driving to the Capital Genji was haunted by the image of the sorrow-stricken figure that had watched their departure. Small blame to her if at the moment she was feeling bitterly towards him !

It was quite dark when they arrived. So soon as the carriages had been drawn in, Shōshō and the nurse began looking about them at the splendours amid which they were now destined to reside. They felt indeed (coming as they did from rural and quite unpretentious surroundings) somewhat awestruck and ill at ease. But when they were shown the apartments which had been set aside for the new arrival, with a tiny bed, screens-of-state, and everything which a little lady could require, all beautifully set out and arranged, they began to take heart. The nurse's own room was in the corridor leading to the western wing, on the north side of the passage.

The child had fallen asleep during the journey and while she was carried into the house had not cried or seemed at all put out. She was taken straight to Murasaki's room

---

[1] The sword was the emblem of the child's royal blood. The Heavenly Children were dolls which were intended to attract evil influences and so save the child from harm.

and there given her supper. After a while she began to look round her.

She evidently wondered why her mother was nowhere to be seen, and after a further search her little lips began to tremble. The nurse was sent for and soon succeeded in distracting her attention. If only, thought Genji, who had witnessed this scene—if only the mother in that slow country home could be as easily comforted! But now there was no way to make amends to her, save to see to it that never in one jot should the child's care and upbringing fall short of what its mother might in her wildest dream have craved for it. For the moment indeed he accounted it a blessing that Murasaki had not borne him a child of her own, and was thus free to devote herself to the reparation of the wrong which he had inflicted upon this little newcomer by the circumstances of its birth. For some days the child continued occasionally to ask for its mother or some other person whom it had been used to see daily at Ōi, and when they could not be produced it would have a fit of screaming or of tears. But it was by nature a contented, happy little thing, and soon struck up a friendship with its new mother, who for her part was delighted to take charge of a creature so graceful and confiding. She insisted on carrying it about in her own arms, attended herself to all its wants and joined in all its games. Gradually the nurse became a personal attendant upon Lady Murasaki rather than the under-servant she had been before. Meanwhile a lady of irreproachable birth happened to become available as a wet-nurse and was accordingly added to the establishment. The ceremony of her Initiation did not involve any very elaborate preparations, but the child's little companions were naturally aware that something was afoot. Her outfit, so tiny that it looked as though it came out of a doll's-house, was a charming sight. So many people came in and out of the house all day even at ordinary times that they hardly noticed the guests who had assembled in their little mistress's honour. It was only when she raised her arms for the Binding of the Sleeves that the unwonted gesture caught their attention; they had never seen her in so pretty a pose before.

Meanwhile the mother at Ōi was all the more wretched because she now felt that her misery was self-inflicted. Had she been firm, the child might still be with her and life in some measure endurable. She could not believe that so extreme a course could really have been indispensable to its interests and bitterly repented of her docility. Even the grandmother, who had been foremost in urging the sacrifice, missed the baby sadly and went about the house with tears in her eyes. But news had reached them of the pains which Genji was bestowing upon its upbringing, and she felt no doubt that she had advised for the best.

A peculiar compunction prevented the Lady of Akashi from sending any gift or message to the child which was no longer hers, but she took immense pains in contriving presents for all its companions and attendants from the nurse downwards, and would spend hours in the matching of colours and the choosing of stuffs.

Genji did not at all want her to think that, now she had parted with the child, his visits were going to become any the less frequent, and though it was very difficult to arrange, he made a point of going out to Ōi before the turn of the year. It must at the best of times, he thought, be an uninteresting place to live in; but at any rate she had had the child to look after, and (what with getting it up and putting it to bed) that seemed to occupy a good deal of time. How she managed to get through the day now he could not imagine, and coming away from this visit with a heavy heart he henceforward wrote to her almost daily. Fortunately Murasaki no longer showed any jealousy on this score, feeling, as it seemed, that the surrender of so exquisite a child needed whatever recompense Genji found it in his heart to bestow.

The New Year [1] was ushered in by a spell of bright, clear weather. At the Nijō-in everything seemed to be going particularly well and, now that all the improvements were completed, an unusually large number of guests was entertained during the period of festivities. The older, married visitors came, as is customary, on the seventh day, bringing with them their children to assist in the ceremonies of congratulation; and these young visitors all seemed to be in excellent health and spirits. Even the lesser gentlemen and retainers who came to pay their respects, though no doubt many of them had worries and troubles enough of their own, managed to keep up, during these few days at any rate, an outward appearance of jollity.

The lady from the Village of Falling Flowers, who was now installed in the new eastern wing, seemed completely satisfied by her new surroundings. She had her work cut out for her in keeping up to the mark all the writing-women and young girls whom Genji had allotted to her service. Nor could she feel that she had gained nothing by her present proximity; for whenever he had a few moments to spare, he would come round and sit with her. He did not however visit her by previous appointment or stay at all late at night in her apartments. Happily she was by nature extremely unexacting. If what she wanted did not come her way, she at once assumed that this particular thing was not 'in her destiny,' and ceased to worry about it. This habit of mind made her quite unusually easy to handle, and he for his part lost no opportunity of publicly showing by his manner towards her that he regarded her as of scarcely less

[1] Genji must now have been 30.

consequence than Murasaki; with the result that those who came to the house felt they would be displeasing him if they did not pay their respects to her as well as to his wife; while stewards and servants saw that she was a person whom it would not be advisable to neglect. Thus everything seemed to be working very smoothly, and Genji felt that the arrangement was going to be a great success.

He thought constantly of the country house at Ōi and of the dull hours which the Lady of Akashi must be passing there at this season of festivity. So soon as the New Year celebrations both at his own house and in the Palace were drawing to a close, he determined to pay her another visit, and with this object in view he put on his finest clothes, wearing under his cherry-coloured cloak a matchless vesture of deep saffron hue, steeped in the perfumes of the scented box where it had lain. Thus clad he went to take his leave of Murasaki, and as he stood in the full rays of the setting sun, his appearance was so magnificent that she gazed at him with even greater admiration than was her wont. The little princess grabbed at the ends of his long wide trousers with her baby hands, as though she did not want him to go. When he reached the door of the women's apartments she was still clinging to him and he was obliged to halt for a moment in order to disentangle himself. Having at last coaxed her into releasing him, he hurried down the corridor humming to himself as he did so the peasant-song 'To-morrow I will come again.'[1] At the door he met one of Murasaki's ladies and by her he sent back just that message, 'To-morrow I will come again.' She instantly recognized whence the words came and answered with the poem:

[1] 'Stop your boat, oh cherry-man! I must sow the ten-rood island field. Then I will come again. To-morrow I will come again!' The lady answers: 'To-morrow, forsooth! Those are but words. You keep a girl upon the other side, and **to-morrow you will not come, no, not to-morrow will you come.**'

'Were there on the far shore no person to detain your boat, then might I indeed believe that to-morrow you will come again.' This was brought to him before he drove away, and smiling at her readiness of wit he answered: 'In truth I will but look to my business and come back again; come back to-morrow, though she across the waters chide me as she will.' The little girl did not of course understand a word of all this; but she saw that there was a joke, and was cutting the strangest capers. As usual the sight of her antics disarmed all Murasaki's resentment, and though she would much rather there had been no 'lady on the far shore,' she no longer felt any hostility towards her. Through what misery the mother must be passing, Murasaki was now in a position to judge for herself. She continually imagined what her own feelings would be if the child were taken from her, never for an instant let it go out of her sight, and again and again pressed it to her bosom, putting her lovely teats to its mouth, and caressing it for hours together.

'What a pity that she has never had one of her own!' her ladies whispered; 'To be sure if this were hers, she could not wish it different. . . .'

Meanwhile the Lady of Akashi was setting herself to face with resolute calm the dullness and monotony of country life. The house had a curious charm of its own, which appealed very much to Genji during his visits, and as for its occupant,—he was astonished at the continual improvement in her looks. Indeed, had not that queer father of hers taken such extraordinary pains to prevent her ever mixing with the world, he believed there was no reason why she should not have done extremely well for herself. Yes, all she had needed was an ordinary father; even a rather shabby one would not have mattered. For such beauty and intelligence as hers, if once given the chance, could not have failed to pull her through. Each visit left him restless and unsatisfied, and he found himself spending his time in continual goings and comings, his life ' a tremulous causeway linking dream to dream.'

Sometimes he would send for a zithern and remembering the exquisite music with which she had beguiled those nights at Akashi, he begged her to play to him upon her lute. She would not now play alone; but she sometimes consented to accompany him, doing so with a mastery he could not imagine how she had contrived to acquire. The rest of the time was generally spent in minute recital of the little princess's sayings and doings. Often he had come over on business connected with his new oratory at Saga or his estate at Katsura; and then there would perhaps be only time enough to eat a little fruit and dried rice with her at Ōi before he hurried back to town. On such occasions there was not time for intimacies of any kind; but the mere fact that he snatched at every chance of seeing her and that he did so without any attempt at concealment, marked her as one who held a not inconsiderable place in his affections. She was quite aware of this; but she never presumed upon it, and without any tiresome display of humility she obeyed his orders and in general gave him as little trouble as possible. By all that she could hear, there was not one of the great ladies at Court with whom he was on so intimate a footing as with herself; indeed, he was said to be somewhat stand-offish and difficult of approach. Were she to live closer at hand he would perhaps grow weary of her, and in any case there would certainly be unpleasant rivalries and jealousies. Thus or in some such way may we suppose the Lady of Akashi to have reconciled herself to these brief and accidental visits. Her father, despite his disavowal of all worldly interests, was extremely anxious to hear how Genji was behaving towards his daughter and constantly sent messengers to Ōi to pick up what news they could. Much of what he heard distressed and disappointed him; but frequently too there were signs and indications of a more encouraging kind, and he would grow quite elated.

About this time Lady Aoi's father died. His name had carried great weight in the country and his death was a heavy loss to the present government. It so happened that the period during which he took part in public life had been marked by much disorder and unrest. A renewal of these upheavals was now expected and general depression prevailed. Genji too was much distressed, both for personal reasons and because he had been in the habit of delegating to the old Minister most of the public business which fell to his lot. He had thus managed to secure a reasonable amount of leisure. He saw himself henceforward perpetually immersed in a multiplicity of tiresome affairs, and the prospect greatly depressed him. The Emperor, though still only twelve years old, was extremely forward for his age both in body and mind, and although it was not to be expected that he should act alone, the task of supervising his work was not a difficult one. But for some years such supervision would still be needed, and unfortunately there was no one else to whom Genji could possibly entrust such a task. Thus the prospect of being able to lead the retired life which alone appealed to him was still remote, and he frequently became very discontented.

For some while he was occupied with the celebration of rituals and services on behalf of the dead man's soul; these he carried out even more elaborately than did the sons and grandsons of the deceased. This year, as had been predicted, was marked by a number of disorders and calamities. The Palace was frequently visited by the most disagreeable and alarming apparitions, the motions of the planets, sun and moon were irregular and unaccountable, and clouds of baleful and significant shape were repeatedly observed. Learned men of every school sent in elaborate addresses to the Throne, in which they attempted to account for these strange manifestations. But they were obliged to confess that many of the reported happenings were unique, and of a very baffling character. While speculation thus reigned on every side, Genji held in his heart a guilty secret [1] which might well be the key to these distressing portents.

Lady Fujitsubo had fallen ill at the beginning of the year and since the third month her malady had taken a serious turn. The August visit of the Emperor to her bedside and other unusual ceremonies had already taken place. He was a mere child when she relinquished the care of him, and he had grown up without any very strong feelings towards her. But he now looked so solemn as he stood by the bedside that she herself began to feel quite sad. 'I have for some while felt certain,' she said to him calmly, 'that this would be the last year of my life. But as long as my illness did not prevent me from going about as usual, I gave no hint to those around me that I knew my end was near; for I dreaded the fuss and outcry that such a confession would have produced. Nor did I alter in any way my daily prayers and observances. I longed to visit you at the Palace and talk with you quietly about old days. But I seldom felt equal to so great an exertion. . . . And now it is too late.'

She spoke in a very low, feeble voice. She was thirty-seven years old, but seemed much younger. The Emperor, as he looked at her, was overwhelmed by pity and regret. That just as she was reaching an age when she would need

---

[1] The secret that the Emperor was his son. The safety of the State depended upon the cult of ancestors. This could only be performed by their true descendants. Moreover the occupation of the throne by one who was not by birth entitled to it would arouse the wrath of the Sun, from whom the Emperor of Japan claims descent.

his care, she should, unknown to him, have passed through months of continual suffering, without once having recourse to those sacred expedients which alone might have saved her—this thought made the most painful impression upon him; and now, in a last attempt to rescue her from death, he set in motion every conceivable sort of ritual and spell. Genji too was dismayed at the discovery that for months past she had been worn out by constant pain, and now sought desperately to find some remedy for her condition. But it was apparent that the end was at hand; the Emperor's visits became more and more frequent and many affecting scenes were witnessed. Fujitsubo was in great pain and seldom attempted to speak at any length. But lying there and looking back over the whole course of her career, she thought that while in the outward circumstances of life few women could have been more fortunate than herself, inwardly scarce one in all history had been more continually apprehensive and wretched. The young Emperor was of course still wholly ignorant of the secret of his birth. In not acquainting him with it she felt that she had failed in the discharge of an essential duty, and the one matter after her death in which she felt any interest was the repair of this omission.

Merely in his position as head of the government it was natural that Genji should be gravely concerned by the approaching loss to his faction of so distinguished a supporter, coming, as it seemed likely to, not many months after the death of the old Grand Minister. This public concern could indeed be openly displayed. But concealed from all those about him there was in his inmost heart a measureless sorrow, to which he dared give vent only in perpetual supplication and prayer. That it was no longer possible to renew even such casual and colourless intercourse as had been theirs in recent years was very painful to him.

He hurried to her bedside at the first news of the serious turn which her condition had taken.

To his surprise she did, in a faint and halting manner, contrive to speak a few words to him when she realized that he was near. First she thanked him for carrying out so scrupulously the late Emperor's wishes with regard to the surveillance of his present Majesty. Much had happened in the last years for which she had cause to be grateful to him, and she had often meant to tell him how sensible she was of his kindness. And there was another matter of which she had meant for some time to speak . . . to the Emperor himself. She was sorry she had never . . . Here her voice became inaudible, and tears for a while prevented him from making a reply. He feared that this display of emotion would arouse comment among those who were standing by; but indeed any one who had known her as she used to be might well have been overcome with grief to see her in so woeful a condition. Suddenly he looked up. No thought or prayer of his could now recall her; and in unspeakable anguish, not knowing whether she heard him or no, he began to address her: 'In spite of the difficulties into which I myself have sometimes fallen, I have tried to do my best for His Majesty, or at any rate, what then seemed to me best. But since the death of the old Grand Minister, everything has gone wrong; and with you lying ill like this I do not know which way to turn. Were you now to die, I think I should soon follow you. . . .' He paused, but there was no reply; for she had died suddenly like a candle blown out by the wind, and he was left in bewilderment and misery.

She was, of all the great ladies about the Court at that time, the most tender-hearted and universally considerate. Women of her class do not as a rule expect to compass their own ends without causing considerable inconvenience to ordinary people. Fujitsubo on the contrary invariably released even her servants and retainers from any duty which she felt to be an undue infringement of their liberty.

She was devout; but unlike many religious persons she did not display her piety by impressive benefactions paid for out of funds which other people had collected. Her charities (and they were considerable) were made at the expense of her own exchequer. The ranks, titles and benefices which were at her disposal she distributed with great intelligence and care, and so many were her individual acts of generosity that there was scarcely a poor ignorant mountain-priest in all the land who had not reason to lament her loss. Seldom had the obsequies of any public person provoked so heart-felt and universal a sorrow. At Court no colour but black was anywhere to be seen; and the last weeks of spring lacked all their usual brilliance and gaiety.

Standing one day before the great cherry-tree which grew in front of the Nijō-in Genji suddenly remembered that this was the season when, under ordinary circumstances, the Flower Feast would have been held at the Emperor's Palace. 'This year should'st thou have blossomed with black flowers,'[1] he murmured and, to hide the sudden access of grief that had overwhelmed him, rushed into his chapel and remained there weeping bitterly till it began to grow dark. Issuing at last, he found a flaming sun about to sink beneath the horizon. Against this vivid glow the trees upon the hill stood out with marvellous clearness, every branch, nay every twig distinct. But across the hill there presently drifted a thin filament of cloud, draping the summit with a band of grey. He was in no mood that day to notice sunsets or pretty cloud-effects; but in this half-curtained sky there seemed to him to be a strange significance, and

---

[1] Quoting a poem of Uyeno Mine-o's upon the death of Fujiwara no Mototsune, 891 A.D.

A WREATH OF CLOUD

none being by to hear him he recited the verse : 'Across the sunset hill there hangs a wreath of cloud that garbs the evening as with the dark folds of a mourner's dress.'

There was a certain priest who had for generations served as chaplain in Lady Fujitsubo's family. Her mother had placed extraordinary confidence in him, and she herself had instilled the young Emperor Ryōzen with deep veneration for this old man, who was indeed known throughout the land for the sanctity of his life and the unfailing efficacy of his prayers. He was now over seventy and had for some time been living in retirement, intent upon his final devotions. But recently the occasion of Lady Fujitsubo's death had called him back to the Court, and the Emperor had more than once summoned him to his side. An urgent message, conveyed by Prince Genji, now reached him. The night was already far advanced, and the old man at first protested that these nocturnal errands were no longer within his capacity. But in the end he promised, out of respect for His Majesty, to make a great effort to appear, and at the calm of dawn, at a moment when, as it so happened, many of the courtiers were absent and those on duty had all withdrawn from the Presence, the old man stepped into Ryōzen's room. After talking for a while in his aged, croaking voice about various matters of public interest, he said at last : 'There is one very difficult matter which I wish to discuss with you. I fear I may not have the courage to embark upon it, and I am still more afraid that if I succeed in broaching this topic I may give you great offence. But it concerns something which it would be very wrong to conceal ; a secret indeed such as makes me fear the eye of Heaven. What use is there, now that I am so near my end, in locking it up so tightly in my heart ? I fear that Buddha himself might cast me out should I approach him defiled by this unholy concealment.' He began trying to tell the Emperor something; but he seemed unable to come to the point. It was strange that there should be any worldly matter concerning which the old priest retained such violent emotions. Perhaps, despite his reputation, he had once secretly pursued some hideous vendetta, had caused an innocent person to be entrapped, done away with ... a thousand monstrous possibilities crowded to the Emperor's mind. 'Reverend Father,' he said at last, 'you have known me since I was a baby, and I have never once hidden anything from you. And now I learn that there is something which you have for a long time past been concealing from me. I confess, I am surprised.' 'There is nothing that I have kept from you,' the old man cried indignantly. 'Have I not made you master of my most secret spells, of the inner doctrines that Buddha forbids us to reveal? Do you think that I, who in these holy matters reposed so great a confidence in your Majesty, would have concealed from you any dealing of my own?

'The matter of which I speak is one that has had grave results already and may possibly in the future entail worse consequences still. The reputations concerned are those of your late august Mother and of some one who now holds a prominent place in the government of our country ... it is to Prince Genji that I refer. It is for their sake, and lest some distorted account of the affair should ultimately reach you from other sources, that I have undertaken this painful task. I am an old man and a priest; I therefore have little to lose and, even should this revelation win me your displeasure, I shall never repent of having made it; for Buddha and the Gods of Heaven showed me by unmistakable signs that it was my duty to speak.

'You must know, then, that from the time of your Majesty's conception the late Empress your mother was in evident distress concerning the prospect of your birth. She told me indeed that there were reasons which made the expected child particularly in need of my prayers; but what these reasons were she did not say; and I, being without experience in such matters, could form no conjecture. Soon after your birth there followed a species of convulsion in the state; Prince Genji was in disgrace and later in exile. Meanwhile your august Mother seemed to grow every day more uneasy about your future, and again and again I was asked to offer fresh prayers on your behalf. Strangest of all, so long as Prince Genji was at the Capital he too seemed to be acquainted with the instructions I had received; for on every occasion he at once sent round a message bidding me add by so much to the prayers that had been ordered and make this or that fresh expenditure on some service or ritual. . . .'

The disclosure [1] was astonishing, thrilling, terrifying. Indeed so many conflicting emotions struggled for the upper hand that he was unable to make any comment or reply. The old priest misunderstood this silence and, grieved that he should have incurred Ryōzen's displeasure by a revelation which had been made in His Majesty's own interest, he bowed and withdrew from the Presence. The Emperor immediately ordered him to return. 'I am glad that you have told me of this,' said Ryōzen. 'Had I gone on living in ignorance of it I see that a kind of contempt would have been attached for ever to my name; for in the end such things are bound to be known. I am only sorry that you should have concealed this from me for so long; and tremble to think of the things that in my ignorance I may have said or done. . . .[2] Tell me, does anyone besides yourself know of this, . . .

[1] That Ryōzen was in reality Genji's son.
[2] See above, note on p. 49, and below note on p. 60.

any one who is likely to have let out the secret?' 'Besides myself and your mother's maid Ōmyōbu there is no one who has an inkling of the matter,' the priest hastened to assure him. 'Nevertheless the existence of such a secret causes me grave misgivings. Upheavals of nature, earthquakes, drought and storm, have become alarmingly frequent; and in the State, we have had constant disorder and unrest. All these things may be due to the existence of this secret. So long as your Majesty was a helpless infant Heaven took pity on your innocence; but now that you are grown to your full stature and have reached years of understanding and discretion, the Powers Above are manifesting their displeasure; for, as you have been taught, it frequently happens that the sins of one generation are visited upon the next. I saw plainly that you did not know to what cause our present troubles and disorders are due, and that is why I at last determined to reveal a secret which I hoped need never pass my lips.' The old man spoke with difficulty, tears frequently interrupted his discourse, and it was already broad daylight when he finally left the Palace.

No sooner had he realized the full significance of this astonishing revelation than a medley of conflicting thoughts began to harass Ryōzen's mind. First and foremost, he felt indignant on behalf of the old Emperor, whom he had always been taught to regard as his father; but he also felt strangely uncomfortable at the idea that Genji, who had a much better right to the Throne than he, should have been cast out of the Imperial family, to become a Minister, a mere servant of the State. Viewed from whatever standpoint, the new situation was extremely painful to him, and overcome by shock and bewilderment he lay in his room long after the sun was high. Learning that his Majesty had not risen, Genji assumed that he was indisposed

and at once called to enquire. The Emperor was in tears, and utterly unable to control himself even in the presence of a visitor. But this was after all perhaps not so very surprising. The young man had only a few weeks ago lost his mother, and it was natural that he should still be somewhat upset. Unfortunately it was Genji's duty that morning to announce to his Majesty the decease of Prince Momozono.[1] It seemed to Ryōzen as though the whole world, with all its familiar landmarks and connections, were crumbling about him. During the first weeks of mourning Genji spent all his time at the Palace and paid an early visit to the Emperor every day. They had many long, uninterrupted conversations, during the course of which Ryōzen on one occasion said: 'I do not think that my reign is going to last much longer. Never have I had so strong a foreboding that calamity of some stupendous kind was at hand; and quite apart from this presentiment, the unrest which is now troubling the whole land is already enough to keep me in a continual state of agitation and alarm. Ever since this began I have had great thoughts of withdrawing from the Throne; but while my mother was alive I did not wish to distress her by doing so. Now, however, I consider that I am free to do as I choose, and I intend before long to seek some quieter mode of life. . . .'
'I sincerely hope you will do nothing of the kind,' said Genji. 'The present unrest casts no reflection upon you or your government. Difficulties of this kind sometimes arise during the rule of the most enlightened government, as is proved by the history of China as well as by that of our own country. Nor must you allow yourself to be unduly depressed by the demise of persons such as your respected uncle, who had, after all, reached a time of life when we

[1] Prince Momozono Shikibukyō, brother of the old Emperor and father of Princess Asagao.

could not reasonably expect . . . ' Thus Genji managed, by arguments which for fear of wearying you I will not repeat, to coax the Emperor into a slightly less desperate state of mind. Both were dressed in the simplest style and in the same sombre hue. For years past it had struck the Emperor, on looking at himself in the mirror, that he was extraordinarily like Prince Genji. Since the revelation of his true parentage, he had more frequently than ever examined his own features. Why, of course! There was no mistaking such a likeness! But if he was Genji's son, Genji too must be aware of the fact, and it was absurd that the relationship should not be acknowledged between them. Again and again he tried to find some way of introducing the subject. But to Genji, he supposed, the whole matter must be a very painful one. He often felt that it was impossible to refer to such a thing at all, and conversation after conversation went by without any but the most general topics being discussed; though it was noticeable that Ryōzen's manner was even more friendly and charming than usual. Genji who was extremely sensitive to such changes did not fail to notice that there was something new in the young Emperor's attitude towards him—an air of added respect, almost of deference. But it never occurred to him that Ryōzen could by any possibility be in possession of the whole terrible secret. At first the Emperor had thought of discussing the matter with the maid Ōmyōbu and asking her for a fuller account of his birth and all that had led up to it. But at the last moment he felt that it was better she should continue to think herself the only inheritor of the secret, and he decided not to discuss the matter with any one. But he longed, without actually letting out that he knew, to get some further information from Genji himself. Among other things he wanted to know whether what had happened with regard to his birth was wholly unexampled, or whether it was in point of fact far more common than one would suppose. But he could never find the right way to introduce such a subject. It was clear that he must get his knowledge from other sources, and he threw himself with fresh ardour into the study of history, reading every book with the sole object of discovering other cases like his own. In China, he soon found, irregularities of descent have not only in many cases been successfully concealed till long afterwards, but have often been known and tolerated from the beginning. In Japan he could discover no such instance; but he knew that if things of this kind occurred, they would probably not be recorded, so that their absence from native history might only mean that in our country such matters are hushed up more successfully than elsewhere.

The more he thought about it, the more Genji regretted that Ryōzen should have discovered (as from His Majesty's repeated offers of abdication he now felt certain to be the case) the real facts concerning his birth. Fujitsubo, Genji was sure, would have given anything rather than that the boy should know; it could not have been by her instructions that the secret had been divulged. Who then had betrayed him? Naturally his thoughts turned towards Ōmyōbu. She had moved into the apartments which had been made out of the old offices of the Lady of the Bedchamber. Here she had been given official quarters and was to reside permanently in the Palace. Discussing the matter with her one day, Genji said: 'Are you sure that you yourself, in the course of some conversation with his Majesty, may not by accident have put this idea into his head?' 'It is out of the question,' she replied. 'I know too well how determined my Lady was that he should never discover . . . indeed, the fear that he might one day stumble upon the facts for himself was her constant torment

And this despite the dangers into which she knew that ignorance might lead him.'[1] And they fell to talking of Lady Fujitsubo's scrupulous respect for propriety, and how the fear of scandals and exposures which another woman would in the long run have grown to regard with indifference, had embittered her whole life.

For Lady Akikonomu he had done all and more than all that he led her to expect, and she had already become a prominent figure at Court. During the autumn, having been granted leave of absence from the Palace, she came to stay for a while at the Nijō-in. She was given the Main Hall, and found everything decked with the gayest colours in honour of her arrival. She assumed in the household the place of a favourite elder daughter, and it was entirely in this spirit that Genji entertained and amused her. One day when the autumn rain was falling steadily and the dripping flowers in the garden seemed to be washed to one dull tinge of grey, memories of long forgotten things came crowding one after another to Genji's mind, and with eyes full of tears he betook himself to Lady Akikonomu's rooms. Not a touch of colour relieved the dark of his mourner's dress, and on pretext of doing penance for the sins of the nation during the recent disorders he carried a rosary under his cloak; yet he contrived to wear even this dour, penitential garb with perfect elegance and grace, and it was with a fine sweep of the cloak that he now entered the curtained alcove where she sat. He came straight to her side and, with only a thin latticed screen between them, began to address her without waiting to be announced: 'What an unfortunate year this is! It is too bad that we should get weather like this just when everything in the garden is at its best. Look at the flowers. Are not you

[1] Into performing ceremonies at the grave of his supposed father which unless performed by a true son, were sacrilegious and criminal.

sorry for them? They came when it was their turn, and this is the way they are welcomed.' He leant upon the pillar of her seat, the evening light falling upon him as he turned towards her. They had many memories in common; did she still recall, he asked, that terrible morning when he came to visit her mother at the Palace-in-the-fields? 'Too much my thoughts frequent those vanished days,' she quoted,[1] and her eyes filled with tears. Already he was thinking her handsome and interesting, when for some reason she rose and shifted her position, using her limbs with a subtle grace that made him long to see her show them to better advantage. . . . But stay! Ought such thoughts to be occurring to him? 'Years ago,' he said, 'at a time when I might have been far more happily employed, I became involved, entirely through my own fault, in a number of attachments, all of the most unfortunate kind, with the result that I never knew an instant's peace of mind. Among these affairs there were two which were not only, while they lasted, far more distressing than the rest, but also both ended under a dark cloud of uncharitableness and obstinacy. The first was with Lady Rokujō, your mother. The fact that she died still harbouring against me feelings of the intensest bitterness will cast a shadow over my whole life, and my one consolation is that in accordance with her wishes, I have been able to do something towards helping *you* in the world. But that by any act of mine the flame of her love should thus forever have been stifled will remain the greatest sorrow of my life.' He had mentioned two affairs; but he decided to leave the other part of his tale untold and continued: 'During the period when my fortunes were in eclipse I had plenty of time to think over all these things and worked out a new plan which I hoped

[1] From a poem by Ono no Komachi's sister, say the commentaries; but such a poem is not to be found in her surviving works.

would make every one satisfied and happy. It was in pursuance of this plan that I induced the Lady from the Village of Falling Flowers to take up residence in the new eastern wing. Her own resources are quite inadequate, and I used to feel very uncomfortable about her; it is a great relief to know that she is getting all she needs. Fortunately she is very easy to deal with, we understand each other perfectly and there is (or at any rate I hope so) complete satisfaction on both sides. Soon after I came back a great deal of my time began to be taken up in looking after the young Emperor and helping him to conduct the business of the State. I am not particularly interested in that sort of thing, but I was glad to be of use. It was only when it came to filling his Household that I found myself confronted with a task that was definitely uncongenial. I wonder whether you realize what very strong impulses of my own I had to overcome before I surrendered you to the Palace? You might at least tell me that you feel for me and are grateful; then I should no longer think that this sacrifice was made quite in vain. . . .' She was vexed. Why must he needs start talking in that strain? She made no reply. 'Forgive me,' he said; 'I see that I have displeased you . . . ,' and he began hastily to talk of other matters: 'How much I should like to retire to some quiet place,—to know that for the rest of my life on earth I should have no more anxieties or cares and could devote myself for as long as I liked each day to preparation for the life to come. But of course all this would be very dull if one had nothing interesting to look back upon. There are many things to be thought of first. For example, I have young children, whose place in the world is very insecure; it will be a long time before I can establish them satisfactorily. And here you can be of great use to me; for should you—forgive me for speaking of such a thing—

one day bring increase to his Majesty's house, it would be in your power to render considerable services to my children, even though I should chance no longer to be with you. . . .' It was evident that this sort of conversation was far more to her liking. She did not indeed say more than a word or two at a time; but her manner was friendly and encouraging, and they were still immersed in these domestic projects when darkness began to fall. 'And when all these weighty matters are off my hands,' said Genji at last, 'I hope I shall have a little time left for things which I really enjoy —flowers, autumn leaves, the sky, all those day-to-day changes and wonders that a single year bring forth; that is what I looked forward to. Forests of flowering trees in Spring, the open country in Autumn. . . . Which do you prefer? It is of course useless to argue on such a subject, as has so often been done. It is a question of temperament. Each person is born with " his season " and is bound to prefer it. No one, you may be sure, has ever yet succeeded in convincing any one else on such a subject. In China it has always been the Spring-time with its " broidery of flowers " that has won the highest praise; here however the brooding melancholy of Autumn seems always to have moved our poets more deeply. For my own part I find it impossible to reach a decision; for much as I enjoy the music of birds and the beauty of flowers, I confess I seldom remember at what season I have seen a particular flower, heard this or that bird sing. But in this I am to blame; for even within the narrow compass of my own walls, I might well have learnt what sights and sounds distinguish each season of the year, having as you see not only provided for the springtime by a profusion of flowering trees, but also planted in my garden many varieties of autumn grass and shrub, brought in, root and all, from the countryside. Why, I have even carried hither whole tribes of insects that were wasting their shrill song in the solitude of lanes and fields. All this I did that I might be able to enjoy these things in the company of my friends, among whom you are one. Pray tell me then, to which season do you find that your preference inclines?' She thought this a very difficult form of conversation; but politeness demanded some sort of reply and she said timidly: 'But you have just said you can never yourself remember when it was you saw or heard the thing that pleased you most. How can you expect me to have a better memory? However, difficult as it is to decide, I think I agree with the poet [1] who found the dusk of an autumn evening " strangest and loveliest thing of all." Perhaps I am more easily moved at such moments because, you know, it was at just such a time . . .' Her voice died away, and knowing well indeed what was in her mind Genji answered tenderly with the verse: 'The world knows it not; but to you, oh Autumn, I confess it: your wind at night-fall stabs deep into my heart.'[2] 'Sometimes I am near to thinking that I can hold out no longer,' he added. To such words as these she was by no means bound to reply and even thought it best to pretend that she had not understood. This however had the effect of leading him on to be a little more explicit; and matters would surely have come a good deal further had she not at once shown in the most unmistakable manner her horror at the sentiments which he was beginning to profess. Suddenly he pulled himself up. He had been behaving with a childish lack of restraint. How fortunate that she at least had shown some sense! He felt very much cast down; but neither his sighs nor his languishing airs had any effect upon her. He saw that she was making as though to steal quietly and unobtrusively

[1] Anon, in *Kokinshū*, No. 546.
[2] He identifies Akikonomu with the Autumn.

from the room, and holding her back he said: 'I see that you are terribly offended; well, I do not deny that you have good cause. I ought not to be so impetuous; I know that it is wrong. But, granted I spoke far too suddenly—it is all over now. Do not, I beg of you, go on being angry with me; for if you are unkind . . .'[1] And with that he retired to his own quarters. Even the scent of his richly perfumed garments had become unendurable to her; she summoned her maids and bade them open the window and door. 'Just come over here and smell the cushion that his Highness was sitting on!' one of them called to another. 'What an exquisite fragrance! How he contrives to get hold of such scents I simply cannot imagine. "If the willow-tree had but the fragrance of the plum and the petals of the cherry!" So the old poet wished, and surely Prince Genji must be the answer to his prayer, for it seems that in him every perfection is combined.'

He went to the western wing; but instead of going straight into Murasaki's room, he flung himself down upon a couch in the vestibule. Above the partition he could see the far-off flicker of a lamp; there Murasaki was sitting with her ladies, one of whom was reading her a story. He began to think about what had just occurred. It was a sad disappointment to discover that he was still by no means immune from a tendency which had already played such havoc with his own and other people's happiness. Upon what more inappropriate object could his affections possibly have lighted? True, his chief offence in old days had been of far greater magnitude. But then he had the excuse of youth and ignorance, and it was possible that, taking this into consideration, Heaven might by this time have forgiven the offence. But on this occasion he could

---

[1] 'If you are unkind, I too by unkindness will teach you the pain that unkindness can inflict.' Anonymous poem.

hardly plead inexperience; indeed, as he ruefully admitted to himself, he ought by now to have learnt every lesson which repeated failure can teach.

Lady Akikonomu now bitterly repented of having confessed her partiality for the autumn. It would have been so easy not to reply at all, and this one answer of hers seemed somehow to have opened up the way for the distressing incident that followed. She told no one of what had occurred, but was for a time very much scared and distressed. Soon however the extreme stiffness and formality of address which Genji henceforth adopted began somewhat to restore her confidence.

On entering Murasaki's room at a later hour in the day of the incident, he said to her: 'Lady Akikonomu has been telling me that she likes Autumn best. It is a taste which I can quite understand, but all the same, I am not surprised that you should prefer, as you have often told me that you do, the early morning in Spring. How I wish that I were able to spend more time with you! We would pass many hours in the gardens at all seasons of the year, deciding which trees and flowers we liked the best. There is nothing which I more detest than having all my time taken up by this endless succession of business. You know indeed that if I had only myself to consider I should long ago have thrown up everything and retired to some temple in the hills. . . .'

But there was the Lady of Akashi; she too must be considered. He wondered constantly how she was faring; but it seemed to become every day more impossible for him to go beyond the walls of his palace. What a pity she had got it into her head that she would be miserable at Court! If only she would put a little more confidence in him and trust herself under his roof as any one else would do, he would prove to her that she had no reason for all these reservations and precautions. Presently one of his accustomed excursions to the oratory at Saga gave him an excuse for a visit to Ōi. 'What a lonely place to live in always!' he thought as he approached the house, and even if the people living there had been quite unknown to him he would have felt a certain concern on their behalf. But when he thought how she must wait for him day after day and how seldom her hopes could ever be fulfilled, he suddenly felt and showed an overwhelming compassion towards her. This however had only the effect of making her more than ever inconsolable. Seeking for some means of distracting her mind, he noticed that behind a tangle of close-set trees points of flame were gleaming—the flares of the cormorant-fishers at work on Ōi River; and with these lights, sometimes hardly distinguishable from them, blended the fireflies that hovered above the moat. 'It is wonderful here,' said Genji; 'you too would feel so, were not one's pleasure always spoiled by familiarity.' 'Those lights on the water!' she murmured. 'Often I think that I am still at Akashi. "As the fisher's flare that follows close astern, so in those days and in these has misery clung to my tossing bark, and followed me from home to home."' 'My love,' he answered, ' is like the secret flame that burns brightly because it is hidden from sight; yours is like the fisherman's torch, that flares up in the wind and presently is spent. No, no; you are right,' he said after a pause; 'life (yours and mine alike) is indeed a wretched business.' It happened to be a time at which he was somewhat less tied and harassed than of late, and he was able to devote himself more wholeheartedly than usual to the proceedings at his oratory. This kept him in the district for several days on end, a circumstance which did not often occur and which he hoped would, for the moment at any rate, make her feel a little less neglected.

CHAPTER II

ASAGAO

THE death of Prince Momozono meant, of course, the return to Court of the Kamo Vestal, Lady Asagao; and Genji followed up his letter of welcome by numerous other notes and messages. For it was, as I have said before, a peculiarity of his character that if he had once become fond of any one, neither separation nor lapse of time could ever obliterate his affection. But Asagao remembered only too well the difficulty that she had before experienced in keeping him at arm's length, and she was careful to answer in the most formal and guarded terms. He found these decorous replies exceedingly irritating. In the ninth month he heard that she had moved into her father's old residence, the Momozono Palace, which was at that time occupied by Princess Nyogo, a younger sister of the old Emperor.[1] Here was an opening; for it was perfectly natural and proper that Genji should visit this princess, who had been his father's favourite sister and with whom he had himself always remained on excellent terms. He found that the two ladies were living in opposite wings of the Palace, separated by the great central hall. Though old Prince Momozono had so recently passed away the place had already assumed a rather decayed and depressing

[1] Consequently an aunt both of Asagao and Genji, who were first cousins; Prince Momozono, Asagao's father, being a brother of Genji's father, the old Emperor. Asagao was the one lady whom Genji had courted in vain. See vol. i, p. 68.

air. Princess Nyogo received him immediately. He noticed at once that she had aged very rapidly since he last saw her. She was indeed quite decrepit, and it was difficult to believe that she was really younger than Aoi's mother, who seemed to him never to have changed since he had known her; whereas in the quavering accents and palsied gait of the aged lady who now greeted him it was well nigh impossible to recognize the princess of former days.

'Everything has been in a wretched way since the old Emperor, your poor father, was taken from us, and as the years go by the outlook seems to grow blacker and blacker; I confess, I never have an easy moment. And now even my brother Prince Momozono has left me! I go on, I go on; but it hardly seems like being alive, except when I get a visit like yours to-day, and then I forget all my troubles. . . .' 'Poor thing,' thought Genji, 'how terribly she has gone to pieces!' But he answered very politely: 'For me too the world has been in many ways a different place since my father died. First, as you know, came this unexpected attack upon me, followed by my exile to a remote district. Then came my restoration to rank and privilege, bringing with it all manner of ties and distractions. All this time I have been longing to have a talk with you, and regret immensely that there has never before been an opportunity. . . .' 'Oh, the changes, the changes,' she broke in; 'such terrible destruction I have seen on every side. Nothing seems safe from it, and often I feel as though I would give anything to have died before all this began. But I do assure you I am glad I have lived long enough to witness your return. To die while you were still in such trouble, not knowing how it was all going to end—that would indeed have been a melancholy business.' She paused for a while and then went on in her quavering, thin voice: 'You know, you have grown to be a very handsome man. But I remember that the first time I saw you, when you were only a little boy, I was astonished at you, really I was. I could never have believed that such loveliness would be seen shining in the face of any mortal child! And every time I see you I always feel just as I did then. They say that his present Majesty, the Emperor Ryōzen, is the image of you; but I don't believe a word of it. He may be just a little like; but no one is going to persuade me that he is half as handsome as you.' So she rambled on. Coming from any one else such flattery would have very much embarrassed him. But at this strange old lady's out-pourings one could only be amused. 'Since my exile I have quite lost whatever good looks I may once have possessed,' he said; 'one cannot live for years on end under those depressing conditions without its changing one very much. As for the Emperor, I assure you that his is a beauty of an altogether different order. I should doubt if a better-looking young man has ever existed, and to assert that he is less handsome than me is, if you will forgive my saying so, quite ridiculous.' 'If only you came to see me every day I believe I should go on living for ever,' she burst out. 'I am suddenly beginning to feel quite young, and I am not at all sure that the world is half so bad a place as I made out just now.' Nevertheless it was not long before she was again wailing and weeping. 'How I envy my sister Princess Ōmiya,'[1] she cried; 'no doubt, being your mother-in-law, she sees a great deal of you. I only wish I were in that position. You know, I expect, that my poor brother often talked of affiancing his daughter to you and was very sorry afterwards that he did not do so.' At this Genji pricked up his ears. 'I desired nothing better,' said he, 'than to be connected on close terms with your family, and it would still give me great pleasure to be on a

[1] Aoi's mother.

more intimate footing in this house. But I cannot say that I have hitherto received much encouragement. . . .' He was vexed that he had not discovered this at the time. He looked towards the other wing of the house. The garden under the younger princess's windows was carefully tended. He scanned those borders of late autumn flowers, and then the rooms behind; he pictured her sitting not far from the window, her eyes fixed upon these same swiftly-fading petals. Yes, he must certainly contrive to see her; and bowing to Princess Nyogo he said: 'I naturally intend to pay my respects to your niece to-day; indeed, I should not like her to regard my visit as a mere afterthought, and for that reason I shall, with your permission, approach her apartments by way of the garden instead of going along the corridor and through the hall.' Skirting the side of the house he came at length to her window. Although it was now almost dark, he could see, behind grey curtains, the outline of a black screen-of-state. He was soon observed, and Asagao's servants, scandalized that he should have been left standing even for a moment in the verandah, hurried him into the guest-room at the back of the house. Here a gentlewoman came to enquire what was his pleasure, and he handed to her the following note: 'How this carries me back to the days of our youth—this sending in of notes and waiting in ante-chambers! I had hoped, I confess, that my reticence during the years of your sacred calling would have won for me, still your ardent admirer, the right to a somewhat less formal reception.' It would be hard indeed if she gave him no more encouragement than this! Her answer was brought by word of mouth: 'To come back to this house and find my father no longer here, is so strange an experience that it is difficult to believe those old days were not a mere dream from which I now awake to a fleeting prospect of the most comfortless realities. But in a world where all is change, it would, I confess, be ungracious not to cherish and encourage a devotion so undeviating as that which you have described.'

She need not, he thought, remind him of life's uncertainties. For who had in every circumstance great and small more grievously experienced them than he? In reply he sent the poem: 'Have I not manfully held back and kept cold silence year on year, till the Gods gave me leave?' 'Madam,' he added, ' you are a Vestal no longer and cannot plead that any sanctity now hedges you about. Since last we met I have experienced many strange vicissitudes. If you would but let me tell you a little part of all that I have seen and suffered. . . .' The gentlewoman who took his answer noticed that his badges and decorations were somewhat more dazzling than in old days; but though he was now a good deal older, his honours still far out-stripped his years.

'Though it were but to tell me of your trials and sorrows that you have made this visit, yet even such tidings the Gods, my masters till of late, forbid me to receive.' This was too bad! 'Tell your lady,' he cried peevishly, ' that I have long ago cast my offence [1] of old days to the winds of Shinado; or does she think perhaps that the Gods did not accept my vows?'[2] The messenger saw that though he sought to turn off the matter with these allusions and jests he was in reality very much put about, and she was vexed on his behalf. She had for years past been watching her mistress become more and more aloof from the common interests and distractions of life, and it had long distressed her to see Prince Genji's letters so often left unanswered. 'I did ill to call at so late an hour,' he said; ' I can see that

[1] I.e. making love to her.
[2] Allusion to the poem: 'By the River of Cleansing I tied prayer-strips inscribed " I will love no more "; but it seems that the Gods would not accept my vow.'

the purpose of my visit has been wholly misunderstood.' And sighing heavily he turned to go, saying as he did so: 'This is the way one is treated when one begins to grow old. . . . It is useless, I know, after what has passed, even to suggest that her Highness should come to the window for a moment to see me start . . .' and with that he left the house, watched by a bevy of ladies who made all the usual comments and appraisements. Not only was it delightful weather, but at this moment the wind was making a most agreeable music in the neighbouring trees, and these ladies soon fell to talking of the old days when Prince Momozono was alive; particularly of Genji's visits long ago and the many signs he had given of a deep and unaltering attachment to their mistress.

After his return from this unsuccessful expedition, Genji felt in no mood for sleep, and soon he jumped up and threw open his casement. The morning mist lay thick over the garden of flowers, which, at the season's close, looked very battered and wan. Among them, its blossoms shimmering vaguely, was here and there a Morning Glory,[1] growing mixed in among the other flowers. Choosing one that was even more wilted and autumnal than the rest, he sent it to the Momozono palace, with the note: 'The poor reception which you gave me last night has left a most humiliating and painful impression upon me. Indeed, I can only imagine it was with feelings of relief that you so soon saw my back turned upon your house, though I am loth to think that things can even now have come to such a pass: "Can it be that the Morning Glory, once seen by me and ever since remembered in its beauty, is now a dry and withered flower?" Does it count with you for nothing that I have admired you unrequited, year in year out, for so great a stretch of time? That at least might be put to my

[1] *Asagao.*

credit. . . .' She could not leave so mannerly an appeal quite unheeded, and when her people pressed round her with ink-stone and brush, she yielded to their persuasion so far as to write the poem : ' Autumn is over, and now with ghostly flower the Morning Glory withers on the mist-bound hedge.' ' Your comparison,' she added, ' is so just that the arrival of your note has brought fresh dewdrops to the petals of the flower to whom this reminder was addressed.' That was all, and it was in truth not very interesting or ingenious. But for some reason he read the poem many times over, and during the course of the day found himself continually looking at it. Perhaps what fascinated him was the effect of her faint, sinuous ink-strokes on the blue-grey writing-paper which her mourning dictated. For it often happens that a letter, its value enhanced to us either by the quality of the writer or by the beauty of the penmanship, appears at the time to be faultless. But when it is copied out and put into a book something seems to have gone wrong. . . . Efforts are made to improve the sense or style, and in the end the original effect is altogether lost.

He realized the impropriety of the letters with which he had in old days assailed her and did not intend to return to so unrestrained a method of address. His new style had indeed met with a certain measure of success ; for whereas she had formerly seldom vouchsafed any answer at all, he had now received a not unfriendly reply. But even this reply was far from being such as to satisfy him, and he was unable to resist the temptation of trying to improve upon so meagre a success. He wrote again, this time in much less cautious terms, and posting himself in the eastern wing [1] of his palace he sent a carriage to fetch one of Asagao's ladies, and presently sent her back again with the letter. Her

[1] Where Murasaki would not be likely to come.

gentlewomen would themselves never have dreamed of
discouraging far less distinguished attentions, let alone
those of such a personage as Prince Genji, and they now
urged his claims upon their mistress as one ' for whose sake
a little virtue was surely worth sacrificing.' But after all
her efforts in the past to keep free of such an entanglement,
this was hardly the moment to give in; for she felt that
both he and she had now reached an age when such things
are best put aside. She feared that even her inevitable
allusions to the flowers and trees of the season might easily
be misinterpreted, and even if Genji himself was under no
misapprehension, there are always those who made a
business of getting hold of such things and turning them to
mischief, and in consequence she was careful to avoid the
slightest hint of anything intimate or sentimental. About
this time a rumour ran through the Court to the effect that
Genji was in active correspondence with the former Vestal,
abetted and encouraged by Princess Nyogo and the lady's
other relatives. The pair seemed very well suited to one
another and no one expressed any surprise at the existence
of such an attachment. The story eventually reached
Murasaki's ears. At first she refused to credit it, making
sure that if he were indeed carrying on any such intrigue it
would be scarcely possible for him to conceal it from her.
But observing him with this tale in her mind she thought
that he seemed unusually abstracted and depressed. What
if this affair, which he had always passed off as a mere joke
between himself and his cousin, were to turn out after
all to be something important—the beginning of what she
dreaded day and night? In rank and in accomplishments
perhaps there was little to choose between Asagao and
herself. But he had begun to admire and court this princess
long, long ago; and if an affection grounded so far back in
the past were now to resume its sway over him, Murasaki

knew that she must be prepared for the worst. It was not easy to face what she now believed to threaten her. For years past she had held, beyond challenge or doubt, the first place in Genji's affections—had been the centre of all his plans and contrivings. To see herself ousted by a stranger from a place which long use had taught her to regard as her own by inalienable right—such was the ordeal for which she now began silently to prepare herself. He would not, of course, abandon her altogether; of that she was sure. But the very fact that they had for so many years lived together on terms of daily intimacy and shared so many trifling experiences made her, she felt, in a way less interesting to him. So she speculated, sometimes thinking that all was indeed lost, sometimes that the whole thing was her fancy and nothing whatever was amiss. In his general conduct towards her there was not anything of which she could reasonably complain. But there were from time to time certain vague indications that he was not in the best of tempers, and these were enough whenever they occurred to convince her that she was undone for good and all,—though she showed no outward sign of the despair which had now settled upon her. Genji, meanwhile, spent much of his time in the front [1] of the house and was also frequently at the Emperor's Palace. His leisure was employed in writing endless letters. Murasaki wondered how she could have ever doubted the rumours that were now rampant throughout the Court. If only he would tell, give even the slightest hint of what was in these days passing through his mind!

Winter drew on, and at last the eleventh month came round. But this year there were none of the usual religious festivals and processions [2] to distract him, and Genji became

[1] In the men's quarters.
[2] During the 10th month the Gods withdraw themselves and cannot

more and more restless. One evening when the delicate twilight was sprinkled with a few thin flakes of snow, he determined to set out for the Momozono palace. All day he had been more than usually preoccupied with thoughts of its occupant, and somehow he could not help feeling that she too would on this occasion prove less unyielding. Before starting, he came to take leave of Murasaki in the western wing. ' I am sorry to say Princess Nyogo is very unwell,' he said ; ' I must go and offer her my sympathy.' She did not even look round, but went on playing with her little foster-child as though determined not to be interrupted. Evidently there was going to be trouble. ' There has been something very strange in your manner lately,' he said. ' I am not conscious of having done anything to offend you. I thought we understood one another well enough for me to be able to spend a day or two now and then at the Emperor's Palace without your taking offence. But perhaps it is something else ? ' ' I certainly understand you well enough,' she answered, ' to know that I must expect to put up with a great deal of suffering . . .' and she sank back upon the divan, her face turned away from him. He could never bear to leave her thus, and knew he would be wretched every step of the way to Princess Nyogo's house. But the hour was already late, and as he had promised beforehand that he would call there that evening, it was impossible to defer his departure.

Murasaki meanwhile lay on her couch, continually debating within herself whether this affair might not really have been going on for years past—perhaps ever since his return—without her having any suspicion of it. She went to the window. He was still dressed chiefly in

---

hear our prayers ; their return in the 11th month is celebrated with rejoicing ; but this year, owing to the National Mourning for Fujitsubo's death, these ceremonies were omitted.

grey; but the few touches of colour which his mourning permitted showed up all the more brightly, and as she watched his handsome figure moving against a background of glittering snow, the thought that she might be losing him, that soon, very soon perhaps, he would vanish never to return, was more than she could endure. His cortège consisted only of a few favourite outriders, to whom he said: 'I am not feeling inclined just now to go about paying calls; indeed, you will have noticed that apart from a few necessary visits to Court, I have hardly left home at all. But my friends at the Momozono palace are passing through a very trying time. Her Highness has for years relied upon her brother's aid and, now that he is taken from her, the least I can do is to help her occasionally with a little encouragement and advice. . . .' But his gentlemen were not so easily deceived and whispered among themselves as they rode along: 'Come, come, that will not do. Unless he has very much changed his ways it is not to chatter with old ladies that his Highness sets out at this hour of a winter night. There is more here than meets the eye,' and they shook their heads over his incurable frivolity.

The main gate of the palace was on the north side; but here there was usually a great deal of traffic, and not wishing to attract attention he drove up to a side-entrance, the one which Prince Momozono himself commonly used, and sent in a servant to announce his arrival. As he had promised to appear at a much earlier hour Princess Nyogo had by now quite given up expecting him, and, much put about by this untimely visit, she bade her people send the porter to the western gate. The man made his appearance a moment later, looking wretchedly pinched and cold as he hastened through the snow with the key in his hand. Unfortunately the lock would not work, and when he went back to look for help no other manservant could anywhere be found.

'It's very rusty,' said the old porter dolefully, fumbling all the while with the lock, that grated with an unpleasant sound but would not turn. 'There's nothing else wrong with it, but it's terribly rusty. No one uses this gate now.'

The words, ordinary enough in themselves, filled Genji with an unaccountable depression. How swiftly the locks rust, the hinges grow stiff on doors that close behind us! 'I am more than thirty,' he thought; and it seemed to him impossible to go on doing things just as though they would last . . . as though people would remember . . 'And yet,' he said to himself, 'I know that even at this moment the sight of something very beautiful, were it only some common flower or tree, might in an instant make life again seem full of meaning and reality.'

At last the key turned and with a great deal of pushing and pulling the gate was gradually forced open. Soon he was in the Princess's room, listening to her usual discourses and lamentations. She began telling a series of very involved and rambling stories about things all of which seemed to have happened a great while ago. His attention began to wander; it was all he could do to keep awake. Before very long the Princess herself broke off and said with a yawn: 'It's no good; I can't tell things properly at this time of night, it all gets mixed up. . . .'

Then suddenly he heard a loud and peculiar noise. Where did it come from? What could it be? His eye fell upon the Princess. Yes; it was from her that these strange sounds proceeded; for she was now fast asleep and snoring with a resonance such as he would never have conceived to be possible.

Delighted at this opportunity of escape he was just about to slip out of the room when he heard a loud 'Ahem,' also uttered in a very aged and husky voice, and perceived that some one had just entered the room. 'There! What a shame! I've startled you. And I made sure you heard me come in. But I see you don't know who in the world I am. Well, your poor father, the old Emperor, who loved his joke, used to call me the Grandam. Perhaps that will help you to remember....' Could this be.... Yes, surely it was that same elderly Lady of the Bedchamber who had flirted with him so outrageously years ago, at the time of the Feast of Red Leaves.[1] He seemed to remember hearing that she had joined some lay order and become a pensioner in the late prince's household. But it had not occurred to him that she could possibly still be in existence, and this sudden encounter was something of a shock. 'I am distressed to find,' he answered, 'that those old days are becoming very dim in my mind, and anything that recalls them to me is therefore very precious. I am delighted to hear your voice again. Pray remember that, like the traveller whom Prince Shōtoku[2] found lying at the wayside, I have 'no parent to succour me' and must therefore look to old friends such as you for shelter from the world's unkindness.' It was extraordinary how little she had changed in appearance, and her manner was certainly as arch and coquettish as ever. Her utterance, indeed, suggested that she now had very few teeth left in her head; but she still managed to impart to her words the same insinuating and caressing tone as of old. It amused him that she spoke of herself as though she had been a mere girl when they first met and that she continually apologized for the changes which he must now be noticing in her. He was amused, but also saddened. For he could not help thinking that of all the gentlewomen who had been this lady's rivals scarce one was now left at Court. Most were dead; others had fallen into disgrace and were eking out a

[1] See vol. i, p. 229.   [2] 572–621 A.D.

miserable existence no one knew where. Or again, that a creature such as Lady Fujitsubo should vanish so soon, while this absurd grandam, even in her younger days totally devoid of charm or intelligence, should be left behind! And judging by her appearance, there was every prospect that she would go on happily pottering about and telling her rosary for another twenty years. No; there was no sense, no purpose in all this.

She saw that thoughts which moved him deeply were passing through his mind and at once assumed that he was recalling the details of what she was pleased to think of as their 'love affair'; and now in her most playful voice she recited the poem: 'Though your father called me Granny, I am not so old but that you and I were sweethearts long ago.' He felt somewhat embarrassed but he answered kindly: 'Such motherly care as yours not in this life only but in all lives to come none save a scapegrace would forget.' 'We must meet again at a more convenient time and have a good talk,' he said; and with that he hastened towards the western wing. The blinds were drawn and everything was shut up for the night, save that at one window she[1] had left a lattice half unclosed, feeling that to show no light at all on the evening of his visit would be too pointedly uncivil. The moon had risen and its rays blended with the glitter of the newly-fallen snow. It was indeed a most charming night. 'An old woman in love and the moon at midwinter': he remembered the saying that these are the two most dismal things in the world; but to-night he felt this collocation to be very unjust. He sent in an urgent letter: if despite her scruples she intended ever to admit him for a few moments to her presence, why not take advantage of this excellent opportunity and not subject him to the irritation of purposeless delays?

[1] Asagao.

She did not doubt the reality of his feelings; but if at a time when they were both young enough to be forgiven a few indiscretions, when moreover her father was actually seeking to promote an alliance between them, she had without a moment's hesitation refused to yield herself to him—what sense could there be, now that they were both past the age to which such irresponsible gallantries by right belong, what sense (she asked herself) could there be in parleying with him, indeed, in admitting him into her presence at all? He saw that she was absolutely unmoved by his appeal, and was both astonished and hurt. She meanwhile disliked intensely this frigid interchange of messages and notes, but for the moment saw no way of bringing it to a close. It was now getting late, a fierce wind had begun to blow and Genji, feeling a very real disappointment and distress, was about to make his way homeward, flinging out as he did so the parting verse:

'No penance can your hard heart find save such as you long since have taught me to endure.' As usual her gentlewomen insisted that she must send a reply, and reluctantly she wrote the verse; 'Is it for me to change, for me who hear on every wind some tale that proves you, though the years go by, not other than you were?'

He burst into a great rage when he received her note, but a moment afterwards felt that he was behaving very childishly, and said to the gentlewoman who had brought it: 'I would not for the world have any one know how I have been treated to-night. Promise me, I beg of you, that you will speak of it to no one; stay, you had best even deny that I was here at all. . . .' He whispered this in a very low voice; but some servants who were hanging about near by noticed the aside, and one of them said to another: 'Look at that now! Poor gentleman! You can see she has sent him a very stinging reply. Even if she does not fancy him, she might at least treat him with common civility. For he does not look at all the kind of gentleman who would take advantage of a little kindness. . . .'

As a matter of fact, she had no distaste for him whatever. His beauty delighted her and she was sure that she would have found him a most charming companion. But she was convinced that from the moment she betrayed this liking he would class her among the common ruck of his admirers and imagine that she would put up with such treatment as they were apparently content to endure. A position so humiliating she knew that she could never tolerate. She was resolute, therefore, in her determination never to allow the slightest intimacy to grow up between them. But at the same time she was now careful always to answer his letters fully and courteously, and she allowed him to converse with her at second hand whenever he felt inclined. It was hardly conceivable that, submitted to this treatment, he would not soon grow weary of the whole affair. For her part she wished to devote herself to the expiation of the many offences against her own religion [1] that her residence at Kamo had involved. Ultimately she meant to take orders; but any sudden step of that kind would certainly be attributed to an unfortunate love-affair and so give colour to the rumours which already connected her name with his. Indeed, she had seen enough of the world to know that in few people is discretion stronger than the desire to tell a good story, and she therefore took no one into her confidence, not even the gentlewoman who waited daily upon her. Meanwhile she devoted herself more and more ardently to preparation for the mode of life which she hoped soon to embrace.

She had several brothers; but they were the children of

[1] Buddhism. She had been Vestal in the Shintō temple at Kamo, where no Buddhist prayers or observances were allowed.

Prince Zembo's first wife [1] and she knew very little of them. Other visitors at the Momozono palace became increasingly rare; but the fact that no less a person than Genji was known to be Princess Asagao's admirer aroused a widespread curiosity concerning her.

As a matter of fact, he was not very desperately in love with her; but her apparent indifference had piqued him and he was determined to go on till he had gained his point. He had recently gathered from several sources of information, including persons of every rank in society, but all of them in a position to know what they were talking about, that his own reputation now stood very high in the country. He felt indeed that his insight into affairs had very greatly improved since old days, and it would certainly be a pity if a scandal once more deprived him of popular confidence. Nevertheless, if gossip were to concern itself with the matter at all, he could not help feeling he should prefer to figure in the story as having succeeded than as having been ignominiously repulsed.

Meanwhile his frequent absences from the Nijō-in had already convinced Murasaki that the affair was as serious as it could possibly be. She tried to conceal her agitation, but there were times when it was evident that she had been secretly weeping, and Genji said to her one day: 'What has come over you lately? I cannot imagine any reason why you should be so depressed'; and as he gently stroked the hair back from her forehead they looked such a pair as you might put straight into a picture.

'Since his mother's death,' Genji went on presently, 'the Emperor Ryōzen has been in very low spirits and I have felt bound to spend a good deal of time at the Palace. But that is not the only thing which takes up my time in these days; you must remember that I have now to attend

[1] Rokujō was his second.

personally to a mass of business which the old Minister of the Left used formerly to take off my hands. I am as sorry as you are that we see so much less of one another; but I do my best, and you must really try henceforward to bear with me more patiently. You are no longer a child; yet you make as little effort to enter into my feelings and see my point of view as if you were still in the nursery.' And with that, just as though she were indeed a small child, he put back in its place a lock of her hair that had become disordered while she was weeping.

But still she turned away from him and would not speak a word. 'This is quite new,' he said; ' who has been teaching you these pettish airs and graces?' He spoke lightly; but how long, he wondered, was this going to last, how much time were they going to spend in this dismal fashion, while at any moment one of those countless horrors that life perpetually holds over us might suddenly descend upon them and reconciliation be no longer possible? Determined to bring the matter to a head, he said at last: ' I think you have perhaps been misled by very foolish rumours concerning my friendship with the former Vestal. As a matter of fact, it is of the most distant kind, as in the end you will yourself probably realize. She has always, since I first got to know her years ago, treated me with an exaggerated coldness. This hurts me, and I have more than once remonstrated with her on the subject. As very little now goes on at the Momozono palace, she has a good deal of time on her hands and it amuses her to keep up a desultory correspondence. This is all that has happened between us; and even you will surely admit that is not worth crying about! If it is really this affair that has been on your mind, I assure you that there is no cause whatever for anxiety. . . .' He spent the whole day in trying to win back her confidence, and his patience was at last rewarded.

By this time the snow was lying very deep, and it was still falling, though now very lightly. So far from obliterating the shapes of pine-tree and bamboo, the heavy covering of snow seemed only to accentuate their varying forms, which stood out with strange distinctness in the evening light. 'We decided the other day,' said Genji to Murasaki, ' that Lady Akikonomu's season is Autumn, and yours Spring. This evening I am more sure than ever that mine is Winter. What could be more lovely than a winter night such as this, when the moon shines out of a cloudless sky upon the glittering, fresh-fallen snow ? Beauty without colour seems somehow to belong to another world. At any rate, I find such a scene as this infinitely more lovely and moving than any other in the whole year. How little do I agree with the proverb that calls the moon in winter a dismal sight !' So saying he raised the window-blind, and they looked out. The moon was now fully risen, covering the whole garden with its steady, even light. The withered flower-beds showed, in these cold rays, with painful clearness the ravages of wind and frost. And look, the river was half-choked with ice, while the pond, frozen all over, was unutterably strange and lonesome under its coat of snow. Near it some children had been allowed to make a monster snow-ball. They looked very pretty as they tripped about in the moonlight. Several of the older girls had taken off their coats and set to in a very business-like way, showing all sorts of strange under-garments ; while their brothers, coming straight from their tasks as page-boys and what not, had merely loosened their belts, and there was now a sight of smart coat-tails flapping and long hair falling forwards till its ends brushed the white garden floor—an effect both singular and delightful. Some of the very little ones were quite wild with joy and rushed about dropping all their fans and other belongings in their mad excitement.

The glee imprinted on these small faces was charming to behold. The children made so big a snow-ball that when it came to rolling it along the ground they could not make it budge an inch, and the sight of their frantic endeavours to get it moving provoked much jeering and laughter from another party of children which had just made its appearance at the eastern door.

'I remember,' said Genji, 'that one year Lady Fujitsubo had a snow-mountain built in front of her palace. It is a common enough amusement in winter time; but she had the art of making the most ordinary things striking and interesting. What countless reasons I have to regret her at every moment! I was during the greater part of her life not at all intimate with her and had little opportunity of studying her at close quarters. But during her residence at the Palace, she often allowed me to be of service to her in various small ways, and I frequently had occasion to use her good offices. In this way we were constantly discussing one piece of business or another, and I discovered that though she had no obvious or showy talents, she had the most extraordinary capacity for carrying through even quite unimportant and trivial affairs with a perfection of taste and management that has surely never been equalled. At the same time she was of a rather timid disposition and often took things too much to heart. Though you and she both spring from the same stem and necessarily have much in common, I have noticed that you are a good deal less even in temperament than she.

'Lady Asagao, now, has a quite different nature. If in an idle moment I address to her some trifling fancy she replies with such spirit that I have hard work not to be left lagging. I know no one else at Court to compare with her in this respect.'

'I have always heard,' said Murasaki, 'that Lady Oborozuki is extremely accomplished and quick-witted. I should have thought, too, from all I know of her that she was very sensible and discreet; and that makes me all the more surprised at certain stories that I have heard repeated. . . .'

'You are quite right,' said Genji. 'Among all the ladies now at Court she is the one I should pick out both for liveliness and beauty. As to the rumours you speak of—I know quite well what you are referring to. I bitterly regret what happened; as indeed I regret much else that belongs to that part of my life. And what quantities of things most people must begin to repent of, as the years go by! For compared with almost any of my friends, I have led a very quiet and decorous life.' He paused for a moment; the mention of Oborozuki seemed to have moved him deeply. Presently he continued: 'I have a feeling that you look down upon country people such as the Lady of Akashi. I assure you that, unlike most women in that station of life, she is extremely cultivated and intelligent; though of course people of her class are bound in many ways to be very different from us, and I admit she has certain strained and exaggerated ideas, of which I cannot approve.

'About women of the common sort I know nothing; but among our own people it has always seemed to me that few indeed were in any way remarkable or interesting. An exception however is our guest in the new wing [1]; she remains charming as ever. But though such beauty and intelligence are very rare, she has never cared to parade them; and since the time when I first realized her gifts and hastened to make her acquaintance, she has always continued to show the same indifference to the worldly conquests which she might so easily have secured. We have now been friends for so long that I do not think we are ever

[1] The lady from the Village of Falling Flowers.

likely to part; I at any rate should be very sorry if she were to leave my house.' While he thus talked of one thing and another, it grew very late. The moon shone brighter and brighter, and a stillness now reigned that, after the recent wintry storms, was very agreeable. Murasaki recited the verse: 'The frozen waters are at rest; but now with waves of light the moon-beam ebbs and flows.' She was looking out at the window, her head a little to one side, and both the expression of her face and the way her hair fell reminded him, as so often before, of her whom he had lost. Suddenly his affections, which for many weeks past had to some small extent been divided, were once more hers, and hers alone.

Just then a love-bird[1] cried, and he recited the verse: 'Does it not move you strangely, the love-bird's cry, to-night when, like the drifting snow, memory piles up on memory?' Long after he and Murasaki had retired to rest, recollections of Lady Fujitsubo continued to crowd into his mind, and when at last he fell asleep, a vision of her at once appeared to him, saying in tones of deep reproach: 'It may be that you on earth have kept our secret; but in the land of the dead shame cannot be hid, and I am paying dearly for what you made me do. . . .' He tried to answer, but fear choked his voice, and Murasaki, hearing him suddenly give a strange muffled cry, said rather peevishly: 'What are you doing that for? You frightened me!' The sound of her voice roused him. He woke in a terrible state of grief and agitation, his eyes full of tears which he at once made violent efforts to control. But soon he was weeping bitterly, to the bewilderment of Murasaki, who nevertheless lay all the time stock still at his side. He was now too miserable and distracted to think of sleep, and slipping out of bed presently began writing notes to various temples in the district, directing that certain texts

[1] Generally called by the ugly name 'Mandarin Duck.'

and spells should be recited; he did not however dare to state on whose behalf these things were to be done.

Small wonder that in the dream she turned upon him so bitter and reproachful a gaze, feeling (as by her words he judged she did) that this one sin had robbed her of salvation. He remembered her constant devotions; never since that fatal day had she omitted one single prayer, penance or charity that might serve as atonement for her guilt. Yet all had been in vain, and even in the world beyond, this one crime clung to her like a stain that could not be washed away. In the past he had never thought clearly about such things; but now they lived in his mind with a terrible vividness and certainty. Were there but some spell, some magic that could enable him to seek her out in the obscure region where her soul was dwelling, and suffer in her stead the penalties of his own offence! Yet the truth was that he could not so much as have a few poor Masses said for her soul; for, had he named her, the suspicions of the Court would at once have been aroused.

Concerning the Emperor, too, Genji's conscience was very uneasy; for had Ryōzen indeed discovered the true story of his birth, he must now be living in a state of continual apprehension. It was at about this time that Genji put himself under the especial protection of Amida, Buddha of Boundless Light, beseeching the Blessed One that in due time his soul and that of the lady whom he had undone might spring from the same lotus in His holy Paradise. But of such an issue he had little hope, and often he would disconsolately recite the verse : ' Fain would I follow her, could I but hope to thread my way among the sunless Rivers of the World Below.'[1]

[1] Through each of the Three Evil Realms (of Animals, Hungry Ghosts and Demons) runs a meandering river.

CHAPTER III

THE MAIDEN

IN the spring of the next year [1] the National Mourning for Lady Fujitsubo came to an end. Gay colours began to appear once more at Court, and when the time for summer dresses came round it was seen that the fashions were smarter than ever; moreover, the weather was unusually agreeable and there was every prospect of a fine spell for the Kamo Festival.[2] Lady Asagao gave no outward sign of what reflections passed through her mind while she witnessed the ceremonies in which she herself had a few years ago taken the leading part. But she gazed fixedly at the laurel tree [3] in front of her window; and though there was much beauty in those lank branches, swept to and fro by the roving winds, yet it seemed as if it must be for some other cause that again and again her eyes returned to it. In her ladies, at any rate, the sight of this tree aroused a host of reminiscences and suitable reflections.

From Genji came a note in which he said: 'Does it not give you a strange feeling to witness a Day of Cleansing in which you take no part?' And remembering that she was still in mourning for her father, he added the poem: 'Little thought I that, like a wave in the swirl of the flood, you

[1] Genji is now 33.
[2] In the 4th month.
[3] The laurel and the hollyhock form the garlands worn by worshippers at this festival.

would come back so soon, a dark-robed mourner swept along time's hurrying stream.'

It was written on purple paper in a bold script, and a spray of wistaria [1] was attached to it. Moved by all that was going on around her she replied: ' It seems but yesterday that I first wore my sombre dress; but now the pool of days has grown into a flood wherein I soon shall wash my grief away.' [2] The poem was sent without explanation or comment and constituted, indeed, a meagre reply; but, as usual, he found himself constantly holding it in front of him and gazing at it as though it had been much more than a few poor lines of verse.

When the end of the mourning actually came, the lady who acted as messenger and intermediary in general was overwhelmed by the number of packages [3] from the Nijō-in which now began to arrive. Lady Asagao expressed great displeasure at this lavishness and, if the presents had been accompanied by letters or poems of at all a familiar or impertinent kind, she would at once have put a stop to these attentions. But for a year past there had been nothing in his conduct to complain of. From time to time he came to the house and enquired after her, but always quite openly. His letters were frequent and affectionate, but he took no liberties, and what nowadays troubled her chiefly was the difficulty of inventing anything to say in reply.

To Princess Nyogo, too, Genji sent good wishes on the occasion of her coming out of mourning. This delighted her, and the old lady observed to her maids, whilst reading the letter: ' How strange it is to get this very nice letter

---

[1] Her mourning was of dark blue wistaria-colour.
[2] Her period of mourning is almost over. There is a play of words; *fuji* = wistaria, and *fuchi* = pool.
[3] The presents of gay clothing which are customarily made to a person who has just emerged from a period of mourning.

from Prince Genji! Why, it seems only yesterday that he was a baby-in-arms, and here he is, writing such a sensible, manly letter! I had heard that he had grown up very good-looking; but what pleases me is that he evidently has a quite exceptionally nice disposition.' These outbursts of praise were always greeted with laughter by the younger ladies-in-waiting, among whom Princess Nyogo's weakness for Genji was a standing joke.

The old lady next bustled off to her niece's rooms. 'What do you say to this?' she asked, holding out the letter; 'could anything be more friendly and considerate? But he has always regarded this house as a second home. I have often told you that your poor father was bitterly disappointed that the circumstances of your birth made it impossible for him to offer your hand to this Prince. It was indeed definitely arranged that he should do so, and it was with the greatest reluctance that he consented to your departure. He talked to me about this constantly in after years, and it was obvious that he bitterly regretted not having arranged the marriage at a much earlier period in your life. What held him back from doing so was that my sister Princess Ōmiya had already arranged for the marriage of her daughter, Lady Aoi, to Prince Genji and, frightened of giving offence, he let time slip by without doing anything towards the accomplishment of this favourite project. But Lady Aoi's death has removed the one insurmountable obstacle which before made it out of the question that any person of consequence should offer to this Prince his daughter's hand. For though there are now several ladies in his household, none of them is of the highest rank. Such a person as yourself, for example, would necessarily assume the foremost place, and I confess I cannot see why, if an offer came your way, it would be such a bad thing for you to accept it. At any rate, that is how I feel. He must be very fond of you, or he certainly would not have started writing again directly you came back from Kamo. . . .'

Princess Asagao thought her aunt's way of looking at things very old fashioned and mistaken : ' Having held out for so long against the reproaches of my father, who was, as you will remember, by no means used to being gainsaid, it would be a strange thing if I were now to yield, after all that has happened since, to your or any one else's friendly persuasions.' She looked so reluctant to discuss the subject further that her aunt did not proceed. The whole staff of the Palace, from dames-of-honour down to kitchen-maids, being all of them more or less in love with Genji themselves, watched with great interest to see how he would fare at Princess Asagao's hands, the majority prophesying for him a heavy discomfiture. But Genji himself firmly believed that if only he went on quietly displaying his devotion, sooner or later there would come some sign that she was ready to yield. He had long ago realized that she was not a person who could ever be hustled into acting against her own better judgment and inclination.

It was high time to be thinking about the Initiation of Yūgiri, Aoi's son, who was now twelve years old. It would in many ways have been better that the ceremony should be performed in Genji's palace. But it was natural that the boy's grandmother should be anxious to witness it, and in the end it was decided that it should be performed at the Great Hall. Here the boy had the support of his uncle Tō no Chūjō and of Aoi's other brothers, all of whom were now in influential positions, and as the function was to take place under their own roof they were additionally ready to do whatever they could to help in making the occasion a success. It was an event which aroused very wide interest throughout the country, and what with visitors pouring in from all sides and a mass of preparations to be made for the actual ceremony, there was hardly room to turn round for days beforehand.

He had thought at first of placing Yūgiri in the Fourth Rank; but he was afraid that this would be considered an abuse of power, and there was indeed no hurry; for the boy was still very immature, and affairs being now entirely in Genji's hands he could easily promote him by small steps, till within a comparatively short time it would be possible to put him in the Fourth Rank without attracting an undue amount of attention. When, however, Yūgiri made his appearance at the Great Hall in the light blue decorations of the Sixth Rank, this was more than his grandmother Princess Ōmiya could bear. Genji fortunately realized that she would very likely be somewhat upset. When he went to call upon her she at once began voicing her grievance. 'You must remember,' replied Genji, ' that he is far too young to begin his public career. I would not indeed have performed his Initiation so early save that I designed to make a scholar of him. This will give him profitable employment during two or three years which might otherwise have been completely thrown away. As soon as he is old enough to take public office, he is certain to come quickly to the fore.

'I myself was brought up at the Palace in complete ignorance of the outside world. Living as I did continually at my father the Emperor's side I could not but pick up a certain vague familiarity with writing and books; it was, however, of the most meagre kind. For I could not at the best learn more than he chanced himself to have picked up in the same casual way, so that in every subject I only knew disconnected scraps and had no notion of how they ought to be fitted together. This was the case particularly as regards literature; but even in music my knowledge was hopelessly incomplete, and I acquired no real command over either zithern or flute. It may turn out that he is quicker than I; but on the whole it seems far commoner for children to have less natural aptitude than their parents; and I determined that this child of mine should be educated in a far more thorough way. For if I merely handed on to him the scraps of information which I in my day had picked up from the old Emperor I feared that knowledge might reach him in so attenuated a form as would stand him in very poor stead for the future.

'I have noticed that children of good families, assured of such titles and emoluments as they desire, and used to receive the homage of the world however little they do to deserve it, see no advantage in fatiguing themselves by arduous and exacting studies. Having then in due time been raised to offices for which they have qualified themselves only by a long course of frolics and indiscretions, they are helped out of all their difficulties by a set of time-servers (who are all the while laughing at them behind their backs), and they soon imagine themselves to be the most accomplished statesmen on earth. But however influential such a one may be, the death of some relative or a change in the government may easily work his undoing, and he will soon discover with surprise how poor an opinion of him the world really has. It is *then* that he feels the disadvantages of the desultory education which I have described. For the truth is, that without a solid foundation of book-learning this " Japanese spirit " of which one hears so much is not of any great use in the world.

'So you see that, though at the present moment I may seem to be doing less for him than I ought, it is my wish that he may one day be fit to bear the highest charges in the State, and be capable of so doing even if I am no longer here to direct him. For the moment, though you think that I do not adequately use my influence on his behalf, I will at any rate see to it that he is not looked down upon as a mere starveling aspirant of the Schools.' But the Princess would not part with her grievance : ' I am sure you have thought it all out very carefully,' she said ; ' but his uncles and most other people will not understand a word of this, and will merely think he is being badly treated ; and I am sure the poor boy himself is very disappointed. He has always been brought up with the idea that Tō no Chūjō's children and his other little cousins are in some way inferior to him, and now he sees them all going steadily upwards in rank, while he is treated like this. . . I assure you he found it very painful wearing that light blue dress, and my heart went out to him.' Genji could not help laughing : ' You must not take these things so seriously,' he said. ' What does it all matter ? Please remember that you are talking about a child of twelve years old. You may be sure he understands nothing whatever of all this business. When he has been at his studies for a little while, you will see how much improved he is and be angry with me no longer.'

The ceremony of bestowing the School-name took place in the new part of the Nijō-in palace, a portion of the eastern wing being set aside for the purpose. As such a function seldom takes place in the houses of the great, the occasion was one of great interest, and Princes and Courtiers of every degree vied with one another for the best seats ; the professors who had come to conduct the proceedings were not expecting so large and distinguished an audience, and they were evidently very much put out. 'Gentlemen,' said Genji, addressing them, ' I want you to perform this ceremony in all its rigour, omitting no detail, and above all not in any way altering the prescribed usages either in deference to the company here assembled or out of consideration for the pupil whom you are about to admit into your craft.' The professors did their best to look business-like and unconcerned. Many of them were dressed in gowns which they had hired for the occasion; but fortunately they had no idea how absurd they looked in these old-fashioned and ill-fitting clothes; which saved them from a great deal of embarrassment. Their grimaces and odd turns of speech, both combined with a certain mincing affability which they thought suitable to the occasion—even the strange forms and ceremonies that had to be gone through before any one of them could so much as sit down in his seat—all this was so queer that Yūgiri's cousins, who had never seen anything of the sort in their lives before, could not refrain from smiling. It was therefore as well that, as actual participators in the ceremony, only the older and steadier among the princes of the Great Hall had been selected. They at least could be relied upon to control their laughter, and all was going smoothly, when it fell to the lot of Tō no Chūjō and his friend Prince Mimbuykō to fill goblets out of the great wine-flagon and present them to their learned guests. Being both of them entirely unversed in these academic rites they paused for a moment, as though not quite certain whether they were really expected to perform this task with their own hands. So at any rate the professors interpreted their hesitation, and at once broke out into indignant expostulations: 'The whole proceeding is in the highest degree irregular,'[1] they cried. 'These gentlemen possess no academic qualifications and ought not to be here at all. They must be made to understand that we know nothing of the distinctions and privileges which prevail at Court. They must be told to mend their manners. . . .' At this some one in the audience ventured to titter, and the professors again expostu-

[1] The professors speak in a mixture of antiquated Japanese and classical Chinese the effect of which I do not attempt to reproduce.

lated: 'These proceedings cannot continue,' they said, 'unless absolute silence is preserved. Interruptions are in the highest degree irregular, and if they occur again we shall be obliged to leave our seats.' Several more testy speeches followed, and the audience was vastly entertained; for those who had never witnessed such performances before were naturally carried away by so diverting a novelty; while the few who were familiar with the proceedings had now the satisfaction of smiling indulgently at the crude amazement of their companions. It was long indeed since Learning had received so signal a mark of encouragement, and for the first time its partisans felt themselves to be people of real weight and consequence. Not a single word might any one in the audience so much as whisper to his neighbour without calling down upon himself an angry expostulation, and excited cries of 'disgraceful behaviour!' were provoked by the mildest signs of restlessness in the crowd. For some time the ceremony had been proceeding in darkness, and now when the torches were suddenly lit, revealing those aged faces contorted with censoriousness and self-importance, Genji could not help thinking of the Sarugaku [1] mountebanks with their burlesque postures and grimaces. 'Truly,' he thought, looking at the professors, 'truly in more ways than one an extraordinary and unaccountable profession!' 'I think it is rather fun,' he said, 'to see every one being kept in order by these crabbed old people,' and hid himself well behind his curtains-of-state, lest his comments too should be heard and rebuked.

Not nearly enough accommodation had been provided, and many of the young students from the college had been turned away for lack of room. Hearing this, Genji sent after them with apologies and had them brought back to the Summer House where they were entertained with food

[1] See my *Nō Plays*, p. 15 seq.

and drink. Some of the professors and doctors whose own part in the ceremony was over had also left the palace, and Genji now brought them back and made them compose poem after poem. He also detained such of the courtiers and princes as he knew to care most for poetry; the professors were called upon to compose complete poems [1] while the company, from Genji downwards, tried their hands at quatrains, Teachers of Literature being asked to choose the themes. The summer night was so short that before the time came to read out the poems it was already broad daylight. The reading was done by the Under-secretary to the Council, who, besides being a man of fine appearance, had a remarkably strong and impressive voice, so that his recitations gave every one great pleasure.

That mere enthusiasm should lead young men of high birth, who might so easily have contented themselves with the life of brilliant gaieties to which their position entitled them, to study 'by the light of the glow-worm at the window or the glimmer of snow on the bough,' [2] was highly gratifying; and such a number of ingenious fancies and comparisons pervaded the minds of the competitors that any one of these compositions might well have been carried to the Land Beyond the Sea without fear of bringing our country into contempt. But women are not supposed to know anything about Chinese literature, and I will not shock your sense of propriety by quoting any of the poems —even that by which Genji so deeply moved his hearers.

Hard upon the ceremony of giving the School Name came that of actual admittance to the College, and finally Yūgiri took up residence in the rooms which had been prepared for him at the Nijō-in. Here he was put in charge of the

[1] In eight lines.
[2] Like Ch'e Yün and Sun K'ang, two Chinese scholars who had not money enough to buy candles (4th century A.D.).

most learned masters that could be procured, and his education began in earnest. At first he was not allowed to visit his grandmother at all; for Genji had noticed that she spoiled him shockingly, treating him, indeed, as though he were still a little child, and there seemed a much better chance that he would settle down to his new life if it were not interrupted by constant treats and cossettings at the Great Hall. But Princess Ōmiya took the boy's absence so much to heart that in the end three visits a month were allowed.

Yūgiri found this sudden restriction of liberty very depressing, and he thought it unkind of his father to inflict these labours upon him, when he might so easily have allowed him to amuse himself for a little while longer and then go straight into some high post. Did Genji think him so very stupid as to need, before he could work for the Government, a training with which every one else seemed able to dispense? But he was a sensible, good-natured boy, who took life rather seriously, and seeing that he was not going to be allowed to mix in the world or start upon his career till he had read his books, he determined to get through the business as quickly as possible. The consequence was that in the space of four or five months he had read not only the whole of the *Historical Records*,[1] but many other books as well. When the time came for his Examinations, Genji determined to put him to the test privately a little while beforehand. He was assisted by Tō no Chūjō, by the Chief Secretary of Council, the Clerk of the Board of Rites and a few other friends. The chief tutor was now sent for, and asked to select passages from the *Historical Records*.[1] He went through every chapter,

---

[1] By Ssu-ma Ch'ien, 1st century B.C., a book somewhat longer than Gibbon's *Decline and Fall*; by far the most distinguished Chinese historical work.

picking out the most difficult paragraphs—just such parts indeed as the College Examiners were likely to hit upon—and made his pupil read them out loud. Yūgiri not only read without the slightest stumbling or hesitation but showed clearly in every doubtful or misleading passage that he understood the sense of what he was reading. Every one present was astonished at his proficiency and it was generally agreed that he had the makings of a first-rate scholar. 'If only his poor grandfather could see him!' said Tō no Chūjō with a sigh; and Genji, unable to restrain his feelings, exclaimed with tears in his eyes: 'All this makes me feel very old! Before it has always been other people over whom one shook one's head, saying that they were "getting on in life" or "not so active as they were." But now that I have a grown-up child of my own, I feel (though I am still fortunately some way off my second childhood) that henceforward he will every day grow more intelligent, and I more stupid.' The tutor listened attentively to this speech and felt much comforted by it. Tō no Chūjō had been helping him liberally to wine, and the learned man's gaunt, rugged features were now suffused with smiles of joy and pride. He was a very unpractical man and his worldly success had never been proportionate to his great attainments. At the time when Genji first came across him he was without patronage or any means of subsistence. Then came this sudden stroke of good fortune; he of all people was singled out and summoned to this all-important task. Ever since his arrival he had enjoyed a degree of consideration far in excess of what, in his capacity of tutor, he had any right to expect, and now that the diligence of his pupil had procured for him this fresh ground for Genji's esteem, he looked forward at last to a distinguished and prosperous career.

On the day of the actual examination the College courtyards were crammed to overflowing with fashionable equipages; it seemed indeed as though the whole world had turned out to witness the ceremony, and the princely candidate's entry at the College gates wore the air of a triumphal procession. He looked very unfit to mingle with the crowd (shabby and uncouth as such lads generally are) among whom he now had to take his place, sitting right at the end of the bench, for he was the youngest scholar present; and it was small wonder that he came near to wincing as he took his place amid his uncouth class-mates.

On this occasion also the presence of so large and profane an audience sorely tried the nerves of the academic authorities, and it was to the accompaniment of constant appeals for silence and good manners that Yūgiri read his portion. But he did not feel in the least put out and performed his task with complete success.

This occasion had an important effect upon the fortunes of the College. It began to recover much of its old prestige, and henceforward the students were drawn not only from the lower and middle, but also to a considerable degree from the upper classes, and it became more and more frequent for the holders of high office to have received a certain amount of education. It was found that the possession of Degrees, such as that of Doctor of Letters or even Bachelor, was now an advantage in after life and frequently led to more rapid promotion. This incited both masters and pupils to unprecedented efforts. At Genji's palace too the making of Chinese poems became frequent; both scholars and professors were often his guests, and learning of every kind was encouraged and esteemed in a manner seldom before witnessed at Court.

The question of appointing an Empress now became urgent

The claims of Akikonomu were considerable, since it was the dying wish of Fujitsubo, the Emperor's mother, that her son should be guided by this lady's counsel; and in urging her claims Genji was able to plead this excuse. The great disadvantage of such a choice was that Akikonomu, like Fujitsubo before her, was closely connected with the reigning family, and such alliances are very unpopular in the country. Lady Chūjō [1] had the merit of priority, and to her partisans it appeared that there could be no question of any one else being called upon to share the Throne. But there were many supporters of Lady Akikonomu who were equally indignant that her claims should for an instant be questioned.

Prince Hyōbukyō [2] had now succeeded to the post of President of the Board of Rites, previously held by Asagao's father; he had become a figure of considerable importance at Court and it was no longer deemed politic that his daughter should be refused admittance to the Imperial Household.

This lady, like Akikonomu, had the disadvantage of a close connection with the ruling House; but on the other hand her elevation to the Throne was just as likely to have been supported by the Emperor's late mother as that of Akikonomu, for the new-comer was her brother's child, and it was thought by many people not to be unreasonable that this elder cousin should be called upon to take Fujitsubo's place, as far as watching over the health and happiness of the young Emperor was concerned. The claims, then, were pretty equally divided, and after some hesitation Genji followed his own inclinations by appointing Akikonomu to share the Throne. How strange that in the end this lady

[1] The eldest daughter of Tō no Chūjō.
[2] Murasaki's father, who was anxious to place his younger daughter at Court.

should have risen to an even higher position than her celebrated mother! Such was the comment of the world, and in the country at large some surprise was felt at the announcement of her good fortune, for little was known of her outside the Court.

About this time Tō no Chūjō became Palace Minister and Genji began to hand over to him most of the business of state. Chūjō had a vigorous and rapid mind, his judgment tended to be very sound, and his natural intelligence was backed by considerable learning. Thus, though it will be remembered that at the game of 'covering rhymes'[1] he was badly defeated, in public affairs he carried all before him. By his various wives[2] he had some ten children, who were now all grown-up and taking their places very creditably in the world. Besides the daughter whom he had given in marriage to the Emperor there was another, Lady Kumoi by name, who was a child of a certain princess with whom he had at one time carried on an intrigue. This lady then was not, as far as birth went, in any way her sister's inferior; but the mother had subsequently married a Provincial Inspector who already had a large number of children. It seemed a pity to allow the girl to be brought up by a step-father among this promiscuous herd of youngsters, and Tō no Chūjō had obtained leave to have her at the Great Hall and put her under his mother Princess Ōmiya's keeping. He took far less interest in her, it is true, than he did in Lady Chūjō; but both in beauty and intelligence she was generally considered to be at least her sister's equal. She had during her childhood naturally been brought much into contact with Yūgiri. When each of them was about ten years old they began to live in separate

[1] See vol. ii, p. 86. The rhyme-words at the end of the verses were covered and the competitors had to guess them.
[2] His first wife was a daughter of the Minister of the Right.

quarters of the house. She was still very much attached to him; but one day her father told her that he did not like her to make great friends with little boys, and the next time they met she was careful to be very distant towards him. He was old enough to feel puzzled and hurt; and often when she was in the garden admiring the flowers or autumn leaves or giving her dolls an airing he would follow her about, entreating to be allowed to play with her. At such times she could not bring herself to drive him away, for the truth was that she cared for him quite as much as he for her. Her nurses noticed her changed manner towards him, and could not understand how it was that two children who for years had seemed to be inseparable companions should suddenly begin to behave as though they were almost strangers to one another. The girl was so young that the relationship certainly had no particular meaning for her; but Yūgiri was a couple of years older, and it was quite possible (they thought) that he had tried to give too grown-up a turn to the friendship. Meanwhile the boy's studies began, and opportunities for meeting were rarer than ever. They exchanged letters written in an odd childish scrawl which nevertheless in both cases showed great promise for the future. As was natural with such juvenile correspondents they were continually losing these letters and leaving them about, so that among the servants in both houses there was soon a pretty shrewd idea of what was going on. But there was nothing to be gained by giving information and, having read these notes, the finders hastened to put them somewhere out of sight.

After the various feasts of congratulation were over things became very quiet at Court. Rain set in, and one night when a dank wind was blowing through the tips of the sedges, Tō no Chūjō, finding himself quite at leisure, went to call upon his mother, and sending for Lady Kumoi asked her to play to them on her zithern. Princess Ōmiya herself performed excellently on several instruments and had taught all she knew to her granddaughter. 'The lute,' said Tō no Chūjō, 'seems to be the one instrument which women can never master successfully; yet it is the very one that I long to hear properly played. It seems as though the real art of playing were now entirely lost. True, there is Prince So-and-so, and Genji. . . .' And he began to enumerate the few living persons whom he considered to have any inkling of this art. 'Among women-players I believe the best is that girl whom Prince Genji has settled in the country near Ōi. They say that she inherits her method of playing straight from the Emperor Engi, from whom it was handed on to her father. But considering that she has lived by herself in the depths of the country for years on end, it is indeed extraordinary that she should have attained to any great degree of skill. Genji has constantly spoken to me of her playing and, according to him, it is absolutely unsurpassed. Progress in music more than in any other subject depends upon securing a variety of companions with whom to study and rehearse. For any one living in isolation to obtain mastery over an instrument is most unusual and must imply a prodigious talent.' He then tried to persuade the old princess to play a little. 'I am terribly stiff in the fingers,' she said; 'I can't manage the "stopping" at all.' But she played very nicely. 'The Lady of Akashi,' said Tō no Chūjō presently, 'must, as I have said, be exceptionally gifted; but she has also had great luck. To have given my cousin Genji a daughter when he had waited for one so long was a singular stroke of good fortune. She seems moreover to be a curiously self-effacing and obliging person; for I hear that she has resigned all claim to the child and allows her betters to bring it up as though it were their own.' And he told the whole story, so far as the facts were known to him. 'Women,' he went on, 'are odd creatures; it is no use trying to advance them in the world unless they have exactly the right temperament.' After naming several examples, he referred to the failure of his own daughter, Lady Chūjō: 'She is by no means bad looking,' he said, 'and she has had every possible advantage. Yet now she has managed things so badly that she is thrust aside in favour of some one [1] who seemed to have no chance at all. I sometimes feel that it is quite useless to make these family plans. I hope indeed that I shall be able to do better for this little lady [2]; and there did at one time seem to be a chance that so soon as the Crown Prince [3] was almost old enough for his Initiation I might be able to do something for her in that direction. But now I hear that the little girl from Akashi is being spoken of as the future Empress Presumptive, and if that is so I fear that no one else has any chance.' 'How can you say such a thing?' asked the Princess indignantly. 'You have far too low an opinion of your own family. The late Minister, your father, always believed firmly that we should one day have the credit of supplying a partner to the Throne, and he took immense pains to get this child of yours accepted in the Imperial Household at the earliest possible moment. If only he were alive, things would never have gone wrong like this.' It was evident, from what she went on to say, that she felt very indignant at Genji's conduct in the matter.

It was a very pretty sight to see little Lady Kumoi playing her mother's great thirteen-stringed zithern. Her hair fell forward across her face with a charming effect as she bent over her instrument. Chūjō was just thinking how graceful and distinguished the child's appearance was

---

[1] Akikonomu. [2] Kumoi.
[3] The ex-Emperor Suzaku's little son.

when, feeling that she was being watched, Lady Kumoi shyly turned away, showing for a moment as she did so a profile of particular beauty. The poise of her left hand, as with small fingers she depressed the heavy strings, was such as one sees in Buddhist carvings. Even her grandmother, who had watched her at her lessons day by day, could not hold back a murmur of admiration.

When they had played several duets the big zithern was removed, and Tō no Chūjō played a few pieces on his six-stringed Japanese zithern, using the harsh 'major'[1] tuning which was appropriate to the season. Played not too solemnly and by so skilful a hand as Chūjō's, this somewhat strident mode was very agreeable. On the boughs outside the window only a few ragged leaves were left; while within several groups of aged gentlewomen clustering with their heads together behind this or that curtain-of-state, moved by Chūjō's playing were shedding the tears that people at that time of life are only too ready to let fall upon any provocation. 'It needs but a light wind to strip the autumn boughs,' quoted Chūjō, and continuing the quotation, he added : ' " It cannot be the music of my zithern that has moved them. Though they know it not, it is the sad beauty of this autumn evening that has provoked their sudden tears." But come, let us have more music before we part.' Upon this Princess Ōmiya and her daughter played *The Autumn Wind* and Tō no Chūjō sang the words with so delightful an effect that every one present was just thinking how much his presence added to the amenity of any gathering, when yet another visitor arrived. Yūgiri thinking that such an evening was wasted if not spent in agreeable company, had come over from Genji's palace to the Great

---

[1] Using 'major' and 'minor' as translations of *Yō* and *In*. The six strings were tuned to the 1st, 5th, 9th, and 3rd, 7th, 11th, semitones of the diatonic scale.

Hall. 'Here she is,' said Tō no Chūjō, leading the boy towards the curtain-of-state behind which Kumoi was now sitting. 'You see she is a little shy of you and has taken refuge behind her curtains.' And then looking at Yūgiri: 'I don't believe all this reading is suiting you. Your father himself agrees with me; I know that learning easily becomes a useless and tedious thing if pushed beyond a reasonable point. However, in your case he must have had some particular reason for supposing that academic honours would be useful. I do not know what was in his mind, but be that as it may, I am sure it is bad for you to be bending all day over your books!' And again: 'I am sure that you ought sometimes to have a change. Come now, play a tune on my flute. Your masters can have no objection to that, for is not the flute itself the subject of a hundred antique and learned stories?' Yūgiri took the flute and played a tune or two with a certain boyish faltering, but with very agreeable effect. The zitherns were laid aside and while Chūjō beat the measure softly with his hands, Yūgiri sang to them the old ballad 'Shall I wear my flowered dress?' 'This is just the sort of concert that Genji so much enjoys,' said Tō no Chūjō, 'and that is why he is always trying to get free from the ties of business. Nor do I blame him; for the world is an unpleasant place at best, and surely one might as well spend one's time doing what one likes, instead of toiling day after day at things that do not interest one in the least.'

He passed round the wine-flagon, and as it was now getting dark, the great lamp was brought in, soon followed by supper. When the meal was over, Tō no Chūjō sent Lady Kumoi back to her room. It did not escape the notice of Princess Ōmiya's gentlewomen that Chūjō was anxious to keep Yūgiri and his little daughter as far as possible apart. 'Why, he has sent her away,' they whispered, 'because he does not want her to hear the little gentleman play on the zithern. There will be a sad awakening for him one day, if he goes on treating them like that. . . .' When Tō no Chūjō at length withdrew, he remembered that he had not given certain instructions to one of the Princess's ladies, and stealing back into the room he delivered his message as quietly as possible and was on his way out of the room again, when he caught the sound of his own name. A group of ancient gentlewomen at the far end of the apartment had not noticed his return and their whispering had gone on uninterrupted. He stood still and, listening intently, heard the words: 'He is supposed to be a very clever man. But people are always fools when it comes to dealing with their own children. I could never see any sense at all in that proverb—you know the one I mean—"No one knows a child but its parents." All nonsense, I say,' and she nudged her neighbour expressively. This was a shock to Chūjō. It meant, he realized as he hurried from the room, that the friendship between these two children, which he had hoped to keep within bounds, had already, in the eyes of the household, taken on a romantic tinge. The old ladies within suddenly heard the sharp cry of Chūjō's outriders. 'Well! What do you think of that?' they said. 'He's only just starting! Where has he been hiding all this time? I'll tell you what. He's up to some of his old tricks again, you mark my words!' And another: 'I thought a fresh puff of scent blew this way; but little Prince Yūgiri has got some just like it, and I fancied it was his. Do you think His Excellency was anywhere round here? It would be a terrible thing for all of us if he heard what we said after we thought he had gone away. He's got a hasty temper. . . .' 'Well, after all, there is really nothing to worry about,' thought Tō no Chūjō, as he drove to the Palace. 'It is perfectly natural that they should have made friends.' But it really would be very galling if after the failure of Lady Chūjō to get herself made Empress, Lady Kumoi should through this boy-and-girl affair lose her chance of becoming Empress Presumptive.

Now as always, he was really on very good terms with Genji; but, just as in old days, their interests sometimes clashed, and Chūjō lay awake a long while calling to mind their boyish rivalry and later jealousies. The old princess saw all that was going on; but Yūgiri was her favourite grand-child, and whatever he did she accepted as perfectly justified. But she too was very much irritated by various conversations that she overheard, and henceforward watched over the situation with all the concentration of which her vigorous and somewhat acrid nature was capable.

Only two days later Tō no Chūjō came to his mother's rooms again. The princess was extremely flattered and pleased; it was seldom that he honoured her with two visits in such rapid succession. Before receiving him she had her hair set to rights and sent for her best gown; for though he was her own child he had become so important that she never felt quite sure of herself in his presence, and was as anxious to make a good impression as if he had been a complete stranger. It was soon evident on this occasion that he was in a very bad temper: 'I hesitated to come again so soon,' he said; 'I am afraid your servants must think it very strange. I know I am not so competent as my father and cannot look after you as he did; but we have always seen a great deal of one another and, I hope, always shall. Look back over all that time, and I do not think you will be able to recall one occasion upon which there has been any sort of breach or misunderstanding between us. It never occurred to me as possible that I should ever come here with the express purpose of scolding you, least of all about an affair of this particular sort; but that is why I am here. . . .' The old princess opened her eyes very wide and, under all the powder and paint that she had hurriedly applied when she heard of his coming, she visibly changed colour. ' To what are you alluding ? ' she asked. ' It would indeed be surprising if you suddenly insisted upon picking a quarrel with a woman of my age. I should like to hear what it is all about.' He quite agreed ; it would be lamentable if after so many years of unbroken affection a difference should arise between them. Nevertheless he proceeded : ' The matter is quite simple. I entrusted to your care a child from whom I myself had unfortunately been separated during her early years. I was at the time very much occupied with the future of my other daughter and was much exercised in mind to discover that, despite all my efforts, I could not do for her all that I had planned. But I had absolute confidence that this other child at any rate could be coming to no harm : I now find that quite the opposite is the case, and I think I have every right to complain. You will tell me, I know, that the young gentleman in question is a very fine scholar. He may for all I know be on his way to becoming the most learned man in the world ; but that does not alter the fact that these two are first-cousins and have been brought up together. Should it become known that they are carrying on an intrigue, it would look as though very lax standards prevailed in your house. Such a thing would be considered scandalous even in any ordinary family. . . . I am thinking of Yūgiri's future quite as much as that of my own child. What both of them need is a connection with quite new people ; they would in the end find such an alliance as this too obvious and uninteresting. And if I on my side object to the match on these grounds, you may be sure that Genji, when he hears of it, will insist upon the boy looking further afield. If you could yourself do nothing to forestall this attachment, you might at least have informed me of its existence. I could then have had a chance of arranging the match, despite all its disadvantages, before the matter became the talk of the whole town. You could not have done worse than to leave these young people to their own devices.'

That the matter was so serious as this had never occurred to Princess Ōmiya at all, and she was horrified. ' I entirely agree with you'; she said. ' But how could I possibly know what was going on all the while in the minds of these two children ? I am sure I am very sorry it has happened ; indeed I have quite as much reason to lament over it as you have. But I think it is the young pair themselves, and not I, who ought to bear the blame for what has happened. You have no idea of all that I have done for this girl since you first sent her to me. She has had advantages such as it would never have occurred to you to suggest, and if, through a blindness very natural in a grandmother, I have too long regarded the boy's friendship for her as a matter of no particular consequence, what reason is there to think that any harm has as yet been done ? All your information on the subject is founded on the chatter of good-for-nothings who take a pleasure in damaging the reputations of every one round them. If you were to look into these stories you would probably find they were pure inventions, and stupid inventions at that !' ' Not at all !' said Tō no Chūjō hotly. ' It is not a question of slanders or lies. The way in which these two carry on together is a common matter for jest among your own ladies-in-waiting. It is a most disagreeable situation and I am worried about it'; and with that he left the room.

The news of all this rumpus soon went the round of the aged servants at the Great Hall and there was much wringing of hands. In particular the ladies whose conversation had been overheard felt that, without meaning any harm, they had done irreparable damage, and could not imagine how they could have been so rash as to begin discussing such a subject directly His Excellency left the room.

Tō no Chūjō next looked in upon the young lady herself, and could not help being somewhat melted by her innocent and appealing air. He therefore passed on and went to look for her nurse. 'I understood when I engaged you,' he said, 'that you were young; but one can be young without being infantile, and I supposed you had your wits about you like other people. I seem to have made a great mistake. . . .' To these sarcastic remarks it was impossible to make any reply; but the nurse said afterwards to one of her assistants: 'How is one expected to prevent these things? Just the same might have happened if she had been the Emperor's favourite daughter! In old stories the lovers are generally brought together by some go-between, but we certainly cannot be accused of having played any such part as that, for these two have been allowed to be together as much as they chose for years past; and if my Lady thought they were so young that there was no harm in it, what reason was there for us to interfere? But they have been seeing much less of each other for some while past, and the last thing in the world I should have suspected was that anything wrong could possibly have been going on. Why, the little gentleman looks quite a child; I can't believe such things have ever entered his head.'

So the nurse afterwards declared. But while she was actually being scolded she merely hung her head, and Tō no Chūjō said at last: 'That will do. I am not going to mention this business to anyone else at present. I am afraid a good many people must have heard about it, but you might at least contradict any rumours that you hear going about. ... As for the young lady, I intend to have her moved to my palace as soon as I can arrange it. I think my mother has acted very imprudently; but she could not possibly have foreseen that you nurses would behave with such imbecility.'

So they were all going to move to the Prime Minister's palace! Such was the young nurse's first thought, and she found this prospect so attractive that, though she knew the loss of Lady Kumoi would be a sad blow to the old princess, she could not feel otherwise than elated. 'There now, only think of it!' she said, harping back to Tō no Chūjō's injunction to secrecy. 'And I had half a mind to go round to the Inspector's house and tell the little lady's mama! I should have thought this Prince Yūgiri was good enough for anyone; but of course he does not count as a member of the Royal Family, and they say Lady Kumoi's mama has very grand ideas indeed.' It was clearly no use saying any more to such a featherhead as this, and Kumoi herself was so young that it would be mere waste of breath to lecture her.

The old princess was upset by the affair; but she was fond of both her grand-children, perhaps especially of Yūgiri, and at the bottom of her heart she was extremely gratified at their having taken such a fancy to each other. On reflection it seemed to her that Tō no Chūjō had been very heartless about the matter and had also treated it far more seriously than it deserved. After all he had taken very little trouble about this girl himself, and had never once indicated that he had any ambitious plans for the future. Indeed, it really seemed as though the idea of offering her to the Imperial Household never occurred to him till this trouble arose, and had been invented, thought the old Princess indignantly, merely in order to furnish Tō no Chūjō with a colourable grievance. He had certainly never really counted on this Palace plan; and granted that it was only an afterthought, he must often have contemplated the possibility of the child marrying a commoner. If so, where could a better match be found? Yūgiri was certainly, as regards birth and general advantages, more than the equal of Kumoi; indeed, she could not conceive that any lady would not feel proud to have him as her husband. This no doubt was due to a certain grandmotherly partiality on Ōmiya's part; but be that as it may, she felt very cross with Tō no Chūjō. She was however determined not to let him know it, lest he should become even further incensed against the young people.

Quite unconscious of all the fuss that had been going on at the Great Hall, Yūgiri a few days afterwards again presented himself at his grandmother's apartments. On the last occasion there had been so many people about that he had not managed to get a word in private with Lady Kumoi, and he now arrived very late in the evening, hoping that things would be quieter at such an hour. Old Lady Ōmiya was usually delighted to see him, and full of jokes and nonsense. But to-day she was terribly grave. 'I am very much upset,' she said at last, after talking stiffly of various indifferent matters, 'because your uncle is displeased with you. It is unkind of you to take advantage of us all like this, because naturally I get the blame just as much as you. But that is not why I am talking about it. I mention the matter because you might not otherwise discover that you are in disgrace. . . .' The affair was so much on his mind already that after she had spoken two words he guessed all that was coming. The colour mounted to his cheeks: 'I don't know what he means,' he said. 'Since I began my lessons I have been shut up all the time and have scarcely seen any one. Certainly nothing has happened that my uncle could possibly object to. . . .' It went to her heart to see what pain it cost him to discuss the subject with her. 'There, there,' she said kindly. 'Be careful for the future that is all I ask,' and she turned the conversation on to other matters.

Since in the last month he had done little more than exchange notes with his sweetheart, Yūgiri supposed that even this was considered improper and was very depressed. Supper was served, but he would not eat, and presently it seemed that he had fallen asleep. But in truth he was very wide awake indeed, listening with all his ears till the last sounds of people retiring and settling down for the night had everywhere ceased. Then he stole softly to the door of Lady Kumoi's room, which was usually fastened on a latch, but not bolted or barred. To-night it would not yield an inch. No sound was audible within. With beating heart he leant close up against the door. Despite his care, he had made a certain amount of noise, and this woke her. But now, as she lay listening, she could hear no other sound save that of the wind rustling among the bamboos, and very faint and far away, the mournful cry of wild-geese overhead. Perhaps because, young though she was, the events of the last few weeks had left her far more unhappy than her elders knew, there now came into her head the lines: [1] 'The wild-geese that with sorrowful cry . . . ,' and thinking that no one could hear her, she repeated the poem to herself aloud, causing Yūgiri's heart to beat yet more wildly than before. By what stratagem could he prevail upon her to open the door? 'I am Kojijū,' he said in a feigned childish voice. 'Do let me in!' This Kojijū was the child of Kumoi's old wet-nurse; so desperate was he that any ruse seemed justifiable if he could but bring her to the door. But now all was silent, for

---

[1] 'Some such sorrow as mine they too must know, the wild-geese that with sorrowful cry trail through the country of the clouds.'

Kumoi, ashamed that he should have heard her speaking to herself, lay with her face pressed deep into the pillows. His ruse had not deceived her, and it was misery to picture him standing behind the bolted door. Presently some of the servants in an adjoining room began moving about, and for a moment both he, standing without, and she on her bed within remained rigidly motionless. Soon however all was quiet again and he made his way back to his own bedroom. As he passed by Princess Ōmiya's apartments he heard the noise of some one sighing heavily. Evidently she was still awake; most likely indeed she had heard all that had happened! He crept past the door with the utmost caution and it was with feelings of intense shame and guilt that he at last reached his room. He rose early and wrote a letter to Kumoi which he hoped to convey to her by the hand of that same Kojijū whose voice he had counterfeited in the night. But the child was nowhere to be seen, and Yūgiri left the house in great distress.

What Kumoi on her side could not endure was being scolded by her father and grandmother, and she did all she could to avoid it. But she had not the least idea what they meant when they talked about her 'future' or her 'reputation.' To be whispered about by nurses and servants flattered her vanity and was in itself far from acting as a deterrent. One thing about which her guardians made terrible scenes, seemed to her most harmless of all; this was the writing of letters and poems. But though she had no idea why they forbade it, she saw that it led to scoldings, and henceforward Yūgiri did not receive a single line from her. Had she been a little older she would have found out some way of circumventing these restrictions; and Yūgiri, who already possessed far more capacity to shift for himself, was bitterly disappointed by her tame surrender.

To Princess Ōmiya's great distress Tō no Chūjō no longer paid his customary visits to the Great Hall. Nor did he ever discuss the matter with his wife,[1] who was only able to guess, from his general ill-humour and irritability, that something had gone amiss. He did however one day allude to his disappointment concerning their own daughter, Lady Chūjō: 'I think,' he said, 'that during the ceremonies of Investiture [2] it would be better that our daughter should not be at Court. A quiet time at home would not do her any harm; and although she has been passed over on this occasion she really stands very well with the Emperor. Indeed, she is in such constant attendance upon him that it is a great strain on her gentlewomen who are kept running about at every hour of the day and night...'; and he applied for her release. The Emperor Ryōzen was extremely loth to part with her and at first refused. But Tō no Chūjō seemed to attach such extreme importance to the matter that in the end he agreed to let her spend a short holiday at home. 'I am afraid it will be rather dull for you,' he said to his daughter when she arrived; 'but I have arranged for Kumoi to visit us, so you will have someone to play with. They have been very good to her at her grandmother's; but I find that the house is frequented by a certain rather undesirably precocious child, with whom, as was inevitable, she has struck up a great friendship. She is far too young for that kind of thing....' And he began at once to arrange for Lady Kumoi's removal from the Great Hall.

Princess Ōmiya whose one consolation, since the death of her daughter Aoi, had been the arrival of Lady Kumoi, was appalled at this sudden loss. No hint had been given to her that it was not final, and she saw herself deprived at a stroke of the one happiness which promised to alleviate the

[1] A sister of Kōkiden. [2] Of Akikonomu as Empress.

miseries of old age and decay. And added to all this was the fact that her own son had taken sides against her and become quite indifferent to her sufferings. She charged him with this, but he hotly denied it. 'No, no,' he said, 'it is nonsense to say that I have turned against you. I think that you have behaved foolishly in one particular matter, and shall continue to think so. Lady Chūjō is going through rather a difficult time at Court just now and I have thought it best to withdraw her for a little while. It is very dull at my house and it is a great comfort for her to have a young companion. This is only a temporary measure . . .' and he added: 'Do not think that I am ungrateful for all your kindness to the child. I know that I can never thank you enough. . . .'

Such speeches did little to re-assure her. But it was evident that he was determined to part the two children and it was no use arguing about that. 'How heartless men are!' she said. 'Whatever may have been your reasons for acting like this, the chief result has been that I have lost the confidence of both these children. Perhaps that has not occurred to you? Besides, even if Kumoi is no longer here, Prince Genji, though he is far from being an unreasonable man, is certain to feel that my house is no safe place for young people, and now that he has got Yūgiri at the Nijō-in, he will keep him there permanently.'

Soon afterwards Yūgiri called again at the Great Hall. He was far exceeding the number of visits for which his grandmother had stipulated; but he still hoped that by some accident he might get the chance of speaking a word or two to the playmate who had been so cruelly wrested from him. To his disgust the first thing he saw when he approached the Great Hall was Tō no Chūjō's carriage. He stole away to his old room, which was still kept in readiness for him, and remained in hiding for some while.

Not only Tō no Chūjō but all his sons were there—Kashiwagi, Kōbai, and the rest, but Princess Ōmiya would not receive any of them behind her curtains-of-state. Sayemon no Kami and Gon Chūnagon, who were not her own children but had been born to the late Minister of the Left by another wife, were also in the habit of calling, out of respect to their father's memory, and on this occasion, thinking to please and interest their step-mother, they had brought their little sons with them. But the only result was that, comparing them in her mind with her favourite Yūgiri, she thought them very ugly, unattractive little boys. Yūgiri and Kumoi, these were the only grandchildren for whom she really cared. And now the little girl who had been her delight, upon whom she had lavished so much tenderness and care,—Kumoi, who for all these years had never left her side, was to be taken from her and put into a stranger's hands.

'I have to go to the Palace now,' said Tō no Chūjō quickly. 'I will come back towards nightfall and fetch Kumoi away.'

He had thought the matter out very carefully and decided that even if it should afterwards prove necessary for him to consent to this match, it was not one which he would ever be able to regard with any satisfaction. However, when Yūgiri had begun his career it would be possible to see of what stuff he was made and also to judge the strength of his feeling for Kumoi. If the boy still remained anxious to marry her the betrothal could be announced in a proper way and the whole affair be carried through without discredit to anybody. But so long as they were allowed to frequent the same house, however much they were scolded and watched, it was, considering their age, only to be expected that they would get into a scrape. He could not put it like this to his mother, because to do so would have hurt her feelings; and wishing to avoid any suggestion that Princess Ōmiya had been to blame, he used both at the Great Hall and at his own house the convenient excuse that Lady Chūjō was at home and needed a companion.

Soon after Tō no Chūjō left, Kumoi received a note from Princess Ōmiya : ' Your father is going to take you home with him this evening. I hope you understand that this is entirely his doing. Nothing that happens will ever change my feelings towards you. . . . Come and see me at once. . . .'

The child presented herself immediately. She was dressed in her smartest clothes and, though only eleven and still undeveloped, she had quite the gracious air of a little lady paying a farewell call. She felt very uncomfortable while Princess Ōmiya told her how lonely she would be without any one to play with, and how (though the houses were not far apart) it would seem as though she had gone to live a long, long way off. All this trouble, the child felt dimly, as she listened to the recital of Ōmiya's woe, came from having made friends with that little boy, and hanging her head, she began to weep bitterly. At this moment Yūgiri's old nurse happened to come in. ' Well, I *am* sorry you are going away from us! ' she said to Kumoi. ' I always thought of you as *my* lady, just as much as Prince Yūgiri was *my* little gentleman. We all know what his Excellency means by taking you away like this; but don't you let him down you!' The girl felt all the more wretched and ashamed, but did not know how to reply. ' Don't say such things to the child!' cried Princess Ōmiya. ' It may all come right in the end, without any need to upset the poor little thing like that!' 'The truth is,' answered the nurse indignantly, ' that all of you think my young gentleman is not good enough for her. You and his Excellency may take it from me that Yūgiri is going to be the finest gentleman in the land. . . .' Just as the outraged nurse was voicing this opinion Yūgiri entered the room. He at once recognized the figure of Kumoi behind her curtains-of-state; but there seemed only a very remote chance of getting any conversation with her, and he stood upon the threshold looking so disconsolate that his old nurse could not bear it. A long, whispered consultation took place. At last Ōmiya yielded and under cover of a fading light, at a moment when the movements of the other guests created a useful division, Yūgiri was smuggled behind the little princess's curtains-of-state. They sat looking at one another with nothing to say; they felt very shy and the eyes of both of them began to fill with tears. 'Listen,' said Yūgiri at last. 'Your father thinks that by taking you away from me he can make me stop caring for you. But by all his cruelty he has only made me love you far more than before. Why have I not seen you for so many weeks? Surely we could have found some way. . . .' He spoke childishly; but there was a passion in his voice that strangely stirred her. 'Darling, I wanted to see you,' was all she could say in reply. 'Then you still love me?' She answered with a quick, childish nod.

But now the great lamp was brought in, and a moment afterwards there was a shouting and clatter of hoofs in the courtyard outside. 'There are the outriders, he'll be here in a minute!' cried one of the maids in great alarm, and Kumoi shuddered from head to foot. She attempted indeed to rush from the room; but Yūgiri held her fast. The nurse, who was to go with her to the Prime Minister's Palace, now came to fetch her and to her dismay saw the outline of a boy's figure behind the curtains-of-state. What folly to allow this kind of thing at the last moment! The old princess must suddenly have taken leave of her wits! 'Well, you ought to be ashamed of yourself,' she muttered to Yūgiri as she dived behind the curtains to fetch her charge away. ' I don't know what your uncle would say if he knew this. I have half a mind in any case to tell Madam Inspector,[1] and you'll catch it then. You may be Prince Genji's boy and I don't know what else, but you are only in the Sixth Rank, and have no right to meddle with such a little lady as this! ' It was true enough. He had been kept back, while every one else was promoted; and awakening suddenly to an intense indignation against the powers which had put this affront upon him, he recited the lines: ' Pale was the robe they made me wear; but tears of blood long since have stained it to a hue no tongue should dare deride.' ' Hard driven as we are and thwarted at every hour, how can our love spring upward and put on a deeper hue? ' So Kumoi answered; but she had scarcely said the lines when some one announced that His Excellency was waiting, and the nurse bustled her out of the room. There were three coaches altogether to carry away Tō no Chūjō, the little girl and her belongings. Yūgiri heard them start one after another. Princess Ōmiya presently sent for him to come to her, but he pretended to be asleep. All night he lay sobbing bitterly, and very early next morning, through a world white with frost, he hurried back to the Nijō-in. His eyes were swollen with weeping and he feared that if he stayed longer at the Great Hall his grandmother would insist upon seeing him. All the way home the most melancholy ideas came one after another into his mind. Thick clouds covered the sky and it was still quite dark: ' Unbroken is my misery as this dull sky that day on day has bound the waters of the earth in ice and snow.'

It fell to Genji's lot to supply a dancer for the Gosechi Festival, and though he was merely supposed to choose the girl from among the children of his retainers and leave the rest to her parents, he went much further than this, taking

[1] Kumoi's mother.

a great interest even in the costumes of the little girls who were to wait upon the dancer and hurrying on the seamstresses when he found that they were leaving things to the last moment. The Lady from the Village of Falling Flowers was put in charge of the dresses of those who were to be present at the Early Levee before the ceremony. Genji determined that the dancer supplied by his household should make a brave show, and he equipped her with a body of pages and attendants such as the Empress herself might well have been proud of. Last year, owing to the National Mourning for Fujitsubo, there had been no public festivals or amusements of any kind, so that people looked forward to the coming occasion with an unusual zest, and the families whose turn it was to supply a dancer vied with one another in the pains they took over her training and equipment. One came from the household of the Inspector, one from that of Tō no Chūjō's step-brother Sayemon no Kami, and one from Yoshikiyo, who was now Governor of Ōmi. This year the Emperor had expressed a desire to retain all the dancers in his service at the Palace, and consequently both these gentlemen had chosen daughters of their own to send to the Festival. The dancer from Genji's household was the daughter of Koremitsu, who had now become Governor of the province of Tsu. She had the reputation of being a particularly lively and good-looking child. When Genji first suggested it, Koremitsu did not at all take to the idea, feeling that his family had no claim to such an honour. But every one pointed out to him that the Inspector had shown no hesitation, though he was only offering a bastard daughter; and in the end Koremitsu reluctantly consented, believing like the others that it would give his daughter a chance of permanent service at the Palace. He trained the girl at home, taking endless trouble in teaching her dance-steps and also in selecting the attendants who were to look after her, and on the night before the ceremony he took her to the Nijō-in himself. Meanwhile Genji was inspecting the little train-bearers and pages. They had been chosen from among the prettiest children in the service of the various ladies in his household, and seldom can so engaging a troupe have been collected. His next business was to teach them the curtsey which they would have to make when they were presented to the Emperor, and each one of them showed such readiness and perfect grace in executing the unaccustomed movements that Genji said, laughing: 'We should have no difficulty in producing a second dancer from this household, if one were wanted!' There were still however more of them than were actually required for the ceremony, and since all seemed equally good-looking and equally intelligent, he was obliged to select them according to the rank of their parents.

All this while Yūgiri sat hour after hour in his room, giving no heed to what was going on in this busy house. He was too depressed to work at his books, and lay all day on his couch staring blankly in front of him. But at last he grew tired of doing nothing, and thinking that a little company might distract him, he strolled out to join the throngs who filled the palace.

He was well-born, handsome, and, in a subdued way, very agreeable in his manners. The gentlewomen of the household took no small interest in him, but he remained somewhat of a mystery to them. With Murasaki he had few dealings and was indeed barely acquainted with her. Why it was that he held aloof from her he would have been at a loss to explain. Was it that some dim instinct warned him against a repetition of his father's disastrous entanglements?[1]

The Gosechi dancer had already arrived and a space had been screened up for her to rest in while she was waiting

[1] With Fujitsubo, his father's concubine.

for her rehearsal. Yūgiri sauntered towards the screens and peeped to see what was behind them. There she lay or rather crouched in her corner, looking very miserable. She seemed about the same age as Kumoi but rather taller, and was indeed far more obviously good-looking. It was growing dark and he could not see her features very clearly, but there was certainly something about her which reminded him of the girl he loved. The resemblance was not enough to make him feel in any way drawn towards her; but his curiosity was aroused, and to attract her attention he rustled the train of her skirt. She looked up startled and on the spur of the moment he recited the lines: 'Though you become a servant of Princess Hill-Eternal[1] who dwells above the skies, forget not that to-night I waited at your door.' She heard that he had a pleasant voice, and evidently he was young. But she had not the least idea who he was, and was beginning to feel somewhat nervous when her attendants came bustling along with her dancing-clothes, and as there were now several other people in the room, Yūgiri was obliged to slip away as unobtrusively as he could. He did not like to show himself at the Festival in that wretched blue dress and was feeling very disconsolate at the prospect of being left all alone, when he heard that by Imperial permission cloaks of any colour might be worn at to-day's ceremony, and set off to the Palace. He had no need to hide; for he had a charming young figure upon which, slender though he was, his man's dress sat very well indeed, and every one from the Emperor downwards noticed him on this occasion with particular pleasure and admiration.

At the ceremony of Presentation the dancers all acquitted themselves very creditably and there was little to choose

[1] There is a legend which tells how certain dancing-maidens took the fancy of the gods and were snatched up to the sky.

between the children in any way, though Koremitsu's and the Inspector's were generally voted to have the best of it as regards good looks. But pretty as they all were, none of the others was handsome to anything like the same degree as the girl from Genji's household.[1] She had been brought up in a far humbler way than the others and at any ordinary gathering would have been quite eclipsed by them. But now, when all were dressed for the same part, her real superiority became evident. They were all a little older than the Gosechi dancers usually are, which gave to this year's ceremony a character of its own. Genji was present at the ceremony of Introduction, and the spectacle at once recalled to his mind that occasion, years ago, when he had so much admired one of the Gosechi maidens,—the daughter of the Provincial Secretary.[2] And now on the evening of the Festival Day he sent a messenger to her house with the poem: 'Be thankful that upon the maidens of the Sky time leaves no mark; for upon me, to whom long since you waved your dancing-sleeve, age and its evils creep apace.'

She began to count the years. What a long time ago it had all happened! She knew that this letter did but betoken a brief moment of reminiscent tenderness; but it gave her pleasure that he had succumbed to this feeling, and she answered: 'It needed but your word to bring them back, those winter days; though long since faded is the wreath that crowned them with delight.' Her answer was written on a blue diapered paper in a boldly varied hand, heavy and light strokes being dashed in with an almost cursive sweep,—a somewhat mixed style but, considering the writer's position in life, highly creditable, thought Genji as he examined the note.

Meanwhile with *his* Gosechi dancer Yūgiri made no

[1] Koremitsu's daughter.   [2] See vol. ii, pp. 96 and 129.

further progress, though he thought a good deal about her and would have cultivated her acquaintance, had it been possible to do so without attracting attention. Unfortunately she seemed as a rule to be under extremely close surveillance and he was as yet wholly inexperienced in the art of circumventing such precautions. But he had certainly taken a great fancy to her; and though no one could replace Kumoi, a friendship with this girl might, he felt, do something towards distracting him from his misery.

All four dancers were to be retained at the Palace; but for the moment they had to retire from Court in order to perform the ceremony of Purification. Yoshikiyo's daughter was taken off to Karasaki, Koremitsu's to Naniwa, and soon the dancers had all left Court. A post in the Lady of the Bedchamber's office was vacant, and when the Emperor suggested that Koremitsu's daughter might care to take it Genji naturally accepted for her with alacrity. This was bad news for Yūgiri. Young and unimportant as he was, he could not possibly try to restrain her from accepting such a post; but it would be too bad if she never even found out who it was that had made friends with her that evening at the Nijō-in; and though Kumoi still occupied the chief place in his thoughts, there were times when this subsidiary failure weighed heavily upon him. The girl had a brother who was a page at Court and had also often waited upon Yūgiri at Genji's palace. 'When is your sister going into residence at Court?' he asked the page one day, after making conversation with him for some time. 'I do not know; some time this year, I suppose,' the boy answered. 'She has an extraordinarily beautiful face,' said Yūgiri. 'I envy you for seeing her so constantly. I wish you would arrange for me to meet her again.' 'How can I?' said the boy. 'I am much younger than she. We have not been brought up together, and I do not myself see her except on special occasions. I have no chance of introducing her to gentlemen such as you. . . .' 'But a letter, surely you could manage a letter?' and Yūgiri handed him a note. The boy had been brought up to consider this kind of thing very underhand; but Yūgiri was so insistent that, much against his will, he at last consented. The girl had more taste in such matters than is usual at her age, and the appearance of the note greatly delighted her. It was on a greenish paper, very thin and fine, laid down on a stout backing. The hand was naturally still somewhat unformed; but it did not promise ill for the future. With the letter was a poem: 'Hidden though I was, surely the Maid of Heaven perceived with what enthralment I witnessed the waving of her feathery sleeves?'

Brother and sister were reading the note together when Koremitsu suddenly entered the room and snatched it out of their hands. The girl sat motionless, while the blood rushed to her cheeks. But her brother, indignant at Koremitsu's high-handed manner of dealing with the situation, strode angrily out of the room. 'Who sent this?' Koremitsu called after him. 'Prince Genji's son,' the boy answered, turning back; 'the one who is studying for the College. At any rate it was he who gave me the note and asked me to bring it here.' Koremitsu, who regarded Yūgiri as a mere child, burst into a hearty laugh. 'Well, you have chosen a pretty little prince for your sweetheart,' he said; 'I thought this letter came from some grown-up person. Of course there can be no harm in fun of that sort . . .', and showing the letter to his wife he proceeded to tell her what a nice child Yūgiri was. 'If it ever should happen,' he said to her in an aside, 'that one of these young princes took a fancy to our daughter, we should do much better for her that way than by keeping her at the Palace, where she can never play more than a very humble part,

There's this comfort about it, that if Prince Yūgiri is anything like his father he will continue to show an interest in her when he grows up. You know I have always told you that once Prince Genji takes a fancy to people, he never forgets them, come what may. Look at what he has done for that girl from Akashi.' Nevertheless they hurried on the preparations for their daughter's departure to Court.

After this brief diversion Yūgiri became more than ever pre-occupied with his main misfortune. To Kumoi it was impossible even to send a letter, and all his time was now spent in endless speculations as to where and how he should ever see her again. He no longer visited the Great Hall, for the sight of the rooms where they used to play together evoked memories that he could not endure. But he was almost equally miserable at home, and shut himself up for days on end in his own room. Genji now put him under the care of the Lady from the Village of Falling Flowers. ' His grandmother is not likely to live very long,' Genji said to her. ' You have known him since he was quite small and will be much the best person to look after him.' She always accepted with docility whatever duties he put upon her, and now did her best to look after the boy, of whom she was indeed very fond. Yūgiri liked her, but he did not think she was at all pretty. It seemed to him that Genji, who had gone on being fond of this uninteresting lady for so many years, would surely be able to understand that if one fell in love with a handsome creature like Kumoi one was not likely to give her up all in a minute. No doubt the Lady from the Village of Falling Flowers had quite other qualities to recommend her. She was docile and equable, and Yūgiri saw that it would be very convenient only to fall in love with people of that sort. However, if they were as plain as the lady who had been commissioned to look after him, love would be a painful business. But perhaps his father thought her beautiful or intelligent? The question was hard to answer, but one thing was certain: Genji managed not to spend much time alone with her. 'No,' said Yūgiri to himself, 'I cannot remember his doing more than bring her some little present or chat with her for a few moments from outside her screen ever since I have been in the house.'

About this time old Princess Ōmiya took her vows, and though this necessitated a change of costume, it did not prevent her being as anxious as ever to make a good impression, and she continued to take the greatest possible pains with her appearance. Yūgiri had indeed always known people with whom appearances counted for a great deal; while the lady who had been put in charge of him, having never been particularly handsome, had, now that she was no longer quite young, grown somewhat angular, and her hair was becoming scanty. These things made a disagreeable impression upon him.

As the year drew towards a close, Princess Ōmiya's whole attention became occupied with the delightful task of making ready the young scholar's New Year clothes. It was a splendid costume, *that* he could not deny. But it did not seem to interest him very much. 'I don't know why you have ordered all these clothes,' he said at last; 'I have no intention of going to Court at all on New Year's day. Why did you suppose I meant to?' 'What a way to talk!' she said in bitter disappointment. 'One would think you were already an old gentleman hardly able to drag yourself about!' 'One can have the feeling that one's life is over, without being old,' he muttered, his eyes filling with tears. She knew quite well what was on his mind, and felt very sorry for him. But she thought it better not to discuss the matter and said gently: 'A man ought to bear himself with pride even if he knows that he deserves a higher rank than that which for the moment has been accorded to him. You must not let it depress you so much. Why do you go about looking so wretched nowadays? It really becomes quite insufferable.' 'I don't know what you are talking about,' answered Yūgiri. 'Why should I go to Court if I do not choose to? As a matter of fact, it is very unpleasant to be only in the Sixth Rank. People notice it and make remarks. I know it is only for the present; but all the same I had rather stay at home. I am sure that if my grandfather were alive, he would never allow me to be treated like this. One would think my father might do someting about it; but he does not seem to care what becomes of me. I saw little enough of him before; but now he has put me to live right away in the new eastern wing, and never comes near me at all. The only person who takes any trouble about me is this 'Falling Flowers' whom he keeps there. . . .' 'Poor child,' said Princess Ōmiya, 'it is a terrible misfortune to have no mother, in whatever rank of life one may be. But before long you will be old enough to go out into the world and shift for yourself. Then people will soon learn to respect you. Meanwhile you must try to be patient and not take these things so much to heart. Your grandfather would indeed have done more for you if he were here. For though your father holds the same position, he does not seem to have the same influence over people as your poor grandfather did. They still tell me that your uncle Tō no Chūjō is a man of very remarkable talents, and I used to think so myself. But I have noticed a change in him lately, and it becomes greater every day. However, things must indeed be in a bad way if a young boy like you, with all his life before him, can talk so gloomily about the future. . . .'

On New Year's day Genji, being Grand Minister Extraordinary, did not go to Court, but following the precedent set by Fujiwara no Yoshifusa [1] celebrated the rites of the season at his own palace. On the seventh day a White Horse was presented to the Grand Minister with exactly the same ceremonies as to the Emperor at Court; indeed, in many respects the festivities arranged by Genji exceeded in their magnificence anything that had ever been seen on such occasions save at the Palace itself. Towards the end of the second month came the Imperial Visit to the ex-Emperor Suzaku. It was too early for the blossoms to be quite at their best, but immediately afterwards came the 'month of fasting' in memory of the Emperor's mother, so the Visit could not be postponed. Fortunately the cherry blossom was unusually early this year and in Suzaku's gardens it already made a delightful show. A tremendous cleaning and polishing was set afoot at his palace in preparation for the Emperor's arrival; and meanwhile the noblemen and princes who were to accompany his Majesty thought of nothing but their new clothes. They had been ordered to wear dove-grey lined with pale green; the Emperor himself was to be dressed all in crimson. By special command Genji was also in attendance on the day of the Visit, and he too wore red; so that frequently during the day the figure of the Emperor seemed to merge into that of his Minister, and it was as though the two of them formed but one crimson giant. Every one present had taken unusual pains with his appearance, and their host, the ex-Emperor, who had grown into a far better-looking man than at one time seemed possible, evidently took much more interest in such matters than before, and was himself magnificently apparelled.

Professional poets had not been summoned for the occasion, but only some ten scholars from the College who had the reputation of being able to turn out good verses.

[1] 804–872 A.D.

The subjects chosen were modelled on those given out to the competitors for posts in the Board of Rites. It was thought that it would be a good thing to give Yūgiri some idea of the themes given out at Palace examinations. That his mind might not be disturbed, each poet was set adrift on the lake all by himself, and it was with considerable alarm that these timid scholars, few of whom had ever set foot in a boat before, saw their moorings loosed and felt themselves gliding further and further away from the shore. As dusk drew on, boats with musicians on board began to circle the lake, and their tunes mingled agreeably with the sighing of the mountain wind. Here, thought Yūgiri, was a profession which brought one into pleasant contact with the world and at the same time entailed studies far less arduous than those to which he had been so heartlessly condemned; and he wandered about feeling very discontented.

Later on, the dance called 'Warbling of the Spring Nightingales,' was performed, and Suzaku, remembering that famous Feast of Flowers [1] years ago said to Genji with a sigh: 'What wonderful days those were! We shall not see their like again.' There were indeed many incidents belonging to that time which even now Genji looked back upon with considerable emotion, and when the dance was over, he handed the wine bowl to Suzaku, reciting as he did so: 'Spring comes, and still the sweet birds warble as of old; but altered and bereft [2] are they that sit beneath the blossoming tree.' To this Suzaku replied: 'To-day the nightingales have come to tell me of the Spring. Else had no sunshine pierced the mists that hide my hermit's-dwelling from the world's pomp and pride.' It was now the turn of Prince Sochi no Miya, who had recently become

---

[1] See vol. i, p. 239 seq.
[2] Allusion to the death of the old Emperor, Genji's and Suzaku's father.

President of the Board of War, to present the bowl. He did so, reciting the verse: ' Speak not of change ; unaltered through all ages [1] shall the flute preserve their song, the nightingales that in the spring-time warble on the swaying bough.' This was said with a glance towards the Emperor, and in loud clear voice, that the compliment might not be missed. Ryōzen was indeed gratified by the graceful allusion, but as he took the bowl he answered modestly : ' If birds still sing and a few faded blossoms deck the tree, it is but in remembrance of those happier days when Virtue ruled the world.' This was said with great earnestness and humility. All the above poems were exchanged privately and only overheard by a few privileged persons, and there were others which did not get recorded at all. The pavilion of the musicians was some way off, and Suzaku suggested that those about him should send for their instruments and make a little music of their own. Sochi no Miya accordingly played on the lute, Tō no Chūjō on the Japanese zithern, while Suzaku himself played to the Emperor on the thirteen-stringed zithern. The Chinese zithern was as usual played by Genji. It was seldom that so gifted a band of performers chanced to meet in one place, and the concert that followed was of unforgettable beauty. Several of the courtiers present had good voices, and the songs ' Was ever such a day ! ' and the ' Cherry Man ' [2] were now performed. Finally torches were lit all round the edge of the island in the lake, and so the feast at last came to an end. But late as it was, Ryōzen felt that it would be uncivil on his part if he went away without paying his respects to Suzaku's mother, Lady Kōkiden, who was living in the same house with him. Genji was naturally obliged to

---

[1] The song and dance ' Warbling of the Spring Nightingales ' are attributed to the mythical Chinese Emperor Yao, 3rd millennium B.C.
[2] See above, p. 45.

accompany him. The old lady received them in person and was evidently very much gratified by the visit. She had aged immensely since he last saw her; but here she still was, and it irritated him to think that she should hang on to life in this way, when a much younger woman like Fujitsubo was already in her grave. 'My memory is not so good as it was,' said Kōkiden, ' but this visit of yours has brought back the old days to my mind more clearly than anything that has happened to me for a long time past.' 'Those upon whom I leaned have now been taken from me one after another,' the Emperor replied, ' and hitherto the year has had no spring-time for me. But my visit to your house to-day has at last dispelled my grief; I hope you will permit me to come here often. . . .' Genji too had to make a suitable speech, and had even to ask if he also might venture to call again. The procession left the house amid great scenes of popular enthusiasm, which painfully reminded the old lady of her complete failure to injure Prince Genji's career. To govern he was born, and govern he would despite all her scheming. 'Well, such is fate,' she thought, and was almost sorry that she had wasted time contending against it.

It was natural that this visit should bring Oborozuki to his mind. Not that he had altogether ceased corresponding with her; for lately whenever an opportunity occurred, he had sent her a word or two of greeting. And now there rose before him on his way home many delightful recollections of the hours they had spent together.

As for Kōkiden, despite her professions of good will she did as a matter of fact intensely dislike all contact with the present Emperor and his government. But it was sometimes necessary to communicate with them concerning her own salary, or the preferment of her friends, and on such occasions she often wished that she had not lived to see an age which was in all respects the reversal of what she herself had striven for. Old age had not improved her temper, and even Suzaku found her very difficult to get on with, and sometimes wondered how much longer he would be able to endure so trying a partnership.

So greatly had Yūgiri distinguished himself in the literary competitions which marked that day's festivity, that upon the strength of them alone he was awarded the Doctor's degree. Among those who had competed were many who were far older than he and some who were thought to possess remarkable ability. But besides Yūgiri only two others were passed. When the time of the autumn appointments came round he received the rank of Chamberlain. He longed as much as ever to see Lady Kumoi. But he knew that Tō no Chūjō had his eye upon him, and to force his way into her presence under such circumstances would have been so very disagreeable that he contented himself with an occasional letter. She, meanwhile, was fully as wretched as her young lover.

Genji had long had it in his mind, if only he could find a site sufficiently extensive and with the same natural advantages as the Nijō-in, to build himself a new palace where he could house under one roof the various friends whose present inaccessibility, installed as they were in remote country places, was very inconvenient to him. He now managed to secure a site of four *machi* [1] in the Sixth Ward close to where Lady Rokujō had lived and at once began to build.

The fiftieth birthday of Murasaki's father Prince Hyōbukyō was in the autumn of the following year. The preparations for this event were of course chiefly in her hands; but Genji too, seeing that on this occasion at any rate he must appear to have overcome his dislike of the

[1] A *machi* is 119 yards.

prince, determined to give the affair an additional magnificence by holding the celebrations in his new house; and with this end in view he hurried on the work of construction as fast as he could. The New Year came, and still the place was far from finished. What with spurring on architects and builders, arranging for the Birthday Service, choosing the musicians, the dancers and the like, he had plenty to keep him busy. Murasaki herself had undertaken the decking of the scripture-rolls and images that would be used at the Service; as well as the customary distribution of presents and mementos. In these tasks she was aided by the Lady from the Village of Falling Flowers, and it was at this time that an intimacy sprang up between them such as had never existed before.

The rumour of these preparations soon reached Prince Hyōbukyō's ears. After the general amnesty which succeeded his return from Suma, Genji in general made no difference between those who had remained loyal to his cause and those who had stood aloof from him. But from the first Hyōbukyō felt that in his case an exception was made. Over and over again he found himself treated with marked coldness, and the refusal to accept his younger daughter as a candidate for the Emperor's hand, together with a number of other small but vexatious incidents, finally convinced him that he must at some time have given Genji particular offence. How this had occurred he was at a loss to conjecture; it was indeed the last thing in the world which he would have wished to happen. The fact that, among the many women upon whom Genji had bestowed his favours, it was Murasaki who had been chosen to be the mistress of his house, gave to Hyōbukyō, as her father, a certain worldly prestige. But it could by no means be said that he had hitherto taken a personal share in any of his daughter's triumphs. This time however, a celebration in which Hyōbukyō necessarily played the foremost part was being planned and prepared by Genji himself on a scale which had set the whole country talking. The prince began to hope that his old age would be lightened by a period of belated conspicuity, and he began to feel very well pleased with himself. This intensely irritated his wife, who could not endure that honours should come to him through the influence of her step-child, and saw no reason why Genji should so quickly be forgiven his obstructive attitude concerning the Presentation of her own little daughter.

The new palace was finished in the eighth month. The portions corresponding to the astrological signs Sheep and Monkey[1] were reserved for Lady Akikonomu's occasional use, for they stood on ground that her own suite of rooms had once occupied. The Dragon and Snake quarters were for Genji himself; while the Bull and Tiger corner was to be used by the Lady from the Village of Falling Flowers. Finally the Dog and Wild Boar quarters were made ready for the Lady from Akashi, in the hope that she would at last consent to instal herself under his roof.

He effected great improvement in the appearance of the grounds by a judicious handling of knoll and lake, for though such features were already there in abundance, he found it necessary here to cut away a slope, there to dam a stream, that each occupant of the various quarters might look out of her windows upon such a prospect as pleased her best. To the south-east he raised the level of the ground, and on this bank planted a profusion of early flowering trees. At the foot of this slope the lake curved with especial beauty, and in the foreground, just beneath

---

[1] The points of the compass indicated by these animal designations are, successively S.W., S.E., N.E., N.W. Houses were planned with reference to Chinese astrological conceptions.

the windows, he planted borders of cinquefoil, of red-plum, cherry, wistaria, kerria, rock-azalea, and other such plants as are at their best in spring-time; for he knew that Murasaki was in especial a lover of the spring; while here and there, in places where they would not obstruct his main plan, autumn beds were cleverly interwoven with the rest.

Akikonomu's garden was full of such trees as in autumn-time turn to the deepest hue. The stream above the waterfall was cleared out and deepened to a considerable distance; and that the noise of the cascade might carry further, he set great boulders in mid-stream, against which the current crashed and broke. It so happened that, the season being far advanced, it was this part of the garden that was now seen at its best; here indeed was such beauty as far eclipsed the autumn splendour even of the forests near Ōi, so famous for their autumn tints.

In the north-eastern garden there was a cool spring, the neighbourhood of which seemed likely to yield an agreeable refuge from the summer heat. In the borders near the house upon this side he planted Chinese bamboos, and a little further off, tall-stemmed forest-trees whose thick leaves roofed airy tunnels of shade, pleasant as those of the most lovely upland wood. This garden was fenced with hedges of the white deutzia flower, the orange tree 'whose scent rewakes forgotten love,' the briar-rose, and the giant peony; with many other sorts of bush and tall flower so skilfully spread about among them that neither spring nor autumn would ever lack in bravery.

On the east a great space was walled off, behind which rose the Racing Lodge [1]; in front of it the race-course was marked off with ozier hurdles; and as he would be resident here during the sports of the fifth month, all along the stream at this point he planted the appropriate purple

---

[1] Used for residence during the Kamo Festival.

irises.[1] Opposite were the stables with stalls for his racehorses, and quarters for the jockeys and grooms. Here were gathered together the most daring riders from every province in the kingdom. To the north of Lady Akashi's rooms rose a high embankment, behind which lay the storehouses and granaries, screened also by a close-set wall of pine-trees, planted there on purpose that she might have the pleasure of seeing them when their boughs were laden with snow; and for her delight in the earlier days of the winter there was a great bed of chrysanthemums, which he pictured her enjoying on some morning when all the garden was white with frost. Then there was the mother-oak [2] (for was not she a mother?) and, brought hither from wild and inaccessible places, a hundred other bushes and trees, so seldom seen that no one knew what names to call them by.

The move was to take place about the time of the Festival of the Further Shore.[3] He had at first intended to transfer all the occupants at one time. But it soon became apparent that this would be too vast an undertaking, and it was arranged that Lady Akikonomu should not arrive till somewhat later than the rest. With her usual amiability and good-sense the Lady from the Village of Falling Flowers readily fell in with the suggestion that she and her party should not form a separate cortège, but should join with Murasaki in the ceremony of removal. Genji regretted that the latter was not going to see her new domain at the season for which it had been principally designed; but still, the move itself was a diverting experience. There were fifteen coaches in the procession and almost all the outriders were

[1] Plucked on the 5th day of the 5th month.
[2] *Quercus dentata.*
[3] Lasts for a week, centring round the autumnal equinox. The Further Shore is Nirvāna, to which Buddha carries us in the Ship of Salvation. The festival is peculiar to Japan.

gentlemen of the fourth or fifth rank. The ordering of the procession was not so elaborate as might have been expected, for it seemed likely at the moment that too lavish a display might try the temper of the common people, and some of the more ostentatious forms and ceremonies were either omitted or abridged.

But Genji was careful not to let it seem that any of these restrictions had been carried out to the detriment of one lady rather than another. The Lady from the Village of Falling Flowers had indeed nothing to complain of, for Yūgiri had been told off to wait upon her exclusively during the whole ceremony. The gentlewomen and maids found their quarters in the new house admirably fitted out with every comfort and convenience, and they were louder than ever in Genji's praises. About six days later the Empress Akikonomu arrived from the Palace. The ceremony of her arrival, though it had been intended that the whole move should be as little ostentatious as possible, was necessarily a very sumptuous and imposing affair. Not only had she risen from obscurity to the highest place which a woman can hold in the land, but she had herself advanced so much in beauty and acquired so great a dignity of carriage and mien that she now figured very large in the popular imagination, and crowds flocked the road wherever she was to pass.

The various quarters of which the New Palace was composed were joined by numerous alleys and covered ways, so that access from one to another was easy, and no one felt that she had been bundled away into a corner. When the ninth month came and the autumn leaves began to be at their best, the splendours of Akikonomu's new garden were at last revealed, and indeed the sights upon which her windows looked were indescribably lovely. One evening when the crimson carpet was ruffled by a gusty wind, she filled a little box with red leaves from different trees and sent it to Murasaki. As messenger she chose one of the little girls who waited upon her. The child, a well grown, confident little thing, came tripping across the humped wooden bridge that led from the Empress's apartments with the utmost unconcern. Pleased though Murasaki was to receive this prompt mark of friendship, she could for a while do nothing but gaze with delight at the messenger's appearance, and she quite forgot to be resentful, as some in her place would have been, that an older and more dignified messenger had not been entrusted with the Empress's gift. The child wore a silk shirt, yellow outside and lined with green. Her mantle was of brown gauze. She was used to running about on messages in the Palace, had that absolute faultlessness of turn-out and bearing which seems never to be found elsewhere, and was far from being overawed at finding herself in the presence of such a person as Lady Murasaki. Attached to the box was the poem : 'Though yours be a garden where only Spring-time is of price, suffer it that from my house Autumn should blow a crimson leaf into your hand.' It was amusing to see how while Murasaki read the missive, her ladies crowded round the little messenger and plied her with refreshments and caresses. For answer, Murasaki placed in the lid of the box a carpet of moss and on it laid a very little toy rock. Then she wrote on a strip of paper tied to a sprig of five-pointed pine : 'The light leaf scatters in the wind, and of the vaunted spring no tinge is left us, save where the pine-tree grips its ledge of stone.'

The Empress thought at first that it was a real pine-branch. But when she looked closer she saw that, like the rock, it was a work of art—as delicate and ingenious a piece of craftsmanship as she had ever encountered. The readiness of Murasaki's answer and the tact with which, while not exalting her own favourite season above that of

K

Akikonomu's choice, she had yet found a symbol to save her from tame surrender, pleased the Empress and was greeted as a happy stroke by all the ladies who were with her. But Genji when she showed it to him pretended to think the reply very impertinent, and to tease Murasaki he said to her afterwards: 'I think you received these leaves most ungraciously. At another season one might venture perhaps upon such disparagement; but to do so now that the Goddess of Tatsuta[1] holds us all in sway seems almost seditious. You should have bided your time; for only from behind the shelter of blossoming boughs could such a judgment be uttered with impunity.' So he spoke; but he was in reality delighted to find these marks of interest and good will being exchanged between the various occupants of his house, and he felt that the new arrangement was certain to prove a great success.

When the Lady of Akashi heard of the removal to the New Palace and was told that only her own quarters, as spacious and handsome as any of the rest, now remained untenanted, she determined at last to hold aloof no longer. It was the Godless month when she arrived. She looked around her and, mistrustful though she was, she certainly could see no sign here that as regards either elegance or comfort she would be expected to put up with less than her neighbours. And indeed Genji saw to it that on all occasions she should rank in the eyes of the household rather as mother of the little Princess for whom so brilliant a future was in store, than as the scion of a poor and undistinguished provincial family.

[1] Goddess of the autumn; here compared to Akikonomu. The secondary meaning is 'You must be more civil to Akikonomu now that she is Empress.'

CHAPTER IV

TAMAKATSURA

THOUGH seventeen years had now passed since Yūgao's death,[1] Genji had not by any means forgotten her. He had indeed since those early days seen much of the world and encountered the most divers temperaments. But he had yet to find a disposition such as hers; and it was with feelings of longing and contrition that he looked back upon their intimacy.

Though Ukon was not a creature of much account, she was the one person to whom he could speak of the dead lady. He felt a considerable degree of affection towards her, and during the years after Yūgao's death Ukon had practically lived at the Nijo-in, being allowed to spend most of her time with the older servants in the housekeeper's room. Then came the exile, and with Genji's other servants she went across to the western wing and entered Murasaki's service. She gave the impression of being a harmless, self-effacing creature, and it would have surprised every one very much to know what was all the while going on in her mind. For Ukon, particularly after the move to the New Palace, was constantly appraising the relative positions of the great ladies who ruled the house, and deciding what place her own dear mistress would now be occupying, were she still alive. 'Certainly,' said Ukon to herself, looking critically at the Lady of Akashi, 'my poor lady would not have been eclipsed by such as

See vol. i, chapter iv.

you!' And indeed Ukon had seen for herself that even where his feelings were far less strong than in Yūgao's case, there never came a time when Genji turned aside from those who had opened their hearts to him, or behaved as though his obligations towards them were at an end. However full might be the cup of his affections, he did not allow a drop to spill; and though Yūgao might not perhaps have been able to vie with so great a personage as Murasaki, yet it was certain that were she alive she would now be occupying one of the main apartments in the newly-finished house.

Such were the sad reflections that dwelt constantly in this solitary lady's heart. She had never attempted to get into communication with the family of her late mistress, nor even to discover the present whereabouts of the child [1] whom Yūgao had left behind at the house in the Fifth Ward; partly through fear of being questioned concerning her own part in the unhappy affair, partly because there seemed to be no object in doing so. Moreover, Genji had strictly forbidden her to mention the story to anybody, and though she had sometimes thought of writing to the people at the house, she felt that it would be disloyal to him to do so, and was entirely without news. She did, however, hear long afterwards a report that the husband of the nurse in whose care the child had been left was now working in a provincial Treasury and that his wife was with him. It seemed probable that they had also taken the child.

This was indeed the case. Tamakatsura was four years old when she made the journey to Tsukushi. The nurse, after months of vain endeavour to discover Yūgao's whereabouts, during which she had trudged weary and weeping from quarter to quarter and house to house without finding

[1] Tō no Chūjō's child by Yūgao. Her name was Tamakatsura.

the least glimmer of news, had at last given up all hope. She would have been glad enough for her own sake to keep the child, to whom she had become fondly attached, as a remembrance of the mistress whom she must now regard as forever lost. But there were also the little girl's own interests to consider. 'We are humble people,' thought the nurse, 'and Tsukushi [1] is a long way off. Perhaps it is my duty to tell her father [2] of what has happened and give him the chance of making some more suitable provision for her future.' But it was difficult for such people to communicate with a young gentleman of Tō no Chūjō's quality. 'If I mention the child to its father,' she said to her husband one day, 'he is certain to ask at once how I could have been so foolish as to let our poor young lady out of my sight. And indeed, I don't know how I should answer him. Then again, it isn't as if he had ever seen much of the little creature. It would be like handing her over to strangers, and I do not think that, when the time came, I should ever find it in my heart to let her go. He may of course refuse to do anything for her himself; but one thing is certain: if he hears we are going off to Tsukushi, he will never give me leave to take her with us!' So the nurse declared to her husband and companions. Though Tamakatsura was not much over three years old when her mother disappeared, she had acquired all the airs and graces of a little lady; she was remarkably good-looking and it was apparent that she already had a strong will of her own. But now she was bundled on to a common trading-ship in which no provision whatever had been made for the comfort of the passengers; and as they rowed out into the bay, she began to look very disconsolate. She still thought

---

[1] The large southern island upon which the modern town of Nagasaki stands.
[2] Tō no Chūjō.

a great deal about her mother, and, to re-assure herself, she said out loud : ' I know why we are travelling on this ship ; we are going to see mother ! ' She returned to this idea again and again, but it received no confirmation on any side, and at last she burst into tears. Two young women sitting near by were also weeping, though they suddenly ceased to do so when one of the sailors reminded them that ' tears bring bad luck at sea.'

Skirting along the coast they passed much lovely scenery, and the nurse, remembering what delight her young mistress had taken in such sights as these, wished for a moment that she were here to see them. But then she remembered that but for Yūgao's disappearance she and her husband would never have been driven to accept this wretched post in the provinces, and she gazed regretfully in the direction of the City, envying even the waves that stole back so peacefully towards shores ' that she, perhaps, would never tread again.' Soon the rowers began chanting in their rough, wild voices the song ' Over the distant waves,' and the two young women, who were sitting face to face, again began to weep bitterly. At last the ship rounded the Golden Cape, and knowing that the coast which now came into view belonged not to the mainland, but to the island of Tsukushi, the travellers felt that exile had indeed begun. The old nurse's heart sank ; but she had her little charge to see to and was most of the time far too busy to think of anything else. Now and again she would drop off to sleep and then, as for some time past, she would at once dream that her mistress appeared before her. But always at Yūgao's side there stood the figure of another woman, who seemed to follow her wherever she went. The nurse woke from these dreams sickened and afraid, and she felt, after each such occasion, more certain than ever that Yūgao was no longer alive.

Shōni, the nurse's husband, had only been appointed to his post in Tsukushi for a term of five years. But the position he held was a very humble one and when the time came, he found it difficult to meet the expenses of a long journey. Thus their departure for the capital had to be postponed again and again. At last, after many months of disappointment and delay, Shōni fell seriously ill. Tamakatsura was now ten years old and was growing handsomer every day. Shōni, who knew that his end was near, kept asking himself what would become of her in this desolate place. He had always felt that in bringing her with them they had acted somewhat unfairly to the child. For after all she was Tō no Chūjō's daughter, and her birth entitled her to better surroundings than the cramped and dingy home of a provincial clerk. But five years is not a very long time, and he had always confidently expected that when his term of office ran out he would be able to take her with him to Kyōto and put her into touch with her father. True, it was possible that Chūjō would refuse to acknowledge her. But the City is a big place, and Shōni made no doubt that, once he had settled her there, a girl such as this would not have to wait very long before a satisfactory opening occurred. For this reason he had done everything in his power to raise funds for the journey. But now the last expedient had failed and he knew that for his part he was fated never to leave Tsukushi. During his last days he worried much over the injustice which had been done to the child in detaining her so long away from the Capital, and sending for his sons he said to them: 'As soon as this is over I want you to take Tamakatsura back to the City. The same day. Don't wait for the funeral. . . .'

It was only known to the members of Shōni's family that the little girl was Tō no Chūjō's daughter. To the other government clerks and to the world in general she was a grand-daughter of Shōni's whose parents were in trouble of some kind and had left her in his charge. But in the family she continued to be treated as 'the young lady', and every sacrifice was made that she might have, so far as possible, the upbringing to which her birth entitled her. Shōni's sudden illness and death naturally threw his wife into a piteous state of distraction; but in the midst of her grief, one thought obsessed her; would they ever be able to secure a passage back to the City and restore the little girl to her relations? Unfortunately Shōni had been unpopular with the local people and none of them would give any assistance. Thus the time dragged on, wretched years full of anxiety and discouragement; and still there seemed no prospect of return.

Meanwhile Tamakatsura grew to womanhood. She had all her mother's beauty, and something more besides; for she seemed to have inherited from her father's side a singular air of high breeding, an aristocratic fineness of limb and gesture, that in Yūgao, whose beauty was that of the by-street rather than of the palace, had been entirely lacking. She was of a very generous disposition, and in every way a most delightful companion. Her fame soon spread through the island, and hardly a day passed but some local squire or farmer attempted to get into correspondence with her. These letters, written for the most part in a rustic sprawling hand and very crudely expressed, were thrust upon every member of the household in turn in the hope that he or she would consent to act as a go-between. Clumsy documents of this kind were calculated to arouse nothing but disgust in the breast of any one save an islander, and no attention whatever was paid to them. At last the persistence of her suitors became a nuisance, and the nurse put it about that though the girl looked just like other people, she suffered from a secret deformity which made it impossible for her ever to marry. It had indeed (so the story ran) already been decided that she was to live quietly with her 'grandmother' till the old lady died, and after that was to enter a nunnery. But it soon became so irritating to hear every one saying: 'Isn't it sad about poor Shōni's granddaughter? They say she has got some terrible deformity,' that the old nurse could bear it no longer and again began racking her brains to discover some way of getting the girl back to her father. Was it conceivable that he would refuse to look after her? After all, he had made quite a fuss over her when she was a baby. The old lady prayed fervently to every Buddha and God that some way might present itself of taking Tamakatsura to Kyōto. But the chance of any member of her family getting away from Tsukushi was now remoter than ever. Her daughters had married local people and her sons were employed in the neighbourhood. In her heart of hearts she still cherished all sorts of schemes for compassing the return of the whole family; but every day it became more and more impossible that anything of the kind would ever happen. Thus Tamakatsura grew up amid continual lamentations and repinings and learnt to look upon life as one long succession of troubles and disappointments, varied only by three great bouts of penance and fasting, each January, May and September. The years went by. She was now twenty; her beauty was at its height, and still it was being wasted in this barbarous and sequestered land.

Some while after Shōni's death the family had moved along the coast from Chikuzen to Hizen, hoping for a more peaceful existence in a place where they were not known. But Tamakatsura's reputation had preceded her and, little inclined to credit the stories about her deformity, the notabilities of the neighbouring countryside began pestering her guardians with such assiduity that life soon became as harassing as before.

Among these suitors there was a certain Tayū no Gen who held a small position under the Lord-Lieutenant of Tsukushi. He came of a family that was very influential in Higo and the surrounding country, and on this side of the island he ranked as a person of considerable importance. He had, moreover, greatly distinguished himself in a campaign against the insurgents. To a singular degree of hardihood and endurance there was added in his nature more than a fair share of sensuality. Women were his hobby; he kept a prodigious quantity of them always about him, and was continually on the look-out for opportunities of adding to the collection. The story of the beautiful Tamakatsura and of the secret deformity which prevented her marriage soon reached Tayū's ears. 'Mis-shapen, is she?' he cried. 'Frightened that people will stare? She need not worry about that if she comes to me. I'll keep her locked up all right!' and he wrote at once to Shōni's wife. The old lady, who knew his reputation, was sadly put about. She replied that her grand-daughter was destined for the convent and that no proposals of this kind could be entertained on her behalf. Tayū was not used to be put off like this and, determined at all costs to get his way, he came galloping over to Hizen at full speed. He immediately summoned Shōni's three sons to his lodging and said to them: 'Let me have that girl, and you may count on me as a friend for life. My name goes for something on the Higo side. . . .' Two of the sons were easily won over and promised to do as Tayū asked. They had, it is true, a moment's qualm at the thought of handing over Tō no Chūjō's child to this lawless provincial swashbuckler. But they had their own way to make in the world, and they knew that Tayū had by no means exaggerated the value of his own friendship and protection. On the other hand, life on this part of the island with Tayū against one was a prospect not to be faced with equanimity. If the girl had failed to take in the world the place to which her rank entitled her, that was her father's fault, not theirs. She ought to be grateful that such a man as this (after all, he was the principal person in the neighbourhood) should have taken such a fancy to her. In Tsukushi at any rate there was no prospect of doing better for her, and Tayū, angered by the refusal of his proffered patronage would certainly stick at nothing. . . . So they argued, doing their best to scare their mother into assent by stories of Tayū's violence and implacability. Only the second brother, Bugo no Suke, stood out: 'I know a good deal about this fellow,' he said. 'It's too much of a shame. We simply cannot hand her over to him. . . . Somehow or other one of us ought to do what our father asked us to—take her back to Kyōto. There must be some way of managing it. . . .' Shōni's two daughters stood by weeping. Their mother was utterly heart-broken. What had become now of all her plans for the girl's happy future? Of what use had been all these years of isolation and subterfuge, if at the end Tamakatsura must be handed over to this coarse and unscrupulous barbarian?

It would indeed have astonished Tayū to know that any one in Hizen considered him in such a light as this. He had always regarded his attentions to women as favours bestowed; he flattered himself moreover that he knew as well as any man how to conduct a gallant correspondence, and his letters began to arrive thick and fast. They were written in a clean, bold hand on thick Chinese paper, heavily scented. It was evident indeed that he regarded himself as no mean calligrapher. His style of composition was not an agreeable one, being very tortuous and affected. Soon he made up his mind that the time had come for him to call

in person, and he arranged with the brothers to meet him
at their mother's house. Tayū was a man of about thirty,
tall and solidly built. He was far from ill-looking; but
he had the power (which he frequently exercised) of assuming
the most repulsively ferocious expression. This, however,
was reserved for his followers and opponents. When in
a good temper and engaged upon errands of love he adopted
an entirely different voice and manner. You would have
thought indeed that some little bird was chirruping, so
dexterously did he reduce his rough bass to a small silvery
fluting: 'As a lover, I ought to have come after dark,
ought I not? Isn't that what courting means—coming
at night? So I was always told. What extraordinary
weather for a spring evening! In autumn of course one
expects it. . . .'

Upon a strict undertaking that she would not provoke
Tayū in any way, the old lady's sons had allowed her to
see him. He now turned to her saying: 'Madam, though
I never had the pleasure of meeting your late husband, I
knew him to be a kind-hearted and upright gentleman. I
always hoped that I might one day have an opportunity
of showing him how much I appreciated his excellent
qualities, and it was with deep regret that I heard of his
untimely decease. But though I can no longer do him
any service, I hope that you will allow me to show my regard
for him in some practical way. There is, I think, a young
lady here, (I am right, am I not?) a ward of yours, or
relative of some sort? If I venture to speak of her, it is
with the greatest deference and respect; for I understand
that she is of extremely high birth. I assure you that,
were I ever privileged to make the acquaintance of such a
person, I should kneel before her like a slave, dedicate my
life to her service, humbly petition her. . . . But I see
that you are looking at me somewhat askance. You have

heard stories no doubt. . . . Believe me, there is no truth in them. I have in the past admired one or two of our simple country girls; but surely you can understand that *this* would be a very different matter. Should you admit me to the friendship of your exalted kinswoman, I would set her up as my paragon, my empress, my all-in-all. . . .' He made many fair speeches of this kind. At last the old nurse answered: 'I should indeed consider my granddaughter singularly fortunate to have aroused the interest of so distinguished a gentleman as yourself, were it not for the fact that nature has played upon her a cruel trick at birth. . . . Sir, I have seldom spoken of this to any one before; but I must assure you that the poor girl's unhappy condition has for years past been a sore trouble to me. As for offering her hand in marriage to any one—that is entirely out of the question. . . .' 'Pray don't make so many apologies,' cried Tayū. 'Were she the most blear-eyed, broken-legged creature under Heaven, I'd have her put right for you in a very short while. The truth of the matter is, the Gods and Buddhas in the temples round here owe a good deal to me, and I can make them do pretty much whatever I choose. . . .' So he bragged; but when, assuming that his offer had already been accepted, he began pressing the old lady to name a day, she hastily changed the subject, saying that summer would soon be coming, that the farmers were needing rain, plying him in fact with all the usual topics of the countryside. He felt that before he left he ought to recite a few verses of poetry, and after a long period of silent meditation, he produced the following:

    If she does not want to be married,
    I shall go to the pine-tree Bay
    And complain to the God of the Mirror;[1]
    Then I need hardly say
    That I shall get my way.

[1] The God of the Sacred Mirror, at Matsura, in Hizen.

'I don't think that's such a bad poem,' he said smiling awkwardly. The nurse was in far too agitated a condition to indulge in literary pastimes. Utterly unable to produce any sort of reply, she begged her daughters to answer in her stead. 'But mother darling,' the young ladies protested, 'if *you* cannot think of anything to say, still less can we. . . .' At last after much painful cogitation, the old lady recited the following poem, speaking as though she were addressing herself as much as him: 'Unkind were it indeed should the Guardian of the Mirror frustrate the prayers of one[1] who year on year hath been his and his alone.' 'What's that?' cried Tayū rushing towards her. 'How dare you say such a thing?' So sudden was his onrush that Shōni's wife jumped almost out of her skin, and she turned pale with fright. Fortunately her daughters were not so easily scared, and one of them, laughing as though an absurd misunderstanding had occurred, at once said to Tayū: 'What mother meant was this: she hopes that after all the trouble she has taken praying to the Gods of Matsura on our little niece's behalf, they will not allow the poor girl's deformity to turn you against her. But dear mother is getting old and it is not always easy to make out what she is saying.' 'Oho! Yes, yes, I see,' he said, nodding his head reflectively. 'I don't know how I came to misunderstand it. Ha! ha! Very neatly expressed. I expect you look upon me as a very uncultivated, provincial person. And so I should be, if I were at all like the other people round here. But I've been very fortunate; you would not find many men even at the City who have had a better education than I. You'd be making a great mistake if you set me down as a plain, countrified sort of man. As a matter of fact, there's nothing I have not studied.' He would very much have liked to try his hand

[1] Herself.

at a second poem; but his stock of ideas was exhausted and he was obliged to take leave.

The fact that two of her sons had openly sided with Tayū increased the old lady's terror and despair. All she could now think of was to spirit the girl away from Tsukushi as rapidly and secretly as possible. She besought the other son, Bugo no Suke, to devise some means of conducting the girl to Kyōto; but Bugo no Suke answered: 'I wish I could; but I do not see how it is to be done. There is not a soul on the island who will help me. We three used to hang together in old times; but now they say I am Tayū's enemy and will have nothing to do with me. And with Tayū against one it is a difficult thing in these parts to stir hand or foot, let alone take passage for several persons in an out-going ship. I might find I was doing Lady Tamakatsura a very ill turn. . . .'

But though no one had told the girl of what was going on, she somehow or other seemed to know all about it. She was in a state of the wildest agitation, and Bugo no Suke heard her declare in tones of the utmost horror that she intended to take her own life rather than accept the fate which was in store for her. Bugo was certain that this was no empty threat, and by a tremendous effort he managed to collect a sum sufficient to cover the expenses of the journey. His mother, now getting on in years, was determined not to end her days in Tsukushi. But she was growing very infirm, and it would be impossible for her to accompany them did not one of her daughters consent to come and look after her. The younger sister, Ateki, had been married for several years; but Bugo no Suke prevailed upon her at last to abandon her home and take charge of their mother on the journey. The elder sister had been married much longer; her family was already large and it was obviously impossible for her to get away. The travellers were obliged to leave home hastily late one night and embark at once; for they had suddenly heard that Tayū, who had gone home to Higo, was expected back in Hizen early next day (the twelfth of the fourth month), and he would doubtless lose no time in claiming his bride.

There were distressing scenes of farewell. It seemed unlikely that the elder sister would ever see her mother again. But Ateki took the parting much more calmly; for though Tsukushi had been her home for so long, she was by no means sorry to leave the place, and it was only when someone pointed back to the Matsura temple and Ateki scanning the quay-side recognized the very spot where she had said goodbye to her sister, that she felt at all downcast at the thought of the journey before her. 'Swiftly we row,' she sang; 'the Floating Islands vanish in the mist and, pilotless as they, I quit life's anchorage to drift amid the tempests of a world unknown.' 'No longer men but playthings of the wind are they who in their misery must needs take ship upon the uncertain pathways of the deep.' So Tamakatsura replied, and in utter despair she flung herself face downward upon her seat, where she lay motionless for many hours.

The news of her flight soon leaked out, and eventually reached Tayū's ears. He was not the man to let his prey slip from him in this manner, and though for an instant he was so angry and surprised that he could do nothing at all, he soon pulled himself together, hired a light skiff and set out in pursuit. It was a vessel specially constructed for swift launching, and the wind was blowing hard from shore. He shot across the harbour at an immense speed, with every inch of sail spread, and a moment later was through the Clanging Breakers. Launched upon the calmer waters of the open sea his craft scudded along more swiftly than ever Seeing a small boat chasing after them at reckless speed the captain of the pursued vessel imagined that pirates were on his track and pressed on towards the nearest port. Only Tamakatsura and her companions knew that in that rapidly approaching craft there was one who, by them at any rate, was far more to be dreaded than the most ruthless pirate. Louder and louder beat the poor girl's heart ; so loud indeed that the noise of the breakers seemed to her to have stopped. At last they entered the bay of Kawajiri. Tayū's vessel was no longer in sight, and as their ship approached the harbour, the fugitives began to breathe again. One of the sailors was singing a snatch of the song :

> So I pressed on from China Port to Kawajiri Bay
> With never a thought for my own sad love or the babe
> that wept on her knee.

He sang in an expressionless, monotonous voice, but the melancholy tune caught Bugo no Suke's fancy and he found himself joining in : ' With never a thought . . .' Yes ; he too had left behind those who were dearest to him, with little thought indeed of what was to become of them. Even the two or three sturdy youths who worked for him in the house would have been some comfort to his wife and babes. But these young fellows had clamoured to go with him and he weakly consented. He pictured to himself how Tayū, maddened by the failure of his pursuit, would rush back to Hizen and wreak his vengeance upon the defenceless families of those who had worked against him. How far would he go ? What exactly would he do ? Bugo no Suke now realized that in planning this flight he had behaved with the wildest lack of forethought ; all his self-confidence vanished, and so hideous were the scenes which his imagination conjured up before him that he broke down altogether and sat weeping with his head

L

on his knees. Like the ransomed prisoner in Po Chü-i's poem,[1] though returning to his native place, he had left wife and child to shift for themselves amid the Tartar hordes. His sister Ateki heard him sobbing and could well understand his dismay. The plight of those who had remained at Hizen was indeed a wretched one. Most of all she pitied the few old followers and servants who had consented to come with them from the Capital long ago, believing that in five years they would be back again in their homes. To leave these faithful old people in the lurch seemed the basest of treacheries. They had always (she and her brother) been used to speaking of the City as their ' home '; but now that they were drawing near to it they realized that though it was indeed their native place, there was not within it one house where they were known, one friend or acquaintance to whom they could turn. For this lady's sake they had left what for most of their lives had been their world, their only true home—had committed their lives to the hazard of wind and wave; all this without a moment's reflection or misgiving. And now that their precious cargo was within hail of port, what were they to do with her? How were they to approach her family, make known her presence, prove her identity? Endlessly though they had discussed these points during the journey, they could arrive at no conclusion, and it was with a sense of helplessness and bewilderment that they hurried into the City.

In the Ninth Ward they chanced to hear of an old acquaintance of their mother's who was still living in the neighbourhood, and here they managed to procure temporary lodgings. The Ninth Ward does indeed count as part of Kyōto; but it is an immense distance from the centre, and no one of any consequence lives there. Thus in their effort to find

[1] See my *170 Chinese Poems*, p. 130.

some influential person who would help them to fulfil their mission, the brother and sister encountered only the strangest types of market-women and higglers. Autumn was coming on, they had achieved nothing and there seemed no reason to suppose that the ensuing months would be any more profitable than those which they had just wasted. Ateki who had relied entirely upon her brother and imagined him capable of dealing with any situation that arose, was dismayed to discover that in the City he was like a waterbird on shore. He hung about the house, had no notion how to make enquiries or cultivate fresh acquaintances, and was no better able to look after himself than the youths he had brought with him from Tsukushi. These young fellows, after much grumbling, had indeed mostly either found employment in the neighbourhood or gone back to their native province. It grieved Ateki beyond measure that her brother should be thus stranded in the Capital without occupation or resource, and she bewailed his lot day and night. 'Come, come, Sister,' he would say to her, 'on my account you have no cause to be uneasy. I would gladly come a good deal further than we have travelled and put up with many another month of hardship and waiting, if only I could get our young lady back among the friends who ought to be looking after her. We may have spoilt our own prospects, you and I; but what should we be feeling like to-day, if we consented to let that monster carry her off to his infamous den? But it is my opinion that the Gods alone can help us in our present pass. Not far from here is the great temple of Yawata where the same God is worshipped as in our own Yawata Temples at Hakozaki and Matsura, where mother used to take the young lady to do her penances. Those two temples may be a long way off, but the same God inhabits all three, and I believe that her many visits to Hakozaki and Matsura would now stand her in good stead. What if she were to go to the Temple here and perform a service of thanksgiving for her safe journey to the Capital?' Bugo no Suke made enquiries in the neighbourhood and found out that one of the Five Abbots, a very holy man with whom Shōni had been well acquainted, was still alive. He obtained an interview with the old priest and arranged that Tamakatsura should be allowed to visit the Temple.

After this they visited a succession of holy places. At last Bugo no Suke suggested a pilgrimage to the Temple of the Hasegawa Kwannon. 'There is no deity in Japan,' he said, 'who has in recent times worked so many miracles as this Goddess of Hatsuse. I am told that the fame of her shrine has spread even to China,[1] and far off though Tsukushi is, I know that Lady Tamakatsura has for years past been deeply interested in the achievements of this Divinity and shown an exemplary piety towards her. I believe that a visit to Hatsuse would do more for our young lady than anything else.' It was decided that, to give it a greater significance, the pilgrimage should be made on foot and, despite her great age and infirmity, the old nurse would not be left behind. Tamakatsura, wholly unused to such experiences, felt scared and wretched as, pilgrims in front and behind, she tramped wearily on, turning to right or left when she was bid, but otherwise too deeply buried in her own thoughts to notice what went on around her. What had she done, she asked herself over and over again, to deserve this downtrodden existence? And as she dragged foot after foot along the dusty road she prayed earnestly

---

[1] There is a story in Japan that the wife of the Chinese Emperor Hsi Tsung (874–888 A.D.) was so ugly that she was nicknamed 'Horse-head.' In obedience to a dream she turned to the East and prayed to the Kwannon of Hasegawa in Japan. Instantly there appeared before her a figure carrying Kwannon's sacred water-vessel. He dashed the water over her face and she became the most beautiful woman in China.

to Buddha, saying ' O Much-Honoured One, if my mother is indeed no longer in this world, grant that, wherever it be, her soul may look upon me with compassion and her prayers bring me quick release, that I may take refuge in the place where her spirit dwells. And if she is still alive, grant, O Buddha, that I may one day meet her face to face.' So she prayed, and while she did so suddenly remembered that it was a useless prayer. For she was very young when Yūgao disappeared, had only the haziest recollection of her appearance, and even if the prayer were answered, would certainly pass her mother unrecognized! Dismal as these reflections would at any time have been, they were doubly so now, worn out as she was by the fatigue of the journey. The party had indeed travelled at a very leisurely pace and it was not till the hour of the Snake, on the fourth day, that they at last reached Tsuba Market.[1] Tamakatsura was by this time more dead than alive; they attempted to improvise a carrying-chair, but the pain in her legs was so great that she could not bear to be moved, and there was nothing for it but to let her rest at the inn.

The party consisted of Bugo no Suke, two bowmen and three or four very rough-looking boys to carry the luggage. The three ladies had their skirts tucked in at the belt like country-women, and were attended only by two aged crones who looked like broken-down charwomen. It would indeed have been impossible to guess that any person of quality was among them.

They spent the time till dusk in trimming their holy lamps and preparing such other emblems and offerings as are brought by pilgrims to the Hasegawa Shrine.

Going his rounds at nightfall the priest who owned the inn came upon the two decrepit old serving-women calmly making a bed for Tamakatsura in a corner of the best

[1] A short distance from the Hasegawa Temple.

room of the house. 'These quarters have been engaged for the night by a gentlewoman who may arrive at any minute,' he said in consternation. 'Be off with you at once! Just fancy, without so much as a "by your leave"!' They were still staring at him helplessly, when there was a noise at the door and it became evident that the expected guests had actually arrived. They too seemed to have come on foot. There were two gentlewomen, very well-conditioned, and quite a number of attendants both male and female. Their baggage was on the backs of some four or five horses, and though they wore plain liveries it was evident that the grooms were in good service. The landlord was determined that the newcomers should have the quarters which he had intended for them; but the intruders showed no signs of moving, and he stood scratching his head in great perplexity. It did indeed go to the hearts of Tamakatsura's old servants to turn her out of the corner where she was so comfortably established and pack her away into the back room. But it was soon apparent that the only alternative was to seek quarters in a different inn, and as this would have been both humiliating and troublesome they made the best of a bad job and carried their mistress to the inner room, while others of the party either took shelter in the outhouses or squeezed themselves and their belongings into stray angles and corners of the main house.

The new arrivals did not after all seem to be of such rank and consequence as the priest had made out. But it was hard to guess what manner of people they might be; for they concealed themselves scrupulously from the gaze of their fellow-guests and hardly spoke to one another at all.

In point of fact, the person to whom Lady Tamakatsura had been thus unceremoniously compelled to give place was none other than her mother's faithful maid, Ukon! For years past it had been the one comfort of the solitary and grief-stricken old lady's existence to make this pilgrimage, and Genji had always assisted her to do so with as much comfort as possible. So familiar was the journey that it no longer seemed to her in any way formidable; but having come on foot she was quite ready for a rest, and immediately lay down upon the nearest couch. Beside her was a thin partition of plaited reeds. Behind it she could hear people moving about, and presently some one entered who seemed to be carrying a tray of food. Then she heard a man's voice saying: 'Please take this to my Lady. Tell her I am very sorry it is so badly served; but I have done the best I can.' From the tone in which he spoke it was evident that the lady to whom these apologies were to be conveyed was a person far above him in social position. Ukon's curiosity was aroused. She peeped through a crack in the partition, and at once had the impression that she had seen the young man before. Who could it be? She racked her brains, but could not imagine. It would indeed have been strange had she been able to identify Bugo no Suke, who was a mere child when she last saw him, while now he was a full-grown man, much bronzed from exposure to the sun and winds of Tsukushi, and dressed in the poorest clothes. 'Sanjō, my Lady is asking for you.' So Bugo no Suke now cried, and to her astonishment Ukon saw that the old woman who answered to this name was also certainly some one whom she had once known. But here there could be no mistake. This Sanjō was the one who had been in service with Ukon in Yūgao's house, and had afterwards (like Ukon herself) been one of the few servants whom Yūgao took with her to the house in the Fifth Ward. It seemed like a dream. Who was the Lady whom they were accompanying? She strained her eyes; but the bed in the room behind the partition was surrounded by screens and there was no possibility of seeing its occupant. She had made up her mind to accost the maid Sanjō and question her, when part of her doubt resolved itself spontaneously: the man must be that boy of Shōni's, . . . the one they used to call Hyōtōda, and the lady towards whom they showed such deference could be no other than Tamakatsura, Yūgao's child by Tō no Chūjō. In wild excitement she called to Sanjō by name; but the old woman was busy serving the supper and for the moment she took no notice. She was very cross at being called away from her work like this, but whoever it was that wanted her seemed to be in a great hurry, and presently she arrived, exclaiming: 'I can't make it out. I've spent the last twenty years in service on the island of Tsukushi, and here's a lady from Kyōto calling for me by my own name, as though she knew all about me. Well, Madam, I am called Sanjō. But I think it must be another Sanjō that you are wanting.' As she drew near Ukon noticed that the old woman was wearing the most extraordinary narrow-sleeved overall on top of her frumpy old dress. She had grown enormously stout. The sight of her brought a sudden flush of humiliation to Ukon's cheeks, for she realised that she herself was an old woman, and as Sanjō now looked to her, so must she, Ukon, for years past have appeared to all eyes save her own. 'Look again! Do you not know me?' she said at last, looking straight into Sanjō's face. 'Why, to be sure I do!' cried the old lady, clapping her hands, 'you were in service with my Lady. I was never so glad in my life. Where have you been hiding our dear mistress all this while? . . . Of course she is with you now?' and in the midst of her excitement Sanjō began to weep; for the encounter had brought back to her mind the days when she was young. What times those had been! And how long, how cruelly long ago it all was! 'First,' answered Ukon gravely, 'you must give me a little of your news. Is nurse with you? And what has happened to the baby girl . . . and Ateki, where is she?' For the moment Ukon could not bear to dash Sanjō's hope to the ground; moreover it was so painful to her to speak of Yūgao's death that she now listened in silence to Sanjō's tale: mother, brother and sister were all there. Tamakatsura was grown to be a fine young lady and was with them too. 'But here I am talking,' said Sanjō at last, 'when I ought to have run straight in to tell nurse, . . .' and with this she disappeared. After their first surprise the chief feeling of Ateki and her mother, upon the reception of this news, was one of indignation against Ukon, whom they supposed to have left their mistress in hiding all these years, callously indifferent to the suspense and misery of all her friends. 'I don't feel that I want to see her,' said the old nurse at last, nodding in the direction of Ukon's room, 'but I suppose I ought to go.' No sooner, however, was she sitting by Ukon's couch, with all the curtains drawn aside, than both of them burst into tears. 'What has become of her, where is my lady?' the nurse sobbed. 'You cannot imagine what I have been through in all these years. I have prayed again and again that some sign, some chance word, some dream might tell me where she was hiding. But not one breath of news came to us, and at last I thought terrible things—that she must be very far away indeed. Yes, I have even imagined that she must be dead, and fallen then into such despair that I hated my own life and would have ended it too, had not my love for the little girl whom she left with me held my feet from the Paths of Night. And even so, you see for yourself what I am. . . . It is but a faint flicker of life. . . .'

In this strain the nurse spoke on, supposing all the while that Lady Yūgao herself was somewhere not far away. 'How shall I tell her? What am I to say?' The same questions that tormented Ukon's brain during those first days after the funeral returned to her now with redoubled urgency. But this could not go on; it was impossible not to speak; and Ukon suddenly broke in upon the old nurse's outpourings: 'Listen!' she said. 'It is no use my telling you how it happened. . . . But Lady Yūgao died a long while ago.'

After this there was silence, broken at last by the agonized and convulsive sobbing of these three old women.

It was growing dark, and now with lamps lit and offerings in their hands the pilgrims were about to start for the temple. The women clung to one another till the last moment and, still scarce knowing what they did, were about to set out upon the road together, when Ukon suddenly bethought herself of the astonishment which her attendants must be feeling at this strange addition to the party; moreover Bugo no Suke had as yet heard nothing of the meeting, and for the moment the old nurse had not the heart to enter into a long explanation of what had occurred. The two parties accordingly separated, Ukon scanning with curiosity the pilgrims who filed past her into the street. Among them was a girl, very poorly dressed; her hair was caught up in a thin summer scarf, which held it tight but did not conceal it. In the procession she walked some way ahead, but even the momentary back view which Ukon was thus able to obtain convinced her that the girl was not only of exceptional beauty, but also of a rank in life very different from that of the shabby pilgrims who tramped beside her. When at last they arrived the service was already in full swing and the temple crowded to overflowing; for most of the pilgrims in whose company the party from Tsukushi had set out from the city were sturdy-legged peasants and working people who had pressed on through Tsuba without a moment's rest and long ago secured their places in the holy building. Ukon, being an habitual visitor to the temple, was at once conducted to a place which had been reserved for her immediately to the right of the Main Altar. But Tamakatsura and her party, who had never been there before and had, moreover, the misfortune to fall into the hands of a very unenterprising verger, found themselves bundled away into the western transept. Ukon from her place of privilege soon caught sight of them and beckoned to them to join her. After a hasty consultation with her son, during the course of which the nurse appeared to be explaining, so far as was possible in a few words, who Ukon was and why she had beckoned, the women of the party pushed their way towards the altar, leaving Bugo no Suke and his two followers where the incompetent sacristan had placed them. Though Ukon was in herself a person of no consequence, she was known to be in Genji's service, and that alone, as she had long ago discovered, was sufficient to secure her from interference, even in such a place as this. Let the herd gape if they chose and ask one another with indignation why two ill-dressed women from the provinces, who had arrived at the last minute, were calmly seating themselves in places reserved for the gentry. Ukon was not going to have her young lady wedged into a corner or jostled by the common crowd. She longed to get into conversation at once; but the critical moment in the service had just arrived and she was obliged to remain kneeling with head lowered. So it had come at last, this meeting for which she had prayed year in and year out! And now it only remained that Genji, who had so often begged her to find out what had become of Yūgao's child, should welcome the discovery (as she felt sure he would) and by his influence restore to this unhappy lady the place at Court to which her birth entitled her. Such indeed was the purport of her prayer as she now knelt at the altar by Tamakatsura's side.

In the crowded temple were pilgrims from every province in the land. Among them the wife of the Governor of Yamato Province was conspicuous for her elegance and consequential air, for most of the worshippers were simple country people, very unfashionably dressed. Sanjō, who, after so many years passed in barbarous Tsukushi, had quite forgotten how town people get themselves up for occasions such as this, could not take her eyes off the magnificent lady. 'Hark ye,' she said at last in an awe-struck whisper to the nurse, 'I don't know what you're a-going to pray for to our Lady Kwannon. But I'm a-praying that if our dear young lady can't be wife to the Lord-Lieutenant [1] (as I have always hoped she might be), then let her marry a Governor of this fine province of Yamato. For a grander lady than that one there I'm sure I've never seen! "Just do that," I said to Lady Kwannon in my prayer, "and you'll be surprised at the wonderful offerings poor old Sanjō will bring to your altar."' And smiting her forehead with her hand, she began again to pray with immense fervour. 'Well,' said Ukon, astonished by this extraordinary speech. 'You *have* become a regular country-woman; there's no doubt about it. Don't you know that Madam is Tō no Chūjō's own daughter? That's enough in itself; but now that Prince Genji, who for her mother's sake, would do anything for her, has come into his own again, do you suppose there is any gentleman in the land who would be too good for her? It would be a sad come-down indeed if she were to become some paltry Governor's wife!' But Sanjō was not thus to be put out of countenance.

[1] Of Tsukushi.

'Pardon me,' she said hotly; 'I don't know much about your Prince Genjis or such-like. But I do know that I've seen the Lord-Lieutenant's wife and all her train on their way to the temple of Our Lady Kwannon at Kiyomizu, and I can tell you the Emperor himself never rode out in such state! So don't try to put *me* in my place!' and unabashed the old woman resumed her attitude of prayer.

The party from Tsukushi had arranged to stay three days within the precincts of the temple, and Ukon, though she had not at first intended to stay for so long, now sent for her favourite priest and asked him to procure her a lodging; for she hoped that these days of Retreat would afford her a chance of talking things over quietly with the old nurse. The priest knew by long experience just what she wanted written on the prayer-strips which he was to place in the holy lamps, and at once began scribbling 'On behalf of Lady Fujiwara no Ruri I make these offerings and burn....' 'That is quite right,' said Ukon (for Fujiwara no Ruri was the false name by which she had always referred to Tamakatsura in discussing the matter with her spiritual adviser); 'all the usual texts will do, but I want you to pray harder than ever to-day. For I have at last been fortunate enough to meet the young lady and am more anxious than ever that my prayer for her happiness may be fulfilled.'

'There!' said the priest triumphantly. 'Was there ever a clearer case? Met her? Dear Madam, of course you have. That is just what I have been praying for night and day ever since you were here last.' And much encouraged by this success he set to work once more and was hard at it till daylight came. Then the whole party, at Ukon's invitation, moved to the lodgings that her *daitoko*[1] had reserved for her. Here if anywhere she felt that she

[1] I hesitate to use the word 'Confessor.'

would be able to embark upon the story which she found so difficult to tell.

At last she was able to have a good look at the child for whose happiness she had prayed during so many years. Tamakatsura was undeniably ill-dressed and somewhat embarrassed in the presence of strangers whom she felt to be taking stock of her appearance; but Ukon was unfeignedly delighted with her, and burst out: 'Though I am sure I never had any right to expect it, it so happens that I have had the good luck to see as much of fine ladies and gentlemen as any serving-woman in the City. There's Prince Genji's own lady, Madam Murasaki—I see her nearly every day. What a handsome young thing! I thought there could be no one to compare with her. But now there's this little daughter from Akashi.[1] Of course she is only a child at present. But she grows prettier every day, and it would not surprise me if in the end she put all our other young ladies to shame. Of course they dress that child in such fine clothes and make such a fuss of her that it is hard to compare her with other children. Whereas our young lady (she whispered to the nurse) dressed as she is at this very minute, would hold her own against any of them, I dare swear she would. I have sometimes heard Prince Genji himself say that of the many beauties whom he has known, whether at Court or elsewhere since his father's time, the present Emperor's mother [2] and the little girl born at Akashi stand apart from all the rest. Not one other has he known of whom you could say without fear of contradiction from any living soul that she was perfection itself from tip to toe. Those were his words; but for my own part I never knew Lady Fujitsubo; and charming though the little princess from Akashi may be, she is still little more than a baby, and when Prince Genji speaks

[1] Now about six years old.   [2] Fujitsubo.

of her in these terms, he is but guessing at the future. He did not mention Lady Murasaki at all in this conversation, but I know quite well that in his heart of hearts he puts her above all the rest—so far indeed that he would never dream of mentioning her in such a reckoning as this; and, great gentleman though he is, I have heard him tell her again and again that she deserves a husband a thousand times better than he. I have often thought that having had about him at the start such peerless ladies as those whom I have mentioned, he might well chance to end his days without once finding their like. But now I see that I was wrong; for Madam here is fully their match. Trust me, I shall not say anything high-flown, nor would he listen to fine phrases such as " The light that shines from her countenance is brighter than Buddha's golden rays." I shall just say " See her, and you will not be disappointed." ' So said Ukon, smiling benevolently at the company. But the nurse, who knew nothing, it must be remembered, of Genji's connection with Yūgao nor of any reason why he should interest himself in Tamakatsura, was somewhat disconcerted. 'I am sure I thank you very heartily for suggesting this,' she said; 'and indeed you will believe that no one cares more for this young lady's future than I do, when I tell you that I gave up house and hearth, quitted sons, daughters and friends, and came back to the City which is now as strange to me as some foreign town—all this only for Lady Tamakatsura's sake; for I hated to see her wasting her youth in a dismal place where there was not a soul for her to speak to. . . . No indeed! I should be the last person to interfere with any plan that promises to bring her to her own again; and I am sure that among the grand people whom you have mentioned she would have a much better chance of doing something for herself in the world. . . . But I must say that, with her father at Court all the while, it seems to me a queer thing to quarter her on a perfect stranger. Perhaps I do not quite understand what you propose . . . but wouldn't it be more natural to tell her father that she is here and give him a chance of acknowledging her? That is what we have been trying to do, and we shall be very glad if you would help us.' The conversation was overheard by Tamakatsura; she felt very uncomfortable at being thus publicly discussed and, shifting impatiently in her seat, sat with her back to the talkers. 'I see you think I am taking too much upon myself,' said Ukon. 'I know quite well that I am no one at all. But all the same Prince Genji often sends for me to wait upon him and likes me sometimes to tell him about anything interesting that I have seen or heard. On one occasion I told him the story of Madam here—how she had been left motherless and carried off to some distant province (for so much I had heard). His Highness was much moved by the story, begged me to make further enquiries and at once let him know all that I could discover. . . .' 'I do not doubt,' said the nurse, 'that Prince Genji is a very fine gentleman. But it seems from what you tell me that he has a wife of whom he is fond and several other ladies living with him as well. He may for the moment have been interested in your story; but I cannot imagine why you should suppose he wants to adopt her, when her own father is so close at hand. It would oblige me if you would first help us to inform Tō no Chūjō of Madam's arrival. If nothing comes of that . . .'

Ukon could keep up her end no longer. Unless she told the nurse of Genji's connection with Yūgao, further conversation would be impossible. And having got so far as to confess that Genji had known Yūgao, Ukon plunging desperately on finally managed to tell the whole terrible story. 'Do not think,' she said at last, 'that Genji has forgotten all this, or will ever do so. It has been his one desire since that day to find some means of expiating, in however small a degree, the guilt which brought my lady to her unhappy end; and often I have heard him long that he might one day be able to bring such happiness to Lady Yūgao's child as would in some sort make amends for all that she had lost. Indeed, having few children, he has always planned, if she could but be found, to adopt her as his own, and he begged me to speak of her always as a child of his, whom he had placed with country folk to be nursed.

'But in those days I had seen very little of the world and was so much scared by all that had happened that I dared not go about making enquiries. At last I chanced one day to see your husband's name in a list of provincial clerks. I even saw him, though at some distance, the day he went to the Prime Minister's palace to receive confirmation of his new appointment. I suppose I ought to have spoken to him then; but somehow or other I could not bring myself to do so. Sometimes I imagined that you had left Lady Tamakatsura behind, at the house in the Fifth Ward; for the thought of her being brought up as a little peasant girl on the island was more than I could endure. . . .'

So they spent the day, now talking, now praying, or again amusing themselves by watching the hordes of pilgrims who were constantly arriving at the temple gate. Under their windows ran a river called the Hatsuse, and Ukon now recited the acrostic poem: 'Had I not entered the gate that the Twin Fir-Trees guard, would the old river of our days e'er have resumed its flow?' To this Tamakatsura answered: 'Little knew I of those early days as this river knows of the hill from whence it sprang.' She sat gently weeping. But Ukon made no effort to comfort her, feeling that now all was on the right path. Considering Tamakatsura's upbringing no one would have blamed her if there had been a little country roughness, a shade of over-simplicity in her manner. Ukon could not imagine how the old nurse had achieved so remarkable a feat of education, and thanked her again and again for what she had done. Yūgao's ways had till the last been timid, docile, almost child-like; but about her daughter there was not a trace of all this. Tamakatsura, despite her shyness, had an air of self-assurance, even of authority. 'Perhaps,' thought Ukon to herself, 'Tsukushi is not by any means so barbarous a place as one is led to suppose.' She began thinking of all the Tsukushi people she had known; each individual she could recall was more coarse-mannered and uneducated than the last. No; nurse's achievement remained a mystery.

At dusk they all went back to the temple, where they stayed that night and most of the following day, absorbed in various spiritual exercises. A cold autumn wind was blowing from the valley, and at its cruel touch the miseries of the past rose up one by one before Shōni's widow as she knelt shivering at the Main Altar. But all these sad memories vanished instantly at the thought that the child upon whom she had lavished her care would now take the place that was her birth-due. Ukon had told her about the careers of Tō no Chūjō's other children. They seemed all of them to be remarkably prosperous, irrespective of the rank of their various mothers, and this filled the old lady with an additional sense of security.

At last the moment came to part. The two women exchanged addresses and set out upon their different ways: Ukon to a little house Genji had given her, not far away from his new palace; the others to their lodgings in the Ninth Ward. No sooner had they parted than Ukon was suddenly seized with a panic lest Tamakatsura should attempt to evade her, as Yūgao had fled from Chūjō in days of old; and constantly running between her house and theirs, she had not a moment's peace of mind. It was soon time for Ukon to be back at the new palace, and she was not loath to end her holiday, for she was in a hurry to obtain an interview with Genji and inform him of her success. She could not get used to this new mansion, and from the moment she entered the gates she was always astonished by the vastness of the place. Yet so great was nowadays the number of coaches driving [1] in and out, that the crush was appalling and Ukon began to wonder if she would ever get to the house.

She was not sent for that night, and lay tossing about on her bed, thinking how best to make known her discovery. Next day, though it so happened that a large number of ladies-in-waiting and other young people had just returned from their holidays, Murasaki sent specially for old Ukon, who was delighted by this compliment. 'What a long holiday you have been having!' cried Genji to her when she entered. 'When you were last here you looked like some dismal old widow-lady, and here you are looking quite skittish! Something very nice must have happened to you; what was it?' 'Sir,' she answered, 'it is quite true that I have been away from the City for a whole week; but I don't know whether anything has happened that you would call nice. I have been over the hills to Hatsuse (on foot too!), and came across someone whom I was glad to meet again.' 'Who was that?' asked Genji quickly, and she was about to tell him when it occurred to her that it would be much better to tell him separately, on some occasion when Murasaki was not present. But then perhaps the whole thing would come round to Murasaki's ears and her mistress would be offended that Ukon had not told her first. . . . It was a difficult situation. 'Well then if you

[1] Pulled by servants, the oxen being unyoked at the Gate.

must know...' Ukon was beginning, when suddenly there was a fresh incursion of visitors, and she was obliged to withdraw. But later in the day, when the great lamp had been brought in and Genji was sitting quietly with Murasaki, he said that he would soon be ready for bed, and sent for Ukon to give him his evening massage.

Lady Murasaki was now almost twenty-eight, but never (thought the old woman when she arrived) had she looked so handsome. It seemed indeed as though her full charm had only just matured. Ukon had not seen her mistress at close quarters for some months past, and could now have sworn that even in that short space of time Lady Murasaki had grown twice as handsome. And yet Ukon had no fears for Yūgao's daughter. There was indeed an undeniable difference between this splendid princess and the shy girl from Tsukushi. But it was only the difference between obscurity and success; a single turn of fortune would quickly redress the balance.

'I do not like being massaged by the new young maids,' Genji said to Ukon when she arrived. 'They let me see so plainly how much it bores them to do it. I much prefer some one I have known for a long time... you, for example.' No such preference had ever been noticed by those about him, and smiles were secretly exchanged. They realized that Genji had only said this in order to please and flatter the old lady. But it was far from true that any of them had ever been otherwise than delighted at the reception of such a command, and they thought the joke rather a tiresome one. 'Would you be angry with me, if I took to consorting with elderly ladies?' he whispered to Murasaki. 'Yes,' she nodded, 'I think I should. With you one never knows where one is. I should be very much perturbed....' All the while she was at work Genji amused the old lady with his talk. Never had Ukon seen him so lively and amiable. He had now placed the whole direction of public affairs in Tō no Chūjō's hands; the experiment was working well, and such was Genji's relief at escaping from the burden which had so long oppressed him that he found it impossible to be serious for a minute. To joke with Ukon, a very matter-of-fact old lady, was found by most people to be out of the question. But Genji had a peculiar gift of sympathy, which enabled him to penetrate the most obstinate gloom, the most imperturbable gravity.

'Tell me about the interesting person whom you have discovered,' he went on. 'I believe it is another of your holy men. You have brought him back here, and now I am to let him pray for me. Have I not guessed right?' 'No, indeed,' Ukon answered indignantly; 'I should never dream of doing such a thing!' And then, lowering her voice: 'I have become acquainted with the daughter of a lady whom I served long ago. . . . The mother came to a miserable end. . . . You will know of whom it is I am speaking.' 'Yes,' said Genji . . . 'I know well enough, and your news is indeed very different from anything I had imagined. Where has the child been during all these years?' 'In the country,' answered Ukon vaguely; this did not seem a good moment for going into the whole story. 'Some of the old servants took charge of the child,' she continued, 'and are still in her service now that she has grown up. They of course knew nothing of the circumstances under which their former mistress . . . It was torture to speak of it; but I managed at last to tell them. . . .' 'I think we had better talk about this some other time,' Genji interrupted, drawing Ukon aside. But Murasaki had overheard them. 'Pray do not trouble about me,' she said with a yawn. 'I am half-asleep in any case; and if it is something I am not to hear . . .' So saying she covered her ears with her sleeves.

'Is she as handsome as her mother?' Genji then asked. 'I did not at all expect that she would be,' answered Ukon. 'But I must say that I have seldom seen . . .' 'I am sure she is *pretty*,' he said. 'I wonder whether you mean anything more than that. Compared with my Lady . . . ?' and he nodded towards Lady Murasaki. 'No, indeed,' said Ukon hastily; 'that would be going too far. . . .' 'Come,' he said; 'it would not be going much farther than you go yourself. I can see that by your face. For my part, I must own to the usual vanity of parents. I hope that I shall be able to see in her some slight resemblance to myself.' He said this because he intended to pass off the girl as his own child, and was afraid that part of the conversation had been overheard. Having learnt so much, he could not resist the temptation to hear the whole of Ukon's story, and presently he took her into a side-room, where they could discuss the matter undisturbed. 'Well,' he said, when Ukon had satisfied his curiosity, 'I have quite made up my mind what to do with her. She shall come and live with me here. For years past I have constantly wondered what had become of her, and dreaded lest she should be throwing away her youth in some dismal, unfrequented place. I am delighted indeed that you have re-discovered her. My only misgiving concerns her father. I suppose I ought at once to tell him of her return. But I do not quite see how to set about it; for he knows nothing of my connection with Lady Yūgao, and I have never been able to see that there was any use in enlightening him. He has already more children than he knows what to do with, and the arrival in his house of a fully-grown girl, whom he has not set eyes on since she was a child-in-arms, would merely be a nuisance to him. It seems much simpler that I, who have so small a family, should take charge of her; and it is easy enough to give out that she is a daughter

of mine, whom I have been educating in the quiet of the country. If what you say of her is true, it is certain that she will be a great deal run after. The charge of such a girl needs immense tact and care; I do not think it would be fair to saddle Tō no Chūjō with so great a responsibility.'
'That shall be as your Highness decides,' answered Ukon. 'I am sure, at any rate, that if *you* do not tell Tō no Chūjō, no one else will. And for my part I had rather she should go to you than to any one else. For I am certain you are anxious to make what amends you can for your part in leading Yūgao to her miserable fate; and what better way could there be to do this, than by promoting her daughter's happiness by every means in your power?' 'The fact that I ruined the mother might to some people seem a strange reason for claiming custody of the child,' said Genji smiling; but his eyes were filled with tears. 'My love for her still fills a great part of my thoughts,' he said after a pause. 'You must think that a strange thing for me to say, considering how my household is now arranged. . . . And it is true that in the years since her death I have formed many deep attachments. But, believe it or not as you will, by no one has my heart ever been stirred as it was by your dear mistress in those far-off days. You have known me long enough to see for yourself that I am not one in whom such feelings lightly come and go. It has been an unspeakable comfort to me during all these years that to you at least I could sometimes talk of your mistress, sometimes ease my longing. But that was not enough. I yearned for some object dear to her upon which I could lavish ceaseless pains and care. What could be more to my purpose than that this orphaned child of hers should thus be entrusted to my protection?'

His next step must be a letter to Tamakatsura herself. He remembered Suyetsumu's extreme incapacity in this direction, and feared that Tamakatsura, after her strange upbringing, might prove to be a hundred times more hesitating and inefficient. It was therefore in order to know the worst as soon as possible that he now lost no time in addressing her. His letter was full of the friendliest assurances; in the margin was written the poem: 'It shows not from afar; but seek and you shall find it, the marsh-flower of the Island. For from the ancient stem new shoots for ever spring.'

Ukon herself was the bearer of this letter; she also reported much of what Genji had said to her, especially such expressions of cordiality and goodwill as would tend to allay Tamakatsura's apprehensions. He also sent many handsome stuffs and dresses, with presents for her nurse and other members of the party. With Murasaki's consent the Mistress-of-Robes had gone through all the store-cupboards and laid out before him an immense display of costumes, from which he chose those that were most distinctive in colour and design, thinking to astonish and delight an eye used to the home-spuns of Tsukushi.

Had all this kindness, nay even the smallest part of it, proceeded from her own father, Tamakatsura would indeed have been happy. But to be thus indebted to some one whom she had never seen and upon whom she had not the smallest claim, was an uncomfortable experience. As for taking up residence in his house—the prospect appalled her. But Ukon insisted that such an offer could not be refused; and those about her argued that so soon as she was decently set up in the world, her father would repent of his negligence and speedily lay claim to her. 'That a mere nobody like old Ukon should be in a position to do any service at all is in itself a miracle,' they said, ' and could not have happened were not some God or Buddha on our side. For her to send a message to Tō no Chūjō is, compared with what she has already done, the merest trifle, and so soon as we are all more comfortably settled . . .' Thus her friends encouraged her. But, whether she accepted his invitation or not, civility demanded that she must at least reply to his poem. She knew that he would regard her cadences and handwriting very critically, expecting something hopelessly countrified and out-of-date. This made the framing of an answer all the more embarrassing. She chose a Chinese paper, very heavily scented. 'Some fault there must be in the stem of this marsh-flower. Else it had not been left unheeded amid the miry meadows by the sea.' Such was her poem. It was written in rather faint ink and Genji, as he eagerly scanned it, thought the hand lacking in force and decision. But there was breeding and distinction in it, more indeed than he had dared to look for; and on the whole he felt much relieved.

The next thing was to decide in what part of the house she was to live. In Murasaki's southern wing there was not a room to spare. The Empress Akikonomu was obliged by her rank to live in considerable state. Etiquette forbade that she should ever appear without a numerous train of followers, and her suite had been designed to accommodate an almost indefinite number of gentlewomen. There was plenty of room for Tamakatsura here; but in such quarters she would tend to become lost amid the horde of Akikonomu's gentlewomen, and to put her in such a place at all would indeed seem as though he expected her to assist in waiting upon the Empress. The only considerable free space in the house was the wing which he had built to contain his official papers. These had for the most part been handed over to Tō no Chūjō, and what was still left could easily be housed elsewhere. The advantage of those quarters was that Tamakatsura would here be the close neighbour of the Lady from the Village of Falling Flowers, whose sensible and affectionate nature would, he was sure, prove a great comfort to the new arrival. And now that all was ready, it seemed to him impossible to instal Tamakatsura in his household without revealing to Murasaki the whole truth about the girl's identity and his own dealings with her mother. No sooner had he begun the story than he saw plainly enough that she was vexed with him for having made a mystery of the matter for so long. 'I see that you are vexed,' he said, 'that I did not tell you about all this before. But you have always known quite well that I had many such attachments as this in the days before I knew you, and I have never seen that there was any point in mentioning them, unless some special circumstance made it necessary to do so. In the present case, it is essential that some one should be acquainted with all the facts, and I chose you rather than another merely because you are a thousand times dearer to me than any of the rest.' Then he told her the whole story of his dealings with Yūgao. It was apparent to her that he was deeply moved, and at the same time that he took great pleasure in recalling every detail of their relationship. 'Conversation turns often upon such matters,' he said at last, 'and I have heard innumerable stories of women's blind devotion, even in cases where their love was in no degree reciprocated. Passion such as this is indeed rarely long withstood even by those who have gravely determined to rule out of their lives every species of romance; and I have seen many who have instantly succumbed. But such love as Yūgao's, such utter self-forgetfulness, so complete a surrender of the whole being to one single and ever-present emotion—I have never seen or heard of, and were she alive she would certainly be occupying no less important a place in my palace than, for example, the Lady of Akashi is occupying to-day. . . . In many ways, of course, she fell short of perfection, as indeed is bound to be the case. She was not of great intelligence, nor was her beauty flawless. But she was a singularly lovable creature. . . .' 'Were she as much in your good graces as the Lady of Akashi, she would have nothing to complain of . . .' broke in Murasaki suddenly; for the Akashi episode still rankled sore. The little princess,[1] who constantly visited Murasaki's rooms, was playing with her toys not far away, and Murasaki seeing her look so innocent and pretty, in her childlessness forgave Genji the infidelity which had brought to her so charming a little playmate and companion.

These things happened in the ninth month; but Tamakatsura's actual arrival could not take place for some while afterwards, for though her quarters had been chosen she still lacked attendants. The first thing was to find her some pretty pages and serving-girls. Even in Tsukushi the old nurse had managed to procure some very passable children to wait upon her; for it sometimes happened that some one from the City, having fallen upon evil days, would get stranded on the Island and be glad to place his boy or girl in a respectable home. But in the sudden flight from Tsukushi all these young people had been left behind. Orders were given to market-women and trades-people to keep their eyes open and report upon any suitable children whom they came across; and in this way, as could scarcely fail to happen in so vast a town, a fine batch of attendants was quickly brought together. Nothing was said to them about Tamakatsura's rank, and they were mustered in Ukon's own house, whither Tamakatsura herself now repaired, that her wardrobe might be finally inspected, her staff fitted out with proper costumes and instructed in their duties. The move to Genji's Palace took place in the tenth month. He had already visited the Lady from the

[1] The Lady of Akashi's daughter.

Village of Falling Flowers and prepared her for the arrival of her new neighbours: 'A lady to whom I was much attached, being seized with a sudden melancholy, fled from the Court and soon afterwards ended her days in a remote country place. She left behind a daughter, of whom I could for years obtain no news. All this happened many years ago and this daughter is now of course a full-grown woman; but though I have been making enquiries ever since it was only quite recently (and in the most accidental way) that I at last obtained a clue. I at once determined to invite her to my palace, and I am going to give her quarters close to yours, in the unused Record Office. To one motherless child of mine you have already shown infinite kindness, and have not, I think, found the care of him unduly irksome. If you will do for this new-comer what you have been doing for Prince Yūgiri, I shall be deeply thankful to you. She has been brought up in very humble and rustic surroundings. In many ways she must be ill-prepared for the life which she will lead in such a place as this. I hope that you will instruct her . . .' and he made many suggestions for Tamakatsura's polite education. 'I had no idea,' the Lady replied, 'that you had more than one daughter. However, I am extremely glad, if only for the Akashi child's sake. I am sure she will be delighted to find that she has a sister. . . .' 'The mother,' said Genji, 'was the most gentle and confiding creature I have ever encountered. This girl, Lady Tamakatsura, doubtless resembles her; and since you yourself are the easiest person to get on with . . .' 'I have so much time on my hands,' she answered quickly. 'Some one of my own sort to look after and advise a little. . . . That is just what I long for.'

Genji's own servants and retainers had been told nothing save that a strange lady was shortly to arrive. 'I wonder whom he has picked up this time?' one of them said. 'I don't believe this is a fresh affair,' said another. 'In all probability she is only some discarded mistress who needs looking after for a time. . . .'

The party arrived in three carriages. As Ukon had superintended every detail, the whole turn-out was quite adequately stylish, or at any rate did not betray such rusticity as to attract attention. On their arrival they found their quarters stacked with all sorts of presents from Genji. He gave them time to settle in, and did not call till late the same night. Long, long ago Tamakatsura used often to hear him spoken of in terms of extravagant admiration; 'Genji the Shining One,' that was what people had called him. All the rest she had forgotten; for hers had been a life from which tales of Courts and palaces seemed so remote that she had scarcely heeded them. And now when through a chink in her curtains-of-state she caught a glimpse of him—vague enough, for the room was lit only by the far distant rays of the great lamp beyond the partition—her feeling was one of admiration, but (could it be so, she asked herself) of downright terror.

Ukon had flung open both halves of the heavy main-door and was now obsequiously ushering him into the room. 'You should not have done that,' he protested. 'You are making too much of my entry. No such ceremonies are necessary when one inmate of this house takes it into his head to visit another,' and he seated himself alongside her curtained chair. 'This dim light too,' he continued, addressing Ukon, 'may seem to you very romantic. But Lady Tamakatsura has consented to make believe that she is my daughter, and family meetings such as this require a better illumination. Do you not agree?' And with this he slightly raised one corner of her curtain. She looked extremely shy and was sitting, as he now discovered, with face half-turned away. But he knew at once that as far as looks were concerned she was not going to cause him any anxiety. 'Could we not have a little more light?' he said, turning again to Ukon. 'It is so irritating. . . .' Ukon lit a candle and came towards them holding it aloft in her hand. 'It is rather heavy work to get started!' he whispered, smiling. 'Things will go better presently.' Even the way she hung her head, as though frightened of meeting his eyes, reminded him so vividly of Yūgao that it was impossible for him to treat her as a stranger; instinctively indeed he began to speak to her in a tone of complete familiarity as though they had shared the same house all their lives: 'I have been hunting high and low for you ever since you were a baby,' he said, 'and now that I have found you, and see you sitting there with a look that I know so well, it is more than I can bear. I wanted so much to talk to you, but now . . .' and he paused to wipe the tears from his eyes, whilst there rushed to his mind a thousand tender recollections of Yūgao and her incomparable ways. 'I doubt,' he said at last, reckoning up the years since her death, 'whether true parent has ever reclaimed a child after so long a search as I have made for you. Indeed so long a time has passed that you are already a woman of judgment and experience, and can tell me a far more interesting story of all that has befallen you on that island of yours than could be told by a mere child. I have that compensation at least for having met you so late. . . .'

What would she tell him? For a long while she hung her head in silence. At last she said shyly: 'Pray remember that like the leech-child,[1] at three years old I was set adrift

---

[1] The Royal Gods Izanagi and Izanami bore a leech-child; as at the age of three it could not stand, they cast it adrift in a boat. It made a song which said: 'I should have thought my daddy and mammy would have been sorry for me, seeing that at three years old I could not stand.' See vol. ii, p. 185.

upon the ocean. Since then I have been stranded in a place where only such things could befall me as to you would seem nothing at all.' Her voice died away at the end of the sentence with a half-childish murmur, exactly as her mother's had done long ago. 'I was " sorry for you " indeed,' he said, ' when I heard whither you had drifted. But I am going to see to it now that no one shall ever be sorry for you again.' She said no more that night; but her one short reply had convinced him that she was by no means a nonentity, and he went back to his own quarters feeling confident that there could be no difficulty in launching her upon a suitable career. ' Poor Tamakatsura has lived in the country for so long,' he said to Murasaki later, ' that it would not at all have surprised me to find her very boorish, and I was prepared to make every allowance. . . . But on the contrary she seems very well able to hold her own. It will be amusing to watch the effect upon our friends when it becomes known that this girl is living in the house. I can well imagine the flutter into which she will put some of them,—my half-brother Prince Sochi no Miya for example. The reason that quite lively and amusing people often look so gloomy when they come here is that there have been no attractions of this kind. We must make as much play with her as possible ; it will be such fun to see which of our acquaintances become brisker, and which remain as solemn as ever.' ' You are certainly the strangest " father " ! ' exclaimed Murasaki. The first thing you think of is how to use her as a bait to the more unprincipled among your friends. It is monstrous ! ' ' If only I had thought of it in time,' he laughed, ' I see now how splendidly you would have served for the same purpose. It was silly of me not to think of it ; but, somehow or other, I preferred to keep you all to myself.' She flushed slightly as he said this, looking younger and more charming than ever. Sending for his ink-stone Genji now wrote on a practising-slip the poem: 'Save that both she and I have common cause to mourn, my own is she no more than a false lock worn upon an aged head.'[1] Seeing him sigh heavily and go about muttering to himself, Murasaki knew that his love for Yūgao had been no mere boyish fancy, but an affair that had stirred his nature to its depths.

Yūgiri, having been told that a half-sister (of whose existence he had never heard) was come to live with them in the palace, and that he ought to make friends with her and make her feel at home, at once rushed round to her rooms, saying: 'I do not count for very much, I know; but since we are brother and sister, I think you might have sent for me before. If only I had known who you were, I would have been so glad to help you to unpack your things. I do think you might have told me. . . .' 'Poor young gentleman,' thought Ukon, who was close at hand; 'this is really too bad. How long will they let him go on in this style, thinking all the while she is his sister? I don't think it's fair. . . .'

The contrast between her present way of life and the days at Tsukushi was staggering. Here every elegance, every convenience appeared as though by magic; there the simplest articles could be procured only by endless contriving, and when found were soiled, dilapidated, out-of-date. Here Prince Genji claimed her as his daughter, Prince Yūgiri as his sister. . . . 'Now these,' thought old Sanjō, 'really are fine gentlemen. However I came to have such a high opinion of that Lord-Lieutenant I do not know!' And when she remembered what airs a miserable creature like Tayū had given himself on the Island, she almost expired with indignation.

[1] *Tamakazura* = jewelled wig.

That Bugo no Suke had acted with rare courage and wisdom in planning the sudden flight from Tsukushi was readily admitted by Genji when Ukon had laid all the circumstances before him. It was unlikely that any stranger would serve Tamakatsura with such devotion as this foster-brother had shown, and in drawing up for her a list of gentlemen-in-attendance, Genji saw to it that Bugo no Suke's name should figure among them.

Never in his wildest dreams had it occurred to Bugo no Suke that he, a plain Tsukushi yeoman, would ever set foot in a Minister's palace; nay, would in all his living days so much as set eyes on such a place. And here he was, not merely walking in and out just as he chose, but going with the lords and ladies wherever they went, and even arranging their affairs for them and ordering about their underlings as though they were his own. And to crown his content, no day passed but brought to his mistress some ingenious intention, some well-devised if trifling act of kindness from their host himself.

At the end of the year there took place the usual distribution of stuff for spring clothes, and Genji was determined that the new-comer should not feel that she had come off worse than the greatest ladies in the house. But he feared that, graceful and charming though she was, her taste in dress must necessarily be somewhat rustic, and among the silks which he gave her he determined also to send a certain number of woven dresses, that she might be gently guided towards the fashions of the day. The gentlewomen of the palace, each anxious to prove that there was nothing she did not know about the latest shapes of bodice and kirtle, set to work with such a will that when they brought their wares for Genji's inspection, he exclaimed: 'I fear your zeal has been excessive. If all my presents are to be on this scale (and I have no desire to excite jealousy), I shall indeed be hard put to it.' So saying he had his store-rooms ransacked for fine stuffs; and Murasaki came to the rescue with many of the costly robes which he had from time to time given her for her own wardrobe. All these were now laid out and inspected. Murasaki had a peculiar talent in such matters, and there was not a woman in all the world who chose her dyes with a subtler feeling for colour, as Genji very well knew. Dress after dress was now brought in fresh from the beating-room, and Genji would choose some robe now for its marvellous dark red, now for some curious and exciting pattern or colour-blend, and have it laid aside. 'This one in the box at the end,' he would say, handing some dress to one of the waiting-women who were standing beside the long narrow clothes-boxes; or 'Try this one in your box.' 'You seem to be making a very just division, and I am sure no one ought to feel aggrieved. But, if I may make a suggestion, would it not be better to think whether the stuffs will suit the complexions of their recipient rather than whether they look nice in the box?' 'I know just why you said that,' Genji laughed. 'You want me to launch out into a discussion of each lady's personal charms, in order that you may know in what light she appears to me. I am going to turn the tables. You shall have for your own whichever of my stuffs you like, and by your choice I shall know how *you* regard *yourself*.' 'I have not the least idea what I look like,' she answered, blushing slightly; 'after all, I am the last person in the world to consult upon the subject. One never sees oneself except in the mirror. . . .' After much debating, the presents were distributed as follows: to Murasaki herself, a kirtle yellow without and flowered within, lightly diapered with the red plum-blossom crest—a marvel of modern dyeing. To the Akashi child, a long close-fitting dress, white without, yellow within, the whole seen through an outer facing of shimmering red gauze. To the Lady from the Village of Falling Flowers he gave a light blue robe with a pattern of sea-shells woven into it. Lovely though the dress was as an example of complicated weaving, it would have been too light in tone had it not been covered with a somewhat heavy russet floss.

To Tamakatsura he sent, among other gifts, a close-fitting dress with a pattern of mountain-kerria woven upon a plain red background. Murasaki seemed scarcely to have glanced at it; but all the while, true to Genji's surmise, she was guessing the meaning of this choice. Like her father Tō no Chūjō, Tamakatsura (she conjectured) was doubtless good-looking; but certainly lacked his liveliness and love of adventure. Murasaki had no idea that she had in any way betrayed what was going on in her mind and was surprised when Genji suddenly said: 'In the end this matching of dresses and complexions breaks down entirely and one gives almost at hazard. I can never find anything that does justice to my handsome friends, or anything that it does not seem a shame to waste on the ugly ones . . .' and so saying he glanced with a smile at the present which was about to be dispatched to Suyetsumu, a dress white without and green within, what is called a 'willow-weaving,' with an elegant Chinese vine-scroll worked upon it.

To the Lady of Akashi he sent a white kirtle with a spray of plum-blossom on it, and birds and butterflies fluttering hither and thither, cut somewhat in the Chinese fashion, with a very handsome dark purple lining. This also caught Murasaki's observant eye and she augured from it that the rival of whom Genji spoke to her so lightly was in reality occupying a considerable place in his thoughts.

To Utsusemi, now turned nun, he sent a grey cloak, and, in addition, a coat of his own which he knew she would remember—jasmine-sprinkled, faced with Courtier's crimson and lined with russet. In each box was a note in which the recipient was begged to favour him by wearing these garments during the Festival of the New Year. He had taken a great deal of trouble over the business and could not imagine that any of the presents was likely to meet with a very bad reception. And indeed the satisfaction which he had given was soon evidenced not only by the delighted letters which came pouring in, but also by the handsome gratuities given to the bearers of these gifts. Suyetsumu was still living at the old Nijō-in palace, and the messenger who brought her present, having a quite considerable distance to travel, expected something rather out of the ordinary in the way of a reward. But to Suyetsumu these things were matters not of commerce, but of etiquette. A present such as this was, she had been taught long ago, a species of formal address which must be answered in the same language, and fetching an orange-coloured gown, very much frayed at the cuffs, she hung it over the messenger's shoulders, attaching to it a letter written on heavily scented Michinoku paper, which age had not only considerably yellowed, but also bloated to twice its proper thickness. 'Alas,' she wrote, 'your present serves but to remind me of your absence. What pleasure can I take in a dress that you will never see me wear?' With this was the poem: 'Was ever gift more heartless? Behold, I send it back to you, your Chinese dress,—worn but an instant, yet discoloured with the brine of tears.' The handwriting, with its antique flourishes, was admirably suited to the stilted sentiment of the poem. Genji laughed afresh each time he read it and finally, seeing that Murasaki was regarding him with astonishment, he handed her the missive. Meanwhile he examined the bedraggled old frock with which the discomfited messenger had been entrusted, with so rueful an expression that the fellow edged behind the bystanders and finally slipped out of the room, fearing that he had committed a grave breach of etiquette in introducing so pitiful an object into the presence of the Exalted Ones. His plight was the occasion of much whispering and laughter among his fellow servants. But laugh as one might at the absurd scenes which the princess's archaic behaviour invariably provoked, the very fact that adherence to bygone fashions could produce so ludicrous a result suggested the most disquieting reflexions. 'It is no laughing matter,' said Genji. 'Her "Chinese dress" and "discoloured with the brine of tears" made me feel thoroughly uncomfortable. With the writers of a generation or two ago every dress was "Chinese," and, no matter what the occasion of the poem, its sleeves were invariably soaked with tears. But what about your poems and mine? Are they not every bit as bad? Our tags may be different from those of the princess; but we use them just as hard and when we come to write a poem are as impervious as she is to the speech of our own day. And this is true not only of amateurs such as ourselves, but of those whose whole reputation depends on their supposed poetical gifts. Think of them at Court festivals, with their eternal *madoi, madoi*.[1] It is a wonder they do not grow tired of the word. A little while ago *adabito* "Faithless one" was used by well-bred lovers in every poem which they exchanged. They declined it (" of the faithless one," " from the faithless one " and so on) in the third line, thus gaining time to think out their final couplet. And so we all go on, poring over nicely stitched *Aids to Song*, and when we have committed a sufficient number of phrases to memory, producing them on the next occasion when they are required. It is not a method which leads to very much variety.

[1] 'I go astray.'

'But if we need a change, how much more does this unfortunate princess whose scruples forbid her to open any book except these old-fashioned collections of standard verse, written on dingy, native paper, to which her father Prince Hitachi introduced her long ago? Apart from these the only other reading which he seems to have permitted her was the *Marrow of Native Song*. Unfortunately this book consists almost entirely of " Faults to be avoided; " its comminations and restrictions have but served to aggravate her natural lack of facility. After such an education as this it is no wonder that her compositions have a well-worn and familiar air.'

'You are too severe,' said Murasaki, pleading for the princess. 'Whatever you may say, she managed this time to send an answer, and promptly too. Pray let me have a copy of her poem that I may show it to the Akashi child. I too used to have such books as the *Marrow of Poesy*, but I do not know what has become of them. Probably book-worms got into them and they were thrown away. I believe that to any one unfamiliar with the old phrase-books Suyetsumu's poem would seem delightfully fanciful and original. Let us try. . . .' 'Do nothing of the kind,' said Genji. 'Her education would be ruined if she began to take an interest in poetry. It is an accepted principle that however great the aptitude which a girl may show for some branch of science or art, she must beware of using it; for there is always a risk that her mind may be unduly diverted from ordinary duties and pursuits. She must know just so much of each subject that it cannot be said she has entirely neglected it. Further than this, she can only go at the risk of undermining the fortress of chastity or diminishing that softness of manner without which no woman can be expected to please.'

But all this while he had forgotten that Suyetsumu's

letter itself required a reply; indeed, as was pointed out by Murasaki, the princess's poem contained a hidden meaning which might be construed as a direct plea for further consolation. It would have been very unlike him not to have heeded such an appeal, and feeling that the standard she had set was not a very exacting one, he dashed off the following reply: 'If heartlessness there be, not mine it is but yours, who speak of sending back the coat that, rightly worn, brings dreams of love.'[1]

[1] A coat worn inside out brings dreams of one's lover.

CHAPTER V

THE FIRST SONG OF THE YEAR

WITH the morning of the New Year's [1] Day began a spell of the most delightful weather. Soft air, bright sunshine, and not a cloud to be seen in the whole sky. In every garden, on the humblest piece of waste ground, young shoots that formed each day a clearer patch of green were pushing up amid the snow; while over the trees hung a mist, stretched there, so it seemed, on purpose that the wonders it was hiding might later come as a surprise. Nor was this pleasant change confined to garden and wood; for men and women also, without knowing why, suddenly felt good-humoured and hopeful. It may be imagined then what an enchantment these first spring days, everywhere so delightful, cast upon the gardens of Genji's palace, with their paths of jade-dust, their groves and lakes. It would be impossible here to describe in any way that would not be both tedious and inadequate the beauties of the four domains which Genji had allotted to his favourites. But this I may say, that the Spring Garden,[2] with its great orchards of fruit trees at this moment far excelled the rest, and even behind her screens-of-state Murasaki breathed an atmosphere that was heavily laden with the scent of plum-blossom. Indeed the place was a Heaven upon earth; but a Heaven adapted to human requirements by the addition of numerous comforts and amenities. The Princess [3] from Akashi was

[1] The year began in the spring. Genji was now 36.
[2] Murasaki's.   [3] The child born at Akashi.

still living in Murasaki's apartments. The younger among the gentlewomen-in-waiting had been placed at her disposal; while the older among them, and such as had distinguished themselves in any way, were retained by Murasaki. On the third day they were already gathered together in front of the Mirror Cake [1] reciting 'For a thousand years may we dwell under thy shadow' and other New Year verses, with a good deal of laughter and scuffling, when Genji's unexpected entry suddenly caused many pairs of hands to fly back into an attitude of prayer. The ladies looked so uncomfortable at having been caught treating the ceremonies of the day with undue levity, that Genji said to them laughing: 'Come now, there is no need to take the prayers on our behalf so seriously. I am sure each of you has plenty of things she would like to pray for on her own account. Tell me, all of you, what you most desire in the coming year, and I will add my prayers to yours.' Among these ladies was a certain Chūjō,[2] one of his own gentlewomen, whom he had transferred to Murasaki's service at the time of his exile. She knew well enough, poor lady, what thing *she* most desired. But she only said: 'I tried just now to think of something to pray for on my own account; but it ended by my saying the prayer: "May he endure long as the Mountain of Kagami in the country of Ōmi." [3]

The morning had been occupied in receiving a host of New Year visitors; but now Genji thought he would call upon the various inhabitants of his palace, to give them his good wishes and see how they looked in their New Year clothes. 'Your ladies,' he said to Murasaki, 'do not seem

---

[1] Served on the evening of the third day of the year, with radish and oranges.
[2] She had always been in love with Genji.
[3] Kagami = 'Mirror.'

to take these proceedings seriously. I found them romping together, instead of saying their prayers. You and I will have to hold a service of our own.' So saying he recited the prayer, not without certain additions which showed that he took the business only a trifle more seriously than the ladies whom he had just criticized. He then handed her the poem: 'May the course of our love be clear as the waters of yonder lake, from which, in the spring sunshine, the last clot of ice has melted away.' To this she answered: 'On the bright mirror of these waters I see stretched out the cloudless years love holds for us in store.' Then (as how many times before!) Genji began telling her that, whatever was reported of him or whatever she herself observed, she need never have any anxiety. And he protested, in the most violent and impressive terms, that his passion for her underlay all that he felt or did, and could not be altered by any passing interest or fancy. She was for the moment convinced, and accepted his protestations ungrudgingly.

Besides being the third of the year it was also the Day of the Rat [1] and therefore as fine an occasion for prayers and resolutions as could possibly have been found.

His next visit was to the little girl from Akashi. He found her maids and page-boys playing New Year games on the mound in front of her windows, and pulling up the dwarf pine-trees, an occupation in which they seemed to take a boundless delight. The little princess's rooms were full of sweetmeat boxes and hampers, all of them presents from her mother. To one toy, a little nightingale perched upon a sprig of the five-leafed pine, was fastened a plaintive message: 'In *my* home the nightingale's voice I never hear, . . .' [2] and with it the poem:—

[1] The first of the cyclical signs.
[2] You are silent as this toy bird and send me no New Year greetings.

O nightingale, to one that many months,
While strangers heard you sing,
Has waited for your voice, grudge not to-day
The first song of the year!

Genji read the poem and was touched by it; for he knew that only under the stress of great emotion would she have allowed this note of sadness to tinge a New Year poem. 'Come, little nightingale!' he said to the child, 'you must make haste with your answer; it would be heartless indeed if in the quarter whence these pretty things come you were ungenerous with your spring-time notes!' and taking his own ink-stone from a servant who was standing by, he prepared it for her and made her write. She looked so charming while she did this that he found himself envying those who spent all day in attendance upon her, and he felt that to have deprived the Lady of Akashi year after year of so great a joy was a crime for which he would never be able to forgive himself. He looked to see what she had written. 'Though years be spent asunder, not lightly can the nightingale forget the tree where first it nested and was taught to sing.' The flatness of the verse had at least this much to recommend it—the mother would know for certain that the poem had been written without grown-up assistance!

The Summer Quarters [1] were not looking their best; indeed at this time of year they could hardly be expected not to wear a somewhat uninteresting air. As he looked about him he could see no object that was evidence of any very pronounced taste or proclivity; the arrangements betokened, rather, a general discrimination and good-breeding. For many years past his affection for her had remained at exactly the same pitch, never flagging in the slightest degree, and at the same time never tempting him

[1] Allotted to the Lady from the Village of Falling Flowers.

to the extremer forms of intimacy. In this way there had long ago grown up between them a relationship far more steady and harmonious than can ever exist between those who are lovers in the stricter sense of the term. This morning he spoke to her for a while from behind her curtains-of-state. But presently he cautiously raised a corner of one curtain, and he looked in. How little she had changed! But he was sorry to see that the New Year's dress he had given her was not a great success. Her hair had of late years grown much less abundant, and in order to maintain the same style of coiffure, she had been obliged to supplement it by false locks. To these Genji had long ago grown accustomed. But he now began trying to imagine how she appeared to other people, and saw at once that to them she must seem a very homely, middle-aged person indeed. So much the better, then, that he who loved her had this strange power of seeing her as she used to be, rather than as she was now. And she on her side —what if she should one day grow weary of him, as women often did of those who gave them so little as he had done!

Such were the reflexions that passed through Genji's mind while he sat with her. 'We are both singularly fortunate,' he concluded to himself. 'I, in my capacity for self-delusion; she in hers for good-tempered acceptance of whatever comes her way.' They talked for a long while, chiefly of old times, till at last he found that he ought to be on his way to the Western Wing.

Considering the short time that Tamakatsura had been in residence she had made things look uncommonly nice. The number and smartness of her maids gave the place an air of great animation. The large and indispensable articles of furniture had all arrived; but many of the smaller fittings were not yet complete. This was in a way an advantage; for it gave to her rooms a look of spaciousness and simplicity which had a peculiar charm. But it was the mistress of these apartments who, when she suddenly appeared upon the scene, positively confounded him by her beauty. How perfectly she wore that long, close-fitting robe, with its pattern of mountain-kerria! Here, he thought, contrasting her inevitably with the lady to whom he had just said farewell, here was nothing that it might be dangerous to scrutinize, nothing that kindness bade him condone; but radiance, freshness, dazzling youth from tip to toe. Her hair was somewhat thinned out at the ends, in pursuance, perhaps, of some vow made during the days of her tribulation; and this gave to her movements an ease and freedom which strangely accorded with the bareness of her quarters. Had he chosen any but his present rôle,[1] he would not now be watching her flit unconstrainedly hither and thither across her room. . . . She, however, having by this time grown used to his informal visits, enjoyed his company to the full and would even have had him treat her with a shade less deference . . . when suddenly she remembered that he was only a make-believe father after all, and then it seemed to her that she had already countenanced far greater liberties than their situation demanded. 'For my part,' said Genji at last, 'I feel as though you had been living with us for years, and am certain that I shall never have cause to repent your coming. But you have not progressed so fast in friendship with the other inmates of my household as I have done in mine with you. I notice you do not visit Lady Murasaki. I am sorry for this, and hope that in future you will make use of her apartments without formality of any sort whenever you feel inclined. You could be of great help to the little girl who lives with her. For example, if you would take charge

[1] That of father.

of her music-lessons. . . . You would find every one in that quarter most affable and forthcoming. . . . Do promise me to try!' 'If you wish it,' was all she said; but in a voice which indicated that she really meant to obey.

It was already becoming dark when he arrived at the Lady of Akashi's rooms. Through an open door a sudden puff of wind carried straight towards him from her daïs a blend of perfumes as exquisite as it was unfamiliar. But where was the Lady herself? For a while he scanned the room in vain. He noticed a writing-case, and near it a great litter of books and papers. On a long flat cushion bordered with Chinese brocade from Lo-yang lay a handsome zithern; while in a brazier which, even in the dim light, he could see to be an object of value and importance, there burned some of that incense which is known as 'The Courtier's Favourite.' This was the scent which pervaded the whole room and, blending with a strong odour of musk, created the delicious perfume which Genji had noticed when he first turned into the corridor. Coming close enough to examine the papers which lay scattered about the daïs, he saw that though there were many experiments in different styles, some of them quite interesting, there were no efforts towards the more extravagant and pretentious forms of cursive. Her child's letter of thanks for the toy bird and tree had already arrived, and it was evident that, in her delight, she had just been copying out a number of classic poems appropriate to such an occasion. But among these was written a poem of her own: 'Oh joy untold! The nightingale that, lured by the spring flowers, to distant woods was gone, now to its valley nest again repairs.' She had also copied out the old poems: 'I waited for thy song' and 'Because my house is where the plum-tree blooms,' and many other snatches and fragments such as were likely to run in the head of one to whom a sudden consolation had come. He took up the papers one by one, sometimes smiling, yet ashamed of himself for doing so. Then he wetted the pen and was just about to write a message of his own, when the Lady of Akashi suddenly appeared from a back room. Despite the splendours by which she was now surrounded she still maintained a certain deference of manner and anxiety to please which marked her as belonging to a different class. Yet there was something about the way her very dark hair stood out against the white of her dress, hanging rather flat against it, that strangely attracted him. It was New Year's night. He could not very well absent himself from his own apartments, for there were visitors coming and Murasaki was expecting him. . . .

Yet it was in the Lady of Akashi's rooms that he spent the night, thus causing considerable disappointment in many quarters, but above all in the southern wing, where Murasaki's gentlewomen made bitter comments upon this ill-timed defection.

It was still almost dark when Genji returned, and he persuaded himself that, though he had stayed out late, it could not be said that he had been absent for a night. To the Lady of Akashi, on her side it seemed that he was suddenly rising to leave her just as the night was beginning. Nevertheless, she was enraptured by his visit. Murasaki would no doubt have sat up waiting for him, and he was quite prepared to find her in rather a bad humour. But one never knows, and in order to find out he said: 'I have just had the most uncomfortable doze. It was too childish. . . . I fell asleep in my chair. I wish some one had woken me. It was the most mistaken kindness. . . .' But no! She did not reply, and seeing that for the moment there was no more to be done, he lay back and pretended to be asleep; but as soon as it was broad daylight got up and left the room.

Next day there was a great deal of New Year's entertaining to be done, which was fortunate, for it enabled him to save his face. As usual, almost the whole Court was there, —princes, ministers and noblemen. There was a concert and on Genji's part a grand distribution of trinkets and New Year presents. This party was an occasion of great excitement for the more elderly and undistinguished of the guests; and it may be imagined with what eagerness it was this year awaited by the younger princes and noblemen, who were perpetually on the look-out for adventure and flattered themselves that the new inmate [1] of Genji's palace was by no means beyond their reach. A gentle evening breeze carried the scent of fruit-blossom into every corner of the house; in particular, most fragrant of all, the plum-trees in Murasaki's garden were now in full bloom. It was at that nameless hour which is neither day nor night. The concert had begun; delicate harmonies of flute and string filled the air, and at last came the swinging measure of 'Well may this Hall grow rich and thrive,' [2] with its animated refrain 'Oh, the saki-grass so sweet,' in which Genji joined with excellent effect. This indeed was one of his peculiar gifts, that whatever was afoot, whether music, dancing or what not, he had only to join in and every one else was at once inspired to efforts of which they would not have imagined themselves capable.

Meanwhile the ladies of the household, in the seclusion of their rooms, heard little more than a confused din of horse-

[1] Tamakatsura.

[2] Well may this house grow rich and thrive—
Oh, the saki-grass, the saki-grass so sweet—
Of the saki-grass, three leaves, four leaves, so trim
Are the walls of this house made.'

hoofs and carriage-wheels, their plight being indeed much like that of the least deserving among the Blest, who though they are reborn in Paradise, receive an unopened lotus-bud as their lodging.[1] But still worse was the position of those who inhabited the old Eastern Wing; for having once lived at any rate within ear-shot of such festivities as this, they now saw themselves condemned to an isolation and lack of employment which every year would increase. Yet though they might almost as well have renounced the Court and ensconced themselves 'by mountain paths where Sorrow is unknown,' they did nothing of the kind nor, real though their grievances were, did the slightest complaint ever cross their lips. Indeed, save that they were left pretty much to their own devices, they had little else to complain of. They were housed in the utmost comfort and security. Those of them who were religious had at least the certainty that their pious practices would not be interrupted; while those who cared for study had plenty of time to fill a thousand copy-books with native characters. As regards their lodging and equipment, they had only to express a desire for it to be immediately gratified. And sometimes their benefactor actually called upon them, as indeed happened this spring, so soon as the busy days of the New Festival were over.

Suyetsumu was after all the daughter of Prince Hitachi, and as such was entitled to keep up a considerable degree of state. Genji had accordingly provided her with a very ample staff of attendants. Her surroundings indeed were all that could be desired. She herself had changed greatly in recent years. Her hair was now quite grey, and seeing that she was embarrassed by this and was evidently wondering what impression it would make upon him, he at first kept his eyes averted while he spoke to her. His gaze

[1] And consequently cannot see the Buddha nor hear his Word.

naturally fell upon her dress. He recognized it as that which he had given her for New Year; but it looked very odd, and he was wondering how he had come to give her so unsuitable a garment, when he discovered that the fault was entirely that of the wearer. Over it she had put a thin mantle of dull black crepe, unlined, and so stiff that it crackled when she moved. The woven dress which he had given her was meant to wear under a heavy cloak, and naturally in her present garb she was, as he could see, suffering terribly from the cold. He had given her an ample supply of stuff for winter cloaks. What could she have done with it all? But with Suyetsumu nothing seemed to thrive, every stuff became threadbare, every colour turned dingy, save that of one bright flower. . . .[1] But one must keep such things out of one's head; and he firmly replaced the open flap of her curtain.

She was not offended. It was quite enough that year after year, he should preserve the same unmistakable signs of affection; for did he not always treat her as an intimate and equal, taking her completely into his confidence and addressing her always in the most informal manner imaginable? If this were not affection, what else could it be?

He meanwhile was thinking what a uniquely depressing and wearisome creature she was, and deciding that he must really make up his mind to be a little kinder to her, since it was certain that no one else intended to take the business off his hands.

He noticed that while she talked her teeth positively chattered with cold. He looked at her with consternation. 'Is there no one,' he asked, 'whose business it is to take charge of your wardrobe? It does not seem to me that stiff clumsy over-garments are very well suited to your present surroundings. This cloak of yours, for example.

[1] *Hana* = 'nose' and 'flower.'

If you cannot do without it, then at any rate be consistent and wear it over a dress of the same description. You cannot get yourself up in one style on top and another underneath.' He had never spoken to her so bluntly before, but she only tittered slightly. 'My brother Daigo no Azari,' she said at last, 'promised to look after those warm stuffs for me, and he carried them all off before I had time to make them into dresses. He even took away my sables.[1] I am so cold without them. . . .' Her brother evidently felt the cold even more than she did, and Genji imagined him with a very red nose indeed. Simplicity was no doubt an engaging quality; but really this lady carried it a little too far. However, with her it was certainly no affectation, and he answered good-humouredly: 'As far as those sables are concerned, I am delighted to hear what has become of them. I always thought they were really meant to keep out the rain and snow. Next time your brother goes on a mountain pilgrimage. . . . But there is no need for *you* to shiver. You can have as much of this white material as you like, and there is nothing to prevent your wearing it sevenfold thick, if you find you cannot keep warm. Please always remind me of such promises. If I do not do things at once, I am apt to forget about them. My memory was never very good and I have always needed keeping up to the mark. But now that there are so many conflicting claims upon my time and attention, nothing gets done at all unless I am constantly reminded. . . .' And thinking it safest to act while the matter was still in his mind, he sent a messenger across to the New Palace for a fresh supply of silks and brocades.

The Nijō-in was kept in perfect order and repair; but the fact that it was no longer the main residence somehow or other gave it an air of abandonment and desolation.

[1] See vol. i, p. 200.

The gardens, however, were as delightful as ever. The red plum-blossom was at its best, and it seemed a pity that so much beauty and fragrance should be, one might almost say, wasted. He murmured to himself the lines: ' To see the springtide to my old home I came, and found within it a rarer flower than any that on orchard twigs was hung!'

She heard the words; but luckily did not grasp the unflattering allusion.[1]

He also paid a brief visit to Utsusemi, now turned nun. She had installed herself in apartments so utterly devoid of ornament or personal touches of any kind that they had the character of official waiting-rooms. The only conspicuous object which they contained was a large statue of Buddha, and Genji was lamenting to himself that sombre piety, to the exclusion of all other interest, should have possessed so gracious and gentle a spirit, when he noticed that the decoration of her prayer-books, the laying of her altar with its dishes of floating petals—these and many another small sign of elegance seemed to betray a heart that was not yet utterly crushed by the severities of religion. Her blue-grey curtains-of-state showed much taste and care. She sat so far back as scarcely to be seen. But one touch of colour stood out amid the gloom; the long sleeves of the gay coat he had sent her showed beneath her mantle of grey, and moved by her acceptance of this token he said with tears in his eyes: ' I know that I ought not now even to remember how once I felt towards you. But from the beginning our love brought to us only irritation and misery. It is as well that, if we are to be friends at all, it must now be in a very different way.' She too was deeply moved and said at last: ' How can I doubt your good will towards me, seeing at what pains you have

[1] *Hana* = ' flower' and ' nose.' See above.

been to provide for me, protect me. . . . I should be ungrateful indeed. . . .' 'I daresay many another lover suffered just as I did,' he said, attempting a lighter tone; ' and Buddha condemns you to your present life as a penance for all the hearts you have broken. And how the others must have suffered if their experience was anything like mine! Not once but over and over again did I fall in love with you; and those others . . . There, I knew that I was right. You are thinking, I am sure, of an entanglement beside which our escapade pales into insignificance.' His only intention was to divert the conversation from their own relationship, and he was speaking quite at random. But she instantly imagined that he had in some circuitous way got wind of that terrible story . . .[1] and blushing she said in a low voice: 'Do not remind me of it. The mere fact that you should have been told of it is punishment enough . . .' and she burst into tears.

He did not know to what she referred. He had imagined that her retirement from the world was merely due to increasing depression and timidity. How was he to converse with her, if every chance remark threw her into a fit of weeping? He had no desire to go away; but he could not think of any light topic upon which to embark, and after a few general enquiries he took his leave. If only it were Lady Suyetsumu who was the nun and he could put Utsusemi in her place! So Genji thought as on his way back he again passed by the red-nosed lady's door. He then paid short visits to the numerous other persons who lived upon his bounty, saying to such of them as he had not seen for some time: 'If long intervals sometimes elapse between my visits to you, you must not think that my feelings towards you have changed. On the contrary, I often think what a pity it is that we so seldom meet. For

[1] Her relations with Ki no Kami, her stepson. See vol. ii, p. 257.

time slips away, and bound up with every deep affection is the fear that Death may take us unawares. . . .' Nor was there anything the least insincere in these speeches; in one way or another he did actually feel very deeply about each of the persons to whom they were made. Unlike most occupants of the exalted position which he now held, Genji was entirely devoid of pomposity and self-importance. Whatever the rank of those whom he was addressing, under whatever circumstances he met them, his manner remained always equally kind and attentive. Indeed, by that thread and that alone hung many of his oldest friendships.

This year there was to be the New Year's mumming.[1] After performing in the Imperial Palace the dancers were to visit the Suzaku-in [2] and then come on to Genji's. This meant covering a good deal of ground, and it was already nearing dawn when they arrived. The weather had at first been somewhat uncertain, but at dusk the clouds cleared away, and bright moonlight shone upon those exquisite gardens, now clad in a thin covering of snow. Many of the young courtiers who had recently come into notice showed unusual proficiency on instruments of one kind and another. There were flute-players in abundance, and nowhere that night did they give a more admirable display than when they welcomed the arrival of the mummers in front of Genji's palace. The ladies of the household had been apprised of the ceremony, and they were now assembled in stands which had been set up in the cross-galleries between the central hall and its two wings. The lady of the western side [3] was invited to witness the proceedings in company with the little princess from Akashi,

---

[1] A band of young noblemen going round dancing and singing in various parts of the Palace and at the houses of the great on the 14th day of the 1st month. See vol. i, p. 207.

[2] The residence of the ex-Emperor and his mother, Kōkiden.

[3] Tamakatsura.

THE FIRST SONG OF THE YEAR

whose windows looked out on to the courtyard where the dancing was to take place. Murasaki was their neighbour, being separated from them only by a curtain. After performing before the ex-Emperor the dancers had been summoned to give a second display in front of Kōkiden's apartments. It was consequently even later than had been anticipated when they at last arrived. Before they danced, they had to be served with their 'mummers'' portions. It was expected that, considering the lateness of the hour, this part of the proceedings, with its curious rites and observances, would be somewhat curtailed. But on the contrary Genji insisted upon its being carried out with even more than the prescribed elaboration. A faint light was showing in the east, the moon was still shining, but it had begun to snow again, this time harder than ever. The wind, too, had risen; already the tree-tops were swaying, and it became clear that a violent storm was at hand. There was, in the scene that followed, a strange discrepancy; the delicate pale green cloaks of the mummers, lined with pure white, fluttered lightly, elegantly to the movements of the dance; while around them gathered the gloom and menace of the rising storm. Only the cotton plumes of their head-gear, stiff and in a way graceless as they were, seemed to concord with the place and hour. These, as they swayed and nodded in the dance, had a strangely vivid and satisfying beauty.

Among those who sang and played for the dancers Yūgiri and Tō no Chūjō's sons took the lead. As daylight came the snow began to clear, and only a few scattered flakes were falling when through the cold air there rose the strains of *Bamboo River*.[1] I should like to describe

---

[1] 'In the garden of flowers at the end of the bridge that crosses Bamboo River—in the garden of flowers set me free, with youths and maidens round me.'

the movements of this dance—how the dancers suddenly rise on tip-toe and spread their sleeves like wings—and with how delightful an effect voice after voice joins in the lively tune. But it has truly been said that such things are beyond the painter's art; and still less, I suppose, can any depiction of them be expected of a mere story-teller.

The ladies of the household vied with one another in the decoration of their stalls. Gay scarfs and favours hung out on every side; while shimmering New Year dresses now dimly discovered behind drawn curtains-of-state, now flashing for a moment into the open as some lady-in-waiting reached forward to adjust a mat or rescue a fan, looked in the dawning light like a meadow of bright flowers 'half-curtained by the trailing mists of Spring.' Seldom can there have been seen so strange and lovely a sight. There was, too, a remote, barbaric beauty in the high turbans of the dancers, with their stiff festoons of artificial flowers; and when at last they entoned the final prayer, despite the fact that the words were nonsense and the tune apparently a mere jangle of discordant sounds, there was in the whole setting of the performance something so tense, so stirring that these savage cries seemed at the moment more moving than the deliberate harmonies by which the skilled musician coldly seeks to charm our ear.

After the usual distribution of presents, the mummers at last withdrew. It was now broad daylight, and all the guests retired to get a little belated sleep. Genji rose again towards mid-day. 'I believe that Yūgiri is going to make every bit as good a musician as Kōbai,'[1] he said, while discussing the scenes of the night before. 'I am astonished by the talent of the generation which is now

[1] Tō no Chūjō's son, famous for the beauty of his voice. See vol. ii, p. 87.

growing to manhood. The ancients no doubt far excelled us in the solid virtues; but our sensibilities are, I venture to assert, far keener than theirs. I thought at one time that Yūgiri was quite different from his companions and counted upon turning him into a good, steady-going man of affairs. My own nature is, I fear, inherently frivolous, and not wishing him to take after me I have been at great pains to implant in him a more serious view of life. But signs are not wanting that under a very correct and solemn exterior he hides a disposition towards just those foibles which have proved my own undoing. If it turns out that his wonderful air of good sense and moderation are mere superficial poses, it will indeed be annoying for us all.' So he spoke, but he was in reality feeling extremely pleased with his son. Then, humming the tune [1] that the mummers sing at the moment when they rise to depart, Genji said: ' Seeing all the ladies of the household gathered together here last night has made me think how amazing it would be if we could one day persuade them to give us a concert. It might be a sort of private After Feast.'[2] The rumour of this project soon spread through the palace. On every hand lutes and zitherns were being pulled from out the handsome brocade bags into which they had been so carefully stowed away; and there was such a sprucing, polishing and tuning as you can scarcely imagine; followed by unremitting practice and the wildest day-dreams.

[1] The *Bansuraku* or ' Joy of Ten Thousand Springs.'
[2] The After Feast is held in the Emperor's Palace.

CHAPTER VI

THE BUTTERFLIES

TOWARDS the end of the third month, when out in the country the orchards were no longer at their best and the song of the wild birds had lost its first freshness, Murasaki's Spring Garden seemed only to become every day more enchanting. The little wood on the hill beyond the lake, the bridge that joined the two islands, the mossy banks that seemed to grow greener not every day but every hour—could anything have looked more tempting? 'If only one could get there!' sighed the young people of the household; and at last Genji decided that there must be boats on the lake. They were built in the Chinese style. Every one was in such a hurry to get on board that very little time was spent in decorating them, and they were put into use almost as soon as they would float. On the day when they were launched the Water Music was played by musicians summoned from the Imperial Board of Song. The spectacle was witnessed by a large assembly of princes, noblemen and courtiers, and also by the Empress Akikonomu, who was spending her holidays at the New Palace.

Akikonomu remembered Murasaki's response to her present:[1] it had been tantamount to saying 'Do not visit me now, but in the spring-time when my garden will be at its best.' Genji too was always saying that he wanted

[1] The box of autumn leaves. See above, p. 145.

THE BUTTERFLIES

to show her the Spring Garden. How simple it would all have been if she could merely have walked across to Murasaki's domain when the fancy seized her, enjoyed herself among the flowers and gone away! But she was now an Empress, an August Being hedged round by sacred statutes and conventions. However, if such liberties were hers no longer, there were in her service many who could enjoy them in her stead, and sending for one of the new boats she filled it with some of the younger and more adventurous of her gentlewomen. It was possible to go by water all the way to the Spring Garden, first rowing along the Southern Lake, then passing through a narrow channel straight towards a toy mountain which seemed to bar all further progress. But in reality there was a way round, and eventually the party found itself at the Fishing Pavilion. Here they picked up Murasaki's ladies, who were waiting at the Pavilion by appointment. The boats were carved with a dragon's head at the prow and painted with the image of an osprey at the stern, completely in the Chinese style; and the boys who manned them were all in Chinese costume, with their hair tied up with bright ribbons behind. The lake, as they now put out towards the middle of it, seemed immensely large, and those on board, to whom the whole experience was new and deliciously exciting, could hardly believe that they were not heading for some undiscovered land. At last however the rowers brought them close in under the rocky bank of the channel between the two large islands, and on closer examination they discovered to their delight that the shape of every little ledge and crag of stone had been as carefully devised as if a painter had traced them with his brush. Here and there in the distance the topmost boughs of an orchard showed above the mist, so heavily laden with blossom that it looked as though a bright carpet were spread in mid air. Far away they could just catch sight of Murasaki's apartments, marked by the deeper green of the willow boughs that swept her courtyards, and by the shimmer of her flowering orchards, which even at this distance seemed to shed their fragrance amid the isles and rocks. In the world outside, the cherry-blossom was almost over; but here it seemed to laugh at decay, and round the palace even the wistaria that ran along the covered alleys and porticos was all in bloom, but not a flower past its best; while here, where the boats were tied, mountain-kerria poured its yellow blossom over the rocky cliffs in a torrent of colour that was mirrored in the waters of the lake below. Water-birds of many kinds played in and out among the boats or fluttered hither and thither with tiny twigs or flower sprays in their beaks, and love-birds roamed in pairs, their delicate markings blending, in reflection, with the frilled pattern of the waves. Here, like figures in a picture of fairyland, they spent the day gazing in rapture, and envied the woodman [1] on whose axe green leaves at last appeared.

Many trifling poems were interchanged, such as: 'When the wind blows, even the wave-petals, that are no blossoms at all, put on strange colours; for this is the vaunted cape, the Cliff of Kerria Flowers.' [2] And 'To the Rapids of Idé [3] surely the channels of our spring lake must bend; for where else hang the kerria-flowers so thick across the rocks?' Or this: 'Never again will I dream of the Mountain [4] on the Tortoise's Back, for here in this boat have I found a magic that shall preserve both me and my name forever from the onset of mortality.' And again: 'In the soft spring sunshine even the spray that falls from the rower's

---

[1] See vol. ii, p. 292.
[2] Yamabuki no Saki, a place in Ōmi, referred to in the *Gossamer Diary*. See vol. ii, p. 28.
[3] A place in Yamashiro, also famous for its kerria flowers.
[4] Hōrai, fairyland, the Immortal Island.

oars, sinks soft as scattered petals on to the waveless waters of the lake.'

So captivated were they by this novel experience that they had soon lost all sense of whither they were faring or whence they had come. It was indeed as though the waters had cast a spell of forgetfulness upon their hearts, and when evening came they were still, as it seemed to them, gliding away and away across the lake, to the pleasant strains of the tune called *The Royal Deer*. . . . Suddenly the boats halted, the ladies were invited to go ashore, and to their complete surprise found that they were back again at the Fishing Pavilion.

This place was finished in a manner which combined elegance with extreme simplicity. The rooms were indeed almost bare, and as now the rival parties pressed into them, spreading along the empty galleries and across the wide, deserted floors, there was such an interweaving of gay colours as would have been hard to out-do. The musicians were again called upon, and this time played a sequence of little-known airs which won universal applause. Soon they were joined by a troupe of dancers whom Genji had himself selected, drawing up at the same time a list of pieces which he thought would interest such an audience.

It seemed a pity that darkness should be allowed to interfere with these pleasures, and when night came on, a move was made to the courtyard in front of the palace. Here flares were lit, and on the mossy lawn at the foot of the great Steps not only professional musicians, but also various visitors from Court and friends of the family performed on wind and string, while picked teachers of the flute gave a display in the 'double mode.'[1] Then all the zitherns and lutes belonging to different members of the

---

[1] The mode of the second, beginning on alto A. Being so high it was very difficult to play. It symbolized Spring.

household were brought out on to the steps and carefully tuned to the same pitch. A grand concert followed, the piece *Was ever such a day?* being performed with admirable effect. Even the grooms and labourers who were loitering amid the serried ranks of coaches drawn up outside the great gates, little as they usually cared for such things, on this occasion pricked up their ears and were soon listening with lips parted in wonder and delight. For it was indeed impossible that the strange shrill descants of the Spring Mode, enhanced as they were by the unusual beauty of the night, should not move the most impercipient of human creatures.

The concert continued till dawn. As a return-tune [1] *Gay Springtide Pleasures* was added to the programme, and Prince Sochi no Miya carried the vocal music back very pleasantly to the common mode by singing *Green Willows* [2] in the words of which Genji also joined.

Already the morning birds were clamouring in a lusty chorus to which, from behind the curtains, the Empress Akikonomu listened with irritation.

It would have been hard in these days to find a mote in the perfect sunshine of Genji's prosperity and contentment. But it was noticed with regret by his friends, as a circumstance which must of necessity be painful to him, that Murasaki still bore him no child. It was felt, however, that this misfortune was to some extent remedied by the arrival of his handsome natural daughter (for so Tamakatsura was regarded by the world at large). The evident store which Genji himself set by this lady, becoming a matter

---

[1] The tune which marked the return from the unusual 'Spring' tuning to the ordinary mode.

[2] 'With a thread of green from the willow-tree—Ohé!
The nightingale has stitched himself a hat—Ohé!
A hat of plum-blossom, they say—Ohé!'

THE BUTTERFLIES

of common report, together with the tales of her almost unbelievable beauty, soon induced a large number of suitors to seek her hand; which was precisely what he had anticipated. Those of them whose position in life entitled them to confidence had, through suitable channels, already gone so far as to make hints in this direction; while there were doubtless many petty courtiers the flame of whose love burned secretly as a camp fire buried under a pile of stones.[1]

Tō no Chūjō's sons were, of course, like every one else, under the delusion that she was Genji's child and took a considerable interest in her. But the principal suitor was Genji's half-brother Prince Sochi no Miya. It so happened that he had been a widower for three years; he was tired of this comfortless state of life and had made it clear not only that he considered himself a suitable match for Lady Tamakatsura, but also that he should like the wedding to take place immediately. This morning he was still in a very emotional condition; with a wreath of wistaria flowers about his head, he was indulging in languorous airs which confirmed Genji's previous suspicion that this prince had lately fallen seriously in love. Till now, however, Genji had deliberately pretended not to notice that anything was wrong. When the great tankard was handed round, Prince Sochi said in a doleful voice to Genji: 'You know, if I were not so fond of you, I should long ago have left this entertainment. It has been a terrible night for me . . .' and he recited the poem: 'Because my heart is steeped in a dye too near to its own blood,[2] life do I prize no longer and in the surging stream shall shortly cast myself away.'

[1] Lest the enemy should see it.
[2] He thinks that Tamakatsura is Genji's daughter, and therefore his own niece. Union with a brother's child was ill-viewed. There are numerous puns, which it would be tedious to explain.

So saying he took the wreath of wistaria from his own head and laid it on Genji's, quoting the poem : ' My wreath shall be thine.' Genji laughingly accepted it and replied : ' Watch by the flowers of Spring till the last petal be unfolded ; then will be time enough to talk of whirlpools and despair.' So saying he caught hold of his brother and held him fast in his seat, promising that if he would but stay, he should to-day witness a performance far more entertaining than what had gone before.

It so happened that this day marked the opening of the Empress Akikonomu's Spring Devotions. Most of the visitors not wishing to miss the ceremonies connected with this occasion, asked leave to stay on, and retiring to the guest-rooms, changed into their morning clothes. A few who had urgent business at home reluctantly withdrew from the palace ; but on returning later they found that they had missed nothing, for it was close upon noon before the actual ceremony began. The visitors reached the Empress's apartments in a long procession, headed by Genji himself. The whole Court was there, and though the magnificence of the occasion was partly due to Akikonomu's own position, it was in large measure a tribute to Genji's influence and popularity. At Murasaki's request an offering of flowers was to be made to the presiding Buddha. They were brought by eight little boys disguised some as birds, some as butterflies. The birds carried cherry-blossom in silver bowls ; the butterflies, mountain-kerria in golden bowls. They were in reality quite ordinary flowers such as you might find in any country place ; but in this setting they seemed to acquire an unearthly glint and splendour. The boys arrived by water, having embarked at the landing-stage in front of Murasaki's rooms As they landed at the Autumn domain a sudden gust of wind caught the cherry-blossom in the silver bowls and some of it scattered along the bank. The day was cloudless and it was a pretty sight indeed to see the little messengers come out into the sunshine from behind a trailing patch of mist.

It had not been found convenient to set up the regular Musicians' Tent; but a platform had been constructed under the portico that ran in front of the Empress's apartments, and chairs had been borrowed that the musicians might be seated in foreign fashion.[1] The little boys advanced as far as the foot of the steps, their offerings held aloft in their hands. Here they were met by incense-bearers who conveyed the bowls to the grand altar and adding their contents to that of the holy flower-vessels, pronounced the ritual of dedication. At this point Yūgiri arrived, bearing a poem from Murasaki: 'Lover of Autumn, whom best it pleases that pine-crickets should chirp amid the withered grass, forgive the butterflies that trespass from my garden of flowers.' The Empress smiled. To her own gift of autumn leaves these fictive birds and butterflies were the belated response.

Her ladies, who were at first loyal to the season with which their mistress was identified, had been somewhat shaken in their allegiance by yesterday's astonishing excursion and came back assuring the Empress that her preference would not survive a visit to the rival park.

After the acceptance of their offerings, the Birds performed the Kalyavinka[2] Dance. The accompanying music was backed by the warbling of real nightingales; while afar off, with strangely happy effect, there sounded the faint and occasional cry of some crane or heron on the lake. All too soon came the wild and rapid passage which marks the close.

---

[1] The Japanese, as is well known, squat cross-legged on the ground. But the use of chairs had spread with Buddhism from Central Asia.
[2] One of the magical birds in Amida Buddha's Paradise.

Now it was the turn of the Butterflies, who after fluttering hither and thither for a while, settled at the foot of a tangled thorn-hedge, over which the yellow kerria streamed down in splendid profusion, and here executed their dance.

The Comptroller of the Empress's household, assisted by several courtiers, now distributed largesse to the boy-dancers on her behalf. To the Birds, cherry-coloured jackets; to the Butterflies, cloaks lined with silk of kerria hue. These were so appropriate that they could hardly have been produced on the spur of the moment, and it almost seemed as though some hint of Murasaki's intention had reached the Empress's quarters beforehand. To the musicians were given white, unlined dresses, and presents of silk and cloth according to their rank. Yūgiri received a blue jacket for himself and a lady's costume for his store-cupboards. He was also charged to carry a reply from the Empress: 'I could have cried yesterday at missing it all. . . . But what can I do? I am not my own mistress. " If anything could tempt me to batter down the flowery, eight-fold wall of precedent, it would be the visit of those butterflies who fluttered from your garden into mine." '

You may think that many of the poems which I here repeat are not worthy of the talented characters to whom they are attributed. I can only reply that they were in every case composed upon the spur of the moment, and the makers were no better pleased with them than you are.

On looking back, I see that I have forgotten to mention the presents which Murasaki distributed among her visitors after the ceremonies of the day before. They were, as you may well imagine, very handsome indeed; but to describe all such matters in detail would be very tiresome. Henceforward communication between the Spring and Autumn quarters was of daily occurrence, joint concerts and excursions were constantly planned, and the two parties of gentlewomen began to feel as much at home in one domain as in the other.

Tamakatsura, after that first encounter on the night when the mummers danced in front of the palace, had continued her friendship with Murasaki. The newcomer's evident desire for cordial relations would in any case have been hard to withstand. But it was also apparent that she was extremely intelligent and at the same time very easy to get on with; so that she was soon a general favourite in the palace.

As has been said, her suitors were numerous; but Genji had not as yet shown any sign of encouraging one rather than another. His feelings upon the subject were indeed very fluctuating. To begin with, he had no confidence in his own capacity to go on playing his present fatherly part with success. Something must be done soon; and he often thought that the first step must be to enlighten Tō no Chūjō as to the girl's identity. So long as he hesitated to do so, the situation was very embarrassing. For whereas Yūgiri had formed the habit of going constantly in and out of her room in a manner which very much embarrassed her, but which it was impossible to criticize, since all the world believed him to be her brother (and it must be confessed that he never attempted to behave with anything else than brotherly affection), Tō no Chūjō's sons whose intimacy with Yūgiri brought them frequently to the house, pressed upon her attentions of an unmistakable sort, which she, knowing her true relationship to these young men, was at a loss how to receive. She would very much have liked her real father at any rate to know of her present position; but she made no attempt to get into communication with him, for she had complete confidence that Genji, who would not do so much for her unless he wished her well, must know far better than she what policy it was best to pursue. Her docility touched and delighted him; for though it did not by any means equal Yūgao's, it served constantly to remind him of her. But Tamakatsura was, as he soon discovered, a person of very much stronger character than he had supposed.

The summer came round, bringing with it the distraction of new clothes and an uncertain yet on the whole extremely agreeable weather. Genji had very little business at this season, and there was a great deal of music and entertaining at the New Palace. He heard that love-letters were pouring in to the Western Wing[1] and with the pleasure that one always feels at discovering that one's anticipations are being fulfilled he hastened thither to examine these missives. He took upon himself not only to read all her correspondence, but also to advise her which letters ought to be neglected and which acknowledged with civility. To this advice she listened somewhat coldly. By far the most passionate and profuse of her correspondents seemed to be Prince Sochi no Miya, and Genji smiled as he looked through the thick packet into which that prince's letters had been collected. 'Sochi and I,' he said, 'have always been great friends. With none of the royal princes have I ever been so intimate, and I know that he has always been devoted to me. The only subject upon which we have ever had any difference of opinion is just this matter of love-making. He allowed it to play far too important a part in his life. I am amused and at the same time, in a way, distressed to find him after all these years behaving exactly as he did when we were both boys. However, I should like you to answer him. I know of no other person about the Court with whom it would so well become a lady of consequence to correspond. He is a remarkable man in many ways. His appearance alone would entitle him . . .'

[1] Tamakatsura's quarters.

and more to this effect, designed of course not to blacken Sochi's character, but to portray him in just such a light as would interest an inexperienced girl. These remarks had, however, an exactly opposite effect to that which Genji intended.

Then there was Prince Higekuro. He had always seemed to be a steady-going, capable fellow, successful in everything he undertook. But glancing at his letters Genji feared that upon the hill of Love, where, let it be remembered, even Confucius stumbled,[1] this wise prince too might easily find his undoing. By far the most elegant letter in the whole collection was one written on very dark blue Chinese paper, heavily perfumed with some delicious scent. It was folded up very small, and Genji, whose curiosity would have been aroused by this fact alone, now spread it out, displaying the poem: 'Of my love perchance you know not, for like a stream that is buried under the ground, a moment it springs into the sunlight; then sinks into the cavern whence it sprang.'

It was very well written, in a hand which combined fanciful originality with adherence to the latest fashions. 'Who wrote this?' he asked; but he received only the vaguest replies. Ukon had now joined them and addressing her, Genji said: 'I want you to give your mistress some guidance in the answering of such letters of this kind as may in future arrive. For the unfortunate situations which sometimes result from our present freedom of manners we men are not always to blame. It often happens that a little timely severity on the lady's part would avert the quandaries into which we are led by our determination to treat love as our principal pastime and distraction. At the time (who should know it better than I?) such severity is of course resented by the gentleman, who will rail in the accepted

[1] The married life of Confucius, like that of Socrates, was very unhappy.

style at his lady's "cruelty" and "insensibility." But in the end he will be grateful that the matter was not allowed to go further.

'On the other hand it may happen that some suitor, whose rank is not such that he can be considered as a possible husband, may entertain very serious feelings indeed, yet through fear of giving offence may go no further in his communications than to make a few conventional remarks about the weather or the garden. In such a case, if the lady, insisting upon seeing in such epistles more than is actually expressed, administers a rebuff, the result will only be that the affair is henceforward on a footing of passion, not (as hitherto) of formality. A civil answer, couched in the same conventional terms as the original letter, may instead dispel the lover's romantic notions and lead him to abandon the quest. But whatever happens the lady has done all that ought to be expected of her.

'On the other hand to mistake the idle compliments and attentions which it is now fashionable to scatter in such profusion, and to treat these courtly formalities as signs of genuine feeling, is even more dangerous than to ignore them altogether, and though such a course may lead to a little momentary excitement, it is bound in the long run to produce a disagreeable situation.

'It often happens that a young girl will cast aside all reserve and pursue without thought of the consequences some quite trivial inclination, merely in order to convince the world that she is a woman of feeling. At first the discovery of a new pleasure is in itself sufficient to carry her through; but repetition palls, and after a few months excitement gives place to tedium or even disgust.

'I have, however, reason to believe that both my stepbrother and Prince Higekuro are in this case completely sincere, and whatever her own feelings may be it is improper

THE BUTTERFLIES

that any one in your mistress's position should deal too curtly with offers such as these. As for the rest, I assume that their rank is not such as to make acceptance conceivable, and there can therefore be no objection to your mistress meting out among them such varying degrees of kindness or severity as her fancy dictates.'

While this exposition was in progress at the far end of the room, Tamakatsura sat with her back towards the speakers, occasionally glancing across her shoulder with a turn of the head that showed off her delicate profile to great advantage. She was wearing a long close-fitting robe, pink plum-blossom colour without, and green within; her short mantle matched the flower of the white deutzia, then in full bloom. There was in her style of dress something which made it seem homely without being dowdy or unfashionable. If in her manners any trace of rusticity could still be found, it lay perhaps in a certain lack of self-assurance which she seemed to have retained as a last remnant of her country breeding. But in every other respect she had made ample use of the opportunites afforded her by life at the New Palace. The way she dressed her hair and her use of make-up showed that she observed those around her with an acute and intelligent eye. She had, in fact, since her arrival at Court, grown into a perfectly well turned-out and fashionable beauty, all ready to become, alas, not his own (reflected Genji with chagrin) but some fortunate young man's immaculate bride. Ukon, too, was thinking, as she watched them, that Genji looked much more fit to be her lover than her father. Yes, they were surely made for one another; and Ukon doubted whether, however long he searched, Genji would find her a partner whose looks matched her so well. 'Most of the letters that come,' said the old lady, 'I do not pass on at all. The three or four that you have been looking at, you will agree I could not possibly have returned. But though I delivered them to my mistress, she has not answered them, and though of course she will do so if you insist upon it. . . .' 'Perhaps you can tell me,' broke in Genji, 'who sent this curious note. Despite its minute size there seems to be a great deal of writing in it.' 'Ah, that one . . .' said Ukon, 'if I returned it once I returned it a hundred times! But there was no getting rid of the messenger. It comes from Captain Kashiwagi, His Excellency Tō no Chūjō's eldest son. This gentleman knows little Miruko, my lady's chambermaid, and it was through her that the messenger was first admitted. I assure you no one else but this child Miruko knows anything about the matter at all. . . .' 'But how delightful!' said Genji, much relieved. 'Kashiwagi of course holds a rather low rank, and that is a disadvantage. But no child of such a man as Tō no Chūjō is to be scorned; and there are, in point of fact a great many important officials who in public esteem occupy a far lower place than these young men. Moreover, Kashiwagi is generally considered to be the most serious and competent of the brothers. To receive compliments from such a man is very gratifying, and though he must of course sooner or later learn of his close relationship to you, for the present I see no need to enlighten him.' And still examining the letter, he added 'There are touches in his handwriting, too, which are by no means to be despised.' 'You agree with everything I say,' he continued: 'but I feel that inwardly you are raising objections all the while. I am very sorry not to please you; but if you are thinking that I ought to hand you over to your father without more ado, I simply do not agree with you. You are very young and inexperienced. If you were suddenly to find yourself in the midst of brothers and sisters whom you have never known, I am certain you would be miserable. Whereas if you will

THE BUTTERFLIES

only wait till I have settled your future (in such a way as your father, upon whom there are so many claims, could not possibly manage), there will be time enough afterwards to disclose the story of your birth.'

Though he did not say in so many words that he would far rather have kept her for himself, he more than once came perilously near to hinting something of the kind. Such indiscretions she either misunderstood or ignored. This piqued him; but he enjoyed the visit and was quite unhappy when he discovered that it was high time for him to go back to his own quarters. Before he left she reminded him, in guarded language, of his promise to tell her real father what had become of her. He felt at this more conscience-stricken than he need have done. For in her heart of hearts Tamakatsura was by no means in a hurry to leave the New Palace. She would have been glad to have the inevitable introduction to her real parent safely behind her, chiefly because the prospect of it destroyed her peace of mind. However kind her father might be, it was impossible that he should take more trouble about her than Prince Genji was doing; indeed, Tō no Chūjō, not having once set eyes on her since she was a mere infant, might well have ceased to take any interest in her whatever. She had lately been reading a number of old romances and had come across many accounts of cases very similar to her own. She began to see that it was a delicate matter for a child to force itself upon the attention of a parent who had done his best to forget that it existed, and she abandoned all idea of taking the business into her own hands.

Genji arrived at Murasaki's rooms full of enthusiasm for the lady whom he had just been visiting: 'What a surprising and delightful creature this Tamakatsura is!' he exclaimed. 'Her mother, with whom I was so intimate years ago, had almost too grave and earnest a character.

This girl will, I can see, be more a " woman of the world " ; but she is at the same time evidently very affectionate. I am sure she has a brilliant future before her. . . .' From his manner Murasaki instantly saw that his interest in Tamakatsura had assumed a new character. ' I am very sorry for the girl,' she said. ' She evidently has complete confidence in you. But I happen to know what you mean by that phrase " a woman of the world," and if I chose to do so, could tell the unfortunate creature what to expect. . . .' ' But you surely cannot mean that I shall *betray* her confidence ? ' asked Genji indignantly. ' You forget,' she replied, ' that I was once in very much the same position myself. You had made up your mind to treat me as a daughter ; but, unless I am much mistaken, there were times when you did not carry out this resolution very successfully. . . .' ' How clever every one is ! ' thought Genji, much put out at the facility with which his inmost thoughts were read. But he hastened to rejoin : ' If I were in love with Tamakatsura, she would presumably become aware of the fact quite as quickly as you would.' He was too much annoyed to continue the conversation ; however, he admitted to himself in private that when people come to a conclusion of this kind, it is hardly ever far from the mark. But surely, after all, he could judge better than she ? And Murasaki, he reflected, was not judging this case on its merits, but merely assuming, in the light of past experience, that events were about to take a certain course. . . .

To convince himself that Murasaki had no ground for her suspicions he frequently went across to the Side Wing and spent some hours in Tamakatsura's company.

During the fourth month the weather was rather depressing. But one evening, when it had been raining heavily all day, he looked out and saw to his relief that at last the sky was clearing. The young maples and oak trees in the garden blent their leafage in a marvellous curtain of green. Genji remembered the lines 'In the fourth month the weather grew clearer and still . . .'[1] and thence his thoughts wandered to the girl in the Western Wing. He felt a sudden longing, on this early summer evening, for the sight of something fresh, something fragrant; and without a word to anyone he slipped away to her rooms. He found her practising at her desk in an easy attitude and attire. She was in no way prepared to receive such a visit, and upon his arrival rose to her feet with a blush. Caught thus unawares and informally dressed, she was more like her mother than he had ever seen her before, and he could not help exclaiming: 'I could not have believed it possible! To-night you are simply Yūgao herself. Of course, I have always noticed the resemblance; but never before has it reached such a point as this. It so happens that Yūgiri is not at all like his mother, and consequently I am apt to forget how complete such resemblances can sometimes be.'

A sprig of orange-blossom was stuck among some fruit that was lying on a tray near by. 'As the orange-blossom gives its scent unaltered to the sleeve that brushes it, so have you taken on your mother's beauty, till you and she are one.' So he recited, adding: 'Nothing has ever consoled me for her loss, and indeed, though so many years have passed I shall die regretting her as bitterly as at the start. But to-night, when I first caught sight of you, it seemed to me for an instant that she had come back to me again—that the past was only a dream. . . . Bear with me; you cannot conceive what happiness was brought

[1] From a poem written by Po Chü-i in 821, describing the pleasure of returning to his own house after a spell of duty in the Palace: 'I sit at the window and listen to the wind rustling among the bamboo; I walk on the terrace and watch the moon rising between the trees.'

me by one moment of illusion. But now it is over . . .'
and so saying he took her hand in his. She was somewhat
taken aback, for he had never attempted to do such a thing
before; but she answered quietly: 'Wretched will be
my lot indeed, should the flower's perfume prove hapless
as the flower that was destroyed.'

She felt that things were not going well, and sat staring
at the floor, her chin propped on her fist. This was just
the attitude in which she most attracted him. He noticed
the plumpness of her hand, the softness of her skin, the
delicacy of her whole figure. Such beauty could not,
at these close quarters, in any case have failed to move
him; coupled with the memories which every feature
inspired, it proved irresistible, and to-day his discretion
broke down as never before. True, he did no more than
make a somewhat vague avowal of his feelings towards
her. But Tamakatsura was instantly terror-stricken; of
this there could be no doubt, for she was trembling from
head to foot. 'Come!' he said, 'you need not look so
horrified. There is no harm in my having such feelings,
so long as only you and I are aware of them. You have
known for some time past that I was very fond of you,
and now you have learnt that I care for you even more
than you supposed. But were I drawn towards you by
the blindest passion that has ever darkened the heart of
man, this would not damage your chances with Sochi no
Miya, Higekuro and the rest. For in their eyes you are
my daughter, and it would never occur to them that my
affection for you could in any way hinder their courtship.
My only fear is that you will never find a husband who cares
for you half as much as I do. Such feelings as mine for you
are not as common in the world as you perhaps imagine
them to be. . . .'

He spoke all the while as though what he had said to

her implied nothing more than an unusual access of paternal feeling. It had now quite stopped raining; 'the wind was rustling in the bamboos,'[1] and the moon was shining brightly. It was a lovely and solemn night. Tamakatsura's ladies, seeing that the conversation was beginning to take a somewhat intimate turn, had tactfully withdrawn from her presence.

His visits had for some while been very frequent; but circumstances seldom favoured him as they did to-night. Moreover, now that he had, quite without premeditation, confessed to these feelings, they seemed suddenly to have taken a far stronger hold upon him. Unobtrusively, indeed almost without her being aware of what was happening, he slipped from her shoulders the light cloak which she had been wearing since summer came in, and lay down beside her. She was horrified, but chiefly through the fear that some one might discover them in this posture. Her own father, she ruefully reflected, might refuse to admit his responsibilities towards her and even order her out of his sight, but she could be certain that he would not submit her to such ordeals as she was here undergoing. . . . She did her best to hide her tears, but before long they burst forth in an uncontrollable flood. Genji was dismayed. 'If that is what you feel about it,' he said, 'you must really dislike me very much indeed. I have not attempted to do anything that the world would consider in the least reprehensible, even were I in no way connected with you. But as it is, we have been friends for almost a year. Surely there is nothing very strange in the way I have behaved? You know quite well that I should never force you to do anything you would be sorry for afterwards. Do not, please, be angry with me. Now that you have grown so like your mother, it is an immense

[1] See note on p. 235.

comfort to me simply to be with you. . . .' He spoke then for a long while, tenderly, caressingly. For now that she was lying beside him the resemblance to Yūgao was more than ever complete. But happy though he would have been to remain far longer at her side, he was still able to see that his behaviour had been in the highest degree rash and inconsiderate. It was growing late; at any moment some one might return to the room and discover them. 'Do not think the worse of me for what has happened this evening,' he said at last, rising from the couch; 'it would distress me very much if you did. I know quite well that there are people who never allow their feelings to get the better of them. I can only say that I am differently made. But of this at least I can assure you: whatever you may think of me, such outbursts are not due in my case merely to some frivolous impulse of the moment. Once my affections are aroused they are boundless both in time and extent. You need not fear that I shall ever act in such a way as to harm your good name. All I ask is that I may sometimes be allowed to talk as I have talked to-night; and perhaps I may even hope that you will occasionally answer me in the same spirit.'

He spoke gently, reasonably, but she was now beside herself with agitation, and made no intelligible reply.

'I see that I have made a great mistake,' he said at last. 'I always thought that we got on unusually well together; but it is now clear that the friendship was all on my side. For I cannot think that my showing a little affection would so much perturb you unless you definitely disliked me. . . .' He broke off, and left the room with a final entreaty that she would speak to no one of what had occurred.

Though Tamakatsura was no longer very young, she was still entirely innocent, and this made her judge Genji's conduct more harshly than she would otherwise have done.

THE BUTTERFLIES

He had indeed merely lain down on the same couch; but she, in her inexperience, imagined that in so doing he had taken advantage of her to the utmost possible extent. On returning to the room her gentlewomen at once noticed that she was looking very distraught, and pestered her with tiresome enquiries about her health. No sooner had they withdrawn than Ateki,[1] the daughter of her old nurse, began (irritatingly enough) to congratulate her upon her guardian's extraordinary kindness: 'How gratifying it is,' she said, 'that his Excellency is so admirably attentive to you! With all respect to your own father, I very much doubt whether he would put himself to half as much trouble on your account. . . . Prince Genji seems to take a positive pleasure in looking after you.' But Tamakatsura had been too much surprised and shocked by Genji's conduct to feel, for the moment, any gratitude for the more than parental solicitude by which Ateki was so deeply impressed. She had no desire whatever to see him again, and yet in his absence felt strangely lonely and depressed.

[1] See above p. 159. Ateki of course knew the secret of Tamakatsura's birth.

CHAPTER VII

THE GLOW-WORM

GENJI was now in a singularly fortunate position. The government of the country lay wholly in his hands; but though his power was supreme, he was now seldom troubled by the uninteresting details of public business; for he had some while ago delegated all such minor decisions to Tō no Chūjō, and the arrangement continued to work very successfully. In varying ways and degrees his dependants naturally benefited by his increased leisure and security. Not only was he able to devote far more time to looking after their affairs, but they could also feel that, such as it was, their position was now something permanent and dependable; whereas in the old days, when the powers arrayed against him were still unshaken, they knew quite well that he might at any moment find himself far more in need of patronage than able any longer to dispense it. Most of them, even those who received a very small share of his attentions, were nowadays fairly well content with their lot; but the Princess [1] in the Western Wing continued to view with great apprehension the imprudent turn which her guardian had lately given to their relationship, and different as were his manners from those of her persecutor [2] on the Island, she was now scarcely less alarmed than in the weeks which preceded her flight. She felt that in first insisting on their playing the part of father and daughter, and then suddenly

[1] Tamakatsura.   [2] Tayū.

revealing himself in another character, he had taken advantage of her in a very mean way, and despite his protestations it seemed vain to suppose that, out of consideration for her at any rate, he would restrain himself sufficiently to avoid an open scandal. She had no one to whom she could turn, and now that she was face to face with the actual difficulties of life she realized far more acutely than she had even done as a child the irreparable loss which she had sustained in her mother's death.

Genji, on his side, was exceedingly vexed with himself for having acted so imprudently. He had not breathed a word about the matter to any one, and being anxious to convince himself that his behaviour on that unlucky night had been altogether exceptional, he visited her frequently and, apart from a few rather ambiguous remarks (which however he was careful never to let fall in the presence of her gentlewomen and attendants) he behaved in a manner to which exception could not be taken. Each time that he began to venture on dangerous ground she felt her heart beat violently and, if he had been any one else, would have cut him short and sent him about his business. But as it was she merely pretended not to notice what he was saying.

She was naturally of a very cheerful and lively disposition, so that she made friends easily. Prince Sochi and her other suitors, though they themselves had obtained so little encouragement from her, continued to hear on all sides nothing but praises of her good looks and general charm. They therefore redoubled their efforts; but to their chagrin the rains of the fifth month [1] had already set in without any sign that their industry was likely to be rewarded.

Among some letters which Tamakatsura was showing to him Genji found one from Prince Sochi: 'If you could

[1] It is unlucky to marry in the fifth month.

but find it in your heart to admit me for one single moment to your presence, you would earn my undying gratitude, even though I should never see you again. For I should thus enjoy a respite, the first for many months, from the tortures which I now endure. . . .' 'I have never seen Prince Sochi making love,' said Genji as he read the letter. 'It would be a sight worth seeing. Please tell him he may come,' and he began suggesting the terms in which she should reply. But the idea did not at all appeal to her, and alleging that she was feeling giddy and could not, at the moment, possibly handle a pen, she attempted to lead the conversation into other channels. 'But there is no need that you should write yourself,' said Genji, returning to his project; 'we will dictate a letter between us.'

Among Tamakatsura's gentlewomen there was none in whom she placed any great confidence. The only exception was a certain Saishō no Kimi, a daughter of her mother's younger brother, who seemed to have far more sense than most young women. Hearing that this girl was in difficult circumstances Tamakatsura had sent for her to see what could be done; and finding that Saishō was not only the sort of person whom it would be useful in a general way to have about her, but was also an unusually good penwoman, she retained this young cousin in her service. Genji, who knew that Tamakatsura often used the girl as her amanuensis, now sent for Saishō and proceeded to dictate a letter. For he was consumed by an overwhelming curiosity to see how his half-brother, with whose conduct in all other situations he was so familiar, would conduct himself at such an interview as this. As for Tamakatsura, she had, since the occasion of Genji's unpardonable indiscretion, begun to pay a good deal more attention to the communications of her suitors. She had no reason to give any preference to Prince Sochi; but he, as much as any other husband, represented a way of escape from the embarrassment in which she found herself. She was, however, far from having ever thought of him seriously in this connection.

Little knowing that his success was due to a whim of Prince Genji's rather than to any favourable impression that his own suit had made, Sochi no Miya in great elation rushed round to the New Palace and presented himself at Tamakatsura's door. He could not complain of his treatment; for he was at once accommodated with a divan which was only a few paces from her curtains-of-state. He looked about him. On every side he recognized such presents and appurtenances as far more commonly emanate from a lover than from a parent. The air was laden with costly perfumes. There were hangings, brocades, a thousand trifles any one of which would have been enough to arouse in Sochi's heart the suspicion that Genji, from whom he was convinced that those bounties flowed, was not her father. And if he was not her father, then inevitably, as Sochi ruefully recognized, he must be reckoned with as a serious rival. Tamakatsura herself made no effort to converse with him or even answer his questions. Her maids seemed quite incapable of replying on her behalf, and when even Saishō, reputed to be so capable in every emergency, continued to sit in awkward silence, Genji whispered: 'What is the matter with you all? Have you become rooted to your seats? Get up, do something. . . . Be civil!' But all this had no effect. They merely stared helplessly in front of them.

The evening was now drawing in, and as the sky was very much overcast the room was almost dark. Beyond her curtains Tamakatsura could just discern the motionless form of her suitor, gracefully outlined against the gloom, while from her side a stirring of the evening air would occasionally carry towards him a fragrance enhanced by a strange perfume [1] which, though it was familiar to him, he could not then identify. The room seemed full of diverse and exquisite scents that inflamed his imagination, and though he had previously pictured her to himself as handsome, he now (as these perfumes floated round him) thought of her as a hundred times more beautiful than he had ever done before. Her curtains were thick and it was now quite dark. He could not see her and could only guess that she was still near him; but so vividly did she now appear before his mind's eye that it was as though no barrier were between them, and he began to address her in the most passionate terms. There was now in his style no longer anything of the professional courtier or hardened man-of-the-world. The long outpouring to which Genji, ensconced in his corner of her curtained dais, now listened with considerable emotion, was natural, direct—almost boyish. When it was over, Prince Sochi was rewarded by a note from Saishō, informing him that her mistress had some time ago retired to the inner room! [2] 'This is too bad!' whispered Genji, creeping to the door of her refuge (he had himself been so intent upon his brother's eloquence that he had not seen her slip away). 'You cannot simply disappear while people are talking to you. You are governed by absurd pre-conceived notions, and never stop to consider the merits of the case in question. To treat any visitor, and above all a person of Prince Sochi's standing, in the manner I have just witnessed would not be tolerated in a child; and in your case, seeing that you are a grown woman not without some experience of Court life, such behaviour is insufferable. Even if you are too shy to converse with him, you might at least sit within reasonable distance. . . .'

[1] The rare perfume which Genji wore.
[2] Sochi had been addressing her through her curtains-of-state. She crept away in the darkness as an animal at the Zoo might slink into its back cage. Genji was, of course, all the time with her behind her curtains.

Genji had never yet pursued her into the inner room; but she had no doubt that on the present occasion, in his eagerness to reform her manners, he would have no scruple in doing so; and reluctantly she left her place of retreat and once more seated herself near the edge of her curtained daïs. Sochi now attempted to begin a more general conversation, but no topic seemed to arouse her interest. Suddenly her attention was distracted by a light which had begun to glimmer quite close to where she sat. It seemed to move when Genji moved. She now saw him go to her curtains-of-state and, at a certain point, hook back the inner curtain, leaving only a single thickness of light transparent stuff. Here he suspended something bright, that looked like a paper candle.... What was he doing? She was dumbfounded.

The fact was that on his way to her apartments earlier in the evening Genji had encountered an unusual number of glow-worms. Collecting them in a thin paper bag he had concealed this improvised lantern under the folds of his cloak and, on his arrival, disposed of it in a safe corner. Startled by the sudden glow of light, Tamakatsura snatched up her fan and buried her face behind it, not before Sochi had caught an enchanting glimpse of her beauty. This was just what Genji had intended. The attentions which his brother had hitherto paid to Tamakatsura were, he suspected, due solely to the fact that Sochi had accepted the current story and imagined her indeed to be Genji's daughter. He knew that, despite her fame as a delightful accession to the Court, Prince Sochi could have but a vague conception of her charm; and in order that he might the sooner escape from his own dilemma he was determined that Sochi should no longer merely pay formal court to the girl, but should really lose his head about her. He imagined that he was now at any rate indisputably playing the part of a fond and disinterested parent. A strange delusion! For had he reflected for a moment he would have seen that nothing would ever have induced him so crudely to thrust his own daughter, the Princess of Akashi, upon a suitor's notice. He now stole away by a back door and returned to his own apartments.

Sochi was feeling much encouraged. He now discredited Saishō's note and imagined that the lady had been sitting during the whole time of his discourse in the position where the light of the glow-worms revealed her. 'After all,' he thought to himself, 'I have interested her. She listens patiently and apparently even likes to be near me.' And with that he pulled back the light gauze flap at the part of her curtains where Genji had removed the thick inner hanging. She was now but a few feet away from him, and though a bag of glow-worms makes no very famous [1] illumination, he saw enough by this fitful and glimmering light to confirm his impression that she was one of the most beautiful women he had ever seen. In another moment Tamakatsura's maids, summoned hastily to the scene, had detached the strange lantern and carried it somewhere out of sight.

Genji's stratagem was indeed abundantly successful. This momentary vision of Tamakatsura huddled disconsolately upon her couch had profoundly disturbed him. 'Does the harsh world decree that even the flickering glow-worm, too shy for common speech, must quench the timid torchlight of its love!' So he now recited; and she, thinking that if she appeared to be taking much trouble about her reply, he would suppose she attached more importance to the matter than was actually the case, answered instantly: 'Far deeper is the glow-worm's love that speaks in silent points of flame, than all the passions idle courtiers prate

---

[1] *Oboye-naki* 'fame-less.' I retain this idiom as it corresponds curiously with ours.

with facile tongue.' She spoke coldly; moreover she had now withdrawn to the far side of her dais. For some while he pleaded in vain against this inhospitable treatment. But he soon saw that he would gain nothing, even should he stay where he was till dawn; and though he could hear by the water dripping from the eaves that it was a most disagreeable night, he rose and took his leave. Despite the rain the nightingales were singing lustily; but he was in no mood to enjoy their song and did not pause an instant to hear them.

On the fifth day of the fifth month, business at the Stables brought Genji in the direction of her apartments, and he availed himself of this opportunity to discover what had happened on the night of Sochi's visit. 'Did the prince stay very late?' he asked. 'I hope you did not let him go too far. He is the sort of man who might very easily lose control of himself . . . not that he is worse than others. It is really very unusual indeed to meet with any one who is capable of acting with self-restraint under such circumstances.' And this was the match-maker who on the very occasion to which he was now referring, had driven her into Prince Sochi's arms! She could not help being amused at his unblushing inconsistency. But all the while he was warning her against the very man for whose visit he had himself been responsible. Tamakatsura scanning him in his holiday clothes thought that he could not, by any imaginable touch of art or nature, have looked more beautiful. That thin cloak—what a marvellous blend of colours! Did fairies preside over his dyeing-vats? Even the familiar and traditional patterns, she thought, on such days as this take on a new significance and beauty. And then looking again at Genji: 'If only we were not on this tiresome footing,' she said to herself, 'I believe I should long ago have fallen very much in love with him.'

A letter arrived. It was from Prince Sochi, written on thin white paper in a competent hand, and couched in terms which at the time seemed very spirited and apposite. I fear, however, that were I to reproduce it here, this admired letter would seem in no way remarkable, and I will only record the poem which accompanied it: 'Shall I, like the flower that grows unnoticed by the stream though holiday-makers in their dozens pass that way, find myself still, when this day closes, unwanted and passed-by?' The letter was attached to the tallest and handsomest flag-iris[1] she had ever seen. 'He is quite right,' said Genji; 'to-day there is no escape for you.' And when one after another of her gentlewomen had pleaded with her that this once at any rate she should answer him with her own hand, she produced the following reply, which had, however, very little to do with what was going on in her mind: 'Better had the flower remained amid the waters, content to be ignored, than prove, thus swiftly plucked, how feeble were the roots on which it stood.'

It was an idle repartee, and even the handwriting seemed to Prince Sochi's expectant eye somewhat vague and purposeless. He was, indeed, not at all sure, when he saw it, that he had not made a great mistake. . . . Tamakatsura, on the other hand, was disposed to be in rather a good humour with herself. She had this morning received Magic Balls[2] of the utmost variety and splendour from an unprecedented number of admirers. A more complete contrast than that between her poverty-stricken years on the island and her present pampered existence could hardly be imagined. Her ideas on a variety of subjects were becoming far less rigid than when she first arrived

[1] Irises were plucked on the fifth day of the fifth month.
[2] Balls made of coloured stuffs, with scent-bags in the middle. Supposed to ward off disease.

at the New Palace; and she began to see that provided her relationship with Genji could be maintained upon its present harmless footing she had everything to gain from its continuance.

Later in the day Genji called upon the lady in the Eastern Quarter.[1] 'The young men in the Royal Body Guard are holding their sports here to-day,' he said. 'Yūgiri will be bringing them back with him to his rooms and is counting on you to prepare for their entertainment. They will arrive just before sunset. There will also probably be a great deal of company besides; for ever since a rumour spread round the Court that we were secretly harbouring in the New Palace some fabulous prodigy of wit and beauty, an overwhelming interest has been taken in us, and we have not had a moment's peace. So be prepared for the worst!'

Part of the race-course was not far away from this side of the palace and a good view could be obtained from the porticos and outer galleries. 'You had better throw open all the garden-doors along the passage between this wing and the main house,' he said. 'The young people will see very well from there. The Bodyguard of the Right is exceptionally strong this year. In my opinion they are a far more interesting lot than most of the present high officers at Court.' This whetted, as it was intended to do, the curiosity of the young people in that part of the house, and the galleries were soon thronged. The pages and younger waiting-women from Tamakatsura's wing also came to see the sights and were accommodated at the open doors along the passage, the persons of quality being ensconced behind green shutters or curtains dyed in this new-fashioned way according to which the colour is allowed to run down into the fringe. Among the dresses of the visitors

[1] The Lady from the Village of Falling Flowers.

were many elaborate Chinese costumes, specially designed for the day's festivity, the colour of the young dianthus leaf tending to prevail. The ladies who belonged to this wing had not been encouraged to make any special effort for the occasion and were for the most part in thin summer gowns, green without and peach-blossom colour within. There was a great deal of rivalry and harmless self-display, which was rewarded from time to time by a glance from one of the young courtiers who were assembled on the course.

Genji arrived on the scene at the hour of the Sheep,[1] and found just such a concourse of distinguished visitors as he had predicted. It was interesting to see the competitors, whom he knew only in their official uniforms, so differently arrayed, each with his following of smartly dressed squires and assistants. The sports continued till evening. The ladies, although they had a very imperfect understanding of what was going on, were at least capable of deriving a great deal of pleasure from the sight of so many young men in elegant riding-jackets hurling themselves with desperate recklessness into the fray. The finish of the course was not so very far from Murasaki's rooms, so that her gentlewomen too were able to get some idea of what was going on. The races were followed by a game of polo played to the tune of Tagyūraku.[2] Then came a competition of rival pairs in the Nasori.[3] All this was accompanied by a great din of bells and drums, sounded to announce the gaining of points on one side and another. It was now getting quite dark and the spectators could barely see what was going on. The first part of the indoor entertainment which came next consisted in the distribution of prizes among the successful riders. Then followed a great banquet and it was very late indeed when the guests began

[1] 1 p.m.   [2] 'Hitting the Ball Tune.'
[3] A Korean dance.

to withdraw. Genji had arranged to sleep that night in the Eastern Wing. He sat up a long while talking to the Lady from the Village of Falling Flowers. 'Did you not think to-day,' he said, ' that Prince Sochi was immeasurably superior to any of the other visitors? His appearance is of course not particularly in his favour. But there is something in his manners and mode of address which I at any rate find very attractive. I was able recently to observe him on an occasion when he had no reason to believe that he was being watched, and came to the conclusion that those who so loudly praise his wit and ingenuity have no idea what constitutes his real charm.' 'I know that he is your younger brother,' she answered; ' but he certainly looks considerably older than you. I am told that he has visited here very frequently during the last few months. But as a matter of fact I had not till to-day once set eyes on him since I saw him years ago when my sister was at Court. I confess I then had no idea that he would turn out so well as he has done. In those days it was his younger brother, the Viceroy of Tsukushi, whom I used to admire. But I see now that he had not the same princeliness of air and carriage which you rightly attribute to Prince Sochi.' He saw that, brief as was the time she had spent in Prince Sochi's company that day, she had already completely succumbed to his charms. He smiled, but did not draw her on into a general discussion of his guests and their merits or defects. He had always had a great dislike of those who cannot mention an acquaintance without immediately beginning to pick his character to pieces and make him seem utterly contemptible. When he heard the Lady from the Village of Falling Flowers going into raptures over Prince Higekuro, he did indeed find it hard not to disillusion her, particularly as he was just then beginning to be somewhat alarmed lest this prince, whom he regarded as rather unsuitable, should in the end turn out to be the strongest candidate for Tamakatsura's favour.

He and the Lady from the Village of Falling Flowers had for years past been on terms merely of ordinary confidence and friendliness. It was assumed on this occasion as on others that they would presently retreat each to a separate resting-place. How and why had this assumption first begun? He could not remember, and felt that to-night he would very gladly have broken the rule. But she seemed to take for granted that he would presently wish to retire, and so far from resenting this or seeming to be at all depressed, she evidently felt highly gratified that her own quarters had been selected as the scene of a festivity the like of which she had not witnessed in person for a very great number of years. 'The withered grass that even the woodland pony left untouched, to-day with the wild iris of the pool-side has been twisted in one wreath.' Thus she expressed her gratitude and pride. He was touched that so small an event should mean so much to her, and answered with the verse: 'The colt whose shadow falls upon the waters close where the wild-swan's wing is mirrored in the lake, from iris and sweet marsh-marigold shall ne'er be far away.' How easily was she now contented, and how vague had his own compliments become! 'Though I so seldom manage to see you,' he said, 'I assure you I am never happier than when I am here.' It would have been unlike her to take him to task for the insincerity of this last speech. She merely accepted it quietly and they parted for the night. He found that she had given up her own bed to him, and had all her things carried to another place. Had she not seemed so convinced that anything in the way of greatest intimacy was out of the question, he might have felt inclined on this occasion to suggest a different arrangement.

This year the rainy season lasted much longer than usual, and whereas the monotony of the downpour is usually relieved by an occasional day of sunshine, this time there was nothing but one continuous drizzle for weeks on end. The inhabitants of the New Palace found it very hard to get through the day and tried one amusement after another. In the end they mostly betook themselves to reading illustrated romances. The Lady of Akashi had, among her other accomplishments, a talent for copying out and finely decorating such books as these; and being told that every one was clamouring for some occupation which would help them to get through the day, she now sent over a large supply to the Princess, her daughter. But the greatest enthusiast of all was Lady Tamakatsura, who would rise at daybreak and spend the whole day absorbed in reading or copying out romances. Many of her younger ladies-in-waiting had a vast stock of stories, some legendary, some about real people, which they told with considerable skill. But Tamakatsura could not help feeling that the history of her own life, should it ever come to be told, was really far more interesting than any of the tales with which her ladies sought to entertain her. True the sufferings of the princess in the *Sumiyoshi Tale* [1] had at certain points a resemblance to her own experiences. But she could see no reason why for generations past so many tears of indignation and pity should have been shed over the fate of this princess at the hands of her unscrupulous lover.[2] Judged as an episode, thought Tamakatsura, her own escape from the violence of Tayū was quite as exciting.

One day Genji, going the round with a number of romances

---

[1] The story of a misused step-child. It is no longer extant, the text which bears this name being merely a 15th-century adaptation of the *Room Below Stairs*.
[2] A disagreeable old man to whom her step-mother tried to marry her.

which he had promised to lend, came to Tamakatsura's room and found her, as usual, hardly able to lift her eyes from the book in front of her. 'Really, you are incurable,' he said, laughing. 'I sometimes think that young ladies exist for no other purpose than to provide purveyors of the absurd and improbable with a market for their wares. I am sure that the book you are now so intent upon is full of the wildest nonsense. Yet knowing this all the time, you are completely captivated by its extravagances and follow them with the utmost excitement: why, here you are on this hot day, so hard at work that, though I am sure you have not the least idea of it, your hair is in the most extraordinary tangle. . . . But there; I know quite well that these old tales are indispensable during such weather as this. How else would you all manage to get through the day? Now for a confession. I too have lately been studying these books and have, I must tell you, been amazed by the delight which they have given me. There is, it seems, an art of so fitting each part of the narrative into the next that, though all is mere invention, the reader is persuaded that such things might easily have happened and is as deeply moved as though they were actually going on around him. We may know with one part of our minds that every incident has been invented for the express purpose of impressing us; but (if the plot is constructed with the requisite skill) we may all the while in another part of our minds be burning with indignation at the wrongs endured by some wholly imaginary princess. Or again we may be persuaded by a writer's eloquence into accepting the crudest absurdities, our judgment being as it were dazzled by sheer splendour of language.

I have lately sometimes stopped and listened to one of our young people reading out loud to her companions and have been amazed at the advances which this art of fiction is now making. How do you suppose that our new writers come by this talent? It used to be thought that the authors of successful romances were merely particularly untruthful people whose imaginations had been stimulated by constantly inventing plausible lies. But that is clearly unfair. . . .' 'Perhaps,' she said, 'only people who are themselves much occupied in practising deception have the habit of thus dipping below the surface. I can assure you that for my part, when I read a story, I always accept it as an account of something that has really and actually happened.'

So saying she pushed away from her the book which she had been copying. Genji continued: 'So you see as a matter of fact I think far better of this art than I have led you to suppose. Even its practical value is immense. Without it what should we know of how people lived in the past, from the Age of the Gods down to the present day? For history-books such as the Chronicles of Japan show us only one small corner of life; whereas these diaries and romances which I see piled around you contain, I am sure, the most minute information about all sorts of people's private affairs. . . .' He smiled, and went on: 'But I have a theory of my own about what this art of the novel is, and how it came into being. To begin with, it does not simply consist in the author's telling a story about the adventures of some other person. On the contrary it happens because the story-teller's own experience of men and things, whether for good or ill—not only what he has passed through himself, but even events which he has only witnessed or been told of—has moved him to an emotion so passionate that he can no longer keep it shut up in his heart. Again and again something in his own life or in that around him will seem to the writer so important that he cannot bear to let it pass into oblivion. There must never come a time, he feels, when men do not know about it. That is my view of how this art arose.

'Clearly then, it is no part of the story-teller's craft to describe only what is good or beautiful. Sometimes, of course, virtue will be his theme, and he may then make such play with it as he will. But he is just as likely to have been struck by numerous examples of vice and folly in the world around him, and about them he has exactly the same feelings as about the pre-eminently good deeds which he encounters: they are important and must all be garnered in. Thus anything whatsoever may become the subject of a novel, provided only that it happens in this mundane life and not in some fairyland beyond our human ken.

'The outward forms of this art will not of course be everywhere the same. At the Court of China and in other foreign lands both the genius of the writers and their actual methods of composition are necessarily very different from ours; and even here in Japan the art of story-telling has in course of time undergone great changes. There will, too, always be a distinction between the lighter and the more serious forms of fiction. . . . Well, I have said enough to show that when at the beginning of our conversation I spoke of romances as though they were mere frivolous fabrications, I was only teasing you. Some people have taken exception on moral grounds to an art in which the perfect and imperfect are set side by side. But even in the discourses which Buddha in his bounty allowed to be recorded, certain passages contain what the learned call Upāya or 'Adapted Truth '—a fact that has led some superficial persons to doubt whether a doctrine so inconsistent with itself could possibly command our credence. Even in the scriptures of the Greater Vehicle [1] there are, I confess, many such instances. We may indeed

---

[1] The Mahāyāna, the later development of Buddhism which prevailed in Tibet, China and Japan.

go so far as to say that there is an actual mixture of Truth and Error. But the purpose of these holy writings, namely the compassing of our Salvation, remains always the same. So too, I think, may it be said that the art of fiction must not lose our allegiance because, in the pursuit of the main purpose to which I have alluded above, it sets virtue by the side of vice, or mingles wisdom with folly. Viewed in this light the novel is seen to be not, as is usually supposed, a mixture of useful truth with idle invention, but something which at every stage and in every part has a definite and serious purpose.'

Thus did he vindicate the story-teller's profession as an art of real importance.

Murasaki, who had first taken to reading romances in order to see whether they were suitable for her adopted daughter, the Princess from Akashi, was now deeply immersed in them. She was particularly fond of the *Tale of Komano*[1] and showing to Genji an illustrated copy of it she said one day: 'Do you not think that these pictures are very well painted?' The reason that she liked the illustrations so much was that one of them showed the little girl in the story lying peacefully asleep in her chair, and this somehow reminded Murasaki of her own childhood. 'And do you mean to tell me,' asked Genji, ' that such an infant as that has already, at this early point in the story, been the heroine of gallant episodes? When I remember the exemplary way in which I looked after you during your childhood I realize that my self-restraint is even more unusual than I supposed.' It could not be denied that his conduct was in many ways unusual; but hardly, perhaps, exemplary in the common sense of the word. 'I hope you are very careful not to allow the little princess to read any of the looser stories,' he continued. 'She would realize, I am

[1] Now lost.

sure, that the heroines of such books are acting very wrongly in embarking upon these secret intrigues; but I had much rather she did not know that such things go on in the world at all.' 'This is really too much!' thought Murasaki. 'That he should come straight from one of his interminable visits to Tamakatsura and at once begin lecturing me on how to bring up young ladies!'

'I should be very sorry,' she said, 'if she read books in which licentious characters were too obviously held up to her as an example. But I hope you do not wish to confine her reading to *The Hollow Tree*.[1] Lady Até certainly knows how to look after herself, in a blundering sort of way; and she gets her reward in the end, but at the expense of so grim a tenacity in all her dealings that, in reading the book, we hardly feel her to be a woman at all.' 'Not only did such women actually exist in those days,' replied Genji, 'but I can assure you that we have them still among us. It comes of their being brought up by unsocial and inhuman people who have allowed a few one-sided ideas to run away with them. The immense pains which people of good family often take over their daughters' education is apt to lead only to the production of spiritless creatures whose minds seem to grow more and more child-like in proportion to the care which is lavished on their upbringing. Their ignorance and awkwardness are only too apparent; and after wondering in what, precisely, this superior education consisted, people begin to regard not only the children as humbugs but the parents as well.

'On the other hand if the children happen to have natural talents, parents of this kind at once attribute the faintest sign of such endowment to the efficacy of their own inhuman

---

[1] See vol. ii, p. 15. Lady Até refuses suitor after suitor. Finally she marries the Crown Prince and lives happily ever after. The book seemed as old-fashioned to Murasaki as Hannah More's novels do to us.

system, and become distressingly pleased with themselves, using with regard to some very ordinary girl or stripling terms of the most extravagant eulogy. The world consequently expects much more of the unfortunate creatures than they can possibly perform, and having waited in vain for them to do or say something wonderful, begins to feel a kind of grudge against them. . . .'

'Overpraise,' he added, 'does a great deal of harm to the young. Servants are very dangerous in this respect. . . .' Nevertheless he did not object, as Murasaki had often noticed, to the little Princess from Akashi being praised by any one who came along, and he often put himself to immense trouble in order that she might escape a scolding which he knew she thoroughly deserved.

Step-mothers in books usually behave very spitefully towards the children entrusted to them. But he was now learning by his own experience that in real life this does not always happen. In choosing books for Murasaki and her charge he was therefore careful to eliminate those that depict step-mothers in the traditional light; for he feared she might otherwise think he was trying to give her a quite unnecessary warning.

Yūgiri, as has been said before, saw very little of Murasaki; but it was natural that he should sometimes visit his little sister, the Princess from Akashi, and Genji did not discourage this. On the contrary he was anxious to establish an affectionate relationship between them. For Genji, young though he still was, often thought of what would happen after his death, and he could imagine circumstances in which the princess might stand sorely in need of her brother's help. He therefore gave the boy permission to visit her and even go behind her curtains-of-state as often as he chose, though he still forbad him to enter into conversation with Lady Murasaki's gentlewomen. So few were the children of the house that a great deal more trouble was taken about them than is usually the case. Yūgiri certainly seemed to have repaid this care. In the ordinary affairs of life he showed great judgment and good-sense, and Genji had the comfortable feeling that whatever went amiss, Yūgiri at least could always be relied upon.

The little girl was only seven years old and dolls were still her principal interest. Yūgiri, who a year or two ago used so often to play just such games with his little companion at the Great Hall, made an excellent major-domo of the doll's-house, though the part, bringing as it did a host of recollections to his mind, was often a painful one. Indeed more than once he was obliged to turn away for an instant, his eyes full of tears. During these visits he naturally met many of the princess's other playmates, and a great deal of chattering took place on every conceivable subject. He took his share in these conversations; but he did not get to know any of the little girls at all well, nor did they, so far as he could see, take any particular interest in him. Was all that side of life forever to be closed to him? Yūgiri asked himself. But though this was the thought which instantly recurred to him during these meetings, his outward behaviour seemed only to betoken complete indifference. His green badge![1] Yes, it was that which lay at the bottom not only of these smaller troubles but also of the great disaster [2] which had wrecked all his chances of happiness.

Sometimes the idea came to him that if he simply went straight to Kumoi's father and tackled him about the matter—insisted, shouted, made a great scene—Tō no Chūjō would suddenly give in. But he had suffered enough

---

[1] The mark of the sixth rank. Genji, it will be remembered, had refused to promote him.
[2] His failure to win Tō no Chūjō's daughter, Lady Kumoi.

already in private; there was nothing to be gained by also making himself publicly ridiculous. No, the better way was to convince Kumoi herself by his behaviour, above all by a complete and obvious indifference to the rest of the world, that so far as his own feelings were concerned nothing was altered by one jot or tittle since the day when he first told her of his love.

Between him and her brothers slight difficulties were always arising which resulted, for the time being, in a certain coldness. For example, Kashiwagi, Kumoi's eldest brother, in ignorance of the fact that Lady Tamakatsura was his sister, continued to pay his addresses to her, and finding that his letters often failed to reach their destination, naturally turned to Yūgiri for assistance. Never once did he offer to perform a similar service in return, though it was presumably as easy for him to see Kumoi as it was for Yūgiri to see Tamakatsura. The request irritated him and he firmly refused. Not that they ceased to be friends; for their relationship, like that of their fathers, had always been built up of small rivalries and feuds.

Tō no Chūjō had an unusually large number of children, most of whom had amply fulfilled, as regards both popularity and attainments, the high promise of their early years. His position in the State had enabled him to do extremely well for all his sons. As regards his daughters (who were, however, not so numerous) he had been less fortunate. His plans for the future of the eldest girl had entirely miscarried;[1] he had signified his desire to present Lady Kumoi at Court, but had hitherto received no command to do so. He had not in all these years ever forgotten the little girl who, along with her mother, had so mysteriously disappeared, and sometimes spoke of her to those who had at the time been aware of his attachment to that unhappy

[1] He had hoped to get Lady Chūjō made Empress.

lady. What had become of them both? He imagined that her strange timidity had driven the mother to take flight with that exquisite child into some lonely and undiscoverable place. He fell into the habit of staring hard into the face of every girl whom he met; and the commoner, the more ill-clad and wretched the creature was, the surer he became that this was his lost child. For the lower she had sunk, the less likely it was that she would be able to persuade any one that she was indeed his daughter. It was impossible, he felt, that sooner or later one or other of his agents should not get news of her, and then what reparation he would make for the down-trodden existence that she must now be leading! He told his sons her child-name and begged them to report to him immediately if they should ever come across any one who bore it. 'In my early days,' he said, 'I am afraid I became involved in a great many rather purposeless intrigues. But this was quite a different matter. I cared for the mother very deeply indeed, and it distresses me intensely that I should not only have lost the confidence of the lady herself, but also have been able to do nothing at all for the one child that bore witness to our love.'

For long periods, especially if nothing happened to remind him of the matter, he succeeded in putting it out of his head. But whenever he heard of any one adopting a stray girl or taking some supposed poor relation into their house, he at once became very suspicious, made innumerable enquiries and was bitterly disappointed when it was finally proved to him that his supposition was entirely unfounded.

About this time he had a curious dream, and sending for the best interpreters of the day asked them what it meant. 'It seems to mean,' they said, 'that you have at last heard what has become of a child that you had lost sight of for many years, the reason that you have failed to discover her being that she is thought by the world at large to be some one else's child.' 'Heard what has become . . .'. he faltered. 'No, on the contrary I have heard no such thing. I cannot imagine what you are talking about.'

CHAPTER VIII

A BED OF CARNATIONS

ONE very hot day Genji, finding the air at the New Palace intolerably close, decided to picnic at the fishing-hut on the lake. He invited Yūgiri to come with him, and they were joined by most of the courtiers with whom Genji was on friendly terms. From the Western River on his estate at Katsura *ayu* had been brought, and from the nearer streams *ishibushi* and other fresh-water fish, and these formed the staple of their repast. Several of Tō no Chūjō's sons had called to see Yūgiri, and hearing where he was to be found, joined the picnic. 'How heavy and sleepy one has felt lately!' exclaimed Genji. 'This is certainly a great improvement.' Wine was brought; but he sent for iced water as well. A delicious cold soup was served, and many other delicacies. Here by the lake there was a certain amount of movement in the air; but the sun blazed down out of a cloudless sky, and even when the shadows began to lengthen there was a continual buzzing of insects which was very oppressive. 'I have never known such a day,' said Genji. 'It does not after all seem any better here than it was indoors. You must excuse me if I am too limp to do much in the way of entertaining you,' and he lay back against his cushions. 'One does not feel much inclined for music or games of any kind in such weather, and yet one badly needs something to occupy the mind. I have sometimes wondered lately whether the sun was ever going to set. . . . All the same, the young people on duty at the Emperor's Palace are in a much worse position than we. Imagine not being able to loosen one's belt and ribbons on a day like this! Here at any rate we can loll about just as we please. The only difficulty is to avoid going to sleep. Has not any of you got some startling piece of news to tell us? You need have no fear that I may have heard it already, for I am becoming quite senile; I never hear about anything till every one else has forgotten about it.' They all began wracking their brains to think of some exciting piece of intelligence or entertaining anecdote, but without success; and presently, since their host had invited them to be at their ease, one after another of the visitors somewhat timidly took up a position with his back planted against the cool metal railings of the verandah. ' Well,' said Genji at last, ' as a matter of fact, rarely though this now happens, I myself have picked up a small piece of information. It seems that his Excellency Tō no Chūjō has lately rediscovered and taken to live with him a natural daughter of whom he had lost sight for many years. Come, Kōbai,' addressing Kashiwagi's younger brother, ' you will be able to tell me if there is any truth in this.' ' Something of the kind has happened,' answered the young man, ' though there is a good deal of exaggeration in many of the stories which are being put about. The facts are that last spring, in consequence of a dream, my father asked us to inquire carefully into every case we could discover of a child claiming paternity by him. My brother Kashiwagi did finally hear of a girl who seemed to possess absolute proof that she was an illegitimate child of our father's, and we were told to call upon her and verify this, which we accordingly did. That is all I know about it; and I am sure that there is no one present who has not something a great deal more interesting than that to talk about. I am afraid what I have just told you cannot possibly be of interest to any one but the people actually concerned.' 'So it is true!' thought Genji, wondering whether Tō no Chūjō could have been so misled as to suppose that it was Yūgao's child whom he had rediscovered. 'There are so many of you in the family already,' he said to Kōbai, 'that I wonder your father should search the sky for one stray swallow that has not managed to keep pace with the flock. I, who nurture so small a brood, might be pardoned for such conduct; but in your father it seems somewhat grasping. Unfortunately, though I should feel proud to acknowledge my children, no one shows the slightest inclination to claim me as a father. However, it is no mere accident that Tō no Chūjō is more in request than I am. The moon's image shows dimly in waters that are troubled at the bottom. Your father's early adventures were of a most indiscriminate character, and if you know all your brothers and sisters, you would probably realize that, taken as a whole, you are a very queer family. . . .' Yūgiri, who knew a mass of stories which amply confirmed Genji's last statement, could not help showing his amusement to an extent which Kōbai and his brothers thought to be in exceedingly bad taste. 'It is all very well for you to laugh, Yūgiri,' continued Genji; 'but you would be much better employed in picking up some of those stray leaves than in making trouble for yourself by pressing in where you are not wanted. In so large a garland you might surely find some other flower with which to console yourself!' All Genji's remarks about Tō no Chūjō wore superficially the aspect of such friendly banter as one old friend commonly indulges in concerning another. But as a matter of fact there had for some while past been a real coolness between them, which was increased by Chūjō's scornful refusal to accept Yūgiri as his son-in-law. He realized that he had just been somewhat spiteful; but so far from being uncomfortable lest these remarks should reach his old friend's ears, he found himself actually hoping that the boys would repeat them.

This conversation about the waif whom Tō no Chūjō had recently acknowledged and adopted, reminded Genji that it was becoming high time he should himself make a certain long-intended revelation. Tamakatsura had now lived for over a year at the New Palace; she was definitely accepted as a member of the Court circle, and there was now no fear that her father would be in any way ashamed of her. But the views of Tō no Chūjō were in some ways peculiar. He made an absolutely hard and fast distinction between the 'right' and the 'wrong' people. To those who satisfied his very exacting standards he was extraordinarily helpful and agreeable. As for the others, he ignored them with a sublime completeness that no other Grand Minister had ever equalled. Was it quite certain in which class he would place his own daughter? Then a brilliant idea occurred to Genji. He would introduce Tō no Chūjō to Tamakatsura immediately, but not reveal her identity until Chūjō had once and for all classed her as 'possible.'

The evening wind was by this time delightfully fresh, and it was with great regret that the young guests prepared to take their leave. ' I should be perfectly contented to go on sitting here quietly in the cool; but I know that at your age there are many far more interesting things to be done,' and with that he set out for the Western Wing, his guests accompanying him to the door.

Knowing that in an uncertain evening light all people in Court cloaks look very much alike, Genji at once summoned Tamakatsura to him and explained in a low voice why he had arrived with so large an escort. ' I have been entertaining Tō no Chūjō's sons,' he said, ' Kashiwagi, Kōbai and the rest. It was obvious that they were very anxious to come on here with me, and Yūgiri is such an honest soul, it would have been unkind not to let him come too. Those poor young men, Tō no Chūjō's sons, must really soon be told you are their sister. I am afraid they are all more or less in love with you. But even in the case of quite ordinary families the sudden arrival of some unknown young lady causes endless speculation among those who frequent the house, and though there is intense curiosity to see her, it is apparent that every one has long beforehand made up his mind to fall in love. Unfortunately, even before your arrival, my palace had an undeserved reputation for harbouring bevies of incomparable creatures. Every visitor who comes here seems to arrive primed up with compliments and fine speeches, only to discover that there is no quarter in which they could be employed without impertinence.[1] But you have often asked me about those particular young men and lamented that you never get an opportunity yourself of judging whether they are as intelligent as every one makes out. So I thought you would not mind me bringing them here, and would perhaps like to have a word with one or the other of them. . . .'

While this whispered conversation was going on, the young men were standing in the garden outside. It was not planted in formal borders; but there was a great clump of carnations and a tangled hedge of tall flowering plants, both Chinese and Japanese, with great masses of blossom that stood out vividly in the fading light. True, they had come that evening hoping to pluck a very different flower; but as they sat resting in front of the house they could scarcely restrain themselves from stretching out a hand and filling their laps with these resplendent blossoms.

'They are really very remarkable young men,' Genji went on. 'There is not one of them but in his way shows unmistakable signs of genius, and this is true even of Kashi-

[1] Akikonomu, for example, had become Empress.

wagi, who in outward manner is particularly quiet and diffident. By the way, has he written to you again? I remember we read his poem together. You cannot, of course, under the circumstances risk giving him any definite encouragement; but do not be too hard upon him.'

Even amid these very exceptional young men Yūgiri looked surprisingly handsome and distinguished, and Genji, pointing to him, said to Tamakatsura in a whisper: 'I am terribly disappointed that Tō no Chūjō should take up his present attitude about that boy. It has come to this nowadays, that those people will not look at any one who is not part and parcel of their own gang.[1] A drop of other blood, even if it be that of the Royal House, seems to them a painful blemish. . . .' 'That was not the way Royal Princes were regarded once upon a time,' said Tamakatsura, and quoted the old folk-song *Come to my house*.[2] 'They certainly seem in no hurry to make ready a banquet for poor Yūgiri,' admitted Genji. 'I am extremely sorry for those two. They took a fancy to each other when they were mere children and have never got over it. I know quite well that they have suffered a great deal through this long separation. If it is merely because of Yūgiri's low rank that Tō no Chūjō refuses his consent, he might on this occasion be content to disregard the comments of the world and leave the matter in my hands. He surely does not suppose that I intend the boy to remain in the Sixth Rank for ever. . . .' Again he was speaking of Tō no Chūjō with asperity and, like her brothers a few hours ago, Tamakatsura was perturbed to discover that the breach between them was widening, partly because such a state of

[1] I.e. the Fujiwaras, the clan to which the writer herself belonged.
[2] 'In my house the awnings are at the doors and curtains are hanging about the bed. Come, my Prince! you shall have my daughter for your bride, and at the wedding-feast you shall have the fish you like best, be it *awabi*, oyster or what you will.'

affairs made it all the less probable that Genji would in the near future reveal her identity to Tō no Chūjō.

As there was no moon that night, the great lamp was presently brought in. 'It is now just comfortably warm,' said Genji, 'and the only thing we need is a little more light.' He sent for a servant and said to him: 'One tray of bamboo flares! In here, please.' When they were brought he noticed a very beautiful native zithern and drawing it towards him struck a few chords. It was tuned to the difficult *ritsu* mode, but with remarkable accuracy. It seemed indeed to be an exceptionally fine instrument, and when he had played on it for a little while he said to her: 'I have all these months been doing you the injustice of supposing that you were not interested in these things. What I like is to play such an instrument as yours on a cool autumn evening, when the moon is up, sitting quite close to the window. One then plays in concert with the cicadas, purposely using their chirruping as part of the accompaniment. The result is a kind of music which is intimate, but at the same time thoroughly modern. There is, of course, a go-as-you-please, informal quality about the Japanese zithern which makes it unsuitable for use on ceremonial occasions. But when one remembers that almost all our native airs and measures originated on this instrument, one cannot help regarding it with respect. There are stray references which show that its history stretches back into the dimmest past; but to hear people talk nowadays one would think it had been specially invented for the benefit of young ladies, in whom an acquaintance with foreign arts and usages is considered unbecoming. Above all, do make a practice of playing it in concert with other instruments whenever you get the chance. This will immensely improve your command over it. For though the Japanese zithern is a far less complicated instrument than its rivals, it is by no means so easy to play as most people imagine. At the present time there is no better performer than your father, Tō no Chūjō. You would be astonished at the variety of tone he can get out of a mere succession of open strings; it is as though by some magic he were able in an instant to change his zithern into whatever instrument he pleases. And the volume of sound which he obtains from those few slender strings is unbelievable!'

Tamakatsura had reached a certain point of proficiency herself. But she knew that she had much to learn, and longed to meet with a first-rate performer. 'Do you think I might one day be allowed to hear him?' she asked, not very hopefully. 'I suppose he sometimes plays when he comes here to entertainments. Even among those outlandish people on the Island there were several teachers, and I always supposed that they knew all about it. But from what you have just said I see that such playing as my father's must be something quite different. . . .'

'It is indeed,' he said, 'and you shall certainly hear him play. You know, I expect, that though it is called the Eastern zithern and is said to have come from the other side of the country, it is always played at the beginning of every Imperial concert, being solemnly carried in by the Mistress of the Rolls. As far as our country is concerned (about the history of music in other lands I know very little) it is certainly the parent of all other instruments, and that perhaps the best performer upon it who has ever lived should be your own father is certainly a great stroke of luck for you. He does, as you suggested, play here and at other people's houses from time to time, when there is music afoot; but chiefly on other instruments. It is really very difficult to make him play on the Japanese zithern. Often he begins a tune and then, for some reason, will not go on. It is the same with all great artists. They cannot perform unless they are in the right mood, and the right mood seldom comes. But later on you will, of course, certainly be hearing him. . . .' So saying, he began trying over a few usual chords and runs. Already she wondered how she had managed to tolerate the clumsy twanging of the island-professors. How exciting it would be to live with a father, who, according to Genji's own showing, played far, far better even than this! It was intolerable to feel that all the while she might have been hearing him day after day, in his own home, with nothing to disturb or interrupt him. When, oh when would this new life begin?

Among other old ballads Genji now sang 'Not softlier pillowed is my head,' and when he came to the line ' O lady parted from thy kin ' he could not help catching her eye and smiling. Not only did she find his voice very agreeable, but his improvisations between verse and verse delighted her beyond measure. Suddenly he broke off, saying: ' Now it is your turn. Do not tell me you are shy; for I am certain that you have talent, and if that is so you will forget that there is any one here, once you have become interested in what you are playing. The lady [1] who was " too shy to do anything but go over the tune in her head " wanted all the time to sing the *Sōfuren*,[2] and that is a very different matter. You must get into the habit of playing with any one who comes along, without minding what he thinks of you. . . .' But try as he might, he could not persuade her to begin. She was certain that her teacher on the island, an old lady of whom it was reported that she had once been in some vague way connected with the Capital and even that she was distantly related to the Imperial Family, had got everything wrong from beginning to end.

[1] In some story now lost.
[2] Literally: ' Thinking of a man, and yearning.'

A BED OF CARNATIONS

If only she could persuade Genji to go on playing a little while longer, she felt sure she could pick up enough of the right method to prevent a complete catastrophe, and she sat as near as possible to the zithern, watching his fingers and listening intently. 'Why does it not always produce such lovely sounds as that?' she said laughing. 'Perhaps it depends which way the wind is blowing. . . .' She looked very lovely as she sat leaning towards him, with the lamplight full upon her face. 'I have sometimes known you by no means so ready to listen,' he said, and to her disappointment pushed the zithern from him. But her gentlewomen were passing in and out of the room. Whether for this or other reasons his behaviour to-night continued to be very serious and correct. 'I see no sign of those young men I brought with me,' he said at last, 'I am afraid they grew tired of gazing at every flower save the one they came to see, and went away in disgust. But it is their father's visit to this flower-garden that I ought all the while to be arranging. I must not be dilatory, for life is full of uncertainties. . . . How well I remember the conversation in the course of which your father first told me how your mother had carried you away, and of his long search for you both. It does not seem long ago. . . .' And he told her more than he had ever done before about the rainy night's conversation and his own first meeting with Yūgao.

'Gladly would I show the world this Child-flower's beauty, did I not fear that men would ask me where stands the hedge on which it grew.'[1]

'The truth is, he loved your mother so dearly that I cannot bear the thought of telling him the whole miserable story. That is why I have kept you hidden away like a chrysalis in a cocoon. I know I ought not to have delayed. . . .' He paused, and she answered with the

[1] A reference to Tō no Chūjō's poem, vol. i, p. 59.

verse: 'Who cares to question whence was first transplanted a Child-flower that from the peasant's tattered hedge was hither brought.' Her eyes filled with tears as in a scarcely audible voice she whispered this reply.

There were times when he himself took fright at the frequency of his visits to this part of the house, and in order to make a good impression stayed away for days on end. But he always contrived to think of some point in connection with her servants or household affairs which required an endless going and coming of messengers, so that even during these brief periods of absence she was in continual communication with him. The truth is that at this period she was the only subject to which he ever gave a thought. Day and night he asked himself how he could have been so insensate as to embark upon this fatal course. If the affair was maintained upon its present footing he was faced with the prospect of such torture as he felt he could not possibly endure. If on the other hand his resolution broke down and she on her side was willing to accept him as a lover, the affair would cause a scandal which his own prestige might in time enable him to live down, but which for her would mean irreparable disaster. He cared for her very deeply; but not, as he well knew, to such an extent that he would ever dream of putting her on an equality with Murasaki, while to thrust her into a position of inferiority would do violence to his own feelings and be most unfair to her. Exceptional as was the position that he now occupied in the State, this did not mean that it was any great distinction to figure merely as a belated appendage to his household. Far better, he very well knew, to reign supreme in the affections of some wholly unremarkable Deputy Councillor! Then again there was the question whether he ought not to hand her over to his step-brother Prince Sochi or to Prince Higekuro. Even were this course in every way desirable, he gravely doubted his own capacity to pursue it. Such self-sacrifices, he knew, are easier to plan than to effect. Nevertheless, there were times when he regarded this as the plan which he had definitely adopted, and for a while he could really believe that he was on the point of carrying it out. But then would come one of his visits to her. She would be looking even more charming than usual, and lately there were these zithern lessons, which, involving as they did a great deal of leaning across and sitting shoulder to shoulder, had increased their intimacy with disquieting rapidity. All his good resolutions began to break down, while she on her side no longer regarded him with anything like the same distrust as before. He had indeed behaved with model propriety for so long that she made sure his undue tenderness towards her was a thing of the past. Gradually she became used to having him constantly about her, allowed him to say what he pleased, and answered in a manner which though discreet was by no means discouraging. Whatever resolutions he may have made before his visit, he would go away feeling that, at this point in their relations, simply to hand her over to a husband was more than the most severe moralist could expect of him. Surely there could be no harm in keeping her here a little longer, that he might enjoy the innocent pleasure of sometimes visiting her, sometimes arranging her affairs? Certainly, he could assure himself, his presence was by no means distasteful to her. Her uneasiness at the beginning was due not to hostility but to mere lack of experience. Though 'strong the watchman at the gate', she was beginning to take a very different view of life. Soon she would be struggling with her own as well as his desires, and then all her defences would rapidly give way. . . .

Tō no Chūjō was somewhat uneasy about his newly

discovered daughter.[1] The members of his own household seemed to have a very poor opinion of her, and at Court he had overheard people whispering that she was not quite right in the head. His son Kōbai told him, of course, about Genji's questions, and Tō no Chūjō laughed saying: 'I can quite understand his interest in the matter. A year or two ago he himself took over a daughter whom he had by some peasant woman or other, and now makes an absurd fuss over her. It is very odd: Genji says nothing but nice things about every one else. But about me and every one connected with me he is careful to be as disagreeable as possible. But I suppose I ought to regard it as a sort of distinction even to be run down by him.' 'Father, if you mean the girl who lives in the Western Wing,' said Kōbai, 'I can assure you she is the most beautiful creature you can possibly imagine. Prince Sochi and many of the others have completely lost their hearts to her. . . . Indeed, every one agrees that she is probably one of the handsomest women at Court.' 'You surely do not yourself believe such stories?' said Tō no Chūjō. 'The same thing is always said about the daughters of men in such a position as Genji's; and so oddly is the world made that those who spread such reports really believe in them. I do not for a moment suppose she is anything out of the ordinary. Now that Genji is Grand Minister, faced by an opposition that has dwindled to a mere speck and esteemed as few Ministers before, I fancy the one flaw in his happiness must be the lack of a daughter to lavish his care upon and bring up to be the envy and admiration of the whole Court. I can well imagine what a delight the education of such a child would be to him. But in this matter fate seems to be against him. Of course, there is the little girl who was born at Akashi. Unfortunately her mother's parents are quite humble people

[1] The rustic creature unearthed by Kōbai in his search for Tamakatsura.

and she can never play the part that would naturally have been taken by a child of my sister Lady Aoi or of his present wife, Lady Murasaki. All the same, I have reason to believe that his schemes for her subsequent career are of the most ambitious nature.

'As for this newly-imported princess, it would not surprise me to discover that she is not his child at all. You know as well as I do what Genji's failings are. . . . It is far more probable that she is merely some girl whom he is keeping.' After other somewhat damaging remarks about Genji's habits and character, he continued: 'However, if he continues to give out that she is his daughter, it will soon be incumbent upon him to find her a husband. I imagine his choice will fall upon Prince Sochi, with whom he has always been on particularly good terms. She would certainly be fortunate in securing such a husband; he is a most distinguished character. . . .'

Nothing more exasperated Tō no Chūjō at the present moment than the endless speculations concerning Lady Tamakatsura's future which were now the staple of every conversation at Court. He was sick of hearing people ask 'What are Prince Genji's intentions?' 'Why has he changed his mind?' and so on, while the future of his own daughter, Lady Kumoi, seemed for some reason not to arouse the slightest curiosity. Why should not a little of the energy which Genji expended in dangling this supposed daughter of his before the eyes of an expectant Court be used on Lady Kumoi's behalf? A word whispered by Genji in the Emperor's ear would suffice to secure her future; but that word, it was very evident, had never been spoken.

If Genji (and this seemed hardly credible) were waiting to secure Kumoi for his own son Yūgiri, let him raise the boy to a decent rank. Then, provided suitable overtures were made on Genji's side, he was quite willing to consider the possibility of such a match. As to what the young man's feelings in the matter might be—he did not give the question a moment's thought, having always regarded Yūgiri merely as a nuisance.

One day when he had been reflecting upon this problem more earnestly than usual, Tō no Chūjō determined to thresh the matter out with the girl herself, and taking Kōbai with him he went straight to her room. It so happened that Kumoi had fallen asleep. She was lying, a small and fragile figure, with only a single wrap of thin diaphanous stuff thrown carelessly across her. It was certainly a pleasure on such a day to see any one looking so delightfully cool! The delicate outline of her bare limbs showed plainly beneath the light wrap which covered her. She lay pillowed on one outstretched arm, her fan still in her hand. Her loosened hair fell all about her, and though it was not remarkably thick or long, there was something particularly agreeable in its texture and in the lines it made as it hung across her face. Her gentlewomen were also reposing, but at some distance away, in the room which opened out behind her curtained daïs, so that they did not wake in time, and it was only when Tō no Chūjō himself rustled impatiently with his fan that she slowly raised her head and turned upon him a bewildered gaze. Her beauty, enhanced by the flush of sleep, could not but impress a father's heart, and Tō no Chūjō looked at her with a pride which his subsequent words by no means betrayed. 'I have told you often before,' he said, 'that even to be caught dozing in your seat is a thing a girl of your age ought to be ashamed of; and here I find you going to bed in broad daylight . . . you really must be a little more careful. I cannot imagine how you could be so foolish as to allow all your gentlewomen to desert you in this way. It is extremely unsafe for a young girl to expose herself, and quite unnecessary in your case, since I have provided you with a sufficient number of attendants to mount guard on all occasions. To behave in this reckless manner is, to say the least of it, very bad form. Not that I want you to sit all day with your hands folded in front of you as though you were reciting the Spells of Fudō.[1] I am not one of those people who think it a mark of refinement in a girl to stand on ceremony even with her everyday acquaintances and never to address a word to any one except through a barricade of curtains and screens. So far from being dignified, such a method of behaviour seems to me merely peevish and unsociable. I cannot help admiring the way in which Prince Genji is bringing up this future Empress[2] of his. He takes no exaggerated precautions of any kind, nor does he force her talent in this direction or that; but at the same time he sees to it that there is no subject in which she remains wholly uninitiated. Thus she is able to choose intelligently for herself where other girls would be obliged merely to do as they were told. For the time it may seem that the energies of the mind have been somewhat diffused and extenuated, but in later life, given the best balanced and broadest system of education in the world, idiosyncrasies both of character and behaviour will inevitably reappear. At the present moment the Princess from Akashi is in the first and less interesting stage. I am very curious to see how she will develop when she arrives at Court.' After these preliminaries he embarked at last upon the subject which he had really come to discuss. 'You know,' he said, 'that I have not

---

[1] Of these there are several, the shortest of which runs (in Sanskrit) Namas samanta-vajrānām ham. 'Praise be to all the Thunderbolt-bearers. Ay verily.' Its impressiveness was partly due to the fact that very few Japanese knew what it meant.

[2] The princess from Akashi.

been very successful in my plans for your own future. But I still hope that we may be able to arrange something not too contemptible. I promise you at any rate that you shall not be made ridiculous. I am keeping my ears open and have one or two projects in mind, but for the moment it is exceedingly difficult to arrive at a decision. Meanwhile, do not be deceived by the tears and protestations of young men who have nothing better to do than amuse themselves at the expense of confiding creatures such as you. I know what I am talking about ' . . . and so on, speaking more and more kindly as he went along.

In old days the scoldings which she had received on account of her intimacy with Yūgiri had been the more distressing to her because she had not at that time the least idea what all this fuss was about. But now that she was a little better acquainted with such matters, she recalled with burning shame time after time when she had mentioned to her elders things which she now saw it was the wildest folly ever to have repeated. The old Princess [1] frequently complained that Kumoi never came to see her. This put the child in great embarrassment, for the truth was that she dared not go, for Tō no Chūjō would be sure to think that she was using her duty towards the old lady as a pretext for clandestine meeting with her lover.

But another question was at this time occupying a good deal of Tō no Chūjō's attention. What was to be done with this new daughter of his, the Lady from Ōmi ? If, after going out of his way to track her down, he were now to send her home again merely because certain people had said disobliging things about her, he would himself figure as intolerably capricious and eccentric. To let her mix in general society was, judging by what he had heard and seen of her already, quite out of the question. But if he

[1] Tō no Chūjō's mother, Kumoi's grandmother.

continued to keep her, as he had hitherto done, in the seclusion of her own rooms, it would soon be rumoured at Court that she was some paragon who, just at the right moment, would be produced with dazzling effect and carry all before her. This, too, would be very irritating. Perhaps the best that could be done under the circumstances was to put her into touch with his daughter Lady Chūjō,[1] who happened at the moment to be home from Court. It would then be possible to discover whether, when one got to know her better, this Lady from Ōmi were really such a monster as some people made out. He therefore said to Lady Chūjō one day: 'I am going to send this new sister of yours to see you. It seems that her manners are rather odd, and I should be very much obliged if you would ask one of your older gentlewomen to take her in hand. Young girls are useless in such a case. They would merely lead her on to greater absurdities in order to amuse themselves. Her manner is at present, I gather, somewhat too boisterous'; and he smiled as he recollected some of the anecdotes which had already reached him. 'I will gladly do all I can,' answered Lady Chūjō. 'I see no reason to suppose that the poor creature is anything like so outrageous as people are making out. It is only that Kōbai, wishing to gain credit for his discovery, tended to exaggerate her charms, and people are a little disappointed. I do not think there is any need for you to take alarm. I can quite understand that coming for the first time among surroundings such as these, she feels somewhat lost, and does not always quite do herself justice. . . .' She spoke very demurely. This Lady Chūjō was no great beauty; but there was about her a serene air of conscious superiority which, combined with considerable charm of manner, led most people to accept her as handsome, an impression

[1] On leave from the Palace; she was one of the Emperor's consorts.

shared at this moment by her father as he watched her lips part in a smile that reminded him of the red plum-blossom in the morning when its petals first begin to unfold. 'I daresay you are right,' he replied; 'but all the same I think that Kōbai showed a lack of judgment such as I should have thought he had long ago outgrown. . . .' He was himself inclined to think that the Lady from Ōmi's defects had probably been much exaggerated, and as he in any case must pass her rooms on his way back he now thought he had better go and have another look at her. Crossing the garden he noticed at once that her blinds were rolled back almost to the top of the windows. Clearly visible within were the figures of the Lady herself and of a lively young person called Gosechi, one of last year's Winter Dancers. The two were playing Double Sixes,[1] and the Lady of Ōmi, perpetually clasping and unclasping her hands in her excitement, was crying out 'Low, low! Oh, how I hope it will be low!' at the top of her voice, which rose at every moment to a shriller and shriller scream. 'What a creature!' thought Tō no Chūjō, already in despair, and signalling to his attendants, who were about to enter the apartments and announce him, that for a moment he intended to watch unobserved, he stood near the double door and looked through the passage window at a point where the paper [2] did not quite meet the frame. The young dancer was also entirely absorbed in the game. Shouting out: 'A twelve, a twelve. This time I know it is going to be a twelve!' she continually twirled the dice-cup in her hand, but could not bring herself to make the throw. Somewhere there, inside that bamboo tube, the right number lurked, she saw the two little stones with six pips on each. . . . But how was one to know when to

[1] Sugoroku, a kind of backgammon.
[2] Japanese windows are made of translucent paper, not of glass.

throw ? Never were excitement and suspense more clearly marked on two young faces. The Lady of Ōmi was somewhat homely in appearance; but nobody (thought Tō no Chūjō) could possibly call her downright ugly. Indeed, she had several very good points. Her hair, for example, could alone have sufficed to make up for many shortcomings. Two serious defects, however, she certainly had; her forehead was far too narrow, and her voice was appallingly loud and harsh. In a word, she was nothing to be particularly proud of; but at the same time (and he called up before him the image of his own face as he knew it in the mirror) it would be useless to deny that there was a strong resemblance.

'How are you getting on?' he asked on being admitted to the room. 'I am afraid it will take you some time to get the hang of things here. I wish I could see you more often, but, as you know, my time is not my own. . . .' 'Don't you worry about that,' she answered, screaming as usual at the top of her voice. 'I'm here, a'nt I? And that's quite enough for me. I haven't had the pleasure of setting eyes on you at all for all these years. . . . But I'll own that when I came here and found I shouldn't be with you all the time, like what I'd expected, I was as vexed as though I had thrown a "double-one" at dice.' 'As a matter of fact,' said Tō no Chūjō, 'I have not any one at present to run my messages and look after me generally; I had it in mind that, when you were a little more used to things here, I might train you to help me in that way. But I am not at all sure that such a post would suit you. I do not mean that as a lady-in-waiting in some other family you would not get on very nicely. But that would be different. . . . There would be a lot of other young women. . . . People would not notice so much. . . . I am afraid I am not expressing myself very happily. I only mean that a daughter or sister is bound to attract attention.

People who come to the house ask "Now which of them is the daughter?" "Show me which of them is your sister!" and so on. That sort of thing sometimes makes a girl feel awkward, and it may even be rather embarrassing for the parents. Of course, in your case . .' He broke off.

Despite all his ingenuity he was in the end saying just what he had determined on no account to say. He was merely telling her that he was ashamed of her. But fortunately she did not take it in bad part. 'That's quite right,' she said. 'If you was to put me down among all the fine ladies and gentlemen, I shouldn't know which way to look. I'd far rather you asked me to empty their chamber-pots; I think I might be able to manage that.' 'What odd ideas do come into your head!' laughed Tō no Chūjō. 'But before we go any further, I have a small request to make: if you have any filial feeling whatever towards a father whom you see so seldom, try to moderate your voice a little when you address him. Seriously, you will take years off my life if you persist in screaming at me in this way. . . .' How delightful to find that even a Minister could make jokes! 'It's no good,' she said. 'I've always been like that. I suppose I was born so. Mother was always going on at me about it ever since I can remember, and she used to say it all came of her letting an old priest from the Myōhō Temple into her bedroom when she was lying-in. He had a terrible loud voice, and all the while he was reading prayers with her, poor mother was wondering whether, when I was born, I shouldn't take after him. And sure enough I did. But I wish for your sake I didn't speak so loud. . . .' It was evident that she was sorry to distress him, and touched by this exhibition of filial affection he said to her kindly: 'The fault, then, is evidently not yours but your mother's for choosing her associates among the pious at so critical a moment in her existence. For it is written: "The tongue of the blasphemer shall tremble, his voice shall be silenced," and it seems that, conversely, the voices of the pious generally tend to become more and more resonant.'

He himself stood somewhat in awe of his daughter Lady Chūjō. He knew that she would wonder what had induced him to import, without further enquiries so incongruous a resident into his household. He imagined, too, the pleasantries at his expense which would be exchanged among her people and soon repeated broadcast over the whole Court. He was on the verge of abandoning the plan, when he suddenly decided that it was too late to withdraw: 'I wish you would sometimes go out and see your sister Lady Chūjō while she is staying here,' he said. 'I fancy she could give you one or two useful hints. It is, after all, only by mixing in the society of those who have had greater advantages than themselves, that ordinary people can hope to make any progress. I want you to bear that in mind when you are with her. . . .' 'Well that will be a treat!' she cried delightedly. 'I never thought in my wildest dreams that, even if you one day sent for me, you would ever make me into a great lady like my sister. The best I hoped for was that I might wheedle you into letting me carry pitchers from the well. . . .' The last words were spoken in a tiny, squeaky voice like that of a new-fledged sparrow, for she had suddenly remembered her father's injunctions. The effect was very absurd; but there was no use in scolding her any more, and he said good-humouredly: 'I see no reason why you should draw water, or hew wood either. But if I send you to Lady Chūjō, you must promise me that you have made up your mind never again to model yourself on that pious personage from the Myōhō Temple.' She took this very seriously. 'I'll do my best,' she said.

'When may I go and see her?' Tō no Chūjō was now an important person; indeed, he was reckoned to be the most formidable enemy to the then Minister of State. But the Lady from Ōmi appeared quite unconscious of the subduing effect which his presence had upon every one else, and for her part spoke to him with the utmost confidence and composure. 'I will enquire which day will be the best,' he said. 'But come to think of it, probably one day is quite as good as another. Yes, by all means go to-day . . .' and with that he hastened from the room.

She gazed after him. He was attended by officers of the fourth and fifth ranks, who made a brave show as they escorted him towards the main building. But why were they all nudging one another and laughing? 'Well,' she said at last, 'I have got a fine gentleman for my papa, and no mistake. It does seem queer to think what a funny little house I was brought up in, when by rights I ought to have been in this palace all the while.' 'If you ask my opinion,' said her friend the dancer, 'I think he is far too grand for you. You'd be a great deal better off if you had been claimed by some decent hard-working sort of man, who wouldn't be ashamed of you. . . .' This was too bad! 'There you go again,' the Lady from Ōmi cried, 'trying to put a body down whenever she opens her mouth. But you shan't do it any more, indeed you shan't; for they've made me into a lady now, and you'll have to wait till I choose to let you speak. So there!'

Her face was flushed with anger. Seen thus, showing off in the presence of one whom she now regarded as an inferior, she became suddenly handsome and almost dignified. Only her manner of speech, picked up from the absolute riff-raff among whom she had been educated, remained irredeemably vulgar.

It is indeed a strange thing that a perfectly ordinary

remark, if made in a quiet, colourless voice, may seem original and interesting; for instance, in conversations about poetry, some quite commonplace piece of criticism will be accepted as very profound merely because it is made in a particular tone of voice. Or again, half a verse from the middle of some little-known poem can make, if produced in the right tone of voice, a deep impression even among people who have no notion what the words imply. Whereas if some one speaks in a disagreeable voice or uses vulgar language, no matter how important or profound are the thoughts which he expresses, nobody will believe that it can possibly be worth while to pay any attention to him. So it was with the Lady from Ōmi. She had a loud rasping voice and in general behaved with no more regard for the impression she was making on those around her than a child screaming in its nurse's lap. She thus seemed far sillier than she really was. Indeed, her facility in stringing together poems of thirty-one syllables, of the kind in which the beginning of any one poem might just as well be the end of any other, was quite prodigious.

'But I must be getting ready,' she now exclaimed. 'My father told me I was to call on Lady Chūjō, and if I don't go at once, her ladyship will think I don't want to meet her. Do you know what? I think I'll go this very night, for though I can see that my papa thinks the world of me, I shall never get on in this palace unless the ladies are on my side. . . .' Which again shows that she had more good sense than one would have supposed.

She now sat down at once and addressed the following letter to Lady Chūjō: 'Honoured Madam, though we have been living these many days past with (as the saying goes) scarce so much as a hurdle between us, I have not hitherto, as they say, ventured to tread upon your shadow, for to tell the honest truth I was in two minds whether I should not find " No Admittance " in large letters on your door. But though I hardly like to mention it, we are (in the words of the poet) both "tinged with the purple of Musashi Moor." If I am being too bold, pray tell me so and do not take offence.' All this was written in a rather speckly hand. On the back was the postcript : ' By the way, I have some thoughts of inflicting myself upon you this very same evening. And please forgive these blots, which (as the saying goes) all the waters of Minasé River would not wash away, so what is the use of trying ? ' In the margin was the following extraordinary poem : ' I wonder with as big a query as How Cape on the Sea of Hitachi where the grasses are so young and green, when oh when, like the waves on the shore of Tago, shall we meet face to face ? '

' I'll write no more,' she added at the side of the poem, ' for I declare I feel as flustered as the foam on the great River at Yoshino. . . .'

It was written on a single sheet of blue poetry-paper, in a very cursive style, copiously adorned with hooks and flourishes which seemed to wander about at their own will and stand for nothing at all. The tails of her ' *shi* 's were protracted to an inordinate length, and the lines slanted more and more as the letter went on, till in the end they seemed in danger of falling over sideways. But so delighted was she with her own composition that she could hardly bear to part with it. At last, however, she gave it a final look of admiration, folded it up very small and attaching it to a carnation-blossom, handed it to her favourite messenger, a little peasant-boy who did the dirty work in her part of the palace. He was a good-looking child, and though he had only been in service for a very short while, he had made himself quite at home. Sauntering into Lady Chūjō's apartments, he found his way to the servants' sitting-room and demanded that the note should at once be taken to her

Ladyship. For a moment they surveyed him with astonishment, but presently one of the under-servants exclaimed: 'Why, it's the little boy from the northern wing!', and took the letter, which ultimately reached the hands of a certain gentlewoman named Tayū no Kimi. This lady actually carried it into Lady Chūjō's presence, unfolded it at her bidding and then held it in front of her. The great lady glanced at it, smiled, and indicated that it might now be removed. It happened that a certain Lady Chūnagon was at the moment in attendance. She caught a side view of the letter where it lay, and hoping to be allowed to read it properly, she remarked: 'At a distance, Madam, that looks an uncommonly fashionable note.' Lady Chūjō motioned her to take the letter: 'I cannot make head or tail of it,' she said; 'you will be doing me a service if you can tell me what it is about. Perhaps I am being stupid over these cursive characters. . . .' And a few minutes later: 'How are you getting on? If my answer has no connection with the contents of her letter, she will think me very discourteous. I wish you would write an answer for me, I am sure you would do it very nicely. . . .' The young ladies-in-waiting, though they dared not openly show their amusement, were now all tittering behind their sleeves. Some one came to say that the boy was still waiting for an answer. 'But the letter is just one mass of stock phrases that none of them seem to have anything to do with what she is trying to say,' exclaimed Chūnagon in despair. 'How can I possibly answer it? Besides, I must make it seem to come from you, Madam, not from a third person, or the poor creature's feelings will be terribly hurt.'

'It vexes me,' wrote Chūnagon in her mistress's name, 'to think that we should have been at close quarters for so long without arranging to meet. By all means come. . . .' And at the side she wrote the poem: 'Upon the shore of

Suma, that is on the sea of Suruga in the land of Hitachi, mount, O ye waves, to where the Headland of Hako with pine-woods is clad.' [1]

'I think you have gone too far,' said Lady Chūjō when she saw the letter. 'I certainly hope she will not think it was I who wrote this ridiculous nonsense. . . .' 'I assure you, Madam,' replied Chūnagon, 'there is more sense in it than you think; quite enough at any rate to satisfy the person to whom it is addressed.' And with that she folded the note and sent it on its way. How quickly these great ladies take one's meaning!' exclaimed Ōmi, as she scanned the reply. 'Look, too, how subtly she expresses herself! Merely by mentioning those pine-trees she lets me know, as plain as could be, that she is waiting for me at this minute. . . .' There was no time to be lost. She scented herself by repeated exposure to the fumes of an incense which seemed to contain far too generous an admixture of honey, daubed her cheeks with a heavy rouge, and finally combed out her hair, which being, as I have said, unusually fine and abundant, really looked very nice when she took sufficient trouble about it.

The subsequent interview can hardly have been otherwise than extremely diverting.

[1] The Lady of Ōmi's poem contained three irrelevant place-names. This one contains four, and is intentionally senseless, for Chūnagon had not been able to make out what Ōmi's rigmarole was about.

CHAPTER IX

THE FLARES

IT was now the turn of Lady Ōmi's eccentricities to become the sole topic of conversation at Court. 'All this is very puzzling,' said Genji. 'Her father gave orders that she was to be kept in close confinement; how comes it, then, that every one seems to know so much about her? One hears nothing but stories of her ridiculous behaviour. So far from keeping the poor half-witted creature out of harm's way he seems to be positively making an exhibition of her. Here again I think I see the consequences of his obstinate belief in the impeccability of his own family. He sent for her without making the slightest enquiry, convinced that since his blood ran in her veins she must necessarily be beyond reproach. Finding her an exception to this rule he has taken his revenge by deliberately exposing her to derision. However, I can hardly believe that after all the trouble he has taken, it can really give him much satisfaction that the mere mention of her name should evoke peals of laughter. . . .'

The fate of Ōmi seemed, incidently, to afford some justification for Genji's reluctance to part with Tamakatsura, a fact which she herself recognized. It was by no means safe to assume that Tō no Chūjō would treat a second long-lost daughter any better than the first. The old nurse Ukon, who daily collected for her mistress's benefit some fresh anecdote of Ōmi's discomfiture, vigorously supported the view that Tō no Chūjō was not a father to be lightly adopted. 'True,' thought Tamakatsura, 'Genji's attitude towards me is not quite such as I could wish. But I am bound to confess that hitherto he has never tried to go further than I intend he should, and in practical ways no one could possibly be more kind and considerate.' Thus gratitude was slowly replaced by friendship and even by a certain semblance of intimacy.

Autumn had now come, and with it a bitterly cold wind— the 'first wind' whose chill breath 'only a lover's cloak can nullify.' He made great efforts to keep away from the Western Wing, but all to no purpose; and soon, on the pretext of music-lessons or what not, he was spending the greater part of every day at Tamakatsura's side.

One evening when the moon was some five or six days old he came suddenly to her room. The weather was chilly and overcast, and the wind rustled with a melancholy note through the reeds outside the window. She sat with her head resting against her zithern. To-night too, as on so many previous occasions, he would make his timorous advances, and at the end of it all be just where he started. So Genji grumbled to himself, and continued to behave in a somewhat plaintive and peevish manner during his whole visit. It was however already very late when the fear of giving offence in other quarters drove him from the room. Just as he was leaving he noticed that the flares outside her window were burning very low, and sending for one of his men, he had them kindled anew; but this time at a little distance from the house, under a strangely leaning spindle-tree which spread its branches in the form of a broad canopy, near to the banks of a deep, chilly stream. The thin flares of split pine-wood were placed at wide intervals, casting pale shadows that flickered remotely upon the walls of the unlighted room where she and Genji sat. He caught a glimpse of her hand, showing frail and ghostly against the dark background of her hair. Her face, suddenly illumined by the cold glare of the distant torches, wore an uneasy and distrustful air. He had risen to go, but still lingered. 'You should tell your people never to let the flares go out,' he said. 'Even in summer, except when there is a moon, it is not wise to leave the garden unlighted. And in Autumn . . . . I shall feel very uneasy if you do not promise to remember about this. " Did but the torches flickering at your door burn brightly as the fire within my breast, you should not want for light!"' And he reminded her of the old song in which the lover asks: 'How long, like the smouldering watch-fire at the gate, must my desire burn only with an inward flame?'

'Would that, like the smoke of the watch-fires that mounts and vanishes at random in the empty sky, the smouldering flame of passion could burn itself away!' So she recited, adding: 'I do not know what has come over you. Please leave me at once or people will think. . . .' 'As you wish,' he answered, and was stepping into the courtyard, when he heard a sound of music in the wing occupied by the Lady from the Village of Falling Flowers. Some one seemed to be playing the flute to the accompaniment of a Chinese zithern. No doubt Yūgiri was giving a small party. The flute-player could be none other than Tō no Chūjō's eldest son Kashiwagi; for who else at Court performed with such marvellous delicacy and finish? How pleasant would be the effect, thought Genji, if they would consent to come and give a serenade by the stream-side, in the subdued light of those flickering torches! 'I long to join you,' he wrote, 'but, could you see the pale, watery shadows that the watch-flares are casting here in the garden of the western wing, you would know why I am slow to come. . . .' He sent this note to Yūgiri, and presently three figures appeared out of the darkness. 'I should not have sent for you,' he called to them, 'had you not played "The Wind's voice tells me. . . ." It is a tune that I can never resist.' So saying he brought out his own zithern. When he had played for a while, Yūgiri began to improvise on his flute in the Banshiki mode.[1] Kashiwagi attempted to join in, but his thoughts were evidently employed elsewhere,[2] for again and again he entered at the wrong beat. 'Too late,' cried Genji, and at last Kōbai was obliged to keep his brother in measure by humming the air in a low monotone like the chirping of a meditative grasshopper. Genji made them go through the piece twice, and then handed his zithern to Kashiwagi. It was some while since he had heard the boy play and he now observed with delight that his talent was not by any means confined to wind-instruments. 'You could have given me no greater pleasure,' he said, when the piece was over. 'Your father is reckoned a fine performer on the zithern; but you have certainly more than overtaken him. . . . By the way, I should have cautioned you that there is some one seated just within who can probably hear all that is going on out in this portico. So to-night there had better not be too much drinking. Do not be offended, for I was really thinking more of myself than of you. Now that I am getting on in years I find wine far more dangerous than I used to. I am apt to say the most indiscreet things. . . .'

Tamakatsura did, as a matter of fact, overhear every word of this, as indeed she was intended to, and was thankful that he at any rate saw the necessity of keeping himself in hand. The near presence of the two visitors could not fail to interest her extremely, if for no other reason than merely because they were, after all, though themselves

[1] Corresponding roughly with the white notes from D to D.
[2] He was in love with Tamakatsura.

entirely unaware of the fact, so very closely related to her; and for long past she had surreptitiously collected all possible information concerning their characters and pursuits. Kashiwagi was, as to her distress she had frequently ascertained, very deeply in love with her. Again and again during the course of the evening, he was on the verge of collapsing altogether; but never was the state of agitation through which he was passing for a moment reflected in his playing.

CHAPTER X

THE TYPHOON

THIS year great pains had been taken to improve the Empress Akikonomu's domain; and by now her gardens were aglow with the varied tints of innumerable frost-stained leaves and autumn flowers. Above all, the new pergolas made an admirable show, now that their timber, here stripped of bark, there used in its natural state, was thickly interwoven with blossoming boughs. And when at morning and evening the sun slanted across the dewy gardens, it was as though every flower and tree were decked with strings of glittering pearls. Those who but a few months back had been carried away by the spring-time loveliness of the Southern Garden, could not fail, as they gazed upon the colder beauty of this autumnal scene, with one accord to resume their earlier preference. The lovers of autumn have, I am persuaded, at all times embraced the larger part of mankind; and in thus returning to their allegiance the Empress's companions were but following their natural bent.

So delighted was Akikonomu with the scene I have described that she asked for leave of absence from the Emperor and settled for a while in her own establishment. Unfortunately the anniversary of the late Prince Zembō's [1] death fell in the eighth month, and it was with great anxiety that she watched Autumn's almost hourly advance; for she feared that the best month would be over before she

[1] Her father; Rokujō's husband, who died early.

came out of mourning. Meanwhile she was confined to the house and all amusements were suspended.

The equinoctial gales were this year particularly violent. Then came a day when the whole sky grew black, and an appalling typhoon began. It would have been bad enough wherever one had been to see every tree stripped of its leaves just when they were at their loveliest, every flower stricken to the earth; but to witness such havoc in an exquisite garden, planned from corner to corner with endless foresight and care, to see those dew-pearls unthreaded in an instant and scattered upon the ground, was a sight calculated to drive the onlooker well nigh to madness. As time went on the hurricane became more and more alarming, till all was lost to view in a blinding swirl of fog and dust. But while she sat behind tightly closed shutters in a room that rocked with every fresh blast, it was with thoughts of autumn splendours irrevocably lost rather than with terror of the storm that the Empress's heart was shaken.

The Southern Gardens were just being laid out with wild plants from the countryside when the high winds began, and that impatient longing which the poet attributes to the young lespidezas [1] was indeed fulfilled in all too ample measure. Morning after morning Murasaki too saw the dew roughly snatched from leaf and flower. She was sitting thus one day on watch at her window, while Genji played with the little princess in a neighbouring room. It happened that Yūgiri had occasion to come across from the eastern wing. When he reached the door at the end of the passage he noticed that the great double-doors leading into Murasaki's room were half-open. Without thinking what he was doing, he paused and looked in. Numerous ladies-in-waiting were passing to and fro just inside, and

[1] 'I await your coming eagerly as waits the young lespideza, so heavy with dew, for the wind that shall disburden it.'

had he made any sound they would have looked up, seen
him and necessarily supposed that he had stationed himself
there on purpose to spy upon those within. He saw nothing
for it but to stand dead still. Even indoors the wind was so
violent that screens would not stand up. Those which usually
surrounded the high daïs were folded and stacked against
the wall. There, in full view of any one who came along
the corridor, reclined a lady whose notable dignity of mien
and bearing would alone have sufficed to betray her identity.
This could be none other than Murasaki. Her beauty
flashed upon him as at dawn the blossom of the red flowering
cherry flames out of the mist upon the traveller's still sleepy
eye. It was wafted towards him, suddenly imbued him,
as though a strong perfume had been dashed against his
face. She was more beautiful than any woman he had ever
seen. The hangings of her daïs had broken away from the
poles and now fluttered in the wind like huge flags. Her
ladies made vain attempts to recapture these flapping
curtain-ends, and in the course of the struggle (only half-
visible to Yūgiri) something very amusing evidently occurred,
for Murasaki suddenly burst into peals of laughter. Soon
however she became serious again. For here too, though
in a lesser degree, the wind was working irreparable havoc,
and at each fresh blast he saw her turn a despairing gaze
towards her newly-planted beds. Several of her gentlewomen, thought Yūgiri, as his eye accustomed itself to the
scene, were noticeably good-looking; but there was not
one whose appearance could for more than an instant have
distracted his attention from the astonishing creature at
whose command they served. Now he understood why it
was that Genji had always taken such pains to keep him
away from her. His father was wise enough to know that
no one could possibly see her thus without losing all control
of himself. Genji had indeed, in forbidding him all access

THE TYPHOON

to her rooms, foreseen just such a contingency as had at this moment occurred. The boy, suddenly realizing the extreme insecurity of his hiding-place and at the same time overwhelmed with shame at the mere thought of being discovered in such a situation, was about to dart into safety, when a door on the left opened and Genji himself entered the room. 'What a wind!' he said as he surveyed the exposed condition of her daïs. 'It would really be better just now if you left all the shutters closed. You probably do not realize that you and your ladies are at this moment exposing yourselves completely to the view of any gentleman who may happen to come this way. . . .' Yūgiri had already withdrawn his eye from the crack; but the sound of Genji's voice aroused in him an invincible curiosity, and he returned to his former position. His father was bending over Murasaki and whispering something in her ear; now he was laughing. It seemed to Yūgiri very odd that this high-spirited, handsome, quite young-looking man should really be his father. As for Genji's companion—he could not imagine that she could ever have been more beautiful than at this moment. He gazed spell-bound, and would certainly have crouched at his chink for hours to come, had not the door on the opposite side of the passage suddenly blown wide open, thus leaving his hiding-place embarrassingly exposed. Reluctantly he withdrew (as was now possible, for Murasaki's attendants had all retired to the far end of the room), and working his way round to the verandah, he called to Genji as though he had just arrived from the Eastern Wing. His father answered the greeting and presently joined him, saying to Murasaki as he left the room something which evidently referred to the imperfectly fastened passage-door. 'Look there!' Genji was saying crossly; 'is not that just what I told you? You must really be more careful. . .'

'This,' thought Yūgiri, 'is indeed a tribute to the devotion of her guards during all these years! Only a tempest capable of hurling rocks through the air and uprooting whole forests can so far disarm their vigilance that for a few seconds she is exposed to the curiosity of the passer-by.' He was bound to confess that towards him at any rate the dreaded hurricane had done its best to act a benevolent part.

Several retainers now arrived, reporting that the typhoon was assuming a very serious aspect. 'It is from the north-east,' they said, 'so that here you are comparatively protected and have no notion of its real violence. Both the racing-lodge and the fishing-pavilion are in great danger. . . .' While those people were busy making fast various doors and shutters, and repairing the damage of the previous night, Genji turned to Yūgiri and said : 'Where did you arrive from just now ? ' 'I spent the night at my grandmother's,' he replied. 'But every one says that we are in for a very bad storm, and I felt I ought to come back here and see if I could be of any use. . . . But as a matter of fact it is far worse in the Third Ward than here in the Sixth. The mere noise of the wind, quite apart from everything else, is terrifying at my grandmother's, and if you do not mind I think it would be a good thing if I went back there at once. She is as frightened as though she were a child of two, and it seems unkind to leave her. . . .' 'Yes, by all means go back at once,' answered Genji hastily. 'One sometimes thinks that the notion of old people slipping back into a second childhood is a mere fable ; but I have learnt lately from instances in my own family that it does really happen. Tell her, please, that I have heard how bad things are in the Third Ward and should certainly come myself, were I not satisfied that you will be able to do quite as much for her as I could.'

Yūgiri had a high sense of duty. It was his practice at this time to visit his grandmother at least once a day, and it would have been a ferocious wind indeed that could deter him either from setting out for the Third Ward or returning thence at the hour when his father usually asked for him. There were of course 'times of observance' when he was obliged to remain shut up in the Emperor's Palace for several days on end. But otherwise neither pressure of public business nor attendance at state ceremonies and festivals, however much they might impinge upon his leisure, ever prevented him from calling first at the New Palace and then upon the old Princess, before he dreamt of embarking upon any amusement of his own. Still less upon such a day as this, when, bad as the storm was already, there seemed every prospect that it would soon develop into something more alarming still, could he have brought himself to leave the old lady in solitude.

She was, indeed, delighted that he had not failed her. 'This is the worst typhoon there has ever been in my lifetime,' she said; 'and I can assure you I have seen a good many.' She was trembling from head to foot. Now and again came a strange and terrifying sound; some huge bough that a single breath of the hurricane had twisted from its trunk, crashed in splinters to the ground. Apart from all other dangers, showers of tiles were falling from every roof. To go into the streets at all on such a day was indeed no very safe undertaking, and for a while she listened with mingled gratitude and alarm to the recital of his perils and escapes.

The old Princess's lonely and monotonous existence contrasted strangely with the brilliant scenes amid which she had moved during the days of her husband's remarkable ascendancy. Indeed, that the visits of this staid young grandson should mean so much to her showed only too plainly how far she had fallen from the days when her ante-chambers were thronged by the fashionable world. True, her name was still widely known and even reverenced in the country at large; but this was small consolation for the fact that her own son, Tō no Chūjō, had for some time past been far from cordial in his manner towards her. It was very good of Yūgiri to come on such an evening. But why was it that he looked so thoughtful? Perhaps the noise of the hurricane distracted him. It was certainly very alarming.

If Yūgiri fell into a meditative mood in this house, it was generally with memories of his little playmate[1] that his mind was employed. But to-night he had not, as a matter of fact, thought of her once; nor did the tempest disturb him. It was the face he had seen this morning, in the course of his unintended eavesdropping, which now continually haunted him, till he suddenly checked his imagination and asked himself remorsefully what had come over him that in this of all places another face than Kumoi's should have filled his thoughts during a whole evening. And if it was a crime in him that he should presume to court Tō no Chūjō's daughter, what view would his elders take if they should discover that he spent his leisure in thinking of Genji's wife? He tried hard to think of other things; but after a moment or two the recollection of what he had seen that morning sprang back into his mind. Was all this a mere aberration on his part? He could not believe it; surely her beauty was indisputably of the kind that occurs only once or twice in a century—that a whole epoch may utterly lack? There was nothing to be wondered at in the impression which the sight of her had made upon him; if there was anything strange in the matter at all, it was that Genji, having such a wife as this, could ever have

[1] Kumoi.

taken any interest in such creatures as the lady in the Eastern Wing.[1] That did indeed require some explanation. It was heart-rending that the most beautiful woman of her generation should fall to the lot of one whose other intimacies proved him so completely lacking in discrimination.

It was characteristic of Yūgiri's high sense of propriety that when in his imaginings he became better acquainted with this lovely creature, it was not with Murasaki herself but with someone in every respect exactly like her that he pictured himself spending hours of enchanted bliss. Yes, that was what he needed ; without it life, he had began to discover, was not worth living at all.

Towards dawn the wind became somewhat dank and clammy ; before long sheets of rain were being swept onward by the hurricane. News came that many of the outbuildings at the New Palace had been blown to the ground. The main structure was so solidly built as to defy any storm. In the quarters inhabited by Genji there was, too, a continual coming and going, which served to mitigate the strain of those alarming hours. But the side wings of the palace were very sparsely inhabited. Yūgiri's own neighbour, for example—the Lady from the Village of Falling Flowers —might easily be by this time in a pitiable state of panic. Clearly it was his duty to give her his support, and he set out for home while it was still dark. The rain was blowing crossways, and no sooner had he seated himself in his litter, than an icy douche poured in through the ventilator and drenched his knees. The town wore an inconceivably desolate and stricken air. In his own mind too there was a strange sensation ; it was as though there also, just as in the world outside, the wonted landmarks and boundaries had been laid waste by some sudden hurricane. What had happened to him ? For a moment he could only remember

[1] The Lady from the Village of Falling Flowers.

that it was something distressing, shameful. . . . Why, it was hideous! Yesterday morning. . . . That was it of course. He was mad; nothing more nor less than a raving lunatic. He had fallen in love with Murasaki!

He did indeed find his neighbour in the eastern wing sadly in need of a little support and encouragement. He managed however to convince her that the worst danger was over, and sending for some of his own carpenters had everything put to rights. He felt that he ought now to greet his father. But in the central hall everything was still locked and barred. He went to the end of the passage and leaning on the balustrade looked out into the Southern Garden. Even such trees as still stood were heeling over in the wind so that their tops almost touched the ground. Broken branches were scattered in every direction and what once had been flower-beds were now mere rubbish heaps, strewn with a promiscuous litter of thatch and tiles, with here and there a fragment of trellis-work or the top of a fence. There was now a little pale sunshine, that slanting through a break in the sky gleamed fitfully upon the garden's woe-begone face; but sullen clouds packed the horizon, and as Yūgiri gazed on the desolate scene his eyes filled with tears. How came it, he asked himself, that he should be doomed time and again to long precisely for what it was impossible for him to obtain. He wiped away his tears, came close to Genji's door and called. 'That sounds like Yūgiri's voice,' he heard Genji say. 'I had no notion it was so late. . . .' He heard his father rise. There was a pause, and then Genji laughed, perhaps at some remark that had been inaudible. 'No indeed,' he said. 'You and I have fared better than most lovers. We have never known what it was to be torn from each other at the first streak of dawn, and I do not think that after all these years we should easily reconcile ourselves to such a fate.' Even to overhear such a conversation as this gave Yūgiri a certain kind of pleasure. He could not make out a word of what Murasaki said in reply and judging from the laughter with which the conversation was constantly interrupted it was not of a very serious description. But he felt he could say to himself 'That is what happens when they are alone together,' and he went on listening. Now, however, there was a noise of swift footsteps. Evidently Genji was about to unbolt the door with his own hands. Conscious that he was standing far closer to it than was natural Yūgiri stepped back guiltily into the corridor. 'Well,' asked Genji, 'was the Princess pleased to see you last night?' 'Yes, I think she was,' answered Yūgiri. 'She seems to be very much upset about something that has happened between her and my uncle Tō no Chūjō. She cried a great deal and I was very sorry for her.' Genji smiled. 'Oh, I know all about that business,' he said. 'She will soon get over it. You must persuade her not to brood upon such matters. He thinks she has been indiscreet, and is doing his best to make her feel uncomfortable about it. He cares immensely about the impression which his conduct makes on other people; and as regards his mother—he has always gone out of his way to convince the world that he is a paragon of filial devotion. So far as outward show is concerned, this is true enough. But I fancy that it is all done chiefly for the sake of appearances. The truth of the matter is that he has no very deep feelings towards anybody. This may seem a hard thing to say; but, on the other hand, I freely admit his good qualities. He is extremely well-informed and intelligent; he is musical to an extent which has become very rare in these days. In addition to all that, he is good-looking. As I have said, I think his feelings somewhat superficial. But we all have defects of one sort or another.... By the way, I ought to find out how the Empress has been getting on during this appalling hurricane. I wish you would find out if there is anything I can do for her . . .' and he gave Yūgiri a note in which he said : ' I am afraid the wind prevented you from getting much sleep. I myself find it a great strain and am feeling rather shaky ; otherwise I should have come round to see you long ago. . . .'

On approaching the Empress's apartments he saw a little girl with a cage in her hand trip lightly into the garden ; she had come to give the tame cicadas their morning sip of dew. Further off several ladies were wandering among the flower-beds with baskets over their arms, searching for such stray blossoms as might chance to have survived the tempest. Now and again they were hidden by great wreaths of storm-cloud that trailed across the garden with strange and lovely effect. Yūgiri called to the flower-gatherers. They did not start or betray the least sign of discomposure, but in an instant they had all disappeared into the house.

Being still a mere boy at the time when Akikonomu came to Genji's house, he had been allowed to run in and out of her rooms just as he chose, and had thus become very intimate with several of her gentlewomen. While he was waiting for the Empress's reply, two of these old acquaintances, a certain Saishō no Kimi, and a lady called Naishi, came into view at the end of the passage. He hailed them and had a long conversation. He used to think Lady Akikonomu a very splendid person ; and he was still obliged to confess, as he now looked about him, that she lived in very good style and had shown excellent taste in the furnishing of her quarters. But since those days he had learnt to judge by very different standards, and a visit to this part of the palace no longer interested him in the slightest degree.

On his return to Murasaki's rooms, he found all the shutters unbarred. Everything had resumed its normal course. He delivered the Empress's reply, in which she said: 'It may be very childish, but I own I have been much upset by the storm. I made sure that you would come and see to things here. . . . It would still be a great help to me if you could spare a moment. . . .' 'I remember', said Genji, ' that she was always very easily upset by anything of this kind. I can imagine what a panic she and her ladies must have worked themselves up into during the course of the night! It was wrong of me not to see after her . . .' and he started off towards the Empress's apartments. But he found he had forgotten his cloak, and turning back to the high daïs he raised a corner of the curtain and disappeared within. For a moment Yūgiri caught sight of a light-coloured sleeve; his heart began to beat so loud that it seemed to him every one else in the room must be able to hear it, and he quickly averted his eyes from the daïs. There was an interval during which Genji was presumably adjusting his cloak at the mirror. Then Yūgiri heard his father's voice saying: 'I cannot help thinking that Yūgiri is really looking quite handsome this morning. No doubt I am partial, and to every one else he looks a mere hobbledehoy; for I know that at the between-stage he has now reached young men are usually far from prepossessing in appearance.' After this there was a pause during which he was perhaps looking at his own countenance in the mirror, well content that the passage of time had as yet done so little to impair it. Presently Yūgiri heard him say very thoughtfully: 'It is strange; whenever I am going to see Akikonomu I suddenly begin to feel that I am looking terribly shabby and unpresentable. I cannot think why she should have that effect on one. There is really nothing very remarkable about her, either in intellect or appearance. But one feels, I think, that she is all the while making judgments, which if they ever came to the surface, would seem oddly at variance with the mild femininity of her outward manner. . . .' With these words Genji re-appeared from behind the curtains. The look of complete detachment with which Yūgiri imagined he met his father's gaze was perhaps not so successfully assumed as the boy supposed; for Genji suddenly halted and returning to the daïs whispered to Murasaki something about the door which had been left unfastened yesterday morning. 'No, I am sure he didn't,' answered Murasaki indignantly. 'If he had come along the corridor my people would have noticed. They never heard a sound. . . .' 'Very queer, all the same,' murmured Genji to himself as he left the room. Yūgiri now noticed that a group of gentlemen was waiting for him at the end of the cross-gallery, and he hastened to meet them. He tried to join in their conversation and even in their laughter; but he was feeling in no mood for society, and little as his friends expected of him in the way of gaiety, they found him on this occasion more obdurately low-spirited than ever before.

Soon however his father returned and carried him off to the Eastern Wing. They found the gentlewomen of this quarter engaged in making preparations to meet the sudden cold. A number of grey-haired old ladies were cutting out and stitching, while the young girls were busy hanging out quilts and winter cloaks over lacquered clothes-frames. They had just beaten and pulled a very handsome dark-red underrobe, a garment of magnificent colour, certainly unsurpassed as an example of modern dyeing—and were spreading it out to air. 'Why, Yūgiri,' said Genji, 'that is your coat, is it not? I suppose you would have been wearing it at the Emperor's Chrysanthemum Feast; but of course this odious hurricane has put a stop to everything of that sort. What a depressing autumn it is going to be!'

But Yūgiri could not summon up much interest in the round of visits upon which his father had embarked, and slipped away to the rooms of his little sister, the Princess from Akashi. The child was not there. 'She is still with Madam,' her nurse said. 'She went later than usual to-day. She was so frightened of the storm that it was a long time before she got to sleep, and we had a job to get her out of bed at all this morning.' 'When things began to be so bad,' said Yūgiri, 'I intended to come round here and sit up with her; but then I heard that my grandmother was very much upset, and thought that I had better go to her instead. What about the doll's house? Has that come to any harm?' The nurse and her companions laughed. 'Oh, that doll's house!' one of them exclaimed. 'Why, if I so much as fanned myself the little lady would always cry out to me that I was blowing her dolls to bits. You can imagine, then, what a time we had of it when the whole house was being blown topsy-turvy, and every minute something came down with a crash. . . . You'd better take charge of that doll's house. I don't mind telling you I'm sick to death of it!'

Yūgiri had several letters to write, and as the little girl was still with her step-mother he said to the nurse: 'Might I have some ordinary paper. Perhaps from the writing-case in your own room. . . .' The nurse however went straight to the little Princess's own desk and taking the cover off her lacquered writing-case laid upon it a whole roll of the most elegant paper she could find. Yūgiri at first protested. But after all, was not a rather absurd fuss made about this young lady and her future? There was nothing sacrosanct about her possessions; and accepting the paper, which was of a thin, purple variety, he mixed his ink very carefully and, continually inspecting the point of his brush, began writing slowly and cautiously. The air of serious concentration with which he settled down to his task was very impressive; more so, indeed, than the composition itself, for his education had been chiefly upon other lines.

The poem was as follows: 'Not even on this distracted night when howling winds drive serried hosts of cloud across the sky, do I for an instant forget thee, thou Unforgettable One.' He tied this to a tattered spray of miscanthus that he had picked up in the porch. At this there was general laughter. 'It's clear you haven't read your Katano no Shōshō'[1] said one of the nurses, 'or you would at least choose a flower that matched your paper....' 'You are quite right,' he answered rather sulkily, 'I have never bothered my head about such matters. No doubt one ought to go tramping about the countryside looking for an appropriate flower; but I have no intention of doing so....' He had always seemed to the nurses and other such ladies of the household very difficult to get anything out of. Apparently he did not care what impression he made upon them; and as a matter of fact they were beginning to think him rather priggish and stuck-up.

He wrote a second letter, and sending for his retainer Uma no Suké put this and the original note into the man's hand. But evidently the two letters were to go in quite different directions.[2] For Uma no Suké, having scanned the addresses, entrusted one to a page boy and the other to a discreet, responsible-looking body-servant. These proceedings were accompanied by a great many whispered

---

[1] A tale of the 'perfect lover,' very popular in Murasaki's day, but now lost. Cf. vol. i, p. 39.
[2] One to Kumoi, one to Koremitsu's daughter.

warnings and injunctions. The curiosity of the young nurses knew no bounds ; but it remained wholly unsatisfied ; for hard though they strained their ears, they could not catch a word.

Yūgiri was now tired of waiting and made his way to his grandmother's house. He found her quietly pursuing her devotions, surrounded by gentlewomen not all of whom were either old or ill-looking. But in dress and bearing they formed a strange contrast to the chattering, frivolous young creatures from whom he had just parted. The nuns too, who had come to take part in the service, were by no means decrepit or disagreeable in person, a fact which gave an additional pathos to their assumption of this sombre and unbecoming guise.

Later in the day Tō no Chūjō called, and when the great lamp had been brought in, he and the old Princess had a long, quiet talk. At last she screwed up her courage to say : ' It is a very long time since I saw Kumoi . . .' and she burst into tears. ' I was just going to suggest sending her round here in a day or two,' said Tō no Chūjō. ' I am not very happy about her. She is certainly thinner than she used to be, and there is sometimes a peculiar expression in her face. . . . It is almost as though she had something on her mind. I do not understand how it is that, while I have never had a moment's anxiety over my boys, with these daughters of mine something goes wrong at every turn. And never through any fault of mine. . . .' He said this with an intonation that clearly showed he had not entirely forgiven her. She was sorely wounded by this obstinate injustice, but did not attempt to defend herself.

' Talking of daughters,' he went on, ' you have probably heard that I have lately made a very unsuccessful addition to my household. You have no idea what worries I am going through. . . .' He spoke in a doleful tone, but no sooner were the words uttered than he burst out laughing. 'I cannot bear to hear you talking in that way,' said the old Princess. 'Of one thing I am quite sure: if she is really your daughter she cannot be so bad as people are making out.' 'I think, all the same,' said Tō no Chūjō, 'that it might be possible to put too great a strain upon your habitual indulgence towards everything connected with me. That being so, I have no intention whatever of introducing her to you.'